W9-CDO-289

FATHER
NIGHT

By Eric Van Lustbader

THE JACK McCLURE/ ALLI CARSON NOVELS

First Daughter (2008)
Last Snow (2010)
Blood Trust (2011)
Father Night (2012)

THE PEARL SAGA

The Ring of Five Dragons (2001)
The Veil of a Thousand Tears (2002)
Mistress of the Pearl (2004)

THE SUNSET WARRIOR CYCLE

The Sunset Warrior (1977)
Shallows of Night (1978)
Dai-San (1978)
Beneath an Opal Moon (1980)
Dragons on the Sea of Night (1997)

THE CHINA MAROC SERIES

Jian (1986)
Shan (1988)

THE NICHOLAS LINNEAR/ NINJA CYCLE

The Ninja (1980)
The Miko (1984)
White Ninja (1990)
The Kaisho (1993)
Floating City (1994)
Second Skin (1995)

THE JASON BOURNE NOVELS

The Bourne Legacy (2004)
The Bourne Betrayal (2007)
The Bourne Sanction (2008)
The Bourne Deception (2009)
The Bourne Objective (2010)
The Bourne Dominion (2011)

OTHERS

Sirens (1981)
Black Heart (1983)
Zero (1987)
French Kiss (1989)
Angel Eyes (1991)
Batman: The Last Angel (1992)
Black Blade (1993)
Dark Homecoming (1997)
Pale Saint (1999)
Art Kills (2002)
The Testament (2006)

FATHER
NIGHT

Eric Van Lustbader

A TOM DOHERTY ASSOCIATES BOOK

NEW YORK

FATHER NIGHT

A Forge Book
Published by Tom Doherty Associates, LLC
175 Fifth Avenue
New York, NY 10010

www.tor-forge.com

Forge® is a registered trademark of Tom Doherty Associates, LLC.

Library of Congress Cataloging-in-Publication Data

Lustbader, Eric.
    Father night : a McClure/Carson novel / Eric Van Lustbader. — 1st ed.
        p. cm.
    "A Tom Doherty Associates book."
    ISBN 978-0-7653-3339-1 (hardcover)
    ISBN 978-1-4668-0071-7 (e-book)
    1. National security—United States—Fiction.   2. International
relations—Fiction.   3. Children of presidents—Fiction.   4. United
States. Federal Bureau of Investigation—Fiction.   5. Middle East—
Politics and government—Fiction.   I. Title.
PS3562.U752F38 2012
813'.54—dc23

                                                            2012019935

First Edition: September 2012

Printed in the United States of America

0 9 8 7 6 5 4 3 2 1

Here, on the level sand
Between the sea and land,
What shall I build or write
Against the fall of night?
—A. E. HOUSMAN, *"Smooth*
Between Sea and Land"

FATHER
NIGHT

PROLOGUE

December 4

MOONLIGHT, AND what comes after. The Moskva River shimmered in moonlight. Jack McClure and Annika Dementieva stood on her balcony looking out at snow-covered Red Square. The onion domes gleamed in floodlit splendor. The French doors of Annika's second-floor apartment were thrown open, despite the icy chill. Somewhere beyond Moscow, the stars were out. A crescent moon rode high overhead.

The night sounds of the city were drowned out by Annika's laptop, in split-screen mode, tuned in to both CNN and Al Jazeera. Competing talking heads, one in English, the other in Arabic, were proclaiming the continued rise and spread of what had quickly been dubbed the "Arab Spring," started when the corrupt Mubarak regime in Egypt was ousted by a coalition made up of shopkeepers, teachers, students, doctors, mechanics, bus and taxi drivers, and housewives—everyone, in fact, clamoring, it seemed, for an end to dictatorship and a start to democracy.

"It won't last. A new beginning, indeed," Annika scoffed as she went inside to stare at her laptop screen. "It all sounds so rosy now, everyone, Christian and Muslim, getting along, but it won't last."

"How cynical you are."

"No." She shook her head. "Merely realistic. Every regime in the Middle East is corrupt, it's simply a matter of degree."

Jack tried to get her back outside, but she was too wrapped in her feelings.

She pointed. "Look at them. No one knows what they're talking about. Now that the Muslim Brotherhood has won the election, how long do you think it will take until the army starts muscling in, trying to regain the traditional power it's lost? The Brotherhood knows what I know. Those other factions could never get along; they'll continue to fight and tear each other apart. The Brotherhood was quick to move into the power vacuum."

She turned to look at Jack. "I despised Mubarak, but one thing you could say in his favor, he kept the Brotherhood from insinuating themselves into the fabric of Egypt's government."

"The price was high," Jack said. "Instead of the Brotherhood, the Egyptian military insinuated itself into the fabric of not only Egypt's government, but its economy as well."

"There's no good answer here." Annika shook her head. "When it comes to the Middle East, there never will be. Mark my words, a feeding frenzy for power is going to erupt not only in Egypt, but throughout the Middle East."

Jack closed the browser and shut down the computer. "That's enough of feeling helpless for tonight."

Annika smiled, first slyly, then more broadly. "Who says I feel helpless?"

As he slid his arms around her waist, she said, "There *is* no good answer, you know."

He kissed her. "That's why . . ." He kissed her again. "We're tabling this discussion . . ." And again. "For the rest of the night."

"There *is* an answer, you know," she murmured into his mouth, "but it isn't good."

A high-low siren wailed like a muezzin, approaching along the embankment, before slowly fading away. They heard the hiss of car tires on the road below, and, once, the sharp, demented shout of a drunk, terrified of the demons in his head.

Jack backed her up against the wall. The prints on both sides of them trembled, then rattled. He kissed her hard, and she responded in kind. One of her legs drew up, her bare calf running up the outside of his leg. He rocked her like the sea.

"You should not even be here."

When she spoke, her scent wafted over him, cloves and orange and a peculiar spice all her own.

"You should be with your American friends." Her lips parted and her tongue flicked out. "With your American boss."

"And yet I'm here with you."

"Why? Why are you with me?" The tip of her tongue traced the outer whorls of his ear. "I am a Russian, and a murderer."

"We're all murderers." His voice was thick with desire.

Her palms pressed against his shoulders as he pinned her to the wall. "You know that's not true."

"But it is. For us, killing is as much a part of life as eating or breathing."

"Or making love." Hips insinuating themselves.

"No. Making love is entirely different."

"How?" Her lips slid down the side of his neck. "How is it different? Tell me."

"When we're together, making love, we're different. We're better people."

"Only for a time—the space of a breath." She took his hands, placed them on her buttocks. "Or a sigh." She sighed deeply, an ecstatic explosive.

"Even that is enough." He pulled the fullness of her hips into him. "My fear is that we will become like those before us. Living in the shadows, at the edges of society, gives us certain privileges, privileges that feed our egos, inflate them, until we believe that we are beyond the law."

She unbuckled his belt. "But, darling, we *are* beyond the law."

He unbuttoned her Shantung silk blouse. "Humans, unconstrained, are prone to develop criminal tendencies."

Her fingertips traced a line from just below his navel down to his groin. "Those tendencies were there all the time."

He smiled into the hollow of her throat, dizzy with her scent. "A fundamental illness in the human spirit, a cruelty, a capacity for killing without remorse."

She moved against him, slithering her thighs open farther, pressing the center of herself against him with little grunts of lust. "This isn't the time."

"It's the *only* time." Cupping the back of her head, Jack tilted her up, pressing his lips against hers, feeling them soft beneath his, opening, their tongues twining. He drew back, slowly, reluctantly, because what he had to tell her was an urgency in the pit of his stomach, and needed to be said before their combined desire overwhelmed it and everything else.

"These moments together, no matter how brief, have to be enough to prove to us that we can go on with this life we've chosen." He stared at her bare breasts, his hands seeking them out. "Without them, there's only a descent into a perpetual dark from which we'll never return."

She looked up at him. "Do you think we kill without remorse?"

"I hope not."

"But you don't know." She put her fingers across his lips. "We do what we have to do. There is no choice."

"There's always a choice."

She started to run her hand up and down the length of him. "What? Walking away?" Her voice held an unmistakable mocking note.

"No," he said. "That's not an option."

"Then let's make the most of these moments."

"Let's make the world around us melt away. Let's protect each other."

He rammed her against the wall so hard her body shivered and shook all over. Her legs came off the floor, wound around him, heels drumming against his bare flesh. The wall was their bed; they did not notice how hard it was—they were only aware of each other's bodies as more and more skin appeared. Shadows played over them as they moved in ragged rhythm, their breath mingling, sweat springing out on their flesh, warmed by their mutual heat. Desire and need commingled, fueling their mutual lust. Every moment was breathless, each one another ecstasy, until the frenzy of the end.

The rapturous cries died slowly, the well-oiled bodies sliding against each other in long, languid caresses. Breathing slowed, along with heart rates. Jack watched the endless curves of her body, the mounds, the dells hidden in soft-edged shadow. He thought he had never seen anything more exquisite. His love for her rose like the sun, heating him, the entire room, filling him with a sure sense of iron purpose. Into the silence, he murmured her name.

And that was when he heard it.

He turned his head, saw the knob on the front door turning minutely. Annika's eyes were closed. He kissed her eyelids, each in turn. She murmured, rising up out of the fluttering drowse into which she had descended. When her eyes opened, she smiled. Then, at Jack's silent urging, her gaze followed the direction in which he was pointing.

Then she heard it, too, the slight sound of metal on metal, as someone just outside attempted to pick the lock.

They rolled away from each other, their sticky love now all but forgotten. Jack grabbed a shoe just as the door flew open. He threw the shoe, heel-first. It hit the intruder square in the face. The man's handgun went off, the bullet just missing Annika's bare shoulder. Where it impacted in the corner of the wood dresser, needle-sharp shards sprayed outward. Annika cried out, one hand up to protect her eyes.

The intruder's gun swung around, the muzzle aimed straight at Jack. He leapt directly at the figure, the barrel of the gun slamming into the side of his head as his momentum took them both down across the apartment's threshold. The intruder struck Jack another blow, and Jack reeled. The figure grabbed Jack's throat in a death grip, seeking to crush his larynx, while he brought the gun to bear on Jack's face.

Before the man could pull the trigger, Jack jabbed him in the kidneys, repeatedly smashed his gun hand against the doorframe until the weapon fell to the floor. With the intruder's hand constricting his throat, Jack was losing oxygen at an appalling rate. He jabbed out, his knuckles connecting with the intruder's throat. The man choked, his grip relaxing enough for Jack to sweep his hand away. Then he bore down with both hands in a stranglehold the intruder tried to break. Increasingly desperate, the man's fingers tried to pry Jack's hands away, then scrabbled on the floor for the handgun. But Annika, stepping over them both, picked up the weapon before he could find it.

"Jack," she said. "Jack, stop. That's enough."

But it wasn't, not for Jack. This man had violated their private space at the most intimate of moments. He had fired on Annika and almost hit her. No, it wasn't nearly enough. He pressed in and down, putting his entire body into it, until the intruder's eyes rolled up in their sockets and his breathing stopped.

It was long moments before Annika got through to him, could pull him to his feet. He stood panting over the body.

"Where did our better natures go, Jack?" she said softly. "They were imprisoned and starved to death by our overdeveloped sense of purpose." She looked at him. "Do you understand me?"

He nodded. His chest was still heaving.

"This hit man," she said softly, "I know him." She took Jack's hand in hers. "He works for one of my brothers, Grigori Batchuk."

This name sent a splinter of shock through Jack's brain. "Brothers?"

She nodded. "My father had two children with another woman. Grigori and Radomil."

"Are you telling me that one of your brothers wants you dead?"

"That's precisely what I'm saying. Grigori is determined to kill both me and my grandfather."

"But why?"

"My father—" Her mobile sounded, interrupting her. She padded across the room, picked it up, and listened for a moment.

"Annika," Jack said, coming toward her, "what is it? What's happened?"

Her face looked stricken, and when she spoke her voice was as thin and strained as a wire. "It's Dyadya Gourdjiev. They've just taken him to the hospital."

PART ONE

December 6–December 9

Yesterday is gone. Tomorrow hasn't arrived.
—FRANCISCO DE QUEVEDO (1580–1645)

ONE

ALLI CARSON'S back slammed against the mat.

"I missed my opportunity."

"Patience is opportunity."

She stared up at the broad face with almond eyes and thick black eyebrows.

"I don't understand," she said, regaining her feet. "I missed my chance."

Sensei smiled his enigmatic Ent-like smile. "You mistake chance with advantage."

He squared to her, his bare feet set at shoulder-width. He was small and wiry, yet more powerful than a six-foot-six linebacker. "In hand-to-hand combat you must always seek the advantage. Advantage comes with patience." He cocked his head. "Please explain."

"I can't," Alli said.

"Yes," Sensei insisted, "you can."

Alli screwed up her face, but let her mind wander freely. "Everyone has a weakness."

Sensei's smile widened. "Everyone."

"Even you, Sensei?"

"Together, we shall find out." He lunged at her and she backed away. "Stand your ground. Parry, move not an inch, cede nothing."

For the next five minutes she did as he ordered. She neither retreated nor advanced, no matter the method of his attack, and at the end of that time she saw the opening on his left side every time he advanced. She waited, patient, for his next attack, and when it came, she was ready, feinting left, then right, under his attack. She was just about to land her blow when his right arm whipped around, his hand gripped her shoulder, and he spun her off her feet.

He stood over her for a moment, a big grin on his face. As he leaned over her, he said, "One half learned, one half only." He held out his hand and, after a moment's hesitation, she took it. "You must make certain your opponent is not gulling you into a mistake."

As he pulled her up, she whipped her left leg up, planted her foot on his chest, and pushed from her lower abdomen, the force traveling through her thigh, snapping her bent knee straight, extending through the sole of her foot.

Sensei stumbled backward, but did not let go of her hand. She was yanked forward, a sharp pain in her extended leg. He sought to take advantage of the momentary weakness the pain caused her, wrapping his right arm around her neck as she was falling against him. But she used his own momentum against him, rolling onto her left shoulder, dragging his body up and over her, slamming his shoulder blades against the mat.

Up on one knee, she rested a moment, breathing deeply to allow the pain to flow through her and dissipate. She found that her heartbeat was accelerated; she could hear her pulse in her ears.

Sensei rose to his feet, bowed, and, turning, walked out of the practice room without so much as a backward glance. He said not a word; none was expected. Praise was something Sensei never extended, feeling it gave rise to ego, which had no place in his dojo.

She remained where she was and wiped her damp forehead on her sleeve. Then she collapsed, sitting on the mat in the center of the room, knees drawn up, arms locked around her shins, as she replayed the last two minutes with breathless wonder.

Some moments later, her roommate, Vera Bard, poked her head into the dojo. "Ah, you're finished. Good." Her expression troubled, she stepped into the room and tapped her iPad. "I've got to show you something. It's pretty weird."

As she was about to step onto the mats, Alli waved her back, rose, and came across to her. Plucking her coat off a wooden peg, she slipped into it, and they went outside into the chill December weather. A brilliant blue sky sparkled overhead and frost danced on their exhalations. The campus of Fearington, one of the prime secret services training centers in the D.C. area, surrounded them, the Federal-style buildings interspersed with stands of tall pines and chestnut trees. Farther away, hidden in a series of natural swales, were the Pits: obstacle courses, firing ranges, and the like.

Alli breathed in the fresh air. Her body felt limitless, her mind drunk on her victory over Sensei. She took Vera's iPad and checked out the screen. Vera took it from her and brought up an Internet site titled allicarsonbitch-slave.com.

Alli gave a little gasp. "What the hell?"

"The link to the site was e-mailed to me and to everyone else at Fearington."

"Who sent the e-mails?" Alli asked.

"They were sent by *you*."

"What? But I didn't—"

"Of course you didn't," Vera said.

There were a series of photos of nude girls bound and tied, arms extended over their heads or out to the sides as they sat in a heavy wooden chair. All had Alli's head or face Photoshopped onto them. Below each there was a price for photo sets and short films that could be ordered. Farther down were comments: filthy whore, pervert, hot bitch, and the like, but all of them ended with either a smiley face or LOL, cyber-shorthand for "laugh out loud."

"The good news is that this cyber–smear attack is being viewed as a practical joke inside Fearington. It's likely someone here is the culprit."

"Well, it's not funny." Alli kept reading. "Look here . . . here at the end, a date for my supposed death—December twentieth." She looked up at Vera, appalled. "That's two weeks from now."

"Hey, come on, you can't believe this death threat is real. I mean, someone's gaming you, sure, and we have to stop it, but . . ."

"After what I've been through I take everything seriously," Alli said.

"Okay, but . . . I mean, no one in their right mind would think that's really you in those photos. Look, here and here again, the lighting's off."

But Alli, who had felt a chill run down her spine the moment she saw the images of girls bound into that nightmarish heavy wooden chair, felt plowed under by the intimate eeriness of the photos. And her fear only increased when she saw the date of her supposed death.

"Come on," Vera said. "We'll take this to the authorities. They'll find out who's behind this shit, put him away, and that'll be the end of it."

Alli began to shiver uncontrollably.

At once, Vera put her arm around her roommate's shoulders, pulling her close. "You're cold as ice. What is it?"

Alli remained mute, but her mind was churning with terror. December twentieth was the fifth anniversary of the day she had been kidnapped by Morgan Herr.

ALAN FRAINE, captain of detectives of the Metro Police, was halfway through his strenuous thrice-weekly workout when he saw a man enter the cavernous second floor of Muscle Builders Unlimited, wrap a towel around his neck, and check out the rows of StairMasters. Something familiar about the man made the short hairs at the back of Fraine's neck stir. He continued with his second set of biceps reps, but his mind was no longer in it, and he set the dumbbells aside before he injured himself.

He watched with curiosity as the man strode over to his section. It was then that he recognized Dennis Paull, secretary of the Department of Homeland Security.

Paull straddled the bench next to Fraine and said, "Alan, how's it going?"

Fraine had had occasion to work with Paull and Jack McClure several months ago in connection with Henry Holt Carson and Middle Bay Bancorp. Carson had been part of a conspiracy to frame Fraine's best detective, Nona Heroe. Paull had gotten her out from the Feds' custody.

"Sorry." Fraine tried to hide the depth of his surprise. "I didn't recognize you out of your suit, Mr. Secretary."

"Hardly anyone does," Paull said. "That's a gift sometimes."

"So I imagine," Fraine said. "I had no idea you were a member."

Paull produced a complicit grin. "I joined this morning."

Fraine waited for the shoe to drop. The secretary wasn't here to break a sweat or to exchange pleasantries.

"Alan, I have a proposition for you."

Fraine's ears perked up. "I'm listening."

"I'm putting together a special group."

"What kind of group?"

Paull leaned forward. "A SITSPEC—"

"A what?"

Paull waited while a couple of gym rats passed by, talking reps and sets and punitive diets. "A black-ops group. Situation-specific, hence the acronym."

"Fed-speak."

"What?"

"Nothing. Go on."

Paull nodded, lowering his voice, forcing Fraine to lean toward him. "This one is very special. I'd like you and Nona to be part of it."

"Mr. Secretary, I appreciate the offer, but Nona and I are local and I'm sure your SITSPEC is not. It's probably not even domestic."

"There you're wrong. It *is* domestic and, as of this moment, it's local to the D.C. area."

Fraine considered this possibility. "Why us?"

"I know I can trust you. You and Nona owe me; at the end of the day, I know you won't turn me down." He smiled. "Besides, before it's over, there's a good chance we'll be intersecting with Henry Holt Carson's interests." His smile turned sly. "I know you can't pass up that opportunity."

"THERE'S A time and a place for everything," the General said.

"Even peace?"

"No." The General lit a cigar with a wooden match. He had a head like a helmet, with a fringe of prematurely white hair like a priest's tonsure. "Of course not peace."

The other man, small-boned, sharp-nosed, and gray as a rodent, shifted in his wing chair. He wore a pale-colored suit and a black tie. By his side was a carved hickory walking stick. His name was Werner Waxman, though he also might be known as Smith or Jones, Reilly or Coen, depending on what country and what year he was in. In any case, Waxman was not his real name. "But you said—"

"For me, peace doesn't exist."

The two men were sunk into the dim, woody interior of a hunting lodge deep in the forests of Virginia. Far from the media spotlight glare inside the Beltway, they sat on either side of an enormous fireplace composed of stones as large as their heads. It was late, only a few scattered lamps left on, their pools of lights burnishing the wide polished floorboards. A tray with the remains of coffee and dessert sat unnoticed on a low table nearby.

The General lifted his cleft chin, blew smoke at the coffered ceiling. "I, personally, don't know what peace is, and, frankly, I don't want to know."

Waxman leaned forward, his muscles tense. A blue vein beat at the corner of his left eye. "Peace is death."

The General's gaze came down, fixed Waxman with the accuracy of a lawn dart. "Yes." He seemed as much impressed as he was surprised. "You've caught the essence precisely."

"Well." Waxman inclined his head, a formal Middle European gesture. "That's my job, isn't it?"

"I wouldn't want that." The General rounded the ash crown of his cigar on the lip of his plate. "I wouldn't want the responsibility of making sense of it all."

"We all have our roles to play." Waxman's eyes glinted as he turned his head. "You, General, are a man of action. You carry out a plan to perfection."

The General stirred, wondering now what Waxman wanted. "This enterprise of yours—it had better work."

"Trust me, General."

"The last individual who said that to me is six feet under."

Like a conjuror, Waxman produced a thin smile as if from nowhere. "As to that, I have no worries."

The General sucked on his cigar. "The stakes are astronomical."

"Such melodrama! This isn't Hollywood."

"You can't afford to be wrong." The General stared at the ash at the end of his cigar. "About anything." He glanced up. "Or anyone."

Waxman's thin smile seemed set in cement.

The General regarded Waxman with carefully concealed distaste. He seemed pale and weak, unfit for anything outside a well-ventilated room, but, as he had said, they all had their roles to play, all of them. Each brought a different expertise to the enterprise. They were bound not by friendship, but by need. Better by far than friendship, the General judged. It was unthinkable to betray someone you needed. And betrayal was the one thing they all feared. He knew that, because it was what he feared, the fear muscled way down in the depths of him, but always keeping a wary antenna out for red flags.

The members had made a covenant with each other a long time ago on a dark and turbulent night filled with blood, death, and terror. They were determined to fill the power vacuum Waxman had foretold would come to pass in the Middle East. And, despite Acacia's first failure, he had been right, damnit, all the way down the line, right.

"I know you," Waxman said. "You like to give the people around you a hard time."

"That's *my* job."

Waxman nodded. "The reins of power. I understand."

"What reins? We're all in this together."

Waxman's eyes grew diamond-hard as he sat forward on the edge of his chair. Had it been anyone else, the General might have been alarmed. But Waxman was Waxman; he lived in his own head.

"There's bullshit and then there's bullshit, General. You may have fooled the others, but never for a minute believe that you've fooled me." Waxman inclined his narrow torso like an arrow aimed at the General. "History informs us that while rule by consensus may work for a short time, it breaks down." He spread his white hands. "We're all human, General, we all want what we want—and it's never the common good. You want what you want, General. I know it and you know it."

And what is it exactly that you want, Waxman? the General wondered.

He set aside the remains of his cigar. "You're really in love with that mind of yours, aren't you?"

"Mind games." One corner of Waxman's lips twitched. "You don't want to start with me."

"Is that a threat?" The General's voice was languid as he rose.

Waxman had no choice but to get to his feet. One shoulder was noticeably lower than the other, as if he were poised to make a fast getaway. The General towered over him; nevertheless, he appeared anything but intimidated.

"Sun Tzu wrote, 'All war is deception,' General," Waxman said as, leaning on his stick, he brushed past. "You would do well to keep that in the forefront of your mind."

The tick-tock of the walking stick was like the beating heart of a clock. The General watched Waxman disappear into the innards of the hunting lodge. At length, he turned and picked up his cigar, but it was already cold. The taste he loved was gone.

Two

THE SUNLIGHT in Moscow was white. It fell from a featureless sky cold and hard like sleet. Somewhere there were clouds, Jack McClure thought as he peered through the hospital window, and beyond, hard as it was to believe, a pale blue sky.

Workmen were busy stripping off the gaily colored billboard sheets for the Red Square Circus. Just beyond loomed the blank, brutal faces of the squat Soviet buildings across the street, a reminder of the old guard, as well as the repression and corruption that endured through every regime change. The Russian personality was stronger than communism, social-ism, glasnost, and latter-day imperial fiat.

Hearing Annika call his name, he turned to see her across the corri-dor. She had just emerged from the room where Dyadya Gourdjiev lay beneath rough muslin sheets. Dyadya. Everyone called him Uncle—even Annika—but he was actually her grandfather.

"How is he?" Jack said, stepping across to her.

"The doctors say he's dying, but I don't believe it." She gave him a wan smile. "Neither does he."

He took her in his arms. She had her thick blond hair tied back in a

ponytail, as she had the first time he'd seen her two years ago in the bar
of a hotel across town. The buzzing fluorescent lights turned her carnelian eyes dark as dried blood.

"But if the doctors—"

"The doctors are fools," she said. "They've been saying he's dying for
the better part of a year." Her wide mouth was warm against his cheek.
"He's been asking for you."

"Me?" Jack pulled away to see her expression. "You're joking." But
he could see that she wasn't. "Why would he want to see me?"

She laughed softly. "Don't be an idiot. He liked you even before he
knew you loved me." She tapped his temple with a long forefinger. "He
likes what's inside there, the way you think. He says you remind him of
himself."

Jack stood looking at her, dumbfounded. "He used me just like he
uses everyone else."

"No, not in the same way." She gave him a little push. "Go on,
now. If you wait much longer he'll be asleep."

Jack nodded and, like a sleepwalker, pushed open the blond-wood
door and stepped inside. The first thing he saw was the extremely handsome woman sitting in a chair near the far side of the bed. She turned
as he entered. She wore an oxblood wool suit over a cream-colored silk
blouse, caught at the neck by a magnificent cameo. Vitality usually reserved only for the young blazed through her as if she manufactured sunlight.

With a slight rustle of fabric, she rose. "You must be the Jack Mc-
Clure I've heard so much about." She extended a slender hand, white as
snow, and he took it.

"You have me at a disadvantage, madam."

"You have the honor to meet Katya Tanova," Dyadya Gourdjiev
said from his position propped up in the bed.

Katya Tanova's eyes sparkled like diamonds. As she came around
the end of the bed, Jack saw that she still had magnificent legs. Her figure was slim and elegant. She seemed ageless.

"So you are Annika's lover."

"Katya, please!" Dyadya Gourdjiev protested. "A little decorum."

"At my age, decorum is a useless trait."

Her smile was of the megawatt variety; Jack basked in its warmth. "You don't mind, do you?"

"No, ma'am, not if you call me Jack."

She gave him a formal little nod. "And you must call me Katya. All the family does."

"Katya." There was a warning note in Dyadya Gourdjiev's voice, though it was tempered by an affection he chose not to hide.

"Yes, yes, I know. You men must talk about cabbages and kings." She said this with a mocking tone, waving one hand at the space between Jack and Gourdjiev, then gathered up her things. As she went toward the door, she paused beside Jack. "Try not to tire him out. If you let him, he'll talk all day and all of the night."

"It's a promise," Jack said.

She smiled. "And you're a man who keeps his promises." She put a finger beside her nose and tapped it. "I have a sense about these things."

"She does, you know," Gourdjiev said when she had left. "A sorceress of sorts."

The two men studied each other, the air between them a swirl of difficult memories and bittersweet emotions.

"It's been some time," the old man said.

"Seems like a lifetime."

"And you've been busy, Annika tells me. The Albanians are a ruthless bunch of thugs. Disgusting habits. Thoroughly reprehensible."

Jack said nothing, and the silence deepened. Apart from the beeps and blips of the monitors to which the old man was hooked up, there was no sound at all in the room.

"The way you look at me," Gourdjiev said, "you think I look old."

"You *are* old," Jack said.

The old man gave a wry smile. "It's an act I put on for the doctors. Otherwise, they feel neglected."

Jack laughed and, as was Gourdjiev's intent, the tension was broken. Even so, the levity was short-lived.

The old man nodded. "You'd better say it, get it over with."

"You used me to get to Oriel Batchuk."

Gourdjiev nodded. "In a roundabout way."

"So Annika could kill him."

"Who had a better right?"

"He was her father!"

"A father who kidnapped her when she was just a child, a father who tortured her, who forced her to do unspeakable things, over and over again." His eyes snapped with an inner force. "Do you believe that Annika regrets what she did?"

The old man's monitors revealed his distress.

"Calm down," Jack said, alarmed. He came across and sat on the edge of the bed.

The door opened and a nurse peered in.

"I'm fine," Gourdjiev croaked. "Get out!"

The door sighed shut behind her.

"So?" It was a challenge.

"I believe . . . ," Jack began, "it brought her a kind of peace."

The old man gave a little sigh. "To me, as well."

"Annika said you wanted to see me," Jack said softly, the better to bring Gourdjiev back from the past.

The old man looked him straight in the eye. Unlike most old people, his eyes were as clear as a young man's, they weren't rheumy or watery or lacking in color. On the contrary, Jack could see the lamp of extraordinary intelligence still burning brightly.

"Jack, do you trust me?"

"I think the question is, do you trust me?"

Dyadya Gourdjiev smiled. "You wouldn't be here now if I didn't. Now, come, answer me."

"Trust. That depends on what you mean," Jack said truthfully. "You've lied to me in the past."

"Did things turn out badly?"

"No."

"And it's always turned out for the best, no?"

"That doesn't stop me from feeling used."

The old man took a moment to digest this. "Do you trust me to do no harm?" Like a doctor, the analogy apt, considering their surroundings.

Jack nodded. "It depends on your point of view. I'm never certain whose side you're on."

"Do you trust me to protect Annika, whatever the cost?"

Now Jack's alarm escalated. "Protect her from whom?"

Gourdjiev closed his eyes for a moment, his lids thin as parchment. "Please."

Jack let out a breath he hadn't known he was holding. "Of course I do."

The old man's eyes opened, his gaze steady on Jack. "Then we may proceed." He drew a deep breath, as if preparing for an arduous task. "Listen to me closely. I'm not dying, but it may be that my life is growing short. Who can know, we're all human, yes? The clock keeps ticking." He shrugged. "In any event, the time has arrived for me to plan for a future when I am no longer present."

Jack waited patiently.

"So now I must ask you for a favor."

"Anything."

Gourdjiev slapped him lightly on the forearm. "You agree to such a thing so quickly, without a second thought."

"My second thought would be the same as my first," Jack said seriously.

"Without knowing what this favor might entail."

Jack remained silent, but his gaze remained level on Gourdjiev's face. "So."

The old man pursed his lips, but Jack sensed that he was pleased.

"Well, all right, then. I need you to get me out of here."

"What, the hospital?"

"The hospital, Moscow, Russia."

Jack was puzzled. "But you have so many friends, so much power."

The old man smiled. "The jackals are circling, the hyenas, and now the lions. They're all watching. They all smell blood." He folded his hands on his lap, staring at the tracery of raised blue veins. "Times have changed, Jack. Now money is the only thing that matters. If you have enough money, you buy your way into power. It's easier, you see, than fighting for it yourself. And so much quicker. Shortcuts. These people today, they're lazy, they want everything immediately. Money is the speedway, the rocket to the moon, so to speak."

He shifted slightly, rearranging the sheet over him. "So the old ways are dying, if not already dead, all right, fine, I'm not one to hold on to the past, wringing my hands, mourning for the old days. I think about the future, always, which is why I must make my escape before I get dragged down by what is happening now."

"Which is?"

"A present for which I am unprepared." He shook his head. "Don't look at me like that, I'm neither senile nor paranoid."

"Although in our business," Jack said, "a little paranoia is a good thing."

A small smile played around the corners of Gourdjiev's mouth, but was quickly extinguished. "This escape has to be done now—today."

"Where do you want to go?"

"I'll tell you when we're out of Russia, not before."

"Annika told me that you want to get to a cache of information you've amassed over the years."

"Evidence of wrongdoing, malfeasance, extortion, embezzlement, murder. Documents and photos, taped conversations, videos, that sort of thing." The old man smiled. "There's no such cache."

"Then why did you tell Annik—"

"For her own protection. If she knew everything is inside my head, she'd be paralyzed with fear for me. You understand I can't have that."

Jack did. *Again,* he thought, *who wants her dead? The same jackals, hyenas, and lions that are watching, circling the old man, waiting for an opening; it stands to reason. But who are they?*

Dyadya Gourdjiev tapped the back of Jack's hand with a papery finger. "I wanted you to meet Katya. I love her and she loves me. Now, in my twilight, that's all that's important to me—love. I have no more need of either money or power—they're for younger people, like you and Annika."

With a sudden lunge, he clutched Jack's hand. "You love my granddaughter, yes?"

"Yes," Jack said.

"Because she loves you. This is my beacon in the dark, the only thing I pay attention to now. This is the depth of my trust in you, Jack. Words—words mean nothing, an actor's lines. I want you to remember that. No matter what may occur, you must remember that you love each other, that that love will never change, that it is your true strength, your only salvation."

The old man looked deep into Jack's eyes. "You don't understand this now, but I have faith that one day you will."

Jack sat for a long time, turning over everything Gourdjiev had said. At last, he roused himself. He had a fistful of questions, but he knew the old man well enough not to ask them now. "As to our escape," he said, "I suppose you have a plan."

"When do I not?" That smile again, sharp as a scimitar's blade. "I'm going to have to die."

HENRY HOLT Carson received a call from the president after hours, though, when it came to both men, that phrase hardly existed. Carson was as apt to be up and working at three in the morning as he was at three in the afternoon. His sprawling empire, anchored by his Inter-Public Bancorp, made it imperative that he often transact business in Asia and the Middle East. He was not a man to delegate tasks both difficult and delicate to others just because it might gain him some sack time. "I'll sleep when I'm dead," was Carson's most beloved phrase.

The two men met in the parking lot in back of an enormous Walmart inhabited only by dead-looking trailer trucks unhooked from their cabs and the president's Secret Service detail, which had immediately established a watchful perimeter of granite-faced men linked by a wireless network. Crawford and Carson looked a lot alike. Hands plunged deep in cashmere overcoats, they smiled at each other in a chilly, feral manner, because more often than not the reason for their meetings wasn't pleasant. For both men, business was everything, pleasure a distant memory enjoyed by their younger selves in another, dimly recalled lifetime.

"Making money?" Arlen Crawford said with his just-us-folks Texan heartiness.

"Every minute of every hour of every day," Carson said. "But since you're regularly kept abreast of our mutual holdings I very much doubt that's why we're here in this godforsaken place."

"It suits our purpose." Crawford, tall and rangy, with a cowpoke's rough, wind-reddened skin, indicated that the two should walk. Crawford was not a man who enjoyed being sedentary. Briefings saw him walking back and forth behind the facing sofas in the Oval Office, a habit that still disconcerted some members of his cabinet. This was the very reaction Crawford sought. The president liked everyone off balance, even his closest advisors. "Absent a real live battle," he would say, "it keeps 'em sharp."

The president extracted a pair of Cuban Cohibas from his inside breast pocket, handed one to Carson, then stuck the other between his teeth. The two men paused, bent their heads together as Carson, protected by hunched shoulders and a cupped hand from the wind, lit the cigars. He used one of his prized possessions, a massive silver Ronson lighter, given to him by the premier of China during a pilgrimage Carson had made to Beijing six years ago to clear the way for his brother Edward, then a senator. Also, to consummate a highly lucrative deal with a Chinese high-tech firm headquartered in Shanghai.

The two men continued their leisurely amble around the deserted parking lot, chatting about an upcoming Senate vote, personal golf scores, and Crawford's new press secretary. Nothing important. Carson, walking on the balls of his feet, waited patiently for the current scenario to unfold. The Secret Service perimeter shifted with the location of the POTUS. The men's electronic whispering to each other possessed the hard, dry rustle of an autumn wind.

At last Crawford cleared his throat and said, "I'm growing concerned with Three-thirteen."

The mere mention of the name sent chills through the usually imperturbable Carson. "You're always concerned about Three-thirteen," he said, easily projecting a tone of nonchalance, "though for the life of me I cannot understand why."

The president stopped and turned toward his friend. "Because, Henry, I am growing tired of its monomaniacal focus on Iran."

"I should be the last person on earth to have to remind you of Iran's growing threat in destabilizing the entire Middle East."

"All that is true enough, Henry. But the fact is you neglected to talk to your brother about Three-thirteen."

"Edward was rightly preoccupied with the Russia treaty. Besides, he was hardly in office long enough—"

"I know very well why you didn't tell Edward." The president sucked on his Cohiba, as if to bolster his courage. "He wouldn't have understood. Edward had a highly elevated sense of morality."

"Which we do not."

"We're realists," the president said, "not idealists."

"My brother would never have understood our motivations."

The president regarded the glowing tip of his cigar. "On the contrary, I think Edward would have understood all too well."

Carson turned on the president, his eyes blazing. "What have I told you, Arlen? I do not want to talk about Edward."

"The Good Brother."

Carson, eyes narrowed, took a step closer. "What is it with you tonight, Arlen? Do you have a death wish?"

"Jesus, Henry." Crawford, rearing back, turned pale.

"I made you, Arlen, and I can destroy you. Without my influence, you're a leaky boat dead in the water. If perchance you have forgotten, then consider this your wake-up call. Your last warning. Clear?"

The president continued to suck on his cigar. His hand was trembling.

"I was just . . . I'm voicing a concern . . . for both of us."

"Meaning?"

"Of late, there has been talk among cabinet members," Crawford said. "They're growing uneasy with Three-thirteen's power. They say it should have been shut down long ago. So I want . . . I think for both our sakes it should be dismantled before it takes on a life of its own."

Carson stared at the president with poisonous eyes. He rolled his cigar within the O of his pursed lips. "What you *suggest* . . . can, of course, be accomplished."

"Good." Crawford looked relieved. "I don't want any more questions raised."

Carson felt his heart grow heavy, but he revealed none of his true feelings to the president.

"And, while you're at it, please make sure every trace of the Incident is expunged."

"Let's not start that again."

"The Incident started events spinning out of control."

"The Incident is ancient history. The inquiry following it—"

"Was a sham. We both know it." The ash on Crawford's cigar burned bright for a moment, before falling like snow at his feet. "The inquiry was meant to do one thing only: absolve those involved of any guilt or responsibility."

"Which, at the time, included you and me."

"No, not me." Crawford stared at lights blinking far in the distance as if they had a message for him. "I was on the periphery."

"At the last minute you backed away."

The president winced. "I had other obligations. Important ones." His gray eyes flashed. "That's why I relied on you. The plan was agreed upon. Three-thirteen deployed Acacia to the Horn of Africa, along with a battalion of Marines, for cover. From there, it completely vanished off every grid known to military and man. Twenty-seven hours later, the Incident occurred, causing a cluster-fuck the likes of which I have never seen before or since."

"Which is precisely why it needs to remain buried."

"Ancient history has a way of biting even the most vigilant in the ass. If word of the Incident ever got out, I'd be ruined." The president cleared his throat. "I am thinking more along the lines of incinerated."

Carson waited a moment, marshaling his thoughts. "I think that can be arranged."

"Whatever is done," the president said, "I don't want to know about it."

Of course you don't, Carson thought. *This will happen when and if I give the order, not you.* "Arlen, I want to be clear. There are risks to taking any action whatsoever."

"Deal with them, Henry. Use whatever means. Above all, I want plausible deniability."

Carson nodded, disgusted by the other man's cowardice. On the other hand, if Crawford weren't such a coward, Carson wouldn't be able to exploit him as he did. "I'll take care of it."

They had made a full circle and were now back at where the cars were parked.

President Crawford stuck out his hand. "Henry, good to see you."

Carson grasped it briefly. "As always, Arlen."

The president nodded to his Secret Service detail, letting them know he was ready to leave. "This conversation never happened."

Carson produced a lupine smile. "What conversation?"

NONA HEROE had just come in from the field, where she had been involved in a hostage situation at a stationery store. Before it could get out of hand, she had taken control by entering through the cellar and, coming up behind the perp, disarming him, and taking him into custody. Marching him out the front door, she had announced herself and shoved him over to the uniforms clogging the street. Now, as she strode across the office, she was looking forward to her lunch break so she could visit her brother in the Bethesda Naval Hospital. As often as she went, it never seemed enough.

"Chief of detectives wants to see you," one of her Violent Crimes detectives said when he saw her come in. And then he added, as he watched her make her way to her cubicle, "Now, boss."

"Uh-huh." She turned on her heel and went back down outside, crossed the street to the building opposite the one she worked out of, passed through the marble lobby and into a stainless-steel elevator. She punched nine, then had nothing but her reflection to stare at on the ride up. She saw an imposing woman, with a good figure, the fine, slightly exotic features of her paternal grandmother, and skin the color of bittersweet chocolate. She was still on the good side of forty, but looked more like thirty. Then she turned away, snorting in self-derision.

Exiting, she took a hallway to the end, turned left along another, shorter corridor, and stopped in front of a wood-paneled door. On the

wall to the right was a plaque that read: LEONARD BISHOP, CHIEF OF DE-
TECTIVES.

She rapped once with her knuckles, opened the door, and walked in
just as Bishop said, "Enter."

He stood up when he saw her, but did not come around from behind
his massive oak desk. The walls were hung with decorations, commenda-
tions, and photos of Bishop with various politicos from both parties, past
and present, including President Arlen Crawford, looking red-cheeked,
windblown, and every bit the rangy Texan. There was no picture with
his predecessor, however. Edward Carson must have been killed too soon
after taking office for Bishop to have arranged a photo op.

The CoD's pride in his connections was somewhat justified by his
years getting bloodied on the streets of D.C., though Nona found pride
a repellent trait.

"Take a pew, Detective," Bishop said with a sweeping gesture. "Congratulations. Your quick thinking averted a potential crisis and, quite
possibly, loss of life."

"Thank you, sir."

Bishop seated himself, shuffling some papers aside, bringing others
under his gaze. "I'm putting you in for a commendation."

"That's not necessary, sir." When he glanced up sharply, she altered
her tone. "But much appreciated, sir."

He nodded and dropped his gaze again to the documents in front of
him. "And cut out the 'sir.'" Glancing up briefly again, he added, "When
you're in this office."

He cleared his throat, then looked up and smiled. He was a rather
handsome man, slim, with angular cheekbones, an aggressive nose, wavy
silver hair, and brilliant blue eyes, which looked even better when viewed
through a camera lens.

"Today's heroics only underscore a decision I made this morning,"
he said. "As of next week, you'll be the new coordinator of detectives."

"Sir? Uh, Chief Bishop, I'm not sure I understand."

The CoD spread his hands. "It's a promotion, Nona. Two pay grades
higher and, six months from now, if all goes well, you'll achieve the rank

of deputy chief of detectives." His brow wrinkled. "I must say, you don't look pleased."

"Chief Bishop, correct me if I'm wrong, but isn't coordinator of detectives admin, a desk job?"

"Right as rain." Bishop's smile broadened. "You're being kicked upstairs, Nona. No more looking over your shoulder, waiting for the bullet you never hear. And at your age. I had to pull some strings because of that. Some of my colleagues thought you weren't ready, but I maintained that you are. You don't want to prove me wrong, do you?"

"Of course not." She sat forward, perched on the edge of her chair. "And I don't want to seem ungrateful—"

The CoD's smiled slipped. "Then accept the promotion, and do it graciously."

Nona took a deep breath and let it out. "Look, Chief, I'm a street detective, that's what I've been trained for, that's what I love. It's my life."

"I understand that completely, who better than I? I came up through the ranks just like you."

"I run Violent Crimes; I do it a damn sight better than anyone you might get to replace me."

The CoD nodded sympathetically. "I hear you, but times change, and so must we all. You'll be moving over here."

Away from Alan Fraine and all her friends at Violent Crimes. Nona took a moment to settle the disharmony inside her, to calm down, to find a way to walk the fine line it would take to get what she wanted without terminally pissing off her superior. Bishop was one of a handful of powerful men inside the Metro Police. If he had a mind to, he could ruin her career.

"This is an amazing opportunity, no question about it," she began.

Bishop smiled. "That's more like it."

"But I must respectfully decline."

"You can't decline, Nona, respectfully or otherwise."

"But the street is where I belong, Chief. It's where I do my best work. I am skilled—"

"The time has come to learn new skills."

She stood up. "It seems we're at an impasse."

He pursed his lips. "If there's anything I hate, it's an impasse."

She said nothing, stood primly as a schoolgirl with her hands clasped in front of her.

He leaned back, his fingers steepled, studying her intently. "Have you done something to your hair? A new style?"

The silence stretched and yawned, gaping open to a future she could not abide.

At length, the CoD sighed. "Okay, there is one way to keep the status quo, so to speak, for you to keep your beloved street," he said slowly, as if working it out as he went.

"What?" The eagerness in her voice was unmistakable. "Just tell me."

"It involves me," he said, his words coming ever more slowly as he put emphasis on each one. "And it involves you."

She saw how he undressed her with his eyes, and the revelation hit home. She had been set up. Bishop never expected her to take the coordinator job; he knew her too well and he was too smart to take her off the streets, where, like today, she made him look good. He had wanted this all along, this bending of her to his will, to lord it over her with both power and sex. Under his thumb.

"I could file a report."

"You could," he acknowledged, "but who would see it other than me?"

"Alan."

He cocked his head. "You and Fraine are close, I know. D'you really want to drag your friend into this?"

He was right, she didn't. Hiring a lawyer would get her nowhere except in a career spiral into the toilet. There was nothing else for her to do.

"Well," he said softly, gently. "I'm waiting."

"I want to remain on the street," she said, numb with the ease with which he had turned her world upside down.

"Of course you do." Now he rose and came around from behind his desk. He stood so close to her she could feel the heat coming off him. "And things will be as you wish, Nona. Just as you and I wish."

"PLEASE TELL Annika that it's time," Dr. Zurov, Dyadya Gourdjiev's personal physician, said. He had shown up at the hospital twenty minutes ago and since then had been huddling with his patient. He was a tall, thin individual with a spade beard and a patrician's air.

Jack nodded, rose, and, opening the door, peered out into the corridor, where Annika and Katya were speaking in low tones. At once, Annika broke off the conversation to look at Jack. He nodded to her and she came inside the hospital room and gave Dr. Zurov a meaningful look. Opening her handbag, she took out a plastic device the size and shape of a woman's compact. This she affixed to the underside of the bed. Then she poured her grandfather some water from a plastic pitcher on a rolling tray beside the bed. From his black bag, Dr. Zurov produced a tiny red-coated pill.

"What the hell is that?" Jack said.

"Don't be alarmed," Dyadya Gourdjiev said. He put the pill between his lips and knocked it back with a swallow of water.

Annika reached under the bed to the plastic compact.

"Ten seconds," Dr. Zurov said to his patient. His face looked lined, concentrated, intent.

Dyadya Gourdjiev's eyes rolled up in his head. When he stopped breathing Jack lunged toward him, but Dr. Zurov held him back.

"It's all right," Annika whispered at his side.

A moment later, the steady beeping of the electronic monitors was replaced by a constant shrill sound as all of the old man's vital signs flatlined. A nurse rushed in, took one look at the monitors, and called for a crash cart. Outside in the corridor, they could hear a doctor being urgently paged.

"What happened?" the nurse said as she put a stethoscope over Gourdjiev's heart.

"He had a seizure," Dr. Zurov said. "One minute he was talking, the next he had stopped breathing."

"He's still not breathing," the nurse said as the crash cart was wheeled in.

"I've already pronounced him dead."

The doctor on call rushed in. He asked the same question, to which Dr. Zurov gave the same answer.

"If he's gone, he's gone. He did not want to be resuscitated, he was quite clear on that score." Dr. Zurov produced a signed DNR document, which he handed to the doctor. "Signed and sealed."

Katya, coming into the room, said, "Please leave and let the family grieve in peace."

The doctor, looking bewildered, studied the document, then handed it back with a curt nod. "As you wish." Turning on his heel, he and the nurse left.

Annika was stretched over her grandfather, weeping openly. Katya went to her side and held her around her waist while she stroked her hair.

Dr. Zurov switched off all the monitors. Annika reached beneath the bed and detached the compact, whose electronics had jammed the monitors' signals, and pocketed it.

"He's in the deepest meditative state," Dr. Zurov said. "The drug will last forty minutes."

Katya was already on her cell phone, speaking softly. "The car from the funeral home will be here in ten minutes," she said after she broke the connection.

Jack, astonished at the level of advance planning, said, "I can't see what you need me for."

Annika, who had just placed a kiss in the center of her grandfather's forehead, looked up at him. "You've got the plane standing by at Sherem-etyevo, and it's got diplomatic immunity. Once he's inside and we're air-borne, he's as safe as if he were in a bank vault."

JUST AFTER noon, Alli was summoned to the commander's office. The order was something she had been both expecting and fearing. Bryce Fellows was standing by the window, his hands clasped behind his back. Fellows maintained a stiff military demeanor even during the most informal of Fearington's functions, which, admittedly, were few and far between. His stern countenance was the facade of a man who was both thoughtful and fair-minded.

"I've seen this Web site, Ms. Carson," he said as soon as she entered his office. "It's an abomination, and it has been taken down."

"Thank you, sir." Alli's heart was beating fast.

"That's the good news." Fellows turned from his contemplation of the view outside his office. "The bad news is we have no idea who engineered this attack on you. That being the case, the site, or one very much like it, could pop up on another server at any time."

Alli felt another shiver of dread run through her. She knew Morgan Herr was dead; what was chilling her bones?

"I have no choice but to consider this a direct attack on your person."

"Which is where I come in."

Alli turned to see a familiar face.

"I've been assigned to you," Dick Bridges said.

Bridges had been the head of her father's presidential Secret Service detail. He had been so shaken by his charge's violent death in Moscow that he had disappeared. She had assumed he had retired. Now here he was, as big and robust as ever.

"It's good to see you, Dick," she said.

"You've grown into a fine young woman." He gave her a grim smile. "Sorry this reunion comes under these circumstances."

She shook her head as she turned back to Fellows. "I appreciate your concern, sir, but I'm not going to allow Agent Bridges to follow me around campus. I'm finished being a dog on a leash."

"I'm afraid you don't have a choice, Ms. Carson. Next month, you will graduate Fearington with top honors—in fact, the highest recommendations of any candidate I can recall. I'm not going to allow anyone to harm you."

"I understand your point of view," Alli said. "But please try to understand mine. The moment anyone sees Agent Bridges, they're going to know why he's here."

Fellows nodded. "That's precisely the idea I mean to—"

"With all due respect, sir, everyone will know this person got to me, everyone will know I'm frightened. Especially the person who engineered the attack. That's the wrong message to send."

Fellows opened his mouth, no doubt to refute her, but apparently he thought better of it. He turned to Bridges. "Agent?"

"Unfortunately, Alli's right, Commander."

Fellows shook his head, then addressed Alli. "I'm not prepared to dismiss Agent Bridges, so unless you have an alternative, my order stands."

"I do." Alli came across to where Bridges stood. "Dick stays on campus, but remains in the shadows. Bring him on as part of your visiting instructor program, maybe, that should be easy enough to do."

"He keeps watch over you, but from a distance." Fellows tapped his forefinger against his lips. "Yes, I can see how that would work." He nodded decisively. "It's an excellent compromise, Ms. Carson. Well done."

"It's only well done if it works." Dick Bridges crossed his arms over his chest. "Frankly, Commander, nothing about this assignment satisfies me. It's deeply disturbing that we have not been able to track down the person responsible for the rogue site. Our failure goes against our history in this area. Everyone leaves some form of electronic fingerprint; but his IP address has led us through more than half a dozen countries without gaining a glimpse of his identity. All we get are echoes, never an end address."

"But eventually, you'll find him," Alli said.

Bridges shrugged. "'Eventually' isn't a word you want to hear in this area. I'll be honest, we don't trace him in the first forty-eight hours, it means he's a pro. It'll take a helluva lot of time and manpower to track him down."

IT WASN'T taking off Jack was worried about, it was getting to the airport. Two men from the funeral home, a driver and his assistant, had arrived and had taken Dyadya Gourdjiev out of the hospital on a gurney.

Jack was especially watchful as they accompanied the men from the funeral home into the long ambulancelike van. A frigid wind swept through Moscow. There was snow on the sidewalks and there were icy patches on the roadway, to which the rumbling traffic paid not the slightest attention. Jack was looking for men in parked cars or staring into shop plate-glass windows, which they could use as a reflecting surface to keep an eye on the hospital's entrance.

He was unhappy about being kept out of the loop. Without direct knowledge of Gourdjiev's plan, he felt as if he were in the dark, or at least in a twilight world where he glimpsed shapes and the outlines of things without being able to interpret their meaning.

The interior of the van was cramped. The assistant from the funeral home sat next to the body. He had clamped the gurney down to keep it stationary during the drive to Sheremetyevo. Jack, Annika, Katya, and Boris, the bodyguard who had staked out the hospital lobby, sat on the narrow metal bench that ran along the other side, which was as uncomfortable as it looked.

No one said a word as the van started up and drove away from the reserved space outside the hospital's ER. Jack, hunched to one side, peered out the window of the rear door. The funeral home attendant watched him briefly but said nothing.

Traffic in Moscow was nightmarish, moving either at a glacial pace or at heart-stopping speed, often within the space of the same block. The local taxis—*bombila*—were the most egregious offenders, circling slowly like vultures until they spotted a fare, then accelerating with spine-compressing speed toward their next destination.

There were a number of these *bombila* swerving in and out of the lanes, dodging trucks and ZiL limousines alike. Jack watched them as if he were a spectator at a bumper-car ride. Often, they missed smashing the bumpers or grilles on other vehicles around them by no more than a hairsbreadth.

"Anything?" Annika said.

He shook his head. It seemed inevitable that Gourdjiev's enemies, whose multitude of eyes and ears had by now informed them of the old man's death, would try to get at Annika, now that the old man's protection had ceased to exist. His enemies would consider her an enemy.

The car reached the ring road that circled the inner city. Beyond stretched the highway to the airport. Many of the *bombila* peeled away, using the ring road to race to other parts of the city, but the intercity trucks remained. Also, a couple of ZiLs, the big cars looking like sharks among the whales. Jack concentrated on these limousines. With their smoked windows and armor plating, they made perfect vehicles from which to stage an ambush or an interception.

He had been following the progress of one of the ZiLs, which, to his mind, had been acting suspiciously. It was now directly behind, and pulling closer. When he turned briefly from his observation post to update Annika, he saw her mouth, *We're going in the wrong direction.* He was about to say something, but her eyes cut to the attendant and she placed her forefinger across her lips.

Boris must have become aware of the wrong route. He drew his handgun.

But the attendant already had his own gun out—a Desert Eagle .357 Magnum. He shook his head, said, "Easy, now," as Boris's gun hand twitched. His teeth showed, sharp as needles. "You're ours now."

THREE

"IF THEY can't find the dirtbag," Vera said when Alli had told her about the scene in the commander's office, "then they're incompetents."

"So what do we do?" Alli said.

They were sitting on their beds, facing each other. It was just after midnight, the time they usually spent talking privately.

"Just forget it."

"What?" Alli felt her cheeks flush. How could she forget about December twentieth?

"The site's down, you've already spoken to half the people here and they're all on your side. You came back from Albania a hero. Everyone's calmed down now that the commander's addressed them. There's nothing else to do."

"The hell there isn't," Alli said hotly.

"Alli, it's being dealt with by the authorities. Let them handle it."

Alli jumped up. "You yourself said they're not going to find him."

"I did, but—"

"Then I have to find him!"

She stood up to take Alli's arm, but Alli shook her off. "What's gotten into you?"

"I *am* going to find him." Her eyes were fierce.

"I know that look. Alli, no. This is crazy."

"Don't tell me what's crazy!" Alli shouted.

Vera, taking the measure of her roommate's rapidly escalating agitation, kept her voice calm and even. "Okay, what the hell is going on?"

Alli seemed to collapse, plopping down on the edge of Vera's bed. Vera sat next to her. She had to fight not to call Jack, but he and Annika were in Moscow. Besides, she told herself sternly, she had to handle this on her own. If she went to Jack every time something bad happened she would never become her own person, she would never grow up. She didn't want that.

"Alli," Vera said softly, "talk to me."

When Alli turned her head away, Vera leaned toward her. "Remember when you came back from Albania, when we admitted to each other that we couldn't feel strong emotion toward anyone else?" She bumped her shoulder playfully into Alli's. "Remember what you said?"

Alli took a deep breath and let it out. "Yeah, I said there's only one thing to do—talk about it."

"So." Vera put her hand on Alli's. "How about taking your own advice?"

Their talk back then had been extremely difficult. Vera had confessed that Henry Holt Carson had placed her as Alli's roommate to discover if Alli knew the whereabouts of Caroline, his daughter from his second, failed, marriage. Alli didn't. Caro had vanished years ago, when she was thirteen. No one had seen or heard of her since. When Alli asked why her uncle hadn't come to her himself, Vera shrugged and said, *"He didn't think you'd tell him the truth."*

Vera, it was clear, despised everyone. There was ice in her veins; she had forgotten how to like, never mind love, someone. Alli had opened up about her abduction, the week-long terror at the hands of Morgan Herr, from which Jack had saved her. She had also spoken of Emma McClure, Jack's daughter, who had died four years ago in a car wreck. Alli and Emma had been more than roommates at Langley Fields

College, they had been lovers. Alli had never gotten over that love. It was Alli's most closely guarded secret, because she felt partly responsible for Emma's death. There were only a few people who knew this, and now Vera was one.

For a long time, with these memories swirling, she said nothing, hunched over, elbows on knees, as if drawing in on herself. She knew this pose well; she assumed it whenever she felt emotionally threatened. Physical threats she could handle—she could take direct action, change the situation. But this—this made her feel helpless. And then the fear would rise like a tide, the same fear that had overwhelmed her in that awful room where Morgan Herr had kept her for a week, brainwashing her. It had taken her a long time and a lot of hard work with Jack and Annika's help, but at last she had been certain she had left that nightmare behind. And now it seemed as if it was about to happen all over again, as if Morgan Herr hadn't died, as if he had returned from the dead.

All this she told Vera, and more. At first she did so haltingly, the terror like a ball of needles in her throat, but then the words began to flow more and more easily, and she began to feel an immense sense of relief.

"So, what," Vera said when she had concluded, "you actually think this guy didn't die?"

"That's just it," Alli cried. "I *know* he died. Jack was there. He went out the motel window. He broke his neck and his back. He's dead and buried."

"So what has you so freaked out? You being tied up, the date you were abducted, all this information is public knowledge. Anyone could have—"

"But not the chair." Alli reached over for Vera's iPad, brought up the images she had saved of the nudes with Alli's face. She pointed. "No one but Jack and the cops knew that I had been tied to a chair just like this."

"Now you're getting *me* freaked out," Vera said. "Let's try to think about this rationally."

"There's nothing rational about it."

Alli shivered and Vera put an arm around her.

"This one detail has brought the nightmare rushing back at me. I can't help thinking . . ." Her voice petered out, as if she were afraid to articulate the terrible thoughts whirling through her mind.

Vera took a breath and let it out. "Okay, okay. I agree, this is serious. I'm on board." She reached for her cell. "There's someone who can help us. She's a genius at computer hacking. If anyone can find this cocksucker, it's her."

Alli looked up. "Who is it?"

But Vera had already punched in the number and now held a forefinger across her lips. "Hey, it's me. . . . I know, but this is important. . . . No, no, not me. Alli . . . Carson. . . . Hmmm, okay, but you'll like this one, a real challenge. . . . I agree, let's meet. Tell me where and when. Oh, and, Caro, I'd like to bring her."

Alli stared at Vera as she disconnected. "Caro?"

"Yeah." Vera looked at her in a steady, serious manner. "I've known for a while where your cousin is. I guess we all have angles to play."

THE FUNERAL home van kept up a steady pace along the highway, moving away from Sheremetyevo Airport. Boris sat glowering, having been forced to give up his weapon. Jack was suffused by an icy calm. He tried to make eye contact with Annika, but she was staring fixedly at Gourdjiev, dead asleep in his deep meditative state, helpless as a newborn.

As the car jounced around, Jack began to inch himself farther from Annika. It was imperative that he get as far from her as possible so the gunman would have difficulty keeping a constant eye on both of them. He moved carefully and in inconstant bursts timed to the swaying of the van. Even so, the increasing gap finally became apparent to the gunman, and with a wave of the Magnum's barrel, he indicated that Jack should move back toward Annika.

Jack rose to comply, but instead of moving sideways, he launched himself at the gunman. The Magnum exploded near his left ear, deafening him, but he already had his elbow beneath the gunman's chin, shoving it against his Adam's apple. The gunman struck him on the side of his head, and sparks exploded behind his eyes. He relinquished his grip long enough for the gunman to regain control of the .357 and press its muzzle against Jack's forehead.

Annika had her SIG Sauer out.

"Put the weapon down," the gunman said, staring her down, "or I blow your boyfriend's head—"

Jack slammed his elbow into the attendant's side, cracking a rib. As the man lurched backward, a gunshot tore through the top of the car. Jack grabbed the Desert Eagle, slammed it against the side of the attendant's head. His hand shot out, grabbing Jack around the throat and squeezing hard. Jamming the heel of his hand under the attendant's chin, Jack forced the man's head up, then, with a violent lurch forward, smashed the back of it against the wall. The attendant's eyes rolled up, and Jack wrested the Magnum away from him, slashing the long barrel across the bridge of his nose. The attendant came at him, fingers like claws, and Jack shot him in the head. Katya gave a little cry. The attendant, leaking blood, slid down. Jack rolled him onto the floor.

Annika opened her mouth to say something, but at that moment, the intercom speaker crackled. "Is everything okay back there?"

Leaning over Gourdjiev's body, Jack toggled a switch on the intercom box affixed to the partition. "Fine now," he said a little breathlessly. "The bodyguard tried to make a move and I shot him."

The driver said nothing. Jack looked at Annika. The car slowed, turned off the highway, into a vast industrial open space filled with lines of corrugated metal warehouses.

Jack hunched toward her. "Who are these people?"

"I have no idea."

"They were clever enough to get to these funeral home workers, so they had to have known about the plan. Can you explain that?"

Annika shook her head.

"It's possible, then, that they know we've faked your grandfather's death."

"Impossible."

"Which is what you would have said about suborning these men not ten minutes ago." Jack peered out the window. "We must be going into one of the warehouses."

The van lurched to a stop. They heard the front door slam, saw the driver running for a side door in the warehouse.

"I'm guessing he didn't believe me," Jack said.

Boris, clambering out the back, fired a shot at the driver. The driver whirled, knelt, and returned fire. Boris staggered back as he disappeared into the warehouse. Jack and Annika ran to Boris, who had been shot in the right shoulder. It was a flesh wound. They helped him back into the van, where Annika signed to Katya to take care of him.

Jack indicated the warehouse. "We'll get our answers in there."

Annika eyed the building. "Think this through, Jack. We can't leave my grandfather and Katya. They're too vulnerable out here."

"We need to know who has infiltrated your grandfather's plans. Otherwise, they'll surely try again before we can get to the airport."

She frowned, then nodded. "All right. I'll take care of it while you drive Dyadya and Katya to a safe location."

"I'm not going to let you go in there by yourself."

"Who else is going to do it? Boris is wounded and Katya doesn't drive."

"Annika—"

"Every moment we stand here arguing, my grandfather is at risk." Her carnelian eyes had turned steely.

He nodded, reluctant still. "I'll take him to my plane."

"That's the first thing I thought of," Annika said. "But if we're being observed, then we'll lead the enemy directly to our only source of escape. We can't risk that."

Annika glanced back at the van, where Dyadya Gourdjiev lay, still as death. When she turned back to him, she said, "There's a place you can take him where he'll be safe, at least temporarily." She gave him an address.

Jack hesitated. "What about you?"

"I'll join you as soon as I can."

"Driving what?"

She pointed to a parking lot at the other end of the industrial park. "Any car I can break into."

NONA HEROE rose from the sweat-damp bed, rolled away from Leonard Bishop's naked body, and, spangled in the night glare of Washington's parkway lights, picked her way to the bathroom. She sat on the toilet, her head in her hands, as she relieved herself.

There was still time to walk away from this swamp, she told herself, but that meant abandoning the career she had made for herself, the years of hard work she had put in. She could pack up and move away, perhaps back to her native New Orleans, and remain out on the streets, but to what end? The place was so corrupt a good cop stood a better chance of demotion than rising up the ranks. Besides, she would never feel the adrenaline rush the kinds of cases she encountered here gave her.

She had wanted so badly to tell Alan Fraine about her compromised position, but each time, she had shied away, too humiliated to share her misery even with her friend. He was also her boss and, as such, he would be bound to protect her. But how? Bishop was Alan's boss; he held everyone at Metro in his hand. The only way was to find someone who was more powerful than Bishop and willing to wield that power to free her. But even if she found such a person, whatever he would ask for in return would be too high a price to pay.

The funny thing was that several times she was certain that Alan wanted to say something to her, but he never did. But he had begun to watch her in a different way, as if he were reevaluating her. And once, when she entered his office to hand in a report, she saw her file jacket open on his desk. Then it struck her that she wasn't confiding in him, and she began to wonder whether something basic in their relationship had changed. Did they no longer trust each other? If so, they didn't belong working together. Maybe it *was* time for her to get out of D.C., find a new life, and—

She looked up to see Bishop standing in the doorway.

"Don't you knock?"

"Not in my house." Grinning, he went to the shower and turned on the spray. Steam filled the room. He pulled her to her feet, his eyes running up and down her body, then he shoved aside the shower curtain.

Nona found that her mind had retreated to its paralyzed state.

Bishop pulled her to him, laughing. "Time for round two."

ALAN FRAINE popped a fistful of Bugles in his mouth. He was almost out; next would come the potato chips. He shivered in the dark, even though he was well bundled up. The chill of night seeped its way into the dim interior of his car. His stomach rumbled; he was hungry despite, or possibly because of, the crap he'd been eating since ten P.M. That's when he'd taken up station opposite Leonard Bishop's house.

He hadn't been on a stakeout in years; he'd forgotten just how long and boring it could be. There were times when he wondered whether he had made the right decision. He could have gone into Chris's business. His twin brother had founded and now ran International Perimeter, a top-tier private security firm, whose client list looked like a who's who of giant S&P 500 companies. Nevertheless, IP's largest client was the U.S. government, whose seemingly endless appetite for war had made him a fortune.

Chris, on the cusp of becoming a billionaire, was Alan's polar opposite. He was outgoing, gregarious, a hard-party maniac, a man who made his presence felt in every room he inhabited. People naturally gravitated to him, and it was true that, because of this, IP had the smartest and most highly skilled agents in the insanely competitive field in which IP prospered. Chris was, in short, both the toast of D.C. and the most envied CEO in his field. Alan could have had a piece of IP had he wanted to work for his brother, but he didn't. In fact, despite the legendary intimacy shared by twins, Alan Fraine would have liked nothing better than to be as far away from Chris as he could possibly get. The truth was, Chris's lifestyle embarrassed him. He was like the Hugh Hefner of D.C. Alan didn't think decent people should act like that. Chris called him a Pilgrim, by which he meant Alan was strait-laced, without a sense of fun. He didn't exactly hate Chris and he certainly didn't envy him, sucking at the teat of the federal government. But, no doubt about it, Chris raised the hackles on the back of his neck, especially when he would gift Alan with five-figure checks for his birthday, Christmas, New Year's, even, once, for Valentine's Day. As if Alan were a poor relation. Alan used to tear up the checks, but Chris was so hurt, he soon gave it up, depositing the checks in an account he told no one about, not even his wife. He used to be ashamed of the money, until he hit upon the notion of donating a bit at a time to certain charities he carefully selected.

He yawned mightily, rolled his aching shoulders, and stretched his cramped muscles. At first he had felt guilty following Nona, but now he was glad he had followed his instincts. Something had been up with her, something out of sync, something wrong. Several times during the day he had been certain that she was going to tell him, but in each instance she stopped short. This hesitancy, more than anything else, had set off alarm bells in his head, which was why he had decided to follow her after work.

Nona and Leonard Bishop! The idea of the clandestine liaison made his blood boil. It made no sense. Why would Nona hook up with Bishop? Fraine knew she detested the man. At least, that's what she had told him. Had she been lying to him? Did she have an entire life she held secret from him? Trouble was, he didn't like the answers he was getting.

His salty fingertips found their way to the bottom of the Bugles box. There were still a couple left. He threw the box onto the footwell and stomped on it as if it were Leonard Bishop's head.

ANNIKA SLID herself through the side door to the warehouse. The interior was illuminated only by a horizontal line of narrow windows up near the ceiling, their panes so dirty the light that filtered through was as gray as ash.

The concrete floor was covered with old stains, but bare—no crates or pallets or containers of any kind. A forklift was stashed in one corner, shrouded in gloom. The air was stale, as if the front door hadn't been opened in some time. In the dim light filtering through the filthy windows, she could make out a car along with the hulking silhouette of the forklift. There was no sign of the driver, but she knew he must be here somewhere. She wondered if there were others who had been waiting for him to drive the van inside.

She reached the corner where the forklift rested. She peered up into the dusty cab. The moment she did so, the headlights snapped on, blinding her in their glare.

———

"HOW IN the world do you know Caro Carson?" Alli asked Vera as they got out of the car Vera had driven to the meet. "She's been dead to the world for the last fifteen years. Her father's been searching for her for forever."

"He just didn't know where to look." Vera shook her head. "Bad joke. I knew Caro when we were very young. She was about four years older than I was, but she took an interest in me, God alone knows why. She treated me like a little sister, protecting me and all that. Then she just . . . vanished."

Alli's expression clouded over. "Why should I believe you? You lied to me about your real reason for being at Fearington."

"That's so unfair! I told you your uncle contacted me, pulled strings to get me into Fearington as your roommate."

"After the fact, Vera!"

"Really, Alli? Are we going to do this again? I confessed. Mea culpa. What else can I do?"

"Trust doesn't come so easily, not after what happened. It takes time, it has to be earned."

Some strange, dark thought seemed to flicker behind Vera's eyes, and she opened her mouth, about to say something. But at the last instant she clamped her mouth shut and, nodding, stomped on.

Following her, Alli said, "So, okay, tell me what you know about my vanishing cousin."

"Caro's weird. I haven't a clue what's going on in her head. She contacted me several weeks ago when she got back to D.C."

"Where was she all these years?"

"Here, there, she didn't say, except that it was as far away from her father as she could get, so maybe Asia?"

"My cousin," Alli said in wonderment. "She's gone and now she's back. Why?"

"Who knows?" Vera shrugged. "Maybe she'll tell us tonight. Caro doesn't seem like the kind of person to do anything without a very specific reason. She's kind of scary, really, like a human incarnation of a logic bomb. She's got a mind like . . . well, you'll see."

They met Caroline Lynette Carson outside a twenty-four-hour convenience store down the block from the First New Hope Baptist Church on the corner of Seaton Place and Third Street NE. At this hour of the night the church was closed and the sidewalks were deserted. Now and again, vehicles turned into the convenience store parking lot, a man or woman would get out, go in, make a purchase, and drive off. No one stayed very long and they certainly didn't look around. It was a perfect place for a clandestine meet, Alli thought.

Caro was waiting for them in the shadows at the rear of the lot. As they exited their car, she appeared like an apparition. She wore black jeans, boots, and a thick, sheepskin-lined jacket. Her hands were in her pockets, and for a moment Alli couldn't help but wonder whether she was gripping a pistol. In her maturity, she had blossomed, but her beauty took an altogether different form than her friend's. Whereas Vera was dark-haired, full-figured, with vaguely exotic, sensual features, Caro's face was bare of all makeup, almost ascetic, with a high, broad forehead and hair so blond it was almost white. It was pulled back from her face in a long po-nytail that seemed to turn her slender, boyish figure gaunt as a snowy tree branch.

For a moment she stood frozen, as if shy or unsure as to how to pro-ceed. Then she came forward and kissed Vera lightly on both cheeks in the European manner. When she turned, Alli felt struck by the inten-sity of her emerald-green eyes.

"Alli." Her voice was deep, somehow rough, as if with that single word she were uttering a threat.

Alli did not know what to say or do. She had not seen Caro since they were both children, and then only once or twice when she had come to her uncle's house. She had to remind herself that she had no real memory of Caro, yet she carried with her a sense of her cobbled from the bits and pieces she had heard when Henry Holt Carson had spoken of her to Alli's father.

Now it seemed to her that this real, flesh-and-blood Caro had noth-ing to do with that wild child who had either been kidnapped or had run away from the amoral father she despised, depending on whom you believed, but who, at any rate, had seemed to have vanished off the face of the earth.

Caro cocked her head to one side. "You seem startled."

" 'Startled' is an understatement," Alli said. "I feel like I've been hit by a tidal wave."

Caro laughed, the deep, raspy sound of the inveterate smoker, and now Alli could see the lines at the corners of her mouth and across her forehead, and she wondered how hard Caro's life had been in the intervening years, what she had done, where she had been, who her friends were. It was, she reflected, as if Caro had been beamed down from Mars. She was an alien creature, completely unknown, as if, like Artemis, the powerful goddess of the hunt, she had sprung from the head of a god. She was a myth, come alive.

"We don't know each other at all, do we?" Caro's eyes studied Alli's face. "I know that look, I've seen it many times before." She shook her head. "Don't even try to figure me out."

Caro gestured and she turned, leading them to her car. It smelled of stale smoke and seemed charged with adrenaline. Caro sat alone in the front seat, her back against the driver's-side window, her legs draped over the center console. Alli and Vera made themselves comfortable in the backseat. Caro shook out a cigarette and lit up. As if intuiting their objection, she cracked a window, letting in a knife blade of frigid air. She smoked slowly and languidly. She certainly didn't act like a fugitive, Alli thought, unsurprised at her feeling of admiration. She herself was an outsider. At its deepest level, this was what had bonded her with Vera. She suspected that, whether Caro knew it or not, it would be the same with her. Outsiders had a knack of instantly recognizing one of their own and liking them. They could scarcely help it.

"So," Caro said, picking a piece of tobacco off her lower lip, "you wanted my help?"

Vera handed her the iPad, which was already open to the screen shots she had taken of the Web site when it was still up.

Caro glanced back at them. "You're kidding, right? This is junk, amateur stuff."

"The Feds haven't been able to run down the perp," Alli said.

" 'Perp.' " Caro chuckled. "Listen to you."

Alli pointed. "You see the chair the girls are on? It's identical to the one I was bound to when—"

"Yeah," Caro said, sitting up. "I heard about what happened to you."

"That date of my supposed death, it's when I was abducted."

Caro frowned as she studied the screen shots more carefully. Then she took out a notebook computer and fired it up. Caro had customized it to her own specifications. From what Vera had told her, this notebook was unlike any other in the world.

Caro inputted some information from the screen shots and then did some cyber-digging. "I see what's baffled the Feds," she said. "This guy has sent them bouncing around the world."

"Can you find him?" Alli said.

"No doubt." Caro looked at her. "But not here, not now. It will take a bit of time and craftiness. Plus, I need tools I don't normally carry with me."

"So you'll do it?" Vera said.

Caro looked from one to the other. "Quid pro quo. I want something in return."

"Name it," Alli said immediately. She had a sense that Vera would hesitate, perhaps because she knew Caro.

Vera sighed. "Out with it."

Caro grinned. "I want something that . . ." Her eyes cut toward Vera. "Henry Holt Carson has something I want."

Vera's cheeks flushed deeply. She seemed disconcerted for a moment, before regaining her equilibrium. "You want us to steal this thing, whatever it is?"

"We'll do it!" Alli said, and ignored the venomous look Vera shot her.

"And there you are," Caro said with a good-natured smirk. "The Hardy Girls are born."

JACK DROVE the funeral home van several hundred yards farther into the industrial park until it was hidden between two buildings. Then he got out and sprinted back toward the warehouse into which both the driver and Annika had disappeared.

Finding the side door ajar, he slipped inside. Annika was retreating from a forklift that rumbled relentlessly toward her. Jack shouted, but could not make himself heard over the sound of the forklift's engine. He lifted his Magnum, squeezed off a shot that cracked the driver's-side windshield. Jack glimpsed Annika, making the most of the distraction, leaping up onto the side of the forklift.

ANNIKA GRABBED the operator's door handle as she swung herself all the way up. She saw the shadow of the gun and ducked just as a bullet shattered the side window and whistled past her right ear.

Jack ran toward the forklift. Annika used the butt of her handgun to chop away the shards of remaining glass. She wanted to keep the driver alive, but he seemed determined to kill her.

The driver's thick, muscular arm shot out, his fingers gripping her throat. He began to shake her head back and forth, harder and harder. She lost her sense of balance first, then her vision, which became nothing more than a smeared blur.

Jack, approaching, tried to get a sense of what was happening inside the forklift's cab.

For Annika worse was to come. The driver slammed the side of her head against the cab door. Stars exploded behind her eyes and she felt her gorge rise. He knocked the gun out of her hand and slammed her head into the metal with even more force. A warmth trickled into her mouth, and the taste of copper told her she was bleeding. If he managed to slam her again she felt certain she would lose consciousness. Then she surely would be done for.

Jack raised the Magnum, but Annika and the driver were too closely entwined for him to have a clear shot. He sprinted toward the forklift.

As the driver shook her a third time, Annika managed to raise her arm up as protection, buffering the blow. Then, straining, she leaned in, plunging her forefinger into his right eye. He screamed, and she dug it in farther. His grip on her throat loosened, and she gasped in air, wrenched his hand away.

Jack leapt up onto the forklift, but, clinging with one hand and with the Desert Eagle in the other, he had no leverage. He tried to climb higher to gain better purchase.

Annika saw the gun as the driver brought it to bear on her and knocked it sideways. She had blinded him on her side, forcing him to turn his head full on to her. She smashed his nose with the heel of her hand, and she was totally free. Swinging away, she wrenched open the cab door and kicked him in the face. As he fell back, she grabbed hold of the edge of the roof and wrapped her legs around his neck. His meat-hook hands tore at her, frantically trying to free himself and, at the same time, gouge her. Feeling him prying apart her legs, she locked her ankles behind his ears and exerted as much force as she could muster. For what seemed like endless moments, they were locked in a struggle as much of will as of strength and endurance. Then Annika, using her advantage of leverage, squeezed her thigh muscles with all her force. Still, she was losing the battle; his superior strength was a heartbeat from overwhelming her, freeing himself from her vise.

Leaning in, she smashed her hand into his throat. He coughed, then gagged. Jack, having gained the cab from the other side, jerked open the door and hauled the driver out, dropping him to the concrete floor

Annika, her breathing labored, her heart racing, went slack. "Shit," she said, slipping backward in exhaustion.

JACK CARRIED her down off the forklift. The moment he set her down he got a good look at her face.

"I'm fine," she said.

He took her around the front of the forklift to where the driver, semiconscious, lay on his back.

Jack hauled him into a sitting position, slapped him hard on both cheeks. "Who hired you?"

The driver's eyes fluttered and he sucked in air. Jack repeated the question.

The driver shook his head.

Jack hit him on his right ear.

"Damnit," the driver said, cowed. "I don't know."

Jack slammed him again, this time with the barrel of the Magnum. "Don't fuck with me, I don't have the time."

"Don't kill me."

Jack pressed the muzzle of the Desert Eagle against the driver's right nostril. "I'm not going to kill you," Jack said, "but I will rob you of all your five senses, one at a time, unless you talk."

Jack ripped the gun's muzzle through flesh and skin. The driver cradled his ruined nose with both hands. His eyes were rolling manically. "I was con-contacted by someone who said he worked for the old man. I believed him."

"What did he tell you to do?"

"Just what I did. Take Gourdjiev to this warehouse."

"And then what?"

"Drive the van inside."

"That's it?"

The driver nodded. "Then we were supposed to get out as fast as we could."

Jack shook him. "Who gave you your orders?"

"He said his name was Omega."

Jack looked at him skeptically. "And you took that at face value?"

"I took the ten thousand dollars that arrived at my door at face value."

"Who delivered the money?" Annika said.

The driver shrugged. "A kid. I never saw him before or since."

Remembering the conversation he had had with Annika in her apartment, Jack wondered whether Omega might be Grigori Batchuk. "And this Omega," Jack said, "what did he look like?"

"He was a voice on the phone"—the driver winced in pain—"nothing more."

"Did he call you at home?"

"My mobile," the driver said. "I don't have a landline."

Jack held out his hand. "Let's have it."

The driver took one hand away from his nose and dug in his jacket pocket. As he was about to extract his hand, Jack grabbed his wrist, moved the hand out slowly. It was gripping a mobile phone.

Jack took it from him and turned it on. When the screen lit up, he checked the call log. "What language did you and Omega speak?"

"Russian," the driver said.

"His accent?"

The driver shrugged. "I'm from Moscow and so is he."

Jack was scrolling through the list of recent incoming calls while the driver watched.

"That's the one," the driver said, pointing. "He always called me from that number."

Jack showed it to Annika. "It's a Moscow exchange," she said, "but that's all I can tell."

Jack handed the phone to the driver. "Call it."

The driver glanced up at him, sniffling heavily. "What? I've never contacted him."

"Why not?" Annika asked.

"He told me not to."

"Do it now," Jack said.

Fright leapt into the driver's eyes again. "What d'you want me to say?"

"Tell him the truth—or a version of it. You've run into a problem, your compatriot is dead. You're broken down. Give him your location."

"For real?"

"Yes," Jack said. "And tell him he has to come himself."

"He won't like—"

"Convince him," Jack ordered.

The driver made the call, tilting the mobile so Jack could listen in. The line rang and rang, but no one answered. There was no voice mail, either.

Jack took the mobile away from the driver. "Ten to one it's a dead line," he said. "Omega's moved on."

FOUR

CARO, CYBER–DATA in a flash drive, returned to her penthouse hotel suite, after spending the bulk of the afternoon at lunch in Alexandria and then meeting with certain people for whom she had zero affinity but who were of use to her current plans.

A breathtaking nighttime vista of D.C., the Potomac, and the Tidal Basin greeted her with the affection of old friends. She had rented the suite upon her return to the U.S. on a false passport, after having fled Albania and her former lover and boss, a man known only as the Syrian. Her name was now Helene Simpson. She knew the Syrian had put a price on her head; she knew that he would not rest until she had been hunted down, brought before him, and disemboweled while he watched, hot-eyed and smiling. Such was the price he inflicted on those who betrayed him. She had confided none of this to Vera, nor would she, ever. She had lived too long as her own, sole confidante; she saw no reason to alter that game plan. Nevertheless, she felt the pressure and anxiety of being hunted. She did not sleep well, or, for days at a time, at all, only to fall, at last utterly exhausted, into a shallow sleep, besieged by nightmares of her capture and subsequent death at the hands of her spurned lover.

The Syrian was a notorious recluse. Even those closest to him didn't really know him at all—his origins, his family, even his real name. He had insisted she call him Ashur when they were intimate, but she had no clear idea whether or not the name meant anything, except to him.

Her terror of him provided numerous opportunities for regret; nevertheless, not once did she think leaving him was a mistake. On the contrary, fleeing had saved her from drowning in his power. But now she had become his quarry, and she had no illusions regarding either his ruthlessness or his doggedness in tracking her down. His shadow continued to move on her horizon.

For a long moment, she stood immobile in the center of the living room, studying all the subtle traps she had laid to alert her of an intruder's presence. She had set throw pillows on the sofa in a certain color sequence and in a particular series of angles, she had left sections of *The New York Times* open to different pages, the pages overlapping one another in a specific way.

In the bedroom, the creases in the bedspread were as she had left them and there were no fingerprints or tracks on the dresser tops or handles she had coated with hair spray before she had left. In her clothes closet, she measured the spaces between the hangers over which her dresses and skirts were folded. The cleaning staff were under strict orders not to enter the suite unless she was present. Satisfied that all was in order, she returned to the living room.

Throwing her coat across the sofa, she sat down at her desk, opened her laptop, and inserted the flash drive. Then she took a small gray metal box from the floor of the hall closet, where she had secreted it in a shoe box that housed the Prada shoes she was wearing. This she took back to the desk.

Opening it, she took out *The Little Curiosity Shop*, an old, battered children's book she and Vera had shared. Opening the book to the middle section caused a space to open between the spine and the binding. Slipping her finger into the space, she drew out a micro SD flash memory card, which she fitted into the appropriate slot in her laptop. Navigating to the icon, she double-clicked it, activating the software program of her own design. It was much too valuable to keep on her laptop's hard drive.

When she powered off the laptop, traces of the program were completely wiped, leaving not one byte behind.

Next, she accessed the starting IP address of the Web site she had downloaded from Vera's iPad and ran it beneath her own software program. Instantly, the software used her laptop's souped-up central processor and the Wi-Fi connection to begin its mind-bogglingly rapid calculations, following the IP's trail as it morphed from one address to another.

Caro discovered she was hungry. She punched a key on her cell. "Number Eleven," she said, when the discreet female voice answered. "Ten minutes," the voice replied, and Caro disconnected.

She rose, padded into the bathroom, and scrubbed her hands and face. Toweling off, she stared at herself in the mirror for so long, with her gaze rock steady, that an outsider might have thought she was hypnotizing herself.

The hotel phone rang, and she reached for the receiver beside the sink. "Send him up," she said in response to the query. She left the towel draped over the edge of the granite sink. On her way to the door, she glanced at her laptop's screen. It was filled with rapidly moving calculations that scrolled down the page, replaced by others.

Grunting with satisfaction, she opened the door before the bell could be rung. She stood aside to let the man in, then closed and locked the door, engaging the security chain that she herself had replaced with one made of solid titanium. It could not be cut by anything less powerful than an electric saw with a diamond blade.

By the time she turned around, he had put down his overnight bag, and her silk blouse was already unbuttoned. She wore no undergarments; the inside semicircles of her breasts were bared. She looked into Number Eleven's face and her nipples were suddenly hard. He smiled at her in that way she liked so much, with nothing beneath it but desire for her. She didn't believe his desire was actually for her, but didn't mind the pretense. Sex was all pretense anyway, so why not ride the wave? The Syrian had desired her, but that was very likely as much because she had been of exceptional use to him. Needs often got confused, especially during the sex act. During her time with the Syrian, she had become a master at identifying and manipulating the confusion. It was a distinct relief not to have to do that with Number Eleven. That was the only designation by which she knew him; she had no desire to know his name and every reason not to want to know it.

Number Eleven stood perfectly still as she approached. She clicked open a stiletto switchblade, using it to slice open his clothes layer by layer. She was as careful, as precise as a surgeon slicing through skin, fascia, and muscle, down to the bone, which, in Number Eleven's case, was his softly pearled flesh.

When they were both standing naked in front of each other, she threw the knife across the room. "Now," she said, "take me."

This he did, with singular strength and grace. The first time, he had tried to kiss her. Don't, she had said, turning her head. No kisses on the lips. Even the thought of it frightened her, as if a kiss were an intimacy she could not tolerate, as if in exhaling into his mouth she would lose a part of herself that she could never get back.

Number Eleven possessed extraordinary staying power, giving her time to climax five times, at the end of which she would allow him to abandon himself to her. Midway through this, the chime on her laptop rang. Without a word, she rose, ignoring him as he slipped out of her. Picking her way across the room, she leaned over her laptop, her skin pink with friction, glistening with their mingled secretions.

A Cheshire Cat smile stole across her lips. Her software had completed its scouring of the Web and had found the perpetrator of the Web site, despite a dizzying trip through servers around the globe that wound in concentric circles.

WHEN NONA Heroe exited Bishop's house just after dawn, she saw tendrils of smoke seeping out of a car window cracked open. As she crossed the street, her heart sank when she recognized the vehicle. The driver's-side window slid down as she neared.

"I know you must be tired," her boss said, "but get the fuck in here anyway."

Sighing, Nona went around the front, hauled open the passenger's door, and slid inside. Alan Fraine fired the ignition and pulled out into the deserted street, rolling away from what he must surely think of as the scene of the crime. For her part, Nona was sick to her stomach. What with the smell of cigarettes mixed with Bugles and Fritos, it was all she could do not to vomit.

"Nona—"

"I wish you would keep quiet," she said.

"Sorry, no can do." He made a left turn. "Now you're in the confessional, it's time to unburden yourself."

"You unholy little shit, you followed me."

"True enough"—Fraine nodded—"except for the 'unholy little shit' part."

She grunted, folding her arms across her breasts. "You didn't even give me the benefit of the doubt." She turned to him. "Where did the trust between us go?"

He thought about this a moment. It was a crucial question. "It's not you I don't trust, Nona. It's everyone else."

"That's what my daddy used to tell me when he was teaching me how to drive."

"Nothing ever changes, does it?"

She leaned her head against the window, staring out at the street. The garbage pileup was staggering. She thought she saw a rat running between the black plastic bags.

"How's Frankie?" Fraine said. He knew that Nona tried to visit her brother every day. Occasionally he went with her.

"The same."

"He know you were there?"

"My heart says he did."

Fraine made another turn. They were in a seedy part of D.C. "How about some breakfast?" He shot her a quick glance. "If your stomach's up for it. You look a little green around the gills."

"How the hell can you tell?"

That set them both to laughing, but Nona sobered up quick enough.

"Shit, Alan, I'm in an awful bind."

"I figured." He pulled up in front of their favorite greasy spoon and killed the ignition. "Come on. We'll sort it out over eggs and coffee."

They got out and, hunched over against the wind gusts, went up the concrete steps into the diner. The place was nearly empty and they took their usual window booth. To their left was a long counter with red vinyl stools and, beyond, past the ranks and stands of layer cakes, fruit-filled turnovers, and old-fashioned crullers, was the open kitchen. The interior looked as if it hadn't been cleaned since it had opened in the 1950s. It smelled like it, too, but the thick impasto of grease, sweat, and desperation was all part of the charm. There was even a stained photo of Eisenhower over the pass-through to the steaming kitchen.

Elsie, the old waitress who had been there forever, waddled over, pad and pencil stub clutched in her arthritic hands. "What'll it be, young-uns?"

"The usual," Fraine said, "for both of us."

She nodded. "Prepare your stomach linings, coffee's coming right up."

Fraine pulled out a couple of paper napkins from the chrome container while Nona flipped through the offerings on the table's remote jukebox.

"Nat King Cole or Etta James?" she said.

Fraine grunted. "Etta by a nose."

Nona inserted a quarter and pressed some buttons. A moment later, James's "All I Could Do Was Cry" came wafting through the speakers.

"How appropriate," Fraine said.

"So beautiful, so sad," Elsie said as she set the cups of coffee and the pitcher of cream in front of them. "Eggs and bacon on the griddle."

"Bring another coffee setup," Fraine said as she turned to leave.

Nona frowned. "Someone's joining us?"

"I made the call when you showed. He'll be here shortly."

"Who?"

"Tell me what happened," Fraine said.

Nona recounted her summons from Bishop, how he had extorted her compliance in exchange for keeping her on the street where she belonged.

"I knew he was an unholy little shit," Fraine said, "but he's now graduated to an entirely new level."

Nona smiled thinly at his deliberate use of her own phrase. Elsie arrived with eggs, bacon, and whole-wheat toast, which was Fraine's concession to good nutrition. Immediately, he tucked heartily into his breakfast, but she merely toyed with her food.

After his second mouthful, Fraine looked up at her. "Nona, eat. That's an order."

She nodded, eating with small, deliberate bites. She could taste nothing but ashes. "I didn't want to get you involved, but now . . . I mean, what the hell am I going to do, Alan? Bishop's too powerful for either of us."

Fraine nodded. To her consternation, he seemed unperturbed. "That may be true, but we have friends even Bishop doesn't."

Her head came up. "We do?"

As if on cue, the secretary of homeland security entered the diner.

THE ZOLKA chocolate factory lay in the Chertanovo industrial area, about seven miles south of the center of Moscow.

They had driven out of the industrial park grounds without incident. Annika was driving, while Jack returned to the back to check on Boris. Katya had done a remarkable job, tearing a piece of fabric and tying it in a makeshift but effective tourniquet.

Jack checked Boris's wound, confirming that it was a flesh wound. The bullet went through the triceps and out the other side. The wound looked clean. Katya suffered all the violence and its aftermath more stoically than he could have imagined. When he mentioned this to her, she smiled sadly and said, "I've seen far worse."

She put a hand on his shoulder. "Listen to me, I love Annika dearly, but when it comes to her *dyadya* she can be explosive. He has been mother, father, and mentor to her. He sacrificed to get her back from her despicable father, in the process creating a lifelong enemy, who might have been powerful enough to destroy him were he not so devilishly clever. He has done his best to shield her from her father, while training her to become strong enough in mind, body, and spirit to resist Batchuk. In short, Dyadya Gourdjiev is everything to her. In her mind, her debt to him can never be repaid, not that the old man wanted that. On the contrary, he has done everything for her out of love, for his love long ago outdistanced the guilt, however misguided, not anticipating the depths of her father's depredation—kidnapped from her dying mother's arms while Gourdjiev went about his daily business."

Jack knew most of this family history of obsession and death, but he found it informative to hear it retold from another point of view.

"I have no doubt that she would give up her life for him," Katya went on. "This is the basic problem, one which you need to keep in the forefront of your mind, because when and if she goes down, she'll take everyone close to her down with her."

Jack glanced out the window. Annika was driving very fast. Up ahead loomed the enormous brutalist structures of Chertanovo.

"Does Annika have any idea what we're going to do once we arrive at the Zolka factory?"

"There's a leak in Gourdjiev's inner circle," Katya said. "Someone is gunning for her and Gourdjiev. She's going to find out who that some-one is and kill him."

"No matter who it might be?"

Katya nodded. "That's right." Then she cocked her head. "Why?"

"Because I think Omega is her half-brother, Grigori Batchuk."

"Believe me," Katya said, "that won't stop her."

At that moment, Annika pulled into the Zolka factory parking lot. Jack got out and walked around to the front. Annika was already standing beside the van. She was staring with fixed intensity at the redbrick factory.

"Bring out the driver," she said without looking at him.

"What are you going to—"

"Just do it!" she snapped.

"Annika," he said softly, "I'm not the enemy."

"Good thing, too." She had a murderous look in her eye when she turned to him. "Bring him, Jack."

Against his better judgment, Jack fetched the cowering driver out of the van, where Boris had been keeping a wary eye on him. Taking him by the back of his collar, he brought him to Annika, who stood, spread-legged, staring at him.

"Who do you work for?"

"I already told you."

She hit him, hard, on the point of the chin. His head snapped back, and Jack caught him before he hit the side of the van, brought him upright again.

"Who is Omega?"

"I don't know. Jesus!" he exclaimed as she hit him again. His nose began to bleed again. He whimpered when he wiped it with his sleeve.

"Omega is such a stupid name, I think you made it up."

"What? No, no, of course I didn't! That's who he said—"

Annika hit him a third time, with such force that his head slammed against the side of the van. His knees buckled and Jack raised him up. He opened his mouth to voice a protest, but Annika gave him a sharp shake of her head. Jack had enough experience with interrogation techniques to know that Russians responded to force, and force only. The good cop/ bad cop routine would only make them laugh. Much as he hated to admit it, Annika's approach was the right one. They were in a life-and-death situation. What choice had they been given?

"Listen," the driver said, "I—"

Annika hit him twice, in the mouth and on the nose. He collapsed into Jack's arms, moaning.

"All right, enough. All right." He lifted his bloody face to stare at her. "Omega is a false name, but it's not my invention, it's his."

"Who?" Annika said, her fist cocked.

The driver shuddered. "He'll kill me."

"When we let you go, you'll still have a chance," she said. "Otherwise, you die right here, right now."

The driver nodded, at last admitting defeat. "Omega's real name is Grigori Batchuk."

"I'M OFF caffeine," Dennis Paull said as he sat down. "Just some ice water," he said to Elsie. When she had gone back behind the counter, he affixed a small metal octagon to the window.

"Plate glass is a terrific conductor of vibrations, including voices," he said.

Four suits were in the diner, eyeing the small number of patrons.

Apparently satisfied, they split up into pairs, taking the booths on either side of where the trio sat. They had to displace one guy, hunched over his grits and eggs, moving him to the counter, where he grumbled incessantly. The suit who accompanied him slipped into the kitchen, possibly to interrogate and thoroughly terrify the staff.

"Alan," Paull continued, "I assume you've told her."

"Told me what?" Nona said, suddenly on guard.

"In fact, I haven't," Fraine said. "Not yet, anyway."

Paull drank half his glass the moment it came. Elsie refilled it before she departed. "Why else would you wake me out of a sound sleep?"

"We have a problem," Fraine said.

Paull frowned. "What sort of problem?"

"It involves Leonard Bishop," Nona said.

Her comment caused the secretary to turn, his attention riveted on her. "Please elaborate."

Five minutes later, when Nona had finished telling what had happened to her, Fraine said, "We need you to get Bishop off Nona, as it were."

Paull's lips twitched in the semblance of a sardonic smile. "That's one way to play it," he said.

Nona's stomach contracted. "I beg your pardon, Mr. Secretary, but from where I sit that's the *only* way to play it. You don't know what it's like dealing with this dickwad."

Paull sighed. "I understand your feelings, of course I do."

"All due respect, Mr. Secretary, you're a man."

Paull pursed his lips. "Perhaps I misspoke, and, certainly, if that is your wish I will do my best to see that he no longer molests you." Leaning forward, he placed his forearms firmly on the table, his hands loosely clasped. "But what I'm asking you to do now, Ms. Heroe, is to take a step back, take a look at the big picture before you say another word or make a decision you may come to regret."

"After a night with that piece of shit, nothing's going to change my mind."

"But you'll listen." Taking her silence as assent, Paull continued. "Two days ago, I approached Alan about the two of you joining a

SITSPEC I'm putting together with all due speed." He waited for her to ask what a SITSPEC was, but she remained silent. He continued. "I don't have to detail the momentous events in Egypt over the last year that have rocked the entire Middle East. The political situation there is treacherously fluid. We're still trying to figure out who will be the new power brokers in the Muslim Brotherhood and the Salafis. The Salafis are a loose coalition of Egypt's hard-line sheikhs, who have cleverly embraced Egypt's new wave of populism, gaining power in the first elections. They are honing the politics of resentment that is the staple of right-wing groups the world over.

"The Salafi upsurge has rightfully frightened and angered the Egyptian military. The army has been caught flat-footed, primarily because it's mired in its own internal problems: there's a power struggle going on between the older, Soviet-trained generals who were loyal to Mubarak and the younger, American-trained officers. Still, the military is the key to Egypt's future because it's so deeply entrenched in the country's economy, which literally cannot function without it."

Paull raised his head as the suit returned from his interrogatory tour of the kitchen personnel. Paull nodded minutely, acknowledging the suit's all-clear hand sign.

He returned to his discourse. "On an international level, we not only have the traditional powers of the Great Game—us, England, and Russia—vying for footholds in the new government, but we also have to deal with Israel, the Palestinians, Iran, and China. Egypt may not have the oil reserves of the Saudis, but it controls the Suez Canal. As such, its strategic importance cannot be overstated."

Paull drank off another half glass of water. "As you know, everything in the Middle East, especially the transition of power, is vastly complicated by religious versus secular factions, by Sunni versus Shiite Islamic sectarianism, orthodox versus moderate constituencies, and, of course, by fanatical terrorist groups like al-Qaeda, though by no means limited to it. As of now, all of these disparate elements are vying for power within Egypt's chaotic political structure. Instability is exacerbated by the deep-seated terror the rulers of both Iran and Saudi Arabia have been feeling ever since Mubarak resigned under the duress of the Egyptian people.

With mounting turbulence in Syria, Yemen, Tunisia, Jordan, and Algeria, the question on every entrenched despot's mind is, *Am I next?* Whoever gains ultimate power in Egypt will have the upper hand in deciding who stays and who goes elsewhere in the region."

"Al-Qaeda is likely to worm itself into those breaches," Fraine said.

Paull nodded. "Unfortunately, it's not only al-Qaeda we need to worry about now. All this unrest has emboldened Iran, and, especially because of its nuclear program, what will eventually play out there is really the billion-dollar question."

He paused while Elsie cleared the plates. They all declined the selection of pies and more coffee.

"All these fingers in the pie would be bad enough," Paull said, "but as it happens there is yet another group—a cabal, really—that figures to benefit from Egypt's ongoing chaos. There's no way to say what their goal is as yet. But I strongly suspect that they want to control the Suez Canal, Egypt's decades-old peace treaty with Israel, and the country's influence with the Saudis for exclusive oil contracts."

Nona felt herself getting sucked into the secretary's terrifying scenario. "Who are these people, this cabal? Russian oligarchs, the Irani supreme leader, the Beijing high command?"

"None of the above," Paull said. "The cabal is composed of Americans."

Both Nona and Fraine sat for a moment, stunned into silence.

"Alan, I told you that this SITSPEC was special, even for a black-ops group, and this is why. We'll be going after our own people, and I have no doubt whatsoever that most of them are highly placed government officials."

"How do you know that?" Fraine asked.

"Because," Paull said, "after a great deal of the most boring digging we have managed to identify one of them."

A light suddenly went on in Nona's head. "Oh, no."

Paull nodded. "Oh, yes."

Fraine looked from one to the other. "Who the hell are you two talking about?"

Nona looked at him with a bleak gaze. "Leonard Bishop."

"Fuck me," Fraine said.

Paull, a master of dialogue management, waited a beat. "Nona, I can get him off your back today, this afternoon, if that's still your wish. But I beg you to consider the extraordinary gift we have been given."

Nona closed her eyes for a moment. "I'm already on the inside."

Paull nodded. "And I'd like you to stay there, dig deeper inside, in fact."

"You're pimping her out," Fraine said. "I won't have it."

Nona, smiling, put a hand on his arm. "Easy, there, big fella."

Paull turned to her. "No one can help you here, Nona. You have to listen to your conscience. But consider also your unique qualifications: you know the Middle East, you speak every dialect of Arabic, and, just as important, Farsi. Your brother—"

"Don't bring Frankie into it," Nona said at once.

"I apologize," Paull said in a placating tone, "but let's not kid ourselves, your brother's current condition, the fact that he was grievously wounded in the Horn of Africa, is a factor in your decision process."

"You bastard, that's what this is all about," Fraine cut in angrily. "You came to me to get Nona. You said domestic—"

"I didn't lie, Alan. As I said, these people are American—likely they're all here in the D.C. area, if not all inside the Beltway. To my mind, that makes it domestic."

"But not for Nona."

Paull took a breath and addressed Nona. "I admit that, yes, there may come a time before this is over that we'll need to send you overseas. Are you willing?"

Nona turned to Fraine. "Alan, I know you would move heaven and earth to protect me, and, believe me, I appreciate it more than you can know. To be honest, I despise doing this, but I have to. Secretary Paull is right. If not me, who?"

FIVE

AS JACK and Annika, accompanied by Katya, Boris, and Gourdjiev on the gurney, pushed into the Zolka building, the lobby personnel rushed out to help them.

The lobby was smaller than Jack would have imagined, and dingier, though this was a factory, not a corporate showcase. The profits had obviously been used elsewhere; doubtless, much of it resided in Swiss banks, far away from Moscow's outlaw society, where the government was just as apt to seize your earnings as rival oligarchs were.

Jack pointed to the elevator and led the way over to it. They rolled the gurney inside, then stepped in, and Annika pressed the button for the sixth and top floor. The elevator doors closed and they began their ascent. But just before they reached the fourth floor, the cab lurched to a halt.

KATYA, HOLDING on to Gourdjiev, looked from Jack to Annika for reassurance. They had none. Leaning over, Jack whispered in Annika's ear. Nodding, she helped him pry open the doors. One-third of the elevator was above the fourth floor. One by one, Jack and Annika levered themselves up. Annika, with her ear to the stairway door, heard the tramp of men on the stairs. Now everything depended on timing.

She swung open the stairway door just as three gunmen reached the landing. Jack waited until he heard the male voices raised in query and Annika's deliberately officious responses before he leapt through the open doorway, barreling into the three men as they stood grouped around Annika, consumed by equal parts suspicion and lust.

The goon closest to him went flying into the concrete wall. Annika stepped in between the two other men and Jack, impeding their view. As one moved to shove her to one side, she kneed him hard in the crotch. He doubled over and she slammed him into the stairwell railing. The third man reached out to grab her, a mistake he realized too late. By then she had wrenched his right arm back behind his shoulder blade, making him vulnerable to an elbow to the side of his head. He struck back, delivering a vicious blow to her kidneys. She staggered, and he reversed their position, bending her back over the stairway railing. Lifting her off her feet, he shoved her back, trying to hurl her over. Annika gripped the top rail and kicked out, striking him in the chest. His grip on her loosened, and she kicked again. This time he was ready, dodging her attack and slamming his shoulder into her so hard she felt as if her shoulders had dislocated.

Near their struggle, Jack was entwined with the gunman he had attacked. The man had bounced off the wall, hurling himself bodily into Jack's side, knocking him across the stairwell. Jack stumbled into the man Annika had doubled over and fell to his knees. His antagonist was on him, using hand strikes to keep Jack off balance and disorient him, until he delivered a blow that had Jack on the verge of unconsciousness. Jack struggled to breathe, but something was obstructing his chest. He was being systematically plowed under.

Annika's only chance for survival was to release her grip on the railing. The moment she did so, the gunman, seizing the opening, moved quickly in and leaned forward to tip her over the top. She had counted on this, however, and she used his own momentum against him, swiveling her body at the last moment, her feet on the floor again as she swung him around her, rather than through her, and he pitched over the railing, her intended fate now his. His head and shoulder struck solid concrete and he was dead before his body came to rest on the floor below.

Jack blinked back the darkness that lapped at his consciousness. He felt as if he were in a twilight world, where the only movement he could see were blurred shadows. He had lost all sense of where he was, but he knew what was happening to him, that he was close to death. And then his hand slammed against what seemed like a side of meat. A sharp smell of a foreign body odor acted to clear his mind enough to see that he was lying beside the doubled-over gunman. His own antagonist was astride him, continuing the relentless attack with his fists.

Jack's hand moved, scrabbling inside the jacket of the man lying next to him, and his fingers felt something cold and hard—metallic! Another blow from above splashed his own blood across his face and all the breath went out of him.

Rallying himself, he drew the gun out of its shoulder holster and, turning it in the cramped space, shoved the muzzle into his antagonist's armpit. No time for thought or to aim, he was driven now by pure survival instinct. He pulled the trigger once, twice, and the weight lifted off him as his assailant was slammed against the far wall and collapsed like an abandoned marionette.

DICK BRIDGES had come within a rat's whisker of offing himself. That was during the dark week after his charge, President Edward Carson, had been killed in a car accident on the way from Moscow to the airport during winter's last snow. The limousine had skidded on a patch of black ice and rammed headfirst into a utility pole, which had come down, among a tangle of live wires, onto the limo's top. Carson had been killed; his wife, sustaining grievous internal injuries, had lapsed into a coma from which she never recovered.

Bridges had failed in his primary mission to protect the president with his life, if need be, a sacred duty to which he had, up until the moment of impact, dedicated himself. Without that mission, he had wondered, what was he? How could he look at himself in the mirror without being reminded of that dreadful morning, which for many months he relived in nightmares of excruciating detail?

Now he had been tasked with protecting Alli Carson, the last member of the former first family, and he planned to carry out this mission with precision and valor. He had vowed to himself that nothing would happen to Alli on his watch. She had been incredibly brave in the face of tragedy; more horrifying things had happened to her than most people experience in a lifetime.

Bridges turned these thoughts over once again as he walked across the Fearington campus. He had Alli in sight, hands in his coat pockets, carefully observing the vectors of the students and teachers around her as she moved along the pathways.

This assignment had come as a breath of fresh air; he felt as if he were being given a second chance, a shot most people never received, at redemption. True, he hadn't liked the smell of it, but that hadn't stopped him from insisting on taking it.

Alli was with her roommate, Vera Bard. Bridges could not help wondering about their relationship. He knew how close Alli had been with her former roommate, Emma McClure. He also knew that Alli did not easily form bonds with other people. She was close to Jack Mc-Clure, of course, but to no one in her family, including that prick of an uncle, Henry Holt Carson. Bridges didn't like Edward's older brother, nor did he trust him. There was something of the sly operator, the slick politician, though Henry Holt was a businessman through and through. He liked Alli all the better for her antipathy to her uncle.

Alli and Vera went into one of the classroom buildings and Bridges followed at a discreet distance. Memories flooded through him. He remembered how the interior had the look of an English college, with wooden wainscoting, massive staircases winding upward, and colossal portraits of important-looking men, keen-eyed, square-jawed, staring out at a horizon only they could discern. Some wore the uniforms of various branches of the armed forces. The sun shone at their backs, as if rising at their command. It was all meant to be inspiring, but Bridges found the atmosphere oppressive, as if, come heaven or hell, he could never live up to these men's lofty expectations.

He settled into the hallway outside the classroom Alli and Vera entered, leaning against the wall. Taking out a paring knife, he industriously dug bits of dirt from under his nails. He whistled softly to himself, then shoved off and went to the door, peering in at the candidates sitting attentively in neat rows, typing on their laptops as they transcribed the instructor's lessons.

Seeing that all was well with Alli, he returned to his position holding up the hallway wall. He thought about his ex-wife, about their attempts to have a child—halfhearted because she told him she'd be an unenthusiastic mother, even though he insisted that she couldn't know what sort of mother she'd be until she was holding her own baby in her arms.

It was a moot point now. They'd never had a child, and now they were divorced and hadn't even spoken to each other in a decade. Since then, there had been the occasional girlfriend, but no one had lasted as much as a year. Bridges was the one who wanted a child, and now, with no little irony, he was surrounded by young men and women, any one of whom could have been his. But not in this lifetime. Apparently, he wasn't destined to have much of anything in this lifetime. Once in a very great while, he found himself wondering what terrible crime he had committed in a previous life, to find himself in this current purgatory. Mostly, though, it seemed childish to believe in reincarnation.

All of which explained why it was so important to him to take care of Alli now. Not that he was under any illusion that he could have any kind of friendship with her, but in some faraway island of his mind he could fantasize her being the daughter he never had.

The class was over, the candidates streaming out of the classroom. An hour passed quickly when you were sunk deep inside your own thoughts, Bridges knew. Alli studiously ignored him when she appeared, walking past after she and Vera went their own ways.

He followed her at a discreet distance, out onto the campus grounds. The late afternoon was the color of a spent rifle shell, the temperature had dropped, and, with a shiver, he could sense the incipient fall of night.

Alli cut diagonally across the campus, taking the path that led to the firing range and obstacle courses. Bridges had just enough time to wonder where she was headed when he lost sight of her. Following her into a copse of whip-thin pines, he looked quickly around, but there was no sign of her. He knelt down to check for signs of her passage, but the light had gone out of the sky and under the pines it was already past twilight. He pressed down on the mat of the needles and pine straw, grabbed a handful, and threw it back down, staring at it as if trying to read tea leaves.

He rose, walked farther into the copse and out the other side, his nostrils flaring as if trying to catch a hint of her scent, but she had vanished utterly and completely.

ANNIKA CROSSED to where Jack was woozily getting to his knees.

"My God, your face looks like you've been through a meat grinder." Pulling him up, she ripped off one of the men's shirts and wiped the blood off Jack's face. "Are you okay?"

"In a couple of days, probably." Jack cracked a lopsided grin. "That bastard really packed a wallop."

"We've got to get back to the elevator," Annika said, finishing her cleanup.

It wasn't until he started to move painfully up the stairs that he saw that Annika was limping and turned back to her. "What the hell hap—"

The man Annika had kneed in the groin hurled himself at them. His right hand was filled with an evil-looking switchblade that glinted as it shot out toward Annika's spine. Shoving her roughly aside, Jack felt the blade penetrate his coat, the razor-sharp edge of the blade slicing open a wound in his side. Grasping the man's knife wrist, he pulled him in toward him and smashed his forearm into the man's nose. The man's head shook and he gave an animal snort as blood spattered him, but he managed to get the heel of his hand under Jack's chin, pushing his head up and back. That was when Annika grabbed the gun out of Jack's hand and beat a tattoo with the butt on the man's head. She kept at it, her teeth clamped tight in a fury of blood rage, even after his eyes had rolled up in his head. Jack had to pull her away and turn her to face him so that she slowly refocused.

He wrenched the switchblade from the near-dead man's fist, and together he and Annika sprinted down the fourth-floor hallway.

———

As THEY had agreed during their last class of the day, Alli and Vera met outside the northwest wall of Fearington. Under cover of the gathering darkness, they made their way for about a mile across fields and stands of deciduous trees to the back road where the iron-colored Infiniti sedan sat waiting for them, its engine purring softly.

Vera climbed into the front passenger's seat and Alli got in back.

"Any trouble losing your chaperone?" Caro said from behind the wheel.

"None at all," Alli said. "He wasn't expecting it, but next time won't be easy. He's a clever cookie."

"If this works out right," Caro said, putting the Infiniti in gear, "there won't have to be a next time."

She drove at a sedate pace until the road merged with the highway, and then she put on speed. Alli intuited Caro had no desire to be pulled over by a cop. She hadn't wanted anything to do with Dick Bridges, which was perfectly understandable, given her father's long reach and his enduring efforts to find her. Now that the two of them were in the same city, Caro had to increase her vigilance to keep herself from flying under his extensive radar.

As they sped north, Alli sat back, catching Caro's reflection in the rearview mirror. She had not gotten over the shock of her cousin's sudden appearance from out of nowhere. Caro had remained such a mythic figure in her imagination that adjusting to the real flesh-and-blood person was going to take some getting used to. She kept catching herself thinking of Caro as her uncle had described her. She hated herself for that. Henry Holt Carson had proved himself to be a liar, a chiseler, and, worse, power-hungry. With his younger brother as president, he'd had an unbeatable chip to play. Now he had to deal with Edward Carson's successor, the prickly Arlen Crawford. In a way inexplicable to her, her uncle had managed to forge what seemed to be an alliance with the president. Was he advisor to Crawford as well as being a highly visible lobbyist for the items on the president's foreign and domestic agendas? Jack might know, but Alli didn't.

Alli missed Jack, as she always did when he was far away. She understood her attachment to him in the abstract, but the fact was their relationship was so complex—surrogate father, mentor, friend, and ally—that she had trouble parsing both the depth and the breadth of her feelings for him. When, as now, he was overseas without her, she was terrified he would die in some awful foreign country, that the next time she would see him was in a coffin flown into Dulles on Secretary Paull's official aircraft.

On the surface, her attachment to Jack—and to Annika—seemed to fly in the face of her detachment from everyone around her, but she knew better. Jack had saved her from Morgan Herr. More than that, though, he had believed in her when everyone else had given up on her, including her parents. And there was another aspect she could not discount: he was Emma's dad. Their mutual sorrow at her death bound them more tightly than blood ever could.

"Where are we going?" Alli asked.

"To meet a man," Caro said, her eyes glued to the road.

Alli, heart beating fast, leaned forward, her hands on the back of the front seat. "Does that mean you found who put up the rogue Web site?"

"We're closer than we were yesterday."

"What the hell does that mean?" Vera said.

"I'll let the man we're seeing explain." If Caro was aware of Vera's annoyance she gave no sign of it. "But you were right about one thing, Vera. This is a challenge."

Alli wanted to ask so many more questions, but she could sense that it would be useless to ask. It was clear that Caro had said as much as she was going to on the subject. Reluctantly, Alli melted back into the backseat, brooding about this creature, her cousin, who had suddenly appeared from out of nowhere, who now seemed to have taken over the immediate trajectory of her life.

Fifteen minutes later, Caro pulled the Infiniti into a space on Ninth Street NW, between G and H. Out on the sidewalk, she led them into Spares'n'Strikes, one of those new-style bowling alleys with lounges and party spaces attached. Inside, the atmosphere was totally clublike—there were as many flat-screen TVs blasting a variety of sports matches and music videos as there were bowling lanes. In keeping with the place's play-on-words name, the Stars and Stripes were the decor pattern of choice. All very psychedelic, in a postmodern kind of way.

"You guys go rent shoes and take a lane," Caro said, "while I go take care of business."

She was more enigmatic than the spies Alli knew. She and Vera got shoes that fit tolerably well, then took over Lane 13, which no one else seemed to want. Le Tigre was playing over the loudspeakers. Very retro-chic.

"When was the last time you bowled?" Alli asked as they set them-selves up.

Vera laughed. "I know fuck-all about bowling."

Alli showed her the essentials. As in everything, Vera was a quick study, and by the third frame she had gotten a spare to Alli's two strikes and a missed spare. They were about to order Cokes when Caro ap-peared and sat down beside them.

"What did I miss?" she said, glancing at the score sheet.

"We talked about you incessantly, obsessively," Vera said.

"Happy I didn't hear any of it," Caro said with the same degree of astringency. "And now," she added without turning around, "my con-tact is about to arrive."

"How very mysterioso!" Vera cried in mock excitement.

"None of that while he's with us," Caro said, all banter abruptly drained from her.

"Yes, ma'am," Vera said, staring at her hands clasped demurely in her lap.

Caro snorted, and Alli, hearing a *click-click-click* approaching and thinking of Ahab walking the deck of the *Pequod,* turned her head to see a small man, so unprepossessing he might have been the dormouse at the Mad Hatter's tea party, leaning on a hickory walking stick, mak-ing his way to their lane.

"Alli Carson," Caro said, acting as MC, "this is Werner Waxman."

AT THE top of the stairs they found the floor as silent as a library. Jack had expected a warren of executive offices, but instead was confronted by a cavernous space, divided only by two rows of thick fluted columns with Doric capitals. Instead of half walls and desks, there were bristling stands of electronic equipment, grouped like copses of trees. The space was so vast that its far end was shrouded in a kind of haze, caused by dusty sunlight lancing through small panes of glass. The place smelled faintly of disinfectant and the peculiar but indefinable odor given off by heated electronics.

He walked forward now, into the dusty sunlight, circling around until he faced the islands of electronics. He turned and saw Annika bending over her grandfather's body. She must have done something, given him another drug. Dyadya began to move. He said something to Katya, who was standing beside him. She bent down and kissed him. Then he said something to Annika and she helped him into a sitting position. He swung his legs over the side of the gurney. When he saw where Jack was standing, a smile creased his face.

"You see, Annika, it's as I predicted," the old man said. "Jack knows you triggered our backup plan."

Six

As was his wont, Mr. Waxman inclined his head in the formal European style at Vera's introduction. "Charmed."

"And her friend, Vera Bard."

"Equally," Mr. Waxman said with the precise economy of age.

His face was long and thin, with a nose like a knife blade and thin lips the color of fried liver. Incongruously, he wore a natty porkpie hat similar to the sort sported by fifties jazz musicians and current hipsters. Just below hung elephantine ears, filled with whorled cartilage. He sat with some difficulty between Alli and Vera, as if any movement of his bones pained him.

Turning back to Alli, he said, "Ms. Simpson has apprised me of your current situation. Also of the information she has been able to glean from her scouring of the Internet. She has taken the investigation as far as she can."

"I understand that, and I'm grateful." Alli had to remind herself that Caro's current identity was Helene Simpson. "Can you help?"

"Allow me to explain." Waxman's lips compressed to pencil lines as he smiled. "Ms. Simpson came up against a firewall and she ceased her work immediately. It wasn't that she couldn't get through this particular firewall. On the contrary, I have every confidence that in time she would have breached it if she tried. She chose not to."

Alli glanced at Caro, but she spoke to Waxman. "Why not?"

Waxman had hands like a marmoset, small and neat. He wrapped them over the knobbed head of his walking stick, so that his knuckles, swollen with arthritis, stood out, white as birch bark. "Why not?" he echoed. "Well, for one thing, she's an exceedingly clever creature. For another, infiltrating a government military firewall is a treasonable offense."

Le Tigre had finished, the loudspeakers effortlessly segued into "Who Am I to Feel so Free," from their new incarnation, MEN. The song scarcely registered on Alli; she was too shocked. Her thoughts chased each other madly, her head pounding. Her lips felt glued together.

"I don't . . ." Clearing her throat, she was at last able to speak coherently. "Are you saying that the person who put up that site works for the federal government?"

"Military intelligence," Waxman said, "not to put too fine a point on it."

Alli bent over, head in her hands. Now she understood how this person knew the intimate details of her kidnapping—he was working for the government, protected by it. Which meant that he had been at the crime scene or had been privy to the eyes-only report. She shuddered to think that he had stood in the same room where she had been bound and psychologically beaten by Morgan Herr. A dreadful chill rippled through her. Did that mean he knew her as well as Herr had? *Please, God*, she thought, *don't make it so.*

"Alli?" Vera came and sat next to her, a sheltering arm pulling her close. "Come on. We're all here to help you."

"She's right," Waxman said. "Listen to your friends." His smile was benign, reassuring. "We're all here to help."

Alli shuddered again, her nightmare past roaring back at her full-throttle, overtaking the present. "I think I'm going to be sick." Bolting up, she ran down the aisle behind the lanes, through the lounge, and into the ladies' room, past a pair of girls snorting coke and giggling like mad-women. Slamming into a stall, she had just enough time to bend over before regurgitating the entire contents of her stomach and then some. She held herself up by pressing her palms against the side walls, but her knees felt weak, her consciousness whittled down to the few square feet she currently inhabited.

She was shocked out of her sickly trance by a commanding voice out in the w.c. proper, saying, "Get out! Get out now!"

A moment later, a cool hand pressed itself against her forehead, brushed damp wisps of hair from her forehead and temples. Grateful, she turned, expecting to thank Vera. Instead, she was surprised to see Caro's fierce face.

"The past is a helluva thing, isn't it?" she said.

Pulling on Alli's arm, she directed her out to the line of sinks where the girls had been snorting just a few moments ago. The w.c. had now been swept clear. Caro had made certain of that.

As Alli bent over one of the sinks, washing her face and rinsing out her mouth, Caro stood beside her. "Believe me, I know."

Alli spit out water. "Sorry, but you have no idea what being held against your will feels like. You know what I went through."

"Oh, but I have been held hostage."

Alli picked her head up and stared at her cousin.

"I got trapped into working for a man—"

"That's hardly the same."

"Let me finish," Caro said. For a moment she stared at herself in the mirror above the sinks. "This was a very dangerous man," she said after what seemed a long time.

"Who is he?"

Caro took a paper towel and wiped off the last stray beads of water from Alli's face. "I was, in effect, held hostage by him. And for far lon-ger than a week." She raised both hands. "Not that the amount of time matters. I'm just saying."

Someone shouted on the other side of the door and there was a loud knocking. Caro broke away, crossed to the door, and opened it a sliver. "Fuck off, bitches," she said, and slammed the door closed.

Returning to where Alli stood, she took up where she had left off. "We're similar, you and I, maybe more than you know."

"How d'you mean?"

"Our fathers—the Carson brothers—yin and yang."

"My father was nothing like Uncle Hank."

"Well, no. But Uncle Edward enabled my father to be who he is today."

Alli shook her head. "I don't understand."

Caro crossed her arms over her breasts. "Your father was a good guy—too good, in a way. He covered up for my father. Edward adored his older brother, so much so that he deliberately ignored my father's penchant for power-grabbing, no matter who got hurt. Henry Holt was the doer, Edward was the fixer. Together, they made the perfect team. Trouble was, Edward made an art of looking the other way when Henry skated on the left side of the law or made the most despicable of deals with people he had no business being in bed with."

Alli stared wide-eyed at her cousin. Why hadn't she known this deplorable family history? And then she found herself wondering whether she, in fact, did know, but, like her father, had chosen to turn her attention elsewhere. Her whole family had been in the business of following Edward's lead in idolizing Uncle Henry. Why, she wondered, was it so easy to go through life with blinders on? Humans had the uncanny ability to absorb only what they wanted to see and hear, while blocking out anything and everything that contradicted what they felt was in their best interests.

"Is that why you ran away from home?"

Caro nodded. "Though it wasn't that simple. My father is a determined man with almost unlimited resources."

"It sure it took a shitload of ingenuity and guts," Alli said.

"If only that's all it took." A wistful smile wafted like a cloud across Caro's beautiful face. "I was thirteen. I had raw talent, it's true, but I hardly had the skills I have now." Her gaze turned inward. "I needed help, and the only people who could help me—the only ones powerful enough—were very bad people indeed."

"But you escaped."

Caro's eyes snapped back into focus. "The fact is, I could not have escaped without your help."

Alli took a breath. "*My* help?"

"That's right." Caro nodded. Her eyes glittered. "I was working for the Syrian."

THE GENERAL was not a man to suffer either fools or latecomers. As a result, when Leonard Bishop showed up seven minutes late for dinner, the vampire-thin hostess, following orders to the letter, held him at the podium for precisely that amount of time before she took him to the General's table. During that time, she busied herself answering numerous calls, informing guests at the bar that their tables were ready, and checking the reservations of incoming groups. Beneath theatrically made-up eyelids, she observed Bishop's growing impatience with the waspish schadenfreude endemic to her kind. However, when the required seven minutes had elapsed, she approached Bishop with a warm smile and an outsized menu under one arm. With a ceremonious sweep of her wire-thin arm and a cheerful "This way, Chief Bishop," she led him a circuitous route past closely packed tables, frantic waiters, and loaded-down busboys to the left rear corner of the room, where the General sat, drinking Greenore, Ireland's oldest single-grain whiskey, in a colossal cut-crystal glass the restaurant kept specifically for him.

Bishop took it as an evil sign that the General said not a word as he seated himself in the chair opposite.

"Drink?" the hostess said as she handed him the menu.

"Greenore," Bishop said, a ploy to placate his host. He detested whiskey, and in particular Irish whiskey, which he found lacked the bracing medicinal bite of a fine single-malt scotch.

"Very good," the hostess said, though she was preoccupied taking mysterious visual cues from the General.

Dinnertime swirled around them in a sea of voices, laughter, the chiming of glasses, the clink of cutlery against plates. At the next table, a waiter recited the evening's specials. Bishop heard all of this peripherally; all his attention was focused on the General, who continued to stare at his menu as if it were the Bible.

A waiter set down the glass of Irish, and left.

Bishop, his anxiety level now running off the charts, cleared his throat and said, "What looks good to you, General?"

"A good, heaping helping of being on time," the General said, his head still buried.

"Apologies. The Mall traffic—"

"I don't accept apologies, you know that." The General's eyes snapped to attention and Bishop was immediately in their crosshairs. He carefully laid the menu aside and in a lower tone of voice said, "I only ask for little things, Leonard." He took a sip of his Greenore, savoring the liquor on his tongue, then in the back of his throat, before setting the glass down on the tablecloth. "Understand, when I ask you for something more, it's already too late."

"Understood." Bishop ground his teeth. The humiliations he suffered to get ahead and maintain his edge had turned him into someone who needed to inflict the same on others in order to verify his own worth. He had no other signposts by which to judge. Judge and be judged—if he thought about it that way, his life was simple, bearable, even.

"I think I'll have the shrimp cocktail," the General said to the waiter who had magically appeared tableside. "And then the porterhouse, bloody. Creamed spinach and house potatoes. And don't forget to butter the steak the moment it's taken off the fire."

"Very good, sir." The waiter turned his inquiring face to Bishop. "And you, sir. Have you made your choice?"

Bishop felt a bit panicky, as he always did when sitting down to a meal with the General. He wished his host would give him a clue as to what he should order. His first instinct was to follow the General's lead, but he'd already done that with the drink; continuing down that road was too obvious. His stomach was jumpy anyway, and the damn Irish whiskey had only added to the problem.

"Come on, Bishop," the General snapped. "Out with it."

"A salad and the Dover sole," Bishop said a bit breathlessly. He hated fish, but the sole was the first item his eyes latched onto.

"Any vegetable, sir—or potato?"

"Nothing." Bishop almost shouted in his extreme discomfort.

"As you wish, sir." The waiter gathered the menus and departed.

Now there was nothing between him and the General. Under the table, he felt his right leg begin its nervous pumping.

Across from him, the General took another swig of his vile liquor. When he set his glass down, he said, "Tell me about the girl, Leonard."

The query seemed so far out in left field that Bishop could think of only one response. "What girl?"

"The girl you're currently bedding." The General's fingers rotated the glass slowly, evenly. "She works for you, doesn't she?"

Nona. "As much as the thousand detectives at Metro work for me."

"But she's different, isn't she? She's one of the thousand, but she's not. She's one of the chosen."

"You are correct, sir."

"So my question to you, Leonard, is what are you doing?"

"I don't—"

"You're supposed to be studying her, not bedding her."

"She's difficult to get to know in a professional setting. I know what I'm doing."

The General snapped a breadstick in half and chomped into it. "That what I'm supposed to tell Waxman?"

"I'm telling you, in the office she's like a fucking porcupine."

"Uh-huh." The General chewed and swallowed. It was clear he didn't believe Bishop. "It's been my experience, Leonard, that when men think with their pricks, something bad happens."

"Not this time."

"*Always.*" The General sat back as the appetizers were served. "What about her brother?"

"She visits him every day, almost."

The General closed his eyes for a moment, pressing his fingers into the lids as if Bishop's answer had given him a headache. "I meant his condition, Leonard."

"He's never coming out of his coma, sir. She hasn't given up hope, but I know she's sure of it."

"Well, that's good news." The General pursed his lips, as if about to spit. "We can't have him regaining consciousness. You understand this."

"Yessir."

"But, goddamnit, we can't touch the sonuvabitch."

The General took to tackling his shrimp cocktail, which had been brought in a wide-mouthed martini glass. Dumping the fiery cocktail sauce over the top, he commenced to annihilate the crustaceans between his large, square teeth.

Bishop stared into the green forest of his salad without seeing it. Had the General completed his assessment of the situation with Nona or was the exquisitely humiliating interrogation going to continue? He felt like he had when he was a boy, dressed down by his father for one trespass or another, sometimes real, other times imagined. Any attempt to profess innocence only caused an escalation of whatever punishment his father had decided to mete out. Years later, in the way of life's lessons, it became clear to him that he had been punished for sins his father had committed. His father didn't have to admit to them so long as he punished his son for them.

"Leonard," the General barked, "have you lost your appetite, too?"

Too? Bishop thought with a start. *What else have I lost?*

"IT'S A relief to have you back among the living," Jack said.

"All for a good cause," the old man said. With Annika's help he was regaining the use of his legs. "I had a hunch our escape wasn't going to go smoothly."

Jack turned his attention to him. "Because of Omega." When Gourdjiev gave no reply, Jack continued. "We have information that Omega is Grigori Batchuk."

"That's right." The old man nodded as he led the way to one particular stand of electronics, where Jack saw Boris, his fingers busy on a computer keyboard.

"How's the pain?" Jack said.

"I'm Russian." Boris looked up for a moment, his eyes holding steady on Jack's. "What fucking pain?"

Jack laughed.

"Bring the first one up," Gourdjiev said, and at once Boris pressed a set of keys. Onto the screen flashed live video of a section of the tarmac at Sheremetyevo Airport. Surveillance camera. The old man pointed. "Whoever said a picture is worth a thousand words justly deserves to be lionized."

Jack, peering over the mountain of Boris's shoulder, saw the U.S. government jet that had transported him and Annika to Moscow.

"Second camera," Gourdjiev said.

At once, the image changed, pulling back to show several fistfuls of plainclothes men perhaps a hundred yards from the plane, grouped around their cars. At the old man's command, the image changed to show the other side of the plane, where the tarmac was similarly spattered with plainclothes men, chatting and smoking.

"They're waiting for us," Gourdjiev said, "or, more accurately, for me, though I'm quite certain they would be pleased to drag Annika into their net." He turned to Jack. "So. Now you know. Grigori is not going to allow me access to your plane, Jack."

The old man drifted away, hands clasped behind his back. He looked a whole helluva lot more alive, Jack thought, than he had before.

"He had people at the hospital, which was why it was imperative that you remove me from there as soon as possible. Otherwise, some bogus doctor might have slipped a fast-acting paralyzer in my intravenous, prior to having me whisked me away."

He turned back to face Jack. "You'd have no problem boarding the plane, of course. You're an American citizen."

Jack's mind was racing. "We'll take you on board in a coffin."

"They'll check it."

"Annika will put you under like she did at the hospital."

"The drug is a strain on the system of even a young man." Annika took a step toward them. "He won't tolerate it."

"The scenario is moot," Gourdjiev said. "There's Annika and Katya to consider. I'm not leaving them behind."

Jack thought for a moment. "If we can't go where they expect us, we have to go where they'll never think to look for us."

"Oriel trained his sons well. Grigori thinks of everything," Annika said, hands on her hips. "By now he'll have the city sewn up tighter than a duck's ass."

Jack closed his eyes and cleared his head. On the screen of his mind he brought up a map of Moscow, not as others might see it, in two dimensions, but in the three dimensions in which his mind worked best.

The "map" he reviewed included everything he had seen since he and Annika had flown in the day before. What stood out for him were colors—glorious colors. He watched again the view from the hospital corridor window: the half-stripped poster for the Red Square Circus. Today was its last day in the Russian capital.

"Maybe he does. Then again, maybe not." Smiling mischievously, he turned to Annika and Dyadya Gourdjiev and said, "How are you at lion taming?"

ALLI WAS a bit shell-shocked when she and Caro returned to the bowling alley, where Werner Waxman sat just as they had left him, hands gripping his hickory walking stick. His head was slightly inclined toward Vera as he spoke with her, but they broke off the moment they saw the two young women approach.

"Feeling better?" Waxman said as Alli sat down.

"Of course she isn't." Vera cut Caro a suspicious look that asked, *What the hell happened in the ladies' room?* "She looks like crap."

"I'm fine," Alli said, though she felt far from it.

Waxman nodded, apparently taking her at her word. "I'm afraid the rogue Web site went live in error. An internal investigation revealed one of our people is obsessed with you. He has been stripped from the program. My apologies for any distress it caused you, I can assure you it will not reoccur."

"That's not enough." Alli ignored the tension that came into Waxman's body. "I want to know who posted the site, who Photoshopped my face on those bound nudes."

Waxman's expression grew pained. "I'm afraid his identity is a matter of national security. I'm sure you understand."

"But I don't," Alli said. "There are circumstances that make it imperative I find him."

Waxman shot Caro a lightning glance. He cleared his throat. "If I may ask, *what* circumstances?" He made the common word sound filthy.

Alli hesitated a moment, glanced at Vera, who mouthed, *Go ahead.* "This man knows things—intimate things—about a difficult part of my life that make me exceptionally uneasy."

"Really? Well, now, that *is* troubling." Waxman frowned. "I can certainly see how that might affect you adversely." He sighed. "Hmm, we can't have that, can we? Give me some time. Let me see what can be done." He patted her leg, then rose creakily. "Not to worry, I'm always cleaning up after other people's messes. I imagine that's why my superiors still put up with me."

"Thank you," Alli said, though she sensed that Waxman had no superiors.

"It's nothing." Waxman's hand brushed away her words. "Just another day's work."

When he had left, Caro said, "Okay, it's payback time."

"What, exactly, do you want from Henry Holt?" Vera said.

"A notebook."

Alli cocked her head. "What's in it?"

Caro smiled. "Believe me, it's better if you don't know."

"People say that in films all the time," Alli said. "It's always bad news."

"How will we recognize this notebook?" Vera asked.

"It's made of ray skin—shagreen, decorators call it. Black and shiny, with a raised pearl-colored oval in the center."

"Do you know where it is?"

"If I did I wouldn't need you."

"We'll take care of it, Caro. I promise."

"That's good enough for me."

Vera turned to Alli. "What did you two talk about in the loo?"

Alli arched an eyebrow. "I could ask you the same. You and Waxman were gabbing pretty good when Caro and I came back."

Vera sat back. "Waxman was telling me stories about the old days."

"Which ones?" Caro said.

"The ones where after World War Two the OSS rounded up all the clever Nazis, hid them from the war-crimes tribunals, and hired them for counterintelligence work against the Soviet Union."

Caro shrugged. "Old chestnuts that've been in the fire way past their sell-by date."

"Maybe," Vera said. "Didn't make them any less hair-raising."

"Which story was it, exactly?" Caro asked.

"He was telling me the history of Butterfly—you know, change through chrysalis and all that. Anyway, according to Waxman, Butterfly was the code name for a unit of Nazis working to create false papers— legends—for deep-cover OSS agents being sent into the Soviet Union."

"And?"

"Butterfly also used its skills to ensure some very high-ranking colleagues escaped Germany and justice."

Alli looked from one to the other of her companions. "I can't help but wonder what he thought he was doing."

"What d'you mean?" Vera said.

"I mean our Waxman doesn't strike me as someone who makes idle chitchat."

Caro nodded. "Alli's right. What the hell was Waxman trying to tell us?"

Alli looked at her. "Let's ask another question: If Butterfly still exists, what would it be up to?"

"THERE ARE so many reasons to be happy," Leonard Bishop said, sweat pouring down his bare chest, "why not let this be one of them?"

Nona, seeming to stare up at him with lust-glazed eyes, watched the pattern the streetlights imprinted on the ceiling. Her smile was for him, but her mind was over the hills and far away. In her mind's eye, a big blue swamp moon was rising over Pontchartrain, the lake's indigo water silver-tipped, shivery with a humid wind. That summer, Nona had been sixteen, in the full flower of her first real love, a tall thin biker in stovepipe jeans, cowboy boots, and with ropy tattooed forearms.

His name was Rob—she never did find out his last name—and he claimed he had the cops on his tail. According to Rob, he had held up a liquor store on the interstate, "just for giggles," as he so succinctly put it. Whether this lurid history was true or not, Nona ate it up. She was as much in love with the legend as with Rob himself. When they were together, she was always on the lookout for cop cars—especially the state police—in order to have a hand in saving him from arrest and jail. By way of thanks he laughed at her. There was a cruel streak running through him that caused Nona to shiver with anticipation. But he was never cruel to her, or abusive. In fact, he was gentle with her, his touch always loving, his voice low and mellow. But with others, this streak emerged full-blown and ferocious. He never settled a dispute with words when he could use his fists or, even better, whatever weapon came to hand. She never witnessed him lose a fight, and there were too many to count. People soon learned to give him a wide berth, even other bikers who, unlike Rob, traveled in packs. "I'm a rogue elephant," he told her once. "I crush whatever the fuck's in my path."

In bars, nightclubs, and strip joints, all the low-down, noxious places he took her, he always managed to tangle, to throw his weight around, to lash out with carefully controlled aggression and a cold, cold hatred. The people he put down were bullies—guys bigger, sometimes older than he was. Often there was more than one. Nona stood back in a kind of awe, vibrating from head to toe, while the mayhem ensued. It was like a game for her, like watching her own private 3-D movie, *House of Horrors*, southern style. Always afterward the sex was galactic, making her body arch and her eyes roll up in her head.

One rainy, windswept night, the game abruptly morphed, and it all went off a cliff. Besides his Harley Low Rider, Rob owned a Chevy, souped up and tricked out. As they were speeding down the interstate, the wipers full on to sweep aside the torrential rain, Led Zep's *Houses of the Holy* blasting out of his eight custom speakers, the blurry night was suddenly lit by flashing red lights.

"Cops," Nona breathed, as if this one word would save him.

Rob, singing harmony to Plant's melody, didn't even bother to glance in the rearview mirror. He slowed, though, gradually pulling off to the shoulder. As he did so, he reached under his seat and took out the largest, meanest-looking handgun Nona had ever seen.

"Rob, what do you think you're doing?"

"Just sit tight," he said with his drop-dead grin, "and watch."

By this time the car had rolled to a stop. He kept the car in neutral, rather than park, opened the door, and got out. Nona could hear the electrified voice boom over the bullhorn. "Get back in the car, son."

Ignoring the voice, Rob began to walk back to where the police cruiser had pulled in behind him.

Nona leaned over to the open door. "Rob, come back here! What the hell are you doing?"

He kept walking.

"Son, get back in the car!" the voice shouted. "You will not be warned again!"

Nona could see the cop with the bullhorn. In the driving rain, he was standing next to the cruiser, his free hand on the butt of his service revolver. If there was any traffic on the interstate, it was blurred and indistinct, seeming as far away as the next county.

Rob raised his handgun and squeezed off two rounds. The cop flew backward, his arms outstretched. Nona screamed. More shots, this time fired out the cruiser's rolled-down window. A bullet struck Rob, twisting him sideways. He fired again, was hit again. He fell to his knees and kept on firing until he collapsed onto his face.

Then there was nothing but the sound of rain slamming the car's roof and the hiss of intermittent traffic. The tarmac was stippled like a lake in a storm. Nona sat shaking and crying. Then she crawled across the seat and looked out the open door. Rob wasn't moving and neither was the cop. The bullhorn lay in the road. There was no movement, no sound from the cruiser. Red lights kept blinking emptily.

Hands shaking, Nona slid behind the wheel and, not quite knowing what she was doing, put the car in gear and drove to the local police station, where she staggered up the stairs, crossed the lobby floor, and promptly vomited all over the desk sergeant.

"Nona?"

Because she was black, the white assistant DA tried to have her indicted as an accessory, but there was no case, and his efforts came to nothing, if you discounted two weeks of further terror for Nona.

"Nona?" Bishop slapped her gently on the cheek.

With a feral growl, she leapt up, grabbed him by the throat, shoved him off the bed, and slammed him against the wall.

"Don't ever, *ever* touch me like that again."

Her face was so close to his he had difficulty focusing on her.

"Like what? It was just a tap. What the hell's gotten into you?"

"Did you hear me?" she said. She had not blinked since she had taken hold of him.

"Calm down."

Still not blinking.

"Yes, damnit, yes, I heard you."

Her eyes refocused slowly.

"Let's both just back off," Bishop said slowly and distinctly, "shall we?"

She nodded and stepped back.

"Mistakes were made."

She stared at him as if he were a Martian.

He could not help thinking of his humiliating dinner with the General. Looking into her face, he felt like he had stepped into a steaming pile of something unsettling, something that if he was not exceedingly careful he would slip on and break his neck. What had he done? he wondered. There was a demon inside her he had never before glimpsed. But wasn't there a demon inside everyone?

He massaged his neck, then frowned. "Do I have welts?"

"Let me take care of that."

With a slightly abashed smile, she came into his arms and massaged his neck with a gentle touch so erotic that soon enough they were once again glued to each other. With a dreadful start, she realized that Bishop reminded her of Rob; they shared a monomaniacal look in their eyes. That long-ago night had been a crossroads for her. That night she felt her true calling. That night she decided to be a cop, to stop the Robs of the world—or at least her corner of it—from wreaking their mayhem and destruction. She was still on that path, and now she realized that she could not take another.

THOUGH IT was late, Caro did not return to her apartment. Instead, after dropping Alli and Vera off, she drove herself to Arrows & Quiver, her favorite dive bar minutes off the interstate just this side of the Maryland border. The place was dark, smudgy, with the low metal ceiling of a submarine. She was assaulted by decades of alcohol fumes, and the desultory chatter of the same twenty or so barflies who never seemed to leave the place even after it closed at four A.M. This motley crew was hunched along the oak bar, swaying in a line as if its members were all suffering the same degree of inebriation. On the opposite side of the room, rows of broken-down booths afforded a modicum of privacy, if not comfort. An old juke was playing, Journey's "Wheel in the Sky." It was that kind of place, which was largely why Caro felt comfortable here, stuck in time like a fossil in amber, so that it seemed as if she'd never been away.

As she slid onto a stool, the bartender greeted her with the same salute he had used the first time she had walked in the place. When he pushed her drink across the bartop, she noticed a folded slip of paper, rather than the usual paper napkin, under the glass. She glanced up at the bartender, but he had already turned away, tending to the unending orders from the conga line of sloshed customers.

She lifted the glass and, while she took a lingering sip, unfolded the slip with her free hand, and read what was written on it. Immediately she crushed the note, pulled over a heavy glass ashtray that the bar now used to pile up olive pits, struck a match, and burned the crumpled ball. The flash of flame caught the bartender's interest for maybe a nanosecond, but as it died away, he turned aside.

Caro took her time with another sip, then, glass in hand, she rose and walked across the width of the room. As she did so, she thought about getting the hell out of there as quickly as she could. Practicality stopped her. In this instance, running would do her no good, and she knew it.

She saw him sitting at the booth closest to the rear. His back was to the door and, therefore, to her. That was how certain of himself he was.

He did turn his head, though, when she slid into the booth opposite him.

"Good of you to join me," he said in his trademark deadpan voice.

For some moments, she said nothing, simply stared into his face. And what a beautiful face it was—as if sculpted by a Renaissance master, with its high, wide forehead, large, deeply intelligent eyes, Roman nose, and full lips.

"How did you find me?"

To his credit, he didn't smirk. "I know you better than anyone." He paused a beat for drama's sake. "The only one who knows you at all, I daresay." He paused. "Apart from the Syrian, that is."

"The Syrian saw only what I wanted him to see."

"Don't they all?"

"But not you."

His face was completely still, like a Cretan mask she had seen once in an Athens museum. "Not me."

"So now you're going by Myles Oldham?"

"Is this to be a conversation of non sequiturs?"

"Grigori." She took another sip of her drink. "Now you're Myles." She cocked her head. "Are you—what?—ashamed of Grigori?"

"Myles is so British, isn't it?" he said. "It goes ever so much better with my accent."

"And helped you through Cambridge, no doubt. It falls trippingly on the tongue."

"As Hamlet said." His head dipped in a kind of mock bow. "Your sarcasm is duly noted."

"Or could it be that you're ashamed of your Russian heritage?"

"Half Russian," he said, bristling. "The other half—"

"Yes, yes, your mother was English. Marion Oldham."

"I loved her very much."

"You never knew her, Grigori. Not really."

"Don't." His voice bristled. Then he barked an unkind laugh. "Stop!"

They glared at each other. It was clear the knives were out for real.

Having pushed him to the brink, Caro turned the conversation to other matters. *Time,* she thought, *to bow to the inevitable.* "So. What is it you want?"

"What I've always wanted." He reached for her hands.

PAVEL KURIN, a tall, slope-shouldered man with a long, theatrical mustache that turned up at the ends and eyes like a Mongol, stood amid the rich animal stink in the center of a chaos he controlled. Kurin was the ringmaster and also the manager of the Red Square Circus. Like a philharmonic maestro, he conducted the striking of tents, the feeding of the caged animals, the parade of elephants into their straw-matted box-cars, the disposition of the jugglers, tiny contortionists, brawny strong-men, lithe acrobats, bareback riders, makeupless clowns, aloof trapeze artists, little people, twins and triplets giggling in clusters.

Kurin had been born into circus life. His parents were little people, comfortably retired now in Saint Petersburg. He, however, was over six feet tall—one of those unexplainable quirks that made genetics such a fascinating field of study. He knew this troupe intimately—their loves, their hates, and, most important of all, their friendships and feuds. Despite the inevitable infighting between the acrobats and the trapeze artists, these people were a family. Which meant in times of stress all feuds were forgotten as they banded together, outsiders against a hostile world.

Any group of people who approached the circus when it was down— especially in the rail yard where it was now—were viewed with extreme suspicion. The rail yard was where the local toughs came for payback for supposed cons perpetrated by circus folk. So it was no surprise that at first Kurin refused to talk with Jack, claiming with good reason that he was too busy. Thick-muscled roustabouts appeared, converging. But then Kurin caught sight of the old man, and, thinking of his parents in Saint Petersburg, he signed for his roustabouts to return to their normal duties.

"We'll talk inside," he said, climbing up into his private car. It was painted red and gold, with the Red Square Circus imprint flowing over a cluster of expressionist onion domes. The car was cozy and warm, festooned with a dazzling array of circus memorabilia, as if it were a museum rather than living quarters. A least two dozen photos of Kurin's parents in costume, with animals and with various dignitaries, including Khrushchev and Gorbachev, hung on the walls, between the paraphernalia.

Kurin guided Gourdjiev and Katya to a curvy, tasseled fin-de-siècle love seat, upholstered in worn claret velvet. He stood facing Jack and Annika.

"You have the look of fugitives," he said in his forthright manner.

"And if we are?" Annika said warily.

Kurin spread his arms wide. "We're all fugitives here, in one way or another. We're misfits fleeing the everyday world with its everyday people. We are the opposite of normal; here, in this sanctuary, we can be proud of who and what we are."

"We need safe passage," Jack said.

"Out of Moscow."

Jack nodded. "For a start."

Kurin studied the four of them for a moment, then, abruptly, turned on his heel. "I sense we all could use a drink."

He poured them a very fine vodka he pulled from a small freezer. He served it in jelly jars, but he made no excuse for the service. When they had all taken a sip, he said, "Across the border is where you want to go."

Jack said nothing because the answer was obvious.

"We are headed to Saint Petersburg, so that is good for you. Estonia, Finland are just kilometers away." Kurin took a longer pull of his vodka. "Well, in the circus we are used to the unusual, so anything can be arranged."

"For a price," Annika said.

Kurin regarded her for a moment. "We're not *all* mercenaries, you know."

"Apologies," Jack said.

Kurin fluttered a hand. "I choose not to be offended. I mean, what's the point, yes?" He revisited his jelly jar.

"But surely you understand that we'll be putting you in danger," Jack said.

Kurin laughed. "My dear sir, all of us are here in the circus because we're in love with danger." He shrugged. "What's a little more?"

"This kind of danger is nothing to joke about," Dyadya Gourdjiev said. "My enemies are extremely determined."

Kurin turned to him. "What, now you're trying to talk me out of helping you?"

"We simply want you to be aware of the possible consequences of sheltering us," Annika said.

Kurin spread his hands. "But you see, sheltering is what we do. Without that, what are we? A group of freaks, performing for the yokels."

"Then it's settled?" Annika said.

Kurin smiled, then consulted his watch. "We move out in ninety minutes precisely."

SEVEN

CARO, STARING into Grigori's eyes, could see intimations of both his parents. Not that she would say this to Grigori—she was convinced that his feelings for both of them were pathological. Her hands were still held by his. She allowed this because she needed him to be calm; she knew she could keep him under control—that, apart from his mother, she was possibly the one person who could. But his mother was in Switzerland, in a mountain chalet from which she rarely emerged. She had more money than she knew what to do with, but apart from her son her only passions were skiing and her dogs. Grigori had taken her to the chalet once, and Caro had been introduced to the dogs, a pair of amazing black and white brindled Bernese mountain dogs from the same litter, who acted more human than many Caro had met.

The juke was playing Pat Benatar's "Love Is a Battlefield," its fierce beat impelling a couple of the drunks into the open space for a sloppy dance. The song reminded her of Marion Oldham, a woman of a certain age who was employing every extravagant methodology at her considerable disposal to dig her heels in against the aging process. Caro found her a refreshingly uncomplicated person. She clearly loved her son more than

life itself, but was not the kind of stifling mother that love often gener-
ated. She was warm and affectionate with Caro, which, truth to tell,
freaked Caro out. Something inside her seemed to shrivel at the attention;
all her defenses rose up like a phalanx of spear-carrying warriors. If Marion noticed this, she gave no hint of it, allowing Caro to react as she did
without query or visible judgment.

"He would be cross with me for saying this," Marion had said, "but
he loves you. You're the one woman he has ever loved."

Caro had not known how to respond, so she had remained silent.

When Marion smiled she looked like the carefree adolescent she
must once have been. "I tell you this secret simply because it is a secret.
He would never tell you himself; it's not his way."

Immensely grateful that Marion hadn't asked her if she loved her
son, Caro found her voice at last. "I don't know his way."

Marion's smile was now tinged with sorrow. "You don't know what
he had to endure, growing up. His father . . . and other people . . ." She
shook her head. "And then there was the family."

"It must have been difficult having a father like him."

"His father . . ." Marion looked briefly away. "They were meant to
hate each other."

Caro didn't understand, but before she could form the question Marion gave a dismissive gesture. She had a more important message to im-
part before the interview ended.

"You never met his father. Count yourself lucky. That man was a
demon. When I was around him I quite literally lost all reason, which is
why, in the end, I fled. If I had stayed, he would have destroyed me."

She looked deep into Caro's eyes. "You do take my meaning."

It had taken Caro a moment to work it out. What Marion was saying was that her son's love for Caro was as toxic as Marion's had been for
Oriel.

Marion was so different from the young man holding Caro's hands
now, as if in a desperate attempt to keep her from once again fleeing, as
his mother had fled his father. But history had a way of repeating itself,
whether or not you wanted it to.

"Grigori," Caro said now, her conscious mind returned to the fly-blown D.C. dive, "you can have virtually anything you want."

"And yet it's you I want, Caro."

She glanced furtively around. "Please." No one was paying them the slightest attention; no one was even near them. Across the room, the barflies were half asleep. Nevertheless, they were still knocking back the booze.

"I despise the legend you chose, but all right."

Caro sighed because they were now coming to the nub—the area she did not want to discuss, but which she knew must be discussed.

"It isn't just me you want," she said.

"Whatever do you mean? Epic breasts, legs for days, and a face that launched a thousand ships—"

"I hate when you do that."

"Others wouldn't be so bloody-minded."

She ignored him. "You didn't come all this way, spend time and effort tracking me down, just to hear me say that you can't have me."

So slowly it was almost imperceptible, he uncurled his fingers and let go of her hands. "You really are a bitch, you know that?"

"Only with you."

"Bollocks! With every single bloody person who tries to get near you."

She stared at him. "Are we going to make this personal now?"

"It's always personal with us." He failed to keep the stain of bitterness out of his voice.

"Only because you make it so," she said quietly. Now it was she who took his hands in hers. "Let it go, Grigori."

"I told you—"

"Let it go."

He shook his head mutely, clearly unable to formulate a spoken reply.

"You have no other choice."

There was a kind of desperation in his eyes that she knew could in an instant turn him deadly.

"You have me so . . ." He bit his lip in frustration. "I can only think of a terrible cliché to say this. The heart wants what it wants."

"I think it's the snake between your legs that's doing the wanting."

Color flamed in his cheeks as if she had actually cut through him. "Now you mock me."

She withdrew her hands. "Let's get back to business."

"Business?"

"Of course. It's always business with us, no matter how personal you try to make it. You want—"

"The notebook," Grigori said. "Or, more accurately, what's in it."

"I don't have it."

"But you will. That's why you've come back to D.C. You know where it is."

Her expression hardened. "The notebook is like me: off-limits."

"I knew you'd say that."

"It doesn't have to be this way."

"You know me better than anyone, as you say. So you know it does."

She did, and the certainty of it sent a chill through her because, one way or the other, one of them would not survive the endgame of their years-long struggle.

THE RINGMASTER'S car rattled and shook, causing Jack to peer out the window.

"Unfortunately," Kurin said, "our poor train does not have the speed of the Sapsan trains, which travel as fast as two hundred kilometers per hour. It will take us eight hours to reach Saint Petersburg, so I suggest you sit back and relax as best you can."

The Red Square Circus train had passed the Moscow city limits twenty minutes ago. Jack had sensed the sighs of relief from both Katya and Annika. Dyadya Gourdjiev was his usual sphinxlike self, expressionless, immutable, though he allowed Katya to clutch his hand in hers.

Catching the old man's eye, Jack lifted his chin toward the door that connected the car with the rest of the train. Gourdjiev nodded and, disengaging himself, rose and walked with Jack toward the door. Jack hauled it open.

They stood on the small platform just above the cars' coupling mechanism. Gourdjiev grasped a waist-high metal chain to protect himself from the motion of the train.

Jack put his face close to the old man's. "Now would be a good time to tell me what's going on. Who are your enemies and what do they really want?"

For a long time, Gourdjiev stared out across the tracks to the blurred countryside. They were traveling north by northwest, and the wind was bitter, tasting of industry and soot. At length, he said, "You know, Jack, you're never too old to learn a bitter lesson. I thought, finally, after getting rid of Batchuk, that I had scattered my enemies to the four winds, that without him as leader they would crawl back into the shadows that had been their home."

The train rattled, shaking as it crossed over a second set of rails that led to a siding, and Gourdjiev had to take a moment to steady himself.

"My mistake was in thinking I understood them—or perhaps it would be better to say that I misunderstood the depths of their animosity, their determination to take from me what I had spent decades amassing."

"So the cache of illicit activity you have compiled, the favors outstanding, the quid pro quos, is real."

"Oh, yes." The old man nodded, but it was clear from his gaze that his mind was far away, perhaps already in Estonia or Finland, where he—all of them—would be safe. "It's all true. It all exists."

Jack leaned in, the better to hear and be heard over the noise. "You need to tell me where we're headed, so I can have the plane meet us there."

Gourdjiev shook his head. "Forget your plane, Jack. As you saw for yourself, my enemies are strong at the airports. The instant your pilot files a flight plan they will send agents to its destination."

"Then I'll send it to Estonia while we cross over into Finland, or vice versa, if that's your wish. It'll come to us later."

A small smile appeared on the old man's lips like fire curling tissue paper. "Every time I think you can't surprise me again, you do. Of course you discarded the instinct to send the plane in the opposite direction in which we're headed. They would have thought of that."

"'They.'" Jack took a step toward Dyadya Gourdjiev. "Tell me who you mean."

The old man closed his eyes for a moment, his thin body swaying with the train's movement. When he opened them, they were filled with anguish. "Oriel Jovovich Batchuk and I were friends, then frenemies. When he caused my daughter's death, when he kidnapped Annika, we became implacable foes, bent on destroying each other." His eyes came back into focus. "I thought that war ended with Batchuk's death, but it seems I was wrong."

"Batchuk fathered two children after Annika's mother died—both sons, Grigori and Radomil."

The old man nodded. "Annika told me how you saved her life when one of Grigori's hit men came for her." He passed a hand across his eyes. All of a sudden he looked his age. "I thought I knew every-thing about Oriel Batchuk, but, in the end, he has outfoxed me. It is as if he has returned from the grave. Apparently he trained his sons from a very early age for just such a contingency, and now this one is out for blood—my blood and Annika's blood. From what little I have been able to glean, this vendetta is Grigori's entire reason for being; it has taken over his life completely. Which means that all of us—you included—are in danger."

The wind knifed through Jack, chilling him to the bone. "But surely—"

"No, no, if Grigori isn't stopped, he will destroy all of us, of that I am absolutely certain. You yourself have been witness to his obsession."

"What does Annika plan to do?"

"She is planning Grigori's demise."

"You're allowing—?"

Gourdjiev laughed. "My 'allowing,' as you put it, doesn't enter into this equation. My granddaughter is ruthless—you must know this. The bitterness in her heart was very carefully placed there by her father. It

FATHER NIGHT 115

can be diminished, I've found, but not extinguished. He damaged her too completely. There is a part of her that is black—pitch-black. Neither you nor I have any say in the matter."

"So she is determined to kill Grigori."

"This is part of her mission, yes. Frankly, at this time in my life I welcome her growing power. It's what I have wished for. I want to retire somewhere far, far away and spend the rest of my days with Katya. Having had power for so long, I no longer dream of it. I leave that now to others younger than me."

Jack was appalled. "Is there no other way out of this sibling death match?"

"She's a traitor in Grigori's eyes," Gourdjiev said. "He has every reason to kill her. You must make sure that doesn't happen," the old man said. "She has her assignment. I don't want her distracted."

Jack watched Gourdjiev for some sign of what the other part of Annika's assignment might be, but, of course, none was forthcoming. He could ask the old man, but he knew if Gourdjiev wanted him to know he would have told him. The longer he was around this man, the less he understood his methodology. It was as if he had encountered a modern-day sorcerer. Jack suspected that Gourdjiev had no intention of dying, ever. Nothing seemed capable of killing him, least of all old age. He was as invulnerable as the keep in a fortified castle.

"I want to help," Jack said finally. "Where is Grigori?" He could scarcely draw a breath. "Where is Annika's half-brother?"

"I don't know." Gourdjiev shook his head. "That's the worst of it. Because we have no idea what he calls himself now." The old man's lips gave a curl of distaste. "He hasn't gone by the name Grigori Batchuk since he was seventeen years old."

"IF YOU do that again," Dick Bridges said, "I will report you to Commander Fellows." He stared hard at Alli. "So tell me, where the hell did you disappear to?"

He had waited, coming for her during her first morning class, making a big deal out of asking for her, to maximize her embarrassment, payback for deliberately ditching him the night before.

Alli, who had no intention of telling him what had really transpired, said, "Every now and again Vera and I need to get away from Fearington and its rules and regs. We were just blowing off steam."

Bridges sighed. "Alli, at this point in time, 'just blowing off steam' has the potential to get you into deep trouble. Here in Fearington you're protected."

"Morgan Herr infiltrated Langley Fields."

"Langley Fields is a private school," Bridges pointed out. "Fearington is a government facility with numerous levels of security. Two completely different animals." He put a hand on her shoulder. "Plus, you have me. I'm sworn to protect you. Let me do my job." He stared into her eyes. "Okay?"

She nodded. "Okay."

He opened the door for her and she went back inside the classroom. Everyone was staring at her, but the professor soon got his students back on track. Afterward, Vera and Alli walked across campus to their next class.

"He's behind us," Vera said.

"I know." Alli shifted her laptop from one arm to the other. "He hauled me out of class to read me the riot act. He'll stick like glue now."

"But you can't let him. You can be sure Waxman won't meet you with him around."

"I know, I know," Alli said. "I'll have to think of something." She considered for a moment, then turned to her friend. "Maybe you can help."

THE SLOWING of the train woke Jack. His watch indicated that it was two hours yet before they were scheduled to arrive at Saint Petersburg. Looking around, he saw Annika, Gourdjiev, and Katya still asleep. Pavel Kurin, however, was nowhere in evidence. Tossing aside the blanket that had been given him, he rose, slipped on his shoes, and slid open the door. Kurin was standing on the connecting platform, a pair of field glasses to his eyes.

"What is it?" Jack said. "Why have we slowed down?"

The ringmaster tugged nervously at his mustache. "Actually, we're making an unscheduled stop."

"Why?"

Kurin handed him the field glasses. "See for yourself."

Looking through them, Jack saw a siding in the distance, similar to the one they had passed when he'd been out here talking with Gourdjiev hours ago. The difference was that this siding was open and populated. He saw two cars, along with six men, their eyes on the oncoming train.

Jack handed back the field glasses. "Who are they?"

Kurin shrugged. "State police, FSB, Immigration, who knows?"

"Immigration?"

"We are a world unto ourselves," the ringmaster said. "We shelter all kinds of refugees." He shrugged. "But it hardly matters; whatever their affiliation, their presence is ominous."

"We should wake the others up."

Jack was about to open the car door when Kurin said, "This could go either way. You know that."

"Annika and I are armed," Jack said.

The ringmaster's expression was grim. "That's one of my chief worries. If any of these officials are harmed or killed, the circus will be finished."

"I understand," Jack said, though he had no clear sense that they could successfully emerge from this encounter without gunfire.

Inside the car, Annika was already awake and stirring. He filled her in as to why the train was stopping and asked her to rouse her father and Katya. He crossed to help Kurin take the cushions off the old love seat. Underneath was a plank of wood, worn smooth as a baby's cheek, and the same color. Kurin knelt and inserted a tiny key into an almost invisible hole just beneath the curved arm. An instant later, the plank popped up, revealing a framework of struts and crossbeams.

"Will this work?" Jack said.

"It had better." Kurin lifted the framework out in one piece. Beneath, a hollowed-out space gaped. "Or chances are we're all done for."

———

ALLI GOT the text from Waxman during her last morning class. She had her cell on vibrate mode, so only she knew it had come in. She read it with the cell under the desk, shielded from sight. When she was finished, she looked up to find Vera watching her.

So, Vera texted.

Lunchtime, Alli texted back.

Vera returned a compact complicit smile. Her profound mischievous streak was one of the things Alli liked about her; Vera was always up for anything, no matter how illicit or dangerous. Rebellion was, by and large, how she dealt with what she saw as a deeply hostile world. It had not taken Alli long to understand why she was so closed off, why she lacked sympathy or even empathy for others. She had no idea of what those emotions were; she would not know what to do with them. In fact, when on occasion they did arise, Alli had witnessed Vera shrinking from them like a frightened turtle. Otherwise, however, she was utterly fearless, even, in Alli's opinion, to the point of recklessness. Nevertheless, she was the only ally Alli could count on right now. Even Jack, were he here, would try to stop her from meeting again with Waxman.

Class was dismissed on time at 12:25.

"Lunch," Alli said as she passed Dick Bridges, who lurked in the hallway like Medusa, ready to turn any threatening presence into stone.

"Want to come with?" Vera said to him in her most nonchalant tone. "I guess even you have to eat sometime." This was all according to plan.

The three of them went off-campus to Starstruck Eats, a luncheonette Alli and Vera favored because of its 1960s rock 'n' roll theme. Posters of the Beatles, the Rolling Stones, Muddy Waters, and Elvis vied for attention on the walls. "Please Please Me" was playing from multispeaker outlets as they sat in a high-backed booth covered with lipstick-red vinyl. The table had chromium sides and that iconic period boomerang pattern on its Formica top. The waiters all wore T-shirts with slogans such as MAKE LOVE, NOT WAR, NEVER TRUST ANYONE OVER 30, and YOU ARE A CHILD OF THE UNIVERSE. Their waitress's shirt was emblazoned with

Sex, Drugs and Rock & Roll, which fit both her foxy looks and her demeanor. Alli had to laugh. The waitress dropped off three large menus, filled their water glasses while flirting intensely with Bridges, and was gone, all in an instant.

Bridges frowned to cover his embarrassment. "This place serves liquor. Isn't she too young to work here?"

"What's the matter?" Vera said. "Can't deal with your hard-on?"

Bridges buried his head in the menu while Vera laughed openly.

"Don't pay any attention to her," Alli said. "She's got no inhibitor on her mouth."

Bridges lowered his menu, but his throat still looked scarlet. "This was a mistake."

"What was?"

"Agreeing to come eat with you."

"It's a free country," Vera observed. "Buzz off, if you want."

"Like I said, ignore her." Alli put down her menu. "I'm having a bacon cheeseburger, fries, extra-crispy, and a coffee milkshake. How about you, Dick?"

The Stones' salacious version of Chuck Berry's "You Can't Catch Me" blasted out of the speakers.

"Kids," Bridges muttered.

"We're not kids," Vera said, clearly offended.

"You've still got cast-iron stomachs."

"Oh, come on," Alli said. "Live a little."

He reached into his pocket, popped a couple of Zantacs, crunching down hard on the tablets. He swallowed and, as the waitress appeared, said, "What the hell."

Alli gave their orders. Vera wanted a Caesar salad with a side of bacon. "Cooked fresh," she added. "Don't serve me any of that precooked shit."

"Have you heard anything more from your sources?" Alli asked Bridges in all innocence.

"Blank walls and dead air," he said glumly. "I'm beginning to think this was a fluky one-off."

"Maybe you're right." Alli leaned back and stretched, nonchalant. "I'd like to think so, anyway."

"Hey, Dick," Vera said, "what do you do with yourself when you're off duty? You married?"

"Was," he said sourly. "I'm a walking cliché."

"Girlfriend?"

"Vera!"

"No, it's okay," he said, waving away Alli's protest. "There is someone, but to be honest, she's more interested than I am."

Vera leaned forward. "You interested in anything, then?"

"Keeping Alli safe."

"I mean beyond that."

He shrugged. "Not much."

"Dead man walking, huh? How come?"

He paused for a long time, as if weighing the consequences of his words. "When you fail at the job you love, it changes your perspective on everything."

The Stones' "Play with Fire" ripped through the shocked silence. Vera looked away, unable for the moment to meet his gaze.

"Because of my dad," Alli said at length.

Bridges nodded. "My job was to protect him."

"But no one could've protected him from that accident. You'd have to've been a magician."

"Still."

Alli considered a moment. "Anyway, I imagine that kind of thing would make you think of life as more precious."

"A logical conclusion," Bridges said. "Whatever I'm feeling has nothing to do with logic."

The food came, which afforded Alli time to feel very bad about what they were going to do to him. Still, she reasoned, it couldn't be helped. She had to make her appointment with Waxman in twenty minutes, which would never happen if Bridges was shadowing her.

As they began to eat, she sent a clandestine text message. This was a meal she would normally have savored, but now she could taste none of the food. Halfway through her burger, as, according to her plan, Vera engaged Bridges in a conversation guaranteed to both nettle and distract him, she excused herself, ostensibly to take a pee. Thinking about it beforehand, she figured she'd have no more than three minutes, four at the outside, to slip out of Starstruck Eats and get clear of the immediate area before Bridges grew suspicious.

The early afternoon was chilly but glowing with bright sunshine and promise. She wished it were raining, or at least smudgy with haze, but she had to play the hand dealt her. Besides, without her winter jacket, she was already breaking out in gooseflesh under her turtleneck sweater. The taxi, whose company she had texted from beneath the boomerang-patterned table, drew up just as she turned the corner. Hauling open the rear door, she ducked inside and gave an address eight blocks from the actual meeting point. If she was a few minutes late because she walked part of the way, so be it. She knew better than to leave a trail to where she was actually going.

Waxman had given her an address in the southwest quadrant of Washington, all the way at the end of P Street, where it abutted the Washington Channel. She already knew what was there: a thirteen-foot-tall red granite statue of a partly clothed man with his arms outstretched, a memorial erected to the men who had died saving women and children when the *Titanic* had been hit by an iceberg in the North Atlantic. His pose was the one James Cameron had had Kate Winslet ape at the bow of the ship in the film. Most importantly, the memorial was a block away from Fort McNair, so the meeting spot made perfect sense to Alli. Ideally, she would have taken the subway's Green Line to Waterfront Station, but she could not determine whether it would get her to the rendezvous within a reasonable time frame.

When the taxi pulled over on Eighth Street SW, she paid in cash and exited as quickly as she could. She walked in the opposite direction she needed to until the taxi was out of sight, then turned around and walked quickly down to Fourth Street SW, made a right, and headed toward the junction of P Street SW.

The *Titanic* monument loomed up, but the area around it was cordoned off with wooden sawhorses, so no tourists were around. In fact, the area was deserted.

She saw Waxman when she was still more than a block away. His back was to her, but between his walking stick and his faintly ridiculous porkpie hat, he stood out like a cold sore on a lip.

Coming up to him, she said, "You know, Waxman, you should lose the porkpie and get yourself an ace fedora."

The instant he turned around, she saw it wasn't Waxman who confronted her, but a man who, unfolding himself from a first-rate imitation of Waxman's stance, appeared to be much younger, much more fit.

And then, as he lifted his head, the brim of the porkpie no longer obscured his face, and she felt the blood freeze in her veins.

EIGHT

"THERE IS only one way to play this," Kurin said. They had been joined by Huey, a squat man with red jowls and wisps of hair standing up on top of his semibald pate.

The train, having slowed to the proper speed, was about to be shunted off to the siding, where the men in long leather coats and grim faces were waiting to board and, presumably, go through the cars.

"If it doesn't work we're all in a shit-pile we'll never get out of."

Were they looking for Dyadya Gourdjiev or were they looking for the illegal immigrants the circus was hiding under its multicolored tents? Either way, Jack thought, Kurin was right—gunplay was out of the question if they wanted to get to Saint Petersburg without an official committee waiting to take all of them into custody. Jack was already regretting talking the ringmaster into taking them out of Moscow. There were a lot of innocents on this train, people who depended on the circus for their livelihood. It was their life.

"This goes in two parts," Kurin continued. "Jack and Annika will go with Huey to the elephants. Mr. Gourdjiev and Katya, you're with me."

"I don't like us splitting up," Annika said.

The train clickity-clacked off the main track and onto the siding rails.

"No time for protests now," the ringmaster said. "We have only minutes before we're boarded." He looked from one to the other. "Everyone do as you're told. All right?" He gestured them into action. "Quickly, now."

"YOU'RE NOT listening to me," Vera said with the kind of prurient vitriol only she could muster, but by this time Bridges was immune to her slings and arrows.

"She's gone." Looking up from his cell phone, he threw a wad of bills onto the table and rose. "Come on."

"What? Where do you think—?" Vera gave a little owl hoot as he reached across the table and lifted her bodily to her feet. He was immensely strong, and now, she could tell, immensely determined.

"Did you think you could get away with this a second time?" he said as he herded her out the diner door and down the concrete steps. A dark-colored four-door sedan was waiting for them, its engine humming. Pushing her into the backseat, he climbed in beside her. The sedan took off even before he was fully settled.

"She took a cab to Eighth Street Southwest," the granite-faced driver said. No neck, shoulders as broad as a shithouse, he looked like a corn-fed linebacker on steroids.

As the sedan sped south, Bridges glanced over at Vera, who was intensely studying the apelike back of the driver's neck. "I won't bother asking you where she went—"

"I don't fucking know," Vera snapped. "And even if I did . . ." She didn't bother to end the sentence.

"Cut the attitude," Bridges said. "This idiotic idea could get Alli killed."

Vera curled her upper lip. "Christ, don't go all Jason Bourne on me. Everything's under control. You're the one who's out of—"

"Who is she meeting?"

Vera shrugged. She could feel Bridges's animosity rising like a cobra out of a wicker basket, and this only got her back up even more.

Bridges leaned forward. "Lenny, I need you to get us the fuck there five minutes ago."

"I'm doing the best I can, boss. Look at this fucking traffic."

"If this's your best, I'll come up there and take the wheel myself." Bridges put his face close beside the driver's. "Trust me, Lenny, you don't want that to happen."

"No, boss, I sure as shit don't." Leaning forward himself, Lenny turned the wheel and the sedan jumped the curb, running half along the sidewalk, scaring the crap out of every pedestrian in the vicinity. When they began to scream obscenities, he repeatedly slammed the heel of his hand on the horn to drown them out.

A block and a half later, they had skirted the tie-up and Lenny guided the sedan back onto the street. "There it is," he said, pointing up ahead.

"Keep going. Don't slow down," Bridges commanded. "She's smart enough not to have the taxi let her off at the rendezvous."

He looked around. "We're near Fort McNair."

"Yeah," Lenny said, "and the *Titanic* Memorial."

"Righto, but she could have gone anywhere along here," Bridges said. "Even into a house or an apartment building."

The sedan slowed, cruising while the tension inside ratcheted up to an unbearable level.

Vera stirred beside Bridges, and he turned. "What?" His eyes narrowed, but when he spoke again, his tone had turned conciliatory. "What aren't you telling me?"

"Nothing. She's meeting a contact, that's all."

"A contact?" Bridges turned fully, confronting her. "What the fuck does that mean? Is she a spy now?"

Vera hesitated only a moment. "We got a lead on the guy who—" She stared out the window, unsure now where this was leading or what she should do. "He's military."

"Christ."

"McNair," Lenny breathed.

"Once she's inside, she's beyond our help."

"What the hell are you talking about?" Vera said. She had done some crazy things in her day, but putting someone she liked in jeopardy wasn't one of them. "You're freaking me out."

"How well does Alli know this contact?" Bridges said.

Vera put her head in her hands. "Shit, fuck, shit, fuck."

"Boss," Lenny said, "I got nothing."

Bridges caught Vera's eye. "For God's sake, if you have something, now's the time."

"I don't want anything to happen to her." Vera hauled out her cell and showed it to him. "We agreed she'd leave her GPS on."

Bridges's forefinger stabbed at the screen. "She's on the far side of the memorial, Lenny. Get us near as you can, stat!"

SHE DIDN'T know his name—she didn't have to. He was Morgan Herr resurrected. Alli, thrust into her recurring nightmare, felt paralyzed with fear and loathing. She felt again the straps of the chair into which Morgan Herr had imprisoned her, heard again his singsong voice worming its way into her subconscious, altering her perception of her parents, of herself, relived the stinging humiliation to which he had subjected her. She felt her essence shriveling, as she was diminished by his physical and psychological abuse.

Then, like a shout in her ear, reality snapped back into focus and she was in present time, confronting the terror that had stalked her for months on end following her incarceration. She recoiled, but not fast enough. Reaching out, Herr caught her by the front of her sweater.

He laughed. "I scared you good with that Web site I cooked up."

She twisted away, and the sweater yarn ripped and came away in his fist.

"I know you. I know all about you." He glared at her as she darted to her left, and started to stalk her. "I've burrowed inside your head."

Swinging her body around, she struck out with her extended leg. The impact traveled all the way up to her head, making her teeth clack together painfully. His side was like a block of concrete.

"I'm never going to leave until the moment you die."

Herr grabbed her ankle and twisted, trying to fracture the bones, but Alli was prepared, leaving her feet and twisting her entire body in the same direction. He pushed her away in an attempt to make her land awkwardly, but her muscle memory was excellent, and all of Sensei's lessons now came into play.

Her shock at seeing Herr had kept her brain from working as it should in a dangerous situation. Now she began to search for her adversary's weakness. Instead of retreating, she stood her ground, even if it meant absorbing punishing blows. He was quick and brutal, but he was set in his habits. He had perfected specific strikes and defenses, which she catalogued as their hand-to-hand engagement went on. The problem was the blows she was absorbing were rapidly draining her of strength. Here, her small frame worked against her. Against a foe as powerful as Herr, her stamina was evaporating at a breathtaking pace.

But she thought she had enough of a read on him now, and she retreated, drawing him on, then stepped inside his defenses. Slamming her palms against his ears, she was gratified to see him stagger, and she kicked him as hard as she could in the groin. He groaned, one hand swiped at her, and, ducking under it, she stamped on the inside of his right knee.

Even as he went down, he lunged at her, catching one wrist so hard he almost dislocated her shoulder. The breath hot in her throat, she slammed the heel of her hand between his eyes, and he let her go.

She turned and ran.

"IN HERE," Kurin said.

"Really?" Katya looked skeptically at the space in the hollowed-out love seat.

"Really." Kurin helped her in, then turned to Gourdjiev. "Remember what I told you. As soon as you're settled, stay completely silent and still. This is essential."

The old man nodded and, with Kurin's assistance, gamely stepped into the hollow, slowly disappearing.

The train's brakes were panting like an asthmatic after a run. The train was almost at a full stop.

"I won't forget this service," Gourdjiev said.

"I pray not."

Kurin gave him an encouraging smile, then shut the panel, replaced the cushions, and settled on one of them to wait for the inevitable armed intrusion. His thoughts were with Jack and Annika, who by now must be in the elephant car with Huey, the elephants' trainer. Despite their size, elephants were skittish. They were easily spooked by fire or loud noises, just to name a few of the many possibilities, but they knew and loved Huey, who had been with them for a decade. Kurin, who secretly spoke to God when he was alone and in despair, said a prayer that the beasts would accept the two humans because they were in Huey's company.

"I DON'T see her," Lenny said, slewing the car around at the end of P Street SW.

"Keep Vera here," Bridges said, as he bolted from the sedan. The sunlight struck him a glancing blow, and he squinted into the glare. He drew his service pistol and, leaping over a low fence, headed straight for the *Titanic* Memorial.

Bridges felt the breath hot in his lungs, a constriction in his throat. He had no doubt that Alli had gone to meet someone who claimed to know the identity of the man who had posted the rogue site. Mentally, he kicked himself for not paying enough attention to her obsession with this individual. Jack wouldn't have made that mistake. And now Bridges saw Alli as she had been back at the diner, nonchalantly asking if any progress had been made in IDing the perp, when he was certain now she knew quite well that there hadn't. Somehow, though, she had found a lead and had come up with this elaborate plan to lull Bridges, then ditch him while Vera kept him occupied. He didn't know whether he was more angry at her or terrified for her safety.

He saw the granite man with his arms outstretched, no one nearby, and veered to one side to give himself a view of the rear. Nothing. But now, as he picked his way closer, his heart began to pound in his chest. Directly behind the monument a couple of drops of fresh blood shimmered like jewels in the sunlight.

————

RODYA STAS did not like animals—any animals, but especially the large ones his scientist friend called charismatic megafauna. He smelled them as soon as he swung aboard the train. *Goddamn circuses to the seven levels of hell,* he cursed silently as he made his way through the cars. Two of his men had stayed with the engineer, scaring him so badly he nearly wet his pants.

Stas was FSB, but he took his orders from Grigori Batchuk, who called himself Myles Oldham now that he was out of the country. Grigori wanted Gourdjiev and his granddaughter Annika. So far as Stas could determine, the two of them were quite dangerous and deserved a bullet to the back of their heads. But that wasn't what Grigori wanted; Grigori wanted them alive and well and ready for an extended period of articulated interrogation. In fact, Stas had been in charge of installing the implements of this interrogation in an abandoned warehouse Grigori had purchased for this very purpose. A bristling array of terrifying toys awaited the old man and his granddaughter. Stas was not a forgiving man. Gourdjiev had managed to make a fool of him, not once but twice. Stas found that intolerable. Frankly, at this point he didn't give a shit what Grigori wanted, he had become fixated on what he himself wanted. The repercussions would take care of themselves. He knew Grigori only as a hazy figure, a voice over the phone. The man hadn't been inside Russia in years. In fact, it appeared to Stas as if Grigori had abandoned the motherland entirely.

He passed from one car to another, the animal stench burning his eyes as well as his nostrils, as he headed down the line. He had to force himself not to shoot all the animals and be done with it. The only thing that stopped him was the thought that bigger game awaited him.

The old man had nearly slipped through by faking his own death. Grigori's doctor at the hospital had been fooled, and so had Stas. Up to a point. He'd spent weeks reading up on the old man's MO. He was as slippery as an electric eel, and just as dangerous. It was easy for Stas to test out his theory because he had infiltrated Gourdjiev's organization, which was how he had found out about the fake ambulance. What he hadn't counted on was the old man discovering the men Stas had turned.

Stas and his men had already methodically tossed all the residential cars. He'd leered at the female acrobats, wondering what they would be like in the midst of sexual congress. He pushed aside the midgets. Some held out their papers with trembling hands, but he batted them to the floor. He had no interest in papers. He knew who he was looking for; their faces were etched on the scrim of his mind. He was following up on an anonymous report, relayed to him by one of Grigori's men at the Kursky station, that Gourdjiev was spotted at the rail yards—not the passenger station—an odd place for him to be hanging out unless . . . Stas had checked the departures from that area and had come up with the Red Square Circus.

He gagged as he entered the car with the big cats, lions and tigers and leopards stalking back and forth in their cages. The largest of the male lions must have scented him. He lifted his head, his yellow eyes heavy on Stas. His jaws yawned open and he roared. Teeth like nightmares. Stas got the hell out of there.

The next car brought him to the elephants—a pair of them, their disgusting trunks swaying back and forth. Their trainer was with them, one hand on the flank of both animals, to keep them calm, Stas conjectured. Stas came near them, but they turned their colossal heads and stamped their feet, pale tusks scything through the fetid air, and Stas wanted no more to do with them.

The next two cars were filled with familiar circus paraphernalia: tents, thick ropes coiled like adders, sledgehammers, boxes of wooden pegs, on and on. He soon grew bored and continued to the last car.

The ringmaster was sitting on a poufy love seat when Stas entered. To Stas's cruel eye he looked like a pouf himself, but who could say?

"Name," Stas said, though he already knew it.

"Pavel Kurin." The ringmaster rose slowly, almost reluctantly. "At your service."

Stas began to walk around the interior, in precisely the same way the big cats had stalked their cages. "What have we here, Pavel?"

"I beg your pardon, I didn't catch your name."

"I didn't throw it." He flashed his FSB credentials.

"We're just a circus." Kurin spread his hands. "I don't know what you want with us."

Stas glared hard at him. "No one's just *anything,* Pavel."

"We're simple people." The ringmaster gave him a helpless look. "I don't—"

"None of us are *simply* who we are," Stas explained. "There is nothing *simple* about the human condition, Pavel. There are layers, then layers beneath those layers, but do I really have to belabor this point to a man like you?"

"A man like me?"

Stas continued to circle. "A man who made his break with society a long time ago, a man who harbors freaks, simpletons, children in adult bodies." He glanced around at the walls of photos. "I mean, look at this. You're a fucking freak yourself."

Kurin stood straight, putting steel in his backbone. "I provide a valuable service."

Stas paused, his feet spread at shoulder height. "Indeed you do, Pavel, which brings us to my visit today." As they talked, Stas had been examining every piece of furniture in the car. Now he gestured. "Please step away."

"I beg your—"

"Step away from the love seat, Pavel."

As Pavel did as he was ordered, Stas approached the love seat and produced a long-barreled .357 Magnum. He kicked off the cushions and aimed the Magnum at the wooden plank.

Kurin trembled. "What are you doing? That's a family heirloom. I beg you, don't do anything to—"

Stas squeezed off six shots in succession. The car stank of cordite and aftershock.

"Just to make sure you're not providing *other* valuable services," Stas said. "Services entirely *unrelated* to your little traveling freak show." He reloaded the Magnum and fired another six shots through the wood at point-blank range.

ALLI FELT Herr on her tail as she fled, panting, around a corner. It was at that moment that she sensed a blur of motion from one side. Risking a glance, she saw Dick Bridges tackle Herr. The two of them crashed to the sidewalk, rolling over and over. She stopped and turned. The fall had knocked Bridges's gun out of his hand.

She was about to run to pick it up when she heard her name being called. Waxman was standing beneath a tree. Next to him was a Lincoln Town Car with the passenger's door open.

He gestured with his walking stick, pointing it at her. Something struck her leg and she tried to lift it out of the way. She felt strange and cold.

"Come now, Alli. You're in danger here!"

She pointed at Bridges. "But I know—"

"Yes, I know Dick Bridges. I'll take care of it. Quickly, now! Get in!"

"I can't." She tried to run, but seemed stuck to the ground. "That man was impersonating you. He—"

"Yes, Alli," Waxman said, approaching her. "I know all about it."

She whirled. "What? You?"

She took a stumbling step and fell. Pain seared her knees from the sharp-edged gravel underfoot. She put her hands under her. Looking up, she saw that Waxman's smile seemed as big and wide as the Cheshire Cat's. She shook her head, trying to clear it.

"That won't work," came a voice from above her head. "Nothing will."

Determined, she crawled toward the gun, but already the world was beginning to spin around her. Still, she kept on, drawing closer and closer to Bridges's gun shining on the pavement.

She was only a hand's-breadth from it when Waxman used his walking stick to flick the weapon away. Her head came down, hanging between her shoulders as she tried to marshal her energy, but it was no use. The drug injected into her was too powerful. She fell onto her face. Someone caught her, picked her up, and bundled her into the backseat of the Lincoln.

Dimly, she could see Waxman walking briskly, without his limp, to where Herr and Bridges were grappling hand to hand. She tried to move, but she was paralyzed. She tried to cry out, but she was mute. The muscles of her throat wouldn't work.

"Stop!" Waxman commanded.

At once, Herr pushed Bridges away. Rolling onto his back, Bridges levered himself onto one knee. He scrabbled for his fallen handgun, but Waxman trod hard on his hand.

"That will be enough," Waxman said gruffly.

Herr leapt at Bridges, arms around his neck and the side of his head. Bridges, caught off guard, struggled mightily, but Herr's hold was immovable. Herr gave a powerful wrench, and Bridges's neck cracked. Bridges's eyes rolled up in his head and his hands flopped into his lap. Herr kicked the corpse into the gutter.

Waxman stared down at Herr. "Let that be a lesson to you, Reginald. You should have broken his neck in the first ten seconds."

PART TWO

December 9–December 13

The most secret fear is that a blind,
unthinking passion might rip us away from
the group we belong to, make us guilty of betrayal.
— CARLOS FUENTES, *Diana: the Goddess*
Who Hunts Alone

NINE

ALAN FRAINE had not slept in thirty-six hours. Still, he didn't feel tired, and it wasn't just the caffeine released by the coffee and chocolate circulating in his system. Secretary Paull had assigned him the task of electronically breaking into the group the only known member of which was Leonard Bishop.

Fraine rose from his task chair and, fists pressed to the small of his back, stretched his aching muscles. He walked about the room Paull had provided at the Dupont North Hotel, which, despite its tony name, was a slightly run-down establishment in a not altogether savory neighborhood. Not a good idea to be working on this project within Metro's building, where Bishop held an eagle's-eye view. In fact, the computer Fraine had been working on day and night was not tied into any government server—that would have been too dangerous. Fraine was working with the other member of Paull's SITSPEC, a twenty-one-year-old hacker named Leopard. At least that was his hacker name. Fraine knew him only by this handle, and was glad of it. Leopard knew him only as Alan. He had no idea what Fraine's real job was, and most likely was also glad of it. Compartmentalization was paramount in any black op, but especially this one, where high-level homegrown adversaries were lurking in the tall grass inside the Beltway.

Leopard was a tall, lanky, towheaded kid with angry zits blooming on his forehead and chin. His love of all things junky, greasy, and sugary guaranteed those blemishes weren't going away anytime soon. Still, the computer screen didn't seem to mind, and neither did Fraine. When it came to slipping unnoticed through firewalls, the kid was a stone-cold genius. Plus, he knew how to brew coffee so strong it made Fraine's heart pound. Under what rock Paull had found him was anyone's guess.

Fraine stared out the window at the Hahnemann Memorial in the distance while he sipped some of the kid's liquid caffeine. Hahnemann had been a German doctor, the father of homeopathy. Curious that he would have a statue here.

Fraine turned away, knowing that he was trying to distract himself. He wondered how Nona was handling Bishop; according to Paull's directive, they had had no personal contact since she had agreed to dive into the chief's personal private hell pool. Fraine didn't like it; that wasn't required. Though he felt a natural protectiveness toward her, he also knew she was hard as Satan's heart. She would not break because of what the SITSPEC assignment required of her. But still. Whoring herself out had never been in her job description; taking one for the team had.

"Yo, check it," Leopard said.

He'd been sitting beside Fraine for six hours without getting up even to relieve his bladder. Fraine was beginning to suspect he didn't have one. All that crap went down his throat and got burned up by his furious metabolism. *I should be so lucky,* Fraine thought, as he crossed the room and sat back down.

"Fifteen years ago, this dude Bishop was in the Horn of Africa." Everyone was "dude" to Leopard.

Fraine stared at the document on the screen. It had TOP SECRET and EYES ONLY stamped across the top. "How the fuck did you get this?"

"Firewalls, firewalls, firewalls," Leopard said. "They're all just video game levels to me, puzzles, see, that have to be figured out. You know the code, there's always a path inside, and if you discover the source code, then shit, dude, you got it made."

"Whose firewall?"

"DoD," Leopard said. "But some branch that doesn't exist."

Now we're getting somewhere, Fraine thought. "Officially."

"Well, yes, 'cos here it is." Leopard bobbed his head. "You gotta get all the way to Oz to find it, though."

"This branch have a name?"

"Negatory. Just a number designation: Three-thirteen." The kid picked at a dirty mess of cold fries overlaid with congealed cheese the color of a Day-Glo sun. "So, anyway, Horn of Africa."

The text on the screen began to change so fast Fraine's head hurt.

"Your man Bishop was assigned to a unit, name: Acacia. I've been trying to bring up that name elsewhere in here, to cross-reference, but so far no luck."

Fraine was trying to make sense of the text on the 313 server. "What was Acacia doing in the Horn of Africa?"

"Not clear. Could be anything. One thing I do know, their deployment lasted a month. Then they were flown home and debriefed for a week in DoD HQ."

And apparently let go, because six months later, Bishop joined Metro. Why did he go from a black ops unit of DoD to D.C. police? And how had he risen through the ranks so quickly?

"I want to find out what Acacia's assignment was."

The kid nodded. "Okay, but from the look of things I'd say Acacia was a death squad, deployed maybe to assassinate some politically hot football the Pentagon wanted to get rid of."

"That's quite an imagination you've got there," Fraine said.

Leopard gave him the hairy eyeball. "You think this is *my* first deployment?"

"Clearly not," Fraine said. "I would feel better if we had confirmation. A month's deployment is an awfully long time for a death squad."

"Not if you're ending up elsewhere, like for instance the mountains between Afghanistan and Pakistan."

The kid had a point and Fraine conceded it. "Keep on it." Fraine rose and grabbed his coat. "Meanwhile, I'm going to see if I can find out who Bishop's rabbi was at Metro way back when."

"Dude!"

Fist-bump.

"STAY HERE!" Lenny ordered, already half out of the car.

Vera, filled with fear for Alli, did no such thing. Instead, she went around, felt under the driver's seat, but didn't find what she was looking for: a service pistol. The stiff leather holster bolted to the underside was empty. Hesitating for only a moment, she moved off cautiously, following in Lenny's footsteps.

She hurried across the street, feeling vulnerable in the complete absence of foot traffic, moving from parked car to parked car, crouched down, peering above fenders and around bumpers. She saw Lenny running full-out now, but even when she changed position she could not see any sign of Alli. She kept moving forward, changing her angle of view each time in order to get a sense of the whole scene.

She saw Dick Bridges sitting awkwardly on the street, then Bridges was dead, his neck snapped by a hulking man Vera did not know. And here came Lenny, Glock 9mm in one hand, sprinting toward the men. He yelled something Vera couldn't make out, and Waxman turned toward him. Slowly, almost leisurely, Waxman lifted his walking stick. Something zipped out of its end and struck Lenny, who staggered and went down to his knees. He tried to lift the handgun to aim it at Waxman, but apparently he lacked the strength. The man with Waxman threw Dick Bridges aside and stood up, strode over to Lenny, and kicked him in the face. Lenny keeled onto his back and lay on the ground, unmoving.

At that moment, Waxman looked up, as if he were aware of Vera's presence. She ducked down behind the Chevy van she had been using as a shield, and, keeping herself motionless, held her breath. When she heard footsteps approaching, she slid under the van, keeping herself perfectly still. This was the moment in thriller films when you could hear the woman in peril breathing hard but whoever was after her couldn't. If her situation had not been so dire, Vera would have laughed. Women in those films were so stupid.

She had silently counted off thirty-three seconds when, out of the corner of her eye, she saw the shoes and trouser cuffs. For a moment or two, they stood beside the van, then they proceeded on, the slap of leather soles against tarmac receding to silence. Vera licked her dry lips and allowed herself to breath more deeply. When nothing further happened, she slid out from under the van and risked a glance around its fender. A gleaming black Lincoln Town Car had its rear door open. Waxman, bending down, said something to someone inside. When he moved away, Vera saw that it was Alli. Then Waxman and the man who had killed Dick Bridges got in, and all the doors slammed shut.

She looked around for Dick Bridges or Lenny, but there was no sign that they had ever been there. The bodies must have been stuffed in the Lincoln's trunk, she thought. It was certainly large enough.

As the Town Car backed up to make a U-turn, Vera saw part of the license tag and quickly memorized it as the Lincoln took off.

It was only afterward, upon reflection, that she realized her heart had been in her throat the whole time.

FRAINE KNEW a guy who knew a guy who knew a guy. That's how things worked at Metro. Charlie Patrick was Fraine's guy. Charlie was something of a self-centered prick, but it was just this knack for self-preservation that had kept him at his job through a handful of regime changes and budgetary layoffs at Metro. No one wanted to do without Charlie because he was the one who kept the overtime logs, who figured who was getting how much money above and below the table, so to speak. And, sly as a fox, he had made his software impenetrable to all but himself, so replacing him wasn't an option. In other words, Charlie Patrick was indispensable, which was just the way Charlie Patrick liked his life, because, when you came down to the nub, he was nothing more than a clerk. His office cubicle was the approximate size of a shower stall, without a window or any other means of light besides the three mean fluorescent strips depending from the fiberboard ceiling like stalagmites that had fallen asleep. Looking at the bright side, however, being indispensable was a good enough reason for Charlie not to drink himself into the gutter or to put a gun under his chin and pull the trigger, both popular options for cops who had reached the end of their tether.

Fraine took Charlie Patrick out to Patsy's, the local watering hole where Charlie was a living legend. At Patsy's, at least, Charlie was the unconditional king of the hill.

"Looka those suits ovah there, with their silicone dates," Charlie said darkly. "Only pussies drink wine." Charlie himself never drank anything more potent than beer, and then he limited himself to two at the outside. "I already got me a life," he'd say when queried about not going along with the frequent beer jags for which Patsy's was famous.

They sat in a beery booth whose bones creaked alarmingly with his every move. Charlie was a big man, if you were judging solely by girth. Red-cheeked, flame-haired, nose like Rudolph, he had a notorious Irish temper, especially when someone tried to pee on his territory. Many precinct captains, it was said, were justifiably afraid of him.

"So, Al, long time no see," he said, between ordering a double-meat Coney, plus fries, onion rings, and a beer. Lacing sausage fingers on the tabletop, he added, "What can I do ya for?"

Charlie wasn't one for small talk. "Get the business end out of the way first, then sit back and enjoy the ride," was his oft-stated motto.

"I'm looking for the answer to a question."

"And I'm open for business."

The beers came, along with a plate of pickles and a plastic basket piled high with rolls and prepackaged pats of butter.

"This particular question involves CoD Bishop."

Charlie seemed not to have heard. He tore the tops off three pats and swabbed them all onto a roll. Charlie's massive appetite was a component of his legend at Patsy's.

"CoD Bishop," Charlie said, his cheeks bulging with oily roll flesh. He had a knack of speaking with perfect diction while his mouth was crammed with food. "I hate that snotty fuck." He swallowed. "But I gotta admit he's got a lotta heads up his ass."

"At Metro, you mean."

Charlie sat back, hands in the air, at the ready position, as plates of food were set down in front of him. The Coney turned out to be thick-cut slices of prime rib smothered in melting pools of Cheez Whiz. "I mean everyfuckingwhere." Charlie began to chow down, an astonishing sight any time of the day or night. "Bottom line, he's got major juice behind him."

Fraine automatically lowered his voice. "That's the question needs answering."

Charlie looked up, the lower half of his face glistening like glass. "Headwaters. The source of the Nile." Putting down what was left of one of the Coney pieces, he wiped his lips. He needed three napkins to soak up all the grease. "Well, now, that's a mighty dark continent you're looking to penetrate, Al. You sure you want to go in that direction?"

"I do."

Charlie grunted like a warthog as he devoured the last bites of the Coney wedge, along with a couple of onion rings. "You remember when we scammed that Irish mafia don? We was still wet behind the ears. We're older than that now."

Fraine said nothing.

Charlie sucked a chunk of meat out from between his teeth. "So how long we been singing songs around the same campfire together?"

"A long time," Fraine said. "Too damn long to count."

"You got that right," Charlie snorted. He pointed a fat forefinger. "So I hope to fuck you listen when I tell you not to go down this path. Thorns're likely to eat you alive."

"I hear you, Charlie, but I've got no choice."

The fat man's eyes grew sorrowful. "These days none of us got a choice, seems like."

"It's all a matter of priorities, isn't it?"

Silence grew between them like a vine.

"One more chance, Al."

Fraine could think of nothing to say to this that hadn't already been said.

Charlie sighed deeply and sat back as well as he was able, considering his shape and weight. "Well, then, shit, I gotta guy for you. He don't have what you're lookin' for, he'll know who does."

"What's it going to cost me?"

Charlie Patrick scooped up another messy wedge of the Coney, carved out a mighty bite, and grinned.

THE REPORTS from the shots Stas fired traveled from inside the ringmaster's car, penetrating to where the two elephants, Romulus and Remus, already agitated by Stas's threatening energy, lifted their heads and trumpeted deafeningly.

Jack and Annika had been hiding between them, but now their sanctuary had turned into a death trap. Huey's attempts at calming the animals went for naught; they were too terrorized.

Annika allowed Jack to guide her, the colossal legs just missing them. Jack's brain had mapped the inside of the car and now, because his mind worked at such lightning speed, he was able not only to feel the elephants' extreme agitation but also to accurately predict their responses to it.

Their darting movements were akin to a pair of video game avatars dodging and weaving to avoid enemy attacks. The problem was, they had no way to fight back; their only protection was Jack's mind, making connections Annika could not even dream about.

Remus's backside was jammed against one connecting door, Romulus's tusks poking the other, blocking those routes to safety. Jack, one hand on the leg of each elephant, kept making connections, moving Annika in what seemed a circuitous route toward the sliding door on the side wall.

They were almost there when Romulus bellowed again, as if in pain, and almost smashed Annika between his quivering flank and the wall of the car. At the last instant, Jack pushed her down into a crouch, and drew her quickly under the animal's swaying belly.

Huey grabbed her hand and they ran to the car wall. Jack helped him slide open the side door, and the wide ramp, reinforced to handle the animals' weight, was automatically deployed.

"When they're like this," Huey said breathlessly, "there's nothing I can do. Terror has gripped their hearts. They'll need time to calm themselves."

Then they all had to leap for their lives as Romulus thundered down the ramp, his heart dark with rage.

RODYA STAS pulled up the love seat's shattered bench board and peered inside.

"Look what you've done!" Kurin wailed over and over again.

He appeared on the verge of hysterics when Stas turned and slapped him across the face. "Where are they?"

"Where is who?" Kurin shuddered. "I don't know who you're looking for. And why would you think that person is here?"

Stas checked the space again for any sign of blood or a body. Nothing. He'd pumped enough bullets at close range to kill anyone hiding. Anyway, now that he had a look at it, the space was too small for a person, unless he was curled up in a fetal position.

Thoroughly pissed off, he got up into the ringmaster's face. "Listen, you flyweight pansy, if I find out you had hitchhikers on your pink lady express I'm going to come back here and personally ram your head up your ass, got it?"

Kurin, staring at the pointy toes of his high boots, said nothing.

Stas cursed mightily. The tip had been wrong; he'd been on an hours-long wild goose chase. And, in the meantime, Gourdjiev had surely slipped out of Moscow unseen. Perhaps, knowing the old toad as he did, he'd hired a double to throw Stas off the scent. That would be just like the sonuvabitch.

Shoving Kurin roughly aside, he picked his way across the car and exited through the rear door, where he rendezvoused with his men.

"You checked the undercarriage of every car?"

"Yes, sir."

Stas stood for a moment, hands on hips, as if willing the old man to appear. Then he turned and stalked back to his car. He and his men piled in. At that moment, a door slid open and a ramp slammed down onto the ground near the cars.

Stas turned in his seat in time to see an elephant rampaging down. "Get us out of here!" he called to his driver. "Now."

But the second elephant, thundering down, blocked their way. The driver was in the process of turning around when the first elephant stepped on the second car, demolishing it. Stas's eyes nearly bugged out of his head. He scrabbled for the door handle. Too late, the elephant's eye was fixed on him. Lowering its head, the beast jammed one of its tusks through the car window, impaling Stas. Then, with a powerful flick of its head, it tossed the car high in the air. Tumbling end over end, Stas's car landed on its side, bounced, and slammed upside down with such force that the roof collapsed, crushing its occupants. That didn't stop Romulus, who continued to attack the car with a relentlessness remarkable not only for its vigor but for its clear, almost human sense of revenge.

"NOTHING, SIR," the detective said. "No one on the street or in the area, and the guards at Fort McNair reported no gunshots."

"There were no gunshots," Vera said. "I told you."

"Yes." Elbows on his desktop, Chief of Detectives Bishop steepled his fingers as he studied Vera. "All this happened in total silence."

Vera was about to utter one of her caustic retorts but something in his tone, a steel edge barely perceived, warned her against saying anything at the moment. As soon as the Lincoln Town Car was out of sight, she had risen and begun to run. Then, thinking more clearly, she had returned to Lenny's car and had driven it to Metro police HQ, rather than a precinct. Even so, how she had so quickly gotten bumped up to the chief of detectives was still a mystery. She had prepared an elaborate song and dance to get her moving up the Metro ladder from the detective who took her initial statement to the brass, but as it turned out, the persuasion hadn't been necessary. Now she was terrified that she had made the wrong decision by coming here. The men who had kidnapped Alli were powerful people in a city that ran on power. Who knew how many people they might have in their pockets?

Bishop referred to her statement, which Del Stoddart, the intake detective, had prepared. "You say here that all this happened around the *Titanic* Memorial." He looked up. "Is that right?"

"Yes."

"Yet no one was around, no witnesses."

"That's right. The area is under construction."

Bishop's gaze dropped again to her statement. "I see."

And with those two words, Vera knew that he didn't believe her. *Why* he didn't believe her she couldn't say, but all of a sudden she suspected that she herself was in trouble.

"I've contacted Commander Fellows and he confirms that Alli Carson is not at Fearington." Bishop looked up. "But then neither are you, Ms. Bard. And I can't help wondering—echoing Commander Fellows—why you aren't at Fearington. Technically, you and Ms. Carson are AWOL. I'd very much like to hear why that is."

Vera watched him with both caution and suspicion. He had very deftly turned the interview upside down, making it about offenses that she and Alli had committed, rather than concerning himself with what she had witnessed.

"Two federal agents were killed and my friend has been abducted," Vera said, "and you're asking me why Alli and I are absent without leave?"

"That's right."

"I don't believe this. How the fuck did I land in a Kafka novel?"

"Are you going to answer me, Ms. Bard?"

Her mistake was now writ large in front of her. She should have gone to the Feds right away instead of dicking around with Metro.

"Are you going to inform Secret Service?"

"I have. I've told them that one of their vehicles has been stolen."

"Wait, what? Is that what you think?"

"What else *should* I think, Ms. Bard? You tell me this wild story concerning murder and kidnapping, yet you claim you didn't see any of the perpetrators."

"I was hiding under a car. I couldn't see anything but a bunch of legs."

"Did you get the tags off the Town Car?"

"No." She had decided to lie because she didn't trust this man, didn't trust anyone now. All she wanted was to bolt out of there.

Chief Bishop's phone rang and he fielded the call. He listened, then spoke softly into the mouthpiece before putting the receiver down. He rose. "Wait here a moment, please. Officer McKay will keep you company until I return."

She turned in her chair to see a burly uniform standing just inside the doorway. She spent the next few moments calming herself, then she, too, rose and went to where McKay stood guard.

With her back to him, she stuck her finger down her throat and made herself retch. She groaned. "I think I'm gonna be sick."

McKay looked around, grabbed a metal trash can, and brought it over. Vera took it and smashed it into his face. McKay staggered backward, blood gushing from his nose, and Vera ran past him, then flew through the doorway. She heard his garbled shout as she took the stairs, three at a time, hurried across the echoing lobby, hightailing it out of Metro HQ. She did not stop until she had lost herself in the crosshatching of city streets.

TEN

ONE SUMMER, on a day of dazzling sun and clouds in the shape of African animals, Alli and Caro played in the Barrier Island surf. Alli remembered the smell of Caro, a combination of salt and Coppertone, and the sheer blondeness of her, as if she were an apparition or a child model in one of the slick women's magazines her mother was always leafing through.

Seagulls cawing overhead, the splashing of the surf, the feel of Caro through the water, slick flesh, slippery as a fish. She had not wanted to come out of the water, even when her mother called them, even when Uncle Hank came to gather them in his arms. Alli was docile, but she remembered Caro squirming, crying, fighting. Caro hadn't wanted to leave the surf for the small village of blankets, beach chairs, striped umbrellas, and baskets filled with food and drink.

Alli tried to calm Caro after Uncle Hank set her down on one of the blankets, but nothing would appease her. Alli remembered Caro waiting until her father's back was turned, then running back down to the water. Alli had tried to follow her, but her mother had scooped her up, holding her to her breast as Alli watched Caro hitting the surf. Caro fell, but picked herself up, spitting out seawater, pushing forward, deeper and deeper, until Uncle Hank reached her in long strides. He slapped her bottom over and over as he brought her back to where the family waited. But Caro didn't cry; Caro never cried, at least not in Alli's presence. Instead, she glared straight ahead, through everyone, as if they were ghosts, already dead.

The memory unspooled in Alli's mind with such vividness that she felt as if she were experiencing it all over again, as if she had gone back in time, as if the present had been wiped clean, as if she could start all over again, as if Emma McClure hadn't died, as if she didn't carry around with her a terrible burden of guilt, as if she had never been kidnapped and held captive by Morgan Herr. . . .

Eyes opening, lids gluey, vision blurred and distorted. She felt, rather than saw, that she was surrounded by grayness.

What? Where?

And then the present rushed in like a tidal wave, obliterating the sand-castle dreams her mind had created to protect her from the horror of her new reality. She opened her mouth, she wanted to scream, but nothing came out, not even a squeak. Her tongue hit against something. Thinking there was a dead animal in her mouth, her eyes rounded in terror and she gagged. Then reason overtook irrationality, and she realized a wadded ball of cotton had been stuffed into her mouth to keep her from crying out.

She felt her heart beating so hard it seemed to be painfully expanding and contracting the surrounding ribs. Closing her eyes, she tried to center herself. She breathed through her nose, slowing her breaths, lengthening them in order to get oxygen down into the deepest parts of her. Her heartbeat fluttered, then slowly calmed as she harnessed her mind, turning it to what she needed to do in order to improve her chances of escape.

She opened her eyes again, blinked several times, then tried to assess her surroundings. Grayness, relieved only by a narrow shaft of sunlight heavily filtered, falling from high above her head. She lay on a poured concrete floor. It was unsealed and she felt its powdery residue in her nostrils and at the back of her throat. With an effort, she suppressed the urge to cough, which, with her mouth full, would only cause her to gag again.

She lay on her left side. Looking down her body, she saw her legs tied at the knees and ankles with plastic zip ties as if she were a trussed lamb ready for the slaughter. She tried to move, and pain flared through her. Her arms were tied behind her back, the wrists bound with, she assumed, another zip tie.

It took an alarming amount of effort to roll herself onto her back. Her hands scraped against the floor and her back arched unnaturally. She stared up at the ceiling. Apart from an air vent grille high up, it looked exactly the same as the wall. Turning her head brought the window into her field of vision. It was too small for even her small body to worm through, even if she could somehow free herself and find a way to reach it.

A stainless-steel toilet was attached to a wall beside a tiny sink. A door gleamed dully, so it must be metal, she surmised. A slot at eye level to allow someone from the outside to observe her. In the opposite corner, at the junction of the wall and the ceiling, was a small video camera. So she was being constantly observed. Some kind of a prison cell? All at once, panic filled up her chest as if she were going down for the last time. She was drowning, her nightmare past returning in a terrifying déjà vu. She felt unmoored, alone, adrift, helpless. She shivered violently, hearing Herr's voice in her head, as she did in her nightmares, worming its way into her cortex, as if he had never died, as if in some superhuman effort he had cheated death in order to stalk her, as if he had not finished with her, as if he were about to inflict more damage to her psyche.

She heard a sob escape her, and she bit down on her bottom lip, drawing blood. It was no use. This wasn't a dream. It was real. She was imprisoned again, and there was no way out. She felt as if she were losing her mind. Doubling over, she began to gag, miserable and despairing.

And then, in the deepest mire of her terror, she thought about Jack, about all he had taught her, all she had painfully learned about herself, and she felt the breath rush back into her lungs. She took a step back from her panic until she could hold it at arm's length, so that it no longer engulfed her.

Think, she told herself. *Think rationally.*

She remembered Herr—or the man who looked like Herr—disguised as Waxman, her hand-to-hand with him, then fleeing virtually into the real Waxman's arms. What happened next? Her thoughts darted in and out of her grasp. Waxman had pointed his walking stick at her. The next moment she had felt paralyzed. And she had seen him walking without a limp.

And then, with a wave of despair that threatened to engulf her, she remembered Dick Bridges, who had tried to save her. She had no way of knowing whether he was alive or dead, but the fact that she was here and not safe in Bridges's care made her fear for his life.

She was certain that she had developed a sixth sense that allowed her to spot the minute tics and flaws in human behavior, gaining her an edge when looking for truth and lies. But somehow Waxman had fooled her completely. Maybe she had become complacent, figuring her sixth sense would automatically warn her. Tears of rage and frustration blurred her vision, scalded her cheeks.

"Arrogance is the province of the young," Sensei had told her over and over. But had she listened? It was her arrogance, her total disregard for the rules of safety and caution, that had led her into this situation. Her obsession with Herr had blinded her, and now she was paying the price. All the worse if Bridges had been harmed trying to protect her from herself.

That was when she felt the cool breeze like a kiss against her cheek and, arching her neck, saw Emma standing in the shaft of light that slowly crawled across the floor of her cell. She was colorless, translucent, as if she were made of glass bricks.

"Emma?" she whispered. "Emma."

Emma stepped closer. This was not the first time she had seen Emma's—what?—ghost, anima, spirit, electrical energy?—the definition would depend on your belief system. Alli knew that Emma appeared to

Jack regularly, that he had thought he was going mad with grief until she had come to Alli as well, not as often and not for very long. But she was here now.

"You've found me, Emma."

I will always find you, Alli. You know that. I love you.

Now Alli did cry, the tears rolling freely down her cheeks. "I love you, Emma. I have from the moment we met."

I know. I've always known.

"Emma, where am I?"

You know I can't tell you. I'm not a Get Out of Jail Free card. That's not how it works.

"Tell me how it works."

My current state is as much a mystery to me as it is to you.

"But you're here for a reason."

I'm never anywhere without a reason. Otherwise, I'd simply float away.

"Don't do that, Emma. Please." Alli could no longer tolerate the pain and she rolled back on her left side. "Can you help me?"

I am doing what I can.

"I don't understand."

Yes, you do. Think, Alli.

"Think about what? I'm trapped in a cell, bound hand and foot. I can't even move."

Alli blinked and Emma was gone. A sharp scraping sound filled the cell, and the door swung open, revealing her captor.

WHEN JACK and Annika appeared in the ringmaster's car, Kurin was standing at the window, watching Huey calm Romulus. Remus stood docilely by, her trunk swaying like a metronome.

Annika pulled apart the love seat's bullet-shattered wooden slab. "What happened in here?" she said. "Are Dyadya and Katya all right?"

"Perfectly fine." Kurin smiled as he turned to them.

"Then why aren't you helping them?"

"They don't need help." Kurin looked like a different person. All the fear and subservience he had shown Stas had been replaced by his ringmaster's confidence. He was as good an actor as anyone in the circus. "Come," he said briskly, leading them outside.

"My God," Annika said when she assessed the destruction the elephants had wreaked.

"No one's getting out of that alive," Jack observed.

Kurin nodded. "We all protect our own."

Remus's trunk stopped swaying when she saw them. Her enormous ears flapped and she lumbered over to where they stood beside the ringmaster's car. Her trunk curled up, the end resting first on Jack's head, then on Annika's shoulder. Annika reached up and stroked the trunk.

"She already knows you," Kurin said, as Huey led a now-calmed Romulus back to where Remus stood. The great beasts loomed over them, but there was now a serenity about both of them that soothed the humans' still-jangling nerves.

Pointing to the car's undercarriage, Kurin said, "The floor of my wagon is two and a half feet higher than the bottom." He shrugged. "Emergencies arise from time to time. You never know."

Stepping forward, he pressed the red star that crowned one of the onion domes in the Red Square Circus logo. At once, a panel opened and they could see inside. Gourdjiev and Katya lay within the narrow bay. Annika and Jack helped them out. They blinked in the light.

The old man appeared unperturbed by their close call, but Katya was clearly shaken. Annika put her arm tenderly around the older woman. While they regained their equilibrium, Jack recounted what had happened.

"So, crushed to death," Gourdjiev said, when Jack had concluded. Giving the elephants a wide berth, he picked his way toward the remains of the two cars. "More of Grigori's people dead."

At that moment, Jack's cell buzzed. Seeing it was Secretary Paull, he took the call.

"Get your ass back to D.C. ASAP." Paull's voice was unnaturally tense.

"The situation has blown up here," Jack said. "I've got my hands full."

"Not interested," Paull snapped. "I need you."

Something lurched inside Jack and a certain coolness caused him to look around for any sign of Emma. Suddenly filled with anxiety, he said, "Dennis, what's happened?"

"Alli is missing," Paull replied, "along with Dick Bridges and another Secret Service agent."

WERNER WAXMAN limped into the concrete cell. He did not bother to close the door behind him. Another, far larger man loomed behind him, a chair in one massive hand. When he set it down in front of Alli, she shuddered, recognizing the man who looked just like Morgan Herr.

Waxman sat down, bony hands resting on the knob of his walking stick. "So here we are again, back at the beginning."

Alli stared up at him, mute. The tip of his walking stick flicked out and she flinched, convinced he was going to inject her again. Instead, he manipulated it between her lips, unraveling the ball of cotton and drawing it out of her mouth.

She tried to speak but her throat was dry, her tongue felt swollen. She closed her mouth, tried to gather saliva. There wasn't much on hand.

"Reggie," Waxman said without taking his eyes off her, "would you be kind enough to bring Alli a glass of water?"

Herr turned and, without a word, disappeared into the corridor beyond the doorway. Alli's eyes followed him, but there was nothing to see—the corridor was featureless. Her eyes returned to Waxman, who was gazing at her with the vaguely detached expression of a taxidermist. She shuddered involuntarily.

"Cold?" Waxman said, misinterpreting. He smiled. "It will only get colder."

Herr returned with a glass of water.

"Sit her up," Waxman said.

Herr hauled her into a sitting position, then, bending over, tilted the rim to her lips. He stared at her while she drank greedily, tiny rivulets snaking down the corners of her mouth. When the glass was drained he took it away, but not before baring his teeth at her.

"Better?" Waxman said without a shred of sympathy.

Alli found her voice at last. "Where is Dick Bridges? What happened to him?"

"Ah, Bridges," Waxman said, as if they were speaking about an old mutual friend. "He's dead, I'm afraid."

A needle pierced Alli's heart, but she wondered whether she should believe him. After all, up to this point he had done nothing but lie to her. She wanted so badly for Dick to be alive and well, but she saw again the scene of him tackling Herr, of Waxman standing over him. Then everything had gone blank. Was Dick really dead? He must be, she reasoned. Neither Herr nor Waxman would have left Dick alive as a witness to her kidnapping. No, Waxman must be telling the truth. Dick was gone.

Waxman stared down at her. "Secret Service agents. They're not human, not really. They're trained to react. . . . Oh, but Dick Bridges was the agent who let your father die, yes?" He poked Alli with the tip of his walking stick. "So maybe you don't care that he's dead."

Alli wanted to laugh at that. "What do you want?"

He cocked his head. "Yes, what *do* I want? Why have I gone to all this trouble to bring you here? To begin, we need to talk about Reggie."

"He's the one who created the Web site."

"Yes, he did. On my orders."

"Why?"

Waxman smiled. "A touch of bitter honey to trap this particular fly."

Alli moved her head to indicate Herr. "He's Morgan's brother, isn't he?"

"Better than that." Waxman glanced over his shoulder at Herr, who was standing immobile by the doorway. "Reggie is Morgan's twin."

Alli closed her eyes for a moment. Morgan Herr's twin. The worst of all possibilities. She wished with all her heart that Emma would reappear and tell her what to do, explain how to extricate herself from this nightmare.

Waxman leaned forward, his voice lowered in a whisper that had theatrical overtones. "To be perfectly honest, Herr would like nothing better than to kill you. And who can blame him? You're responsible for his brother's death."

"Morgan became responsible for his own fate when he chose to kidnap me," Alli said. "The same goes for you and the twin."

"Well, I must say I wasn't expecting this display of—what did they call it in the old days? Ah, yes—true grit. Tell me, are you always this feisty?"

Alli kept her voice neutral. "I'm not telling you anything." This surely was a nightmare, but it was one she had already endured. She knew how to protect herself from anything they might do to her.

"I had expected as much." He had the kind of smile that was all teeth. "But, rest assured, there's a long way to go."

"I have to pee," Alli said from her position on the floor.

Waxman contemplated her for a moment, then he raised one hand. Herr obediently returned and, opening a switchblade, cut the three zip ties. He stood over her, watching her as if she were a beetle on its back, as she struggled to regain circulation in her limbs. She was gratified to see the damage she had inflicted on his face. As she rose, he stepped quickly back as if she were radioactive. Turning on his heel, he went back to his post.

Alli took a couple of experimental steps, but one leg, suffering through pins and needles, collapsed under her, and she knelt on one knee until it passed. Then she made her unsteady way to the stainless-steel toilet.

"I'm not going anywhere," Waxman said.

Alli ignored him, pulled down her trousers and underpants, and sat. Elbows on thighs, she stared at Waxman while she relieved herself. The strong stream ricocheted noisily against the metal. He didn't blink and neither did she.

"You know," Waxman said, "it's a pity you're on the wrong side of history. I could have use for someone like you."

"Think how my recruitment would affect the twin over there."

"Rivalry is competition, something I find a healthy incentive for all concerned."

The moment Waxman rose, Herr came and took the chair out of the cell. "Enjoy your moment of peace." He limped across the cell. "I promise you it will be the last in a long, long while."

The cell door banged shut behind him.

ELEVEN

CHESAPEAKE BODYWERKS occupied three contiguous concrete buildings at 1550 Fourteenth Street NW. The facade was unprepossessing. There were six open bays filled with vehicle workstations, including lifts. Two limos and an armored money-delivery truck were being worked on when Fraine drove up. He parked and got out. Someone with a deft hand had painted an American flag over the office door.

He went in and asked one of the two women at the front desk if Andy Beemer was in.

A balding man in jeans, a plaid shirt with the sleeves rolled up, and a Nationals baseball cap looked up. "Depends on who's asking."

"I'm a revenuer."

Beemer had a cheery avuncular laugh. He had a head like a bowling ball and shoulders like a guard or tackle, but his milk-chocolate face looked beaten up. PAL boxing league, Fraine automatically thought, and liked him immediately.

He rose and extended his hand. "Alan, right? Charles said you'd show up." He gave a tilt of his head. "Let's go in back."

They went through one of the bays, which smelled of motor oil, grease, and metal. A couple of Latino men in stained overalls had one of the limos up on a lift and were dismantling a section of the underside, all the while keeping streams of electric-quick street Spanish flowing between them.

Beemer led the way through a dimly lit storeroom that reeked of rubber tires.

"Diet or reg?" he asked.

"I hate Diet anything," Fraine said.

"Mos def."

Banging out a couple of bottles of Coke from an old, rumbling machine, Beemer ambled out a door to a small open area where a lone hawthorn struggled to survive amid ratty tufts of what might be grass, but could just as easily be weeds. Either way, it was unkempt.

Hoisting himself onto an empty oil tub, he handed Fraine one of the frosty bottles, then opened his and took a long swig. He eyed Fraine as if he were assessing him. "How d'you know Charles?"

"We shared the same playpen."

"Ha! Yeah, sure." Beemer shook his head. "None of my bidness." He took another swig and the Coke was gone. "So, what brings you out this way?"

Fraine looked around. "From Charlie to you." His shoulders lifted and fell. "I'm afraid I don't get the connection."

"Yeah, that's kinda the point." Beemer swept a hand to indicate the buildings. "What we work on here are vehicles of a very special nature— the POTUS, veep, cabinet members, certain constituents of the Hill. They all come here. Y'see, I'm bonded in a very special way. *Semper fi,* baby."

"Ex-Marine, huh?"

Beemer nodded. "Been there, done that. But the fact is I'm still on active duty. This here's my last deployment."

"So you don't service Metro police vehicles."

"I believe you know that I do not."

Charlie must have given him more than a heads-up. "How about Leonard Bishop's?"

"Well, shit." Beemer grinned. "The chief is his own special breed of dickhead."

ALLI HAD fallen into a deep sleep when the cell door banged open, bright lights switched on, and the limping gait of Waxman echoed on the concrete floor. When she opened her eyes, he was seated on his chair and Herr was standing by the doorway, an open taunt she ignored.

Every muscle in her body ached. It was freezing in the cell, and not a blanket in sight. Neither was there a bunk; she had slept on the floor and was now chilled to the bone. She clamped her jaws shut to keep her teeth from chattering.

"So," Waxman said. "How are we feeling?"

"What time is it?"

"There's always a chance we can work something out," Waxman said, ignoring her. Like any good interrogator, he was bent on inflicting disorientation, the first step to loss of identity, breaking the spirit, and extracting from her whatever it was he wanted. "But that would entail cooperation on your part."

Alli sat up and ran her tongue over her chapped lips. "Thirsty."

Waxman flicked a hand. "Reggie."

Herr produced a glass of water and stepped back, observing her coldly as she drank. He took the empty glass and retreated.

"I'm curious," Alli said. "What makes Herr loyal to you?"

Across the room Herr twitched. *Score one for me,* Alli thought. She moved, and smelled herself.

Waxman wrinkled his nose, as if her body odor had penetrated his personal private space. "I saved Reggie's life, if you must know. He owes me everything, don't you, Reggie?"

Herr grunted.

Alli seized the opening, even though it was the narrowest of fissures. "He doesn't seem all that happy about it."

"Reggie is not, fundamentally, a happy person." Waxman shifted his walking stick from one hand to the other. "But that's one of the things that makes him so valuable to me."

She lifted her head. "You hear that, Reggie? It pleases old Waxman that you're not happy."

Waxman glared at her. Herr, for his part, continued to watch her as if he were cataloguing her every move.

"Forget that line of reasoning," Waxman said, recovering. "Reggie doesn't care one way or another. His allegiance is set in stone."

"Even stones shift," Alli said, "in ocean tides and earthquakes."

Waxman laughed. "And which one are you, Little Orphan Alli?"

Her stomach rumbled emptily and she felt a wave of dizziness sweep through her. She couldn't recall when she had last eaten. She vowed not to let either of them see her weakness, to get a claw into the fissures in her wall, but her head nodded involuntarily.

"Hungry, are we?" Waxman lifted a hand and Herr brought in food on a small tray, which he set on Waxman's narrow lap. "What have we here?" Waxman looked down. "Ah, chicken salad on whole wheat with mustard and mayonnaise. And what else? A bag of potato chips, a soda, and a slice of chocolate cake." His eyes came up. "You like chocolate cake, don't you, Little Orphan Alli?"

Alli, famished as she was, recognized that she had caused a fundamental shift in him. He had begun needling her; she had gotten under his skin. That knowledge didn't help much, though, as she watched him pick up half the sandwich and begin to consume it in small, delicate bites.

"Delicious," he said, fastidiously wiping his lips. He took another bite, chewed ostentatiously, and swallowed. "I would ask you to join me, but, alas, I cannot." Once again, he smiled with his teeth. "Rules of engagement and all that."

"It doesn't matter."

"Bravely spoken, Little Orphan Alli, but in time—and that time is rapidly approaching—it will." Another tiny bite consumed. "I will tell you frankly that I am keenly anticipating that moment."

Alli knew she needed to husband what positive nuggets she could from the situation. Once again, she fervidly wished Emma were here to help her. But her mind was cast back to their recent conversation.

"Can you help me?" she had said. *I am doing what I can.* "I don't understand." *Yes, you do. Think, Alli.*

Think, Alli. Emma was trying to tell her to use her mind, and this was now what she ordered herself to do. She had already widened the fissure in Waxman's psyche, but that was hardly enough. She knew he was brilliant, certainly clever enough to cotton on to what she was doing sooner rather than later. What she needed was a diversion, a ploy to make him think he knew what she was up to. She realized that she had just the ticket.

"I wonder," Alli said, "what Herr thinks of all your fancy talk."

"Reggie isn't listening."

"What he really means, Reggie, is that you don't think, not for yourself, anyway."

When Waxman continued to eat unabated, Alli said, "Reggie, old Waxman is good at putting words in your mouth. I want to hear what you have to say."

Silence, apart from the walnuts in the chicken salad crunching between Waxman's teeth.

"You won't speak because he doesn't want you to. I mean, that's what your continued silence is telling me. Am I wrong?"

Herr, eyes downcast, picked at a cuticle.

Waxman wiped his mouth, a final act. "Stop this nonsense. It's ludicrous to think you can put a wedge between us. Reggie wants to kill you, not listen to you spout off."

"Too bad," Alli said, "because I know things about his brother I'll bet even he doesn't know."

Herr came off the wall. Sensing the movement, Waxman held up a hand. "She's lying, Reggie. She spent all of one week with him."

Alli kept her gaze steady on Herr. "Like two wartime soldiers in a foxhole. A more intimate week I can't imagine."

"She's right about that," Herr said.

"Use your head, Reggie," Waxman said. "Your brother kidnapped her, strapped her into a chair, kept her in what amounts to solitary for a week, during which time he proceeded to brainwash her. Do you really think he'd reveal anything at all to her? Do you think she'd even be able to absorb it?"

"He did." Alli appealed directly to Herr. "He told me—"

"What?" Waxman advanced on her, teeth bared. "What did he tell you?" He grinned, then turned to Herr. "You see what she's been doing, Reggie. Trying to put a wedge between us." He swung back. "You're clever—more clever than I had imagined." Then he struck her hard across the face with the bulb of his walking stick.

As Alli's head lolled, he took a step back. "Reggie, no one knew Morgan better than I did. We'll never get him back. You must face that sad fact. But the girl knows nothing about him—less than nothing."

Herr seemed to see confirmation in Alli's face. He went swiftly to her and hit her, once, twice, a third time. Waxman did not stop him until the storm had subsided.

"Go now, Reggie," he said quietly. "You'll have your full turn with her, I promise."

Silence. Herr looked from him to Alli before stepping out and closing the door behind him.

Waxman swiveled back. "Now that we've gotten that distraction out of the way, it's time to begin."

Alli lifted up her swollen face. "I'm hungry."

Waxman's face closed like a bank vault. He rose, dragged her up, and bound her to the chair, then grasped the tray. "Hungry? Here!" He threw the tray and its contents onto the floor at her feet. Turning, he limped to the door.

There he turned back for a moment. "Whatever foolish ideas you may still be harboring, you're never getting out of here."

The door slammed behind him. She sat for a moment, immobile. Her empty stomach growled, then rebelled, and she retched violently. A moment later, the lights were extinguished and she was plunged into absolute darkness.

"It's all arranged," Dyadya Gourdjiev said, pocketing his cell. "A car will be waiting to take us to the Nevsky airstrip outside the city."

"And the plane?" Annika said.

"An Antonov An-2," her grandfather said.

"Are you kidding? That's a single-engine biplane, used mainly for agricultural dusting. It must be fifty years old."

"It's the only thing available at such short notice," he said. "You can fly it, yes?"

"Of course I can," Annika said. "I can fly anything."

The train continued to snake its way into Saint Petersburg without further delay. After wiping the blood off Romulus's tusks, Huey had been able to herd the two elephants back into their car, but only after Romulus, who insisted on going first, checked around with trunk and tusks to make sure no other intruders lurked in the shadows.

From this gilded, historic city it was only a hop, skip, and a jump to Finland. Once they crossed the border, Jack could phone the pilot of his plane, which had landed in Tallinn hours ago, and it would come pick them up at the Lappeenranta airport in southwest Finland.

They arrived at Ladoga Rail Terminal, on the western side of the Neva River, the industrial southwest of the city. They thanked Kurin for his help, but lost no time in exiting the train. Jack felt certain that the courageous ringmaster was relieved to be rid of them, even though Dyadya Gourdjiev gave him a generous gift that would pay for substantial upgrades for the circus.

The large Lada was waiting for them. It was surrounded by four armed men, one of whom grinned broadly and, throwing open his arms, embraced the old man, kissing him warmly on both cheeks.

"Everything is in readiness," he said as he ushered them to the Lada, its huge engine gurgling mightily.

Gourdjiev introduced him as Toma. His handshake was firm and dry and he looked each of them in the eye.

"Hurry, now," he said. "The quicker we get to the airstrip, the happier I'll be."

He and one other man got into the car with them. Even though the Lada's interior was roomy, it was a close fit for seven people, including the driver. The two other gunmen watched them as they drove off.

"It's approximately a forty-minute drive to the strip," Toma said from the front seat. "Meanwhile, you'll find vodka, bottled water, and food in the pockets of the seats in front of you."

FRAINE WAS being followed. *That didn't take long,* he thought as he exited a deli on K Street NW. Andy Beemer didn't know who Bishop's original rabbi was, but he claimed to know someone who did. Charlie had cautioned that it might work this way, so Fraine wasn't surprised. It was lunchtime and he was famished. Besides, he needed to log some time at Metro HQ, otherwise people would start talking, and that talk would eventually flow upward to Bishop. From the time of his recruitment into Paull's SITSPEC, Fraine had been scrupulous about making sure he did not show up on the chief of detectives' radar. When it came to Bishop, Fraine had determined there was no such thing as being too cautious. From the deli, he had called Leopard, but the kid had nothing to report. He was still working on finding out where the Acacia unit had been deployed after landing in the Horn of Africa.

Fraine had eaten his corned beef sandwich, wishing he was in Katz's on NYC's Lower East Side. The pickles were good, though, as was the carrot cake. He had eaten leisurely, trying and failing to form a mental picture of the kind of man who would mentor a total shit like Bishop. The rabbi had to be a total shit, as well, but clearly he was someone with the juice to launch Bishop on the fast track inside Metro without causing major waves among the city's top brass.

He'd paid his check and then, toothpick in one corner of his mouth, had ambled outside to take the temperature of D.C. His attention was drawn to a man staring into a shop window across the street, ostensibly eying the display of shoes. Fraine could see his own reflection in the window, which was what the man was actually watching. Fraine began a circuitous route that would eventually take him back to Metro HQ. He wasn't going near Beemer's contact until he was free and clear of tags.

As he walked, he heard from behind him the cough of an SUV engine starting up. He waited in vain for the vehicle to pass him, but it didn't. It might have been going in the opposite direction, except he continued to hear the engine. The SUV was following him. Tags on the ground *and* on wheels. Someone was taking no chances. Twice, he caught a glimpse of the man who had been watching his reflection in the shoe shop window. He was of average height, slightly younger than middle age, neither heavy nor slim, with about the blandest face Fraine had ever seen. A professional tag, in other words. So, not Metro. A Fed, in all probability, which both narrowed the field and upped the stakes.

A sudden thought caused him to pull out his cell and call the SITSPEC number Paull had given him.

"Fraine," he said when he connected. "Do you have a tail on me?"

"Negative."

"Someone else does, then."

"Location."

When Fraine gave it, the voice said, "Don't go anywhere fast."

Fraine knew what that meant.

THE LADA exited the highway and, slowing, headed down a secondary road lined with tall, stately firs on the right and a sheer split of blue and ocher rock face on the left. They were coming off high ground, slaloming down into the shallow bowl of what would in summer be a verdant valley. Now it was filled with narrow brown furrows of earth turning fallow, in the middle of which was a tarmac landing strip. A small shack sat off to the side at one end, at the other a wind sock on a tall pole. The Antonov An-2 biplane was sitting at the shack end of the runway, two men waiting impatiently beside it. One of them with field glasses apparently saw them because he gestured to his compatriot, then waved his arm back and forth, signaling that they had been spotted.

"The Antonov looks in good shape," Annika said, clearly relieved as she sat forward and peered out through the windshield.

"I never thought I'd say this," Katya said, "but I'll be most happy to leave Russia."

"Have you ever been outside the country?" Annika said.

Katya smiled. "Not as an adult, but my father was an exporter, and once, for my sixteenth birthday, he took my mother and me to Paris. That was an eye-opener, let me tell you. The architecture! I couldn't stop looking. And I can still taste the delicious ice cream he bought me on the Île Saint-Louis in a shop called—what was it?"

"Berthillon," Annika said.

"Yes, yes, that's it!" She was delighted, and was about to voice that delight, when something hit the Lada. The sedan slewed, but its weight stopped it from losing the road. The driver fought to regain control.

"It must be a blown tire," said someone, maybe Toma or one of his men. Nevertheless, their handguns were drawn.

The driver, apparently believing the same thing, slowed down, but when the Lada was hit a second time, the force launched it forward, spinning out of control. The car slammed head-on into a fir with such force the entire front crumpled. The wheel and dashboard served as battering rams to instantly crush the four men in the front seat and violently jolt those in the back.

ALLI, BOUND in place on the chair, had been contemplating why she could not read Waxman's body language when the door grated open. She shielded her eyes against the expected glare, but it never came. Nor did she hear Waxman's familiar step-tap-step across the concrete. Instead, she heard the quiet tread of a much larger and heavier man.

She sensed who it was even before he said, "What do you know about my brother?"

Reggie Herr stood directly in front of her.

"Tell me." His voice came from lower down. He must have crouched down to her level.

"Why did he hate me so much?" Alli said.

A quiet breathing. "He didn't hate you, he didn't think about you at all. You were a means to an end, nothing more."

"A thing."

"Yes."

"So killing a human being was nothing to him."

"Like swatting a fly."

"You, as well."

"We were two peas in a stinking pod." His quiet breathing filled the cell. "Now tell me."

"You help me," Alli said, "and I'll help you."

She heard his knees creak as he stood up. Then the stealthy padding as he crossed to the door. He closed it just as stealthily behind him, and that told her what she needed to know.

JACK AWOKE in a coughing fit. Black smoke, seeping in through the shattered windows, filled the interior of the Lada, obscuring his view. The car was a twisted mass; the entire front had collapsed and been jolted backward. His body ached but his limbs seemed intact. He had turned to check on Annika when he became aware of shadows approaching the Lada. The smoke obscured their identities. They could be the two men he had seen down at the airstrip, or they could be the crew that had attacked the car, for there was no doubt in his mind that the Lada had come under attack from small rocket fire.

He slapped Annika's cheek as he crawled over her and out one of the windows. Someone grabbed him, hauling him roughly to his feet.

"Check on the others," a harsh voice said.

As the man began to shake him, Jack slammed his fist into the man's solar plexus, then followed it up with a kidney chop. In the maelstrom of choking smoke, Jack felt the cold metal of a submachine gun and wrenched it away. As the man came awkwardly after it, Jack broke his jaw with the butt, then kicked him off his feet. The man's forehead struck the Lada's rear fender and he went down heavily.

Jack could just make out a second man poking his assault rifle through the window Jack had crawled out of. Jack raised his weapon and squeezed off a short blast. The man jumped, his body plastered against the twisted metal of the Lada, blood spurting.

Jack heard his name being screamed and, peeling the body off the side of the car, he saw Annika pushing her grandfather through the ruined window.

"He's okay," she said. "Just stunned."

Jack grasped the old man under the arms and pulled him clear of the car. As he did so, he saw in the corner of his eye a spark ignite through the swirling smoke. Flames whooshed up. Once they reached the gas tank the car would go up like a Roman candle.

"Katya?"

"Going back for her now," Annika said, turning her back on him.

Hoisting Gourdjiev over his shoulder, Jack staggered a hundred yards away—a safe distance, he judged, even if the Lada should go up. As he was setting the old man down, a battered Volga chugged up. Jack grabbed one of the assault rifles, but the two men who jumped out belonged to the old man.

He told them as well as he could what had happened and one of them set off at a run. The other helped tend to Gourdjiev. Jack heard Annika screaming and he rose, sprinting back into the smoke and flames.

"You've got to get her out right now," he said as he knelt beside the window. "Hand her to me."

"I can't." Annika's voice was breathless and, for the first time since he'd known her, tinged with panic.

The moment he poked his head in, he saw the problem. "Is it both her legs or just one?"

"I don't know." Annika was tugging at the front seat assembly without any luck. Then she turned her head. "Jack, one of her legs is crushed all the way up to the thigh."

"We'll never get her out."

Annika was tugging again. "We have to try, don't we?"

The flames were rising higher. He could feel their suffocating heat. "If I can get to the seat from the front, maybe the two of us will have enough leverage to unpin her leg."

He rose and kicked in the glass of the front window, but when he crouched down, he saw that it was useless. The four corpses were mashed between the dash and the seat backs. The wheel was buried in the driver's shattered chest. He tried to reach over them, but he could not get a grip on the seat, let alone gain the leverage needed to shift it.

"There's no way to move the corpses out of the way," he shouted to Annika over the crackling of the fire. "You've got to get out now!"

Annika was still tugging at the seat. "If I can just move it a little, I think I can—"

"We've run out of time!" Jack reached through the rear window and grabbed hold of her.

"No! No, I can't leave her!" Annika was crying. "How can I—"

A small explosion cut her off. The back of the rear seat burst into flames and, as she recoiled toward him, Jack hauled her bodily through the open window. Still she fought him, as he lifted her and carried her to where the men were tending to their leader.

The old man opened his eyes. He saw Jack setting Annika down beside him. Soot and ash were churning like snow in hell.

"What happened?" he said in a tissue-thin voice.

Then the Lada exploded in a fireball of crimson flame and black smoke rising high into the still air.

TWELVE

FORTY MINUTES of waiting in vain for someone from Paull's SITSPEC team to show up gave Fraine the impression that he was on his own. Either the team was not the well-oiled machine Paull had represented it to be or something unexpected had come up. Just as well, he thought. He preferred being on his own; then the only mistakes were his. But he wasn't going to make one.

He had been sitting in a window seat of a Starbucks, sipping a latte and not tasting it. The car was parked across the street. Three minutes after he had sat down, Bland Man, his walking tail, had come in, ordered, and was standing at the counter between a businessman barking orders into his cell and a heavyset young woman shopping on her iPad. Bland Man had no problem keeping Fraine in sight out of the corner of his eye. Several minutes ago, Bland Man had left, exiting through the front door and disappearing down the street.

Now Fraine rose, dumped his paper container in the trash, and made his way to the rear of the store. He had chosen this particular Starbucks because it had two entrances. The rear entrance gave out onto an indoor shopping arcade with a curved, coffered roof of green glass squares.

Fraine spotted Bland Man right away, lurking in front of a shop directly across from the Starbucks entrance. He loved his reflections, that one.

Turning right, Fraine sifted his way through the thickening late afternoon crowd until he came to a shirt shop he knew well. He went in and immediately made himself invisible to anyone peering in through the window. It wasn't long—three and a half minutes, to be exact—before Bland Man grew anxious enough to step into the shop to find out where he was.

Fraine picked up a couple of shirts on hangers and, making sure Bland Man saw him, went into a changing room. He waited a minute, watching the seconds tick by on his watch, then pulled open the door, grabbed Bland Man by his lapels, head-butted him, and shoved him into the changing room. Fraine delivered a kidney blow that drove the man to his knees. Then he slammed Bland Man's forehead against the rear wall.

Reaching beneath him, Fraine relieved Bland Man of his sidearm in its spring-loaded armpit holster and his wallet. He holstered the gun, stepped out of the changing cubicle, and quickly and unobtrusively exited the store.

In a deserted side alley, Fraine took a closer look at Bland Man's handgun. It was a CZ 75 SP-01 Phantom with polymer grips, which made it a good deal lighter and with far less recoil than the all-steel model. It had a fully loaded eighteen-round magazine and one 9mm bullet in the chamber. The CZ was of Czech manufacture, and while it was one of the best handguns available, so far as Fraine knew it was not standard issue with any law enforcement or clandestine service.

Next, he opened the wallet, which contained a driver's license, two credit cards, approximately a thousand dollars in cash, and, apart from a slip from a Chinese fortune cookie saying, "You are in line to be richly rewarded," not much else. The license and cards were in the name of Milton P. Stirwith, a name that meant nothing to Fraine. He searched in vain for anything else to give him a clue as to who Milton P. Stirwith worked for, but there was no sign of a helpful matchbook cover or a business card to provide a convenient lead. He accessed the Internet on his cell. A quick Google search of the name came up with no one remotely as bland as Stirwith.

Fraine took the shirts he had picked out and paid for them. Carrying the package under his arm, he whistled all the way back to Metro HQ.

"AND THE craziest thing," Vera said in conclusion, "was that the cops seemed convinced I'd stolen the Secret Service car!" Her agitation had climbed during her retelling of the events surrounding Alli's abduction. She was now quite certain she had made a grievous mistake in going to the Metro Police. The only solace she could give herself was that she had been in shock, and wasn't quite in her right mind when she drove there.

Caro, who had responded immediately to her call, said, "Didn't he address the fact that two agents were missing?"

"He said there was no report of agents missing. But they *are* missing because they're fucking dead." Vera looked at her friend. "Why would a chief of detectives lie?"

Caro's brow furrowed. "Curiouser and curiouser."

"You're telling me."

"But then, if it's become a matter of national security there would be nothing else for him to do but lie."

"I didn't like him," Vera said, "and I don't trust him. I don't trust any of them. Which is why I called you."

Vera had sounded so desperate that Caro, though initially suggesting a public meet, had agreed to have her come up to her hotel suite, though it went against her heightened sense of security. They were sitting on a sweeping expanse of beige sofa set facing the panoramic view of Washington through the picture windows. There was a tray with a full tea service on the low glass-top table in front of them.

"Did you tell them you saw Waxman and the others?"

"No."

"Good. You had at least some of your wits about you."

"Bishop's a fucking creep. He kept checking out my tits when he thought I wasn't looking."

Caro laughed. "I would, too, if I were him."

"This is no joke," Vera said, more hotly than she had intended.

Caro cocked her head. "Wait a minute, are those tears I see?" She leaned toward Vera. "You're not crying, are you?"

"What if I am?" Vera said, feeling inordinately defensive.

"You never cry." Caro appeared genuinely fascinated. "Neither of us feel anything for anyone."

"Speak for yourself, Sis." To her horror, Vera felt herself shaking. She took her teacup in both hands and drank in an attempt to calm herself. Previously, she was quite certain that she had ice in her veins. Nothing rattled her. That was the only way she could deal with her father, which, she knew, was true of Caro, as well.

Caro, leaning in, peered at her. "This is about Alli, isn't it?"

Vera said nothing, looked away, chewing her lower lip. Finally, she turned back. "What I can't understand is how you don't seem to care!"

"I am appalled by Waxman's behavior. It's wholly unexpected. What else do you want me to say?"

Vera wiped her eyes with the back of her hand. "You really don't know."

"No," Caro said. "I don't."

"It's Alli. She—"

"Hold on a fucking minute," Caro said with some force. "This is the woman who you've lied to."

"We all lie," Vera said dismissively.

"Not about something as fundamental as who you are. Vera, for Christ's sake, she has no idea we're sisters, that Henry Holt Carson is your father as well as mine. Why haven't you told her?"

Vera turned away. "I don't know."

"Don't give me that. Of course you know." She waited patiently for her sister to turn back to her.

"I'm ashamed, all right? I'm ashamed to be his daughter, to be the child of one of his many affairs. Alli never knew me when we were growing up; he was careful about keeping me at arm's length, out of his life. That's the truth of it. And now it's gone too far. She'll never understand why I kept lying to her."

"So?"

Vera wanted to hit Caro. "She and I are friends now. I like her. I don't want to do something to fuck that up."

Caro shook her head. The two women sat rigid with anger, daring each other to take the next step.

Caro finally took it. "We both deal with HH in such fucked-up ways."

"I think he likes it that way—at least with me."

Caro laughed until she realized that Vera wasn't joking. "Say what?"

"I'm dead serious. I drive him crazy when I rub up against him or spread my legs while he's looking." A mischievous smile wreathed her lips. "Then I take it all away from him."

"Honestly, Vera." Caro was laughing in a wholly different way. "You've got a pair of brass balls."

"It's the only way I know to get back at him."

Caro looked at her levelly. "But that's not all of it, is it?" When Vera remained silent, she added, "You do his bidding from time to time. You're still his daughter."

"So are you."

"But I'm not," Caro said with a care that was palpable. "I'm entirely divorced from him. I no longer have any interest in what happens to him."

"In whether he lives or dies."

"He's already dead to me."

Vera rose and, without a word, padded to the bathroom. When she returned, she said, "You've got to find some way to get Alli back."

"Me?"

"Yeah," Vera said acidly, "you're the brainiac who introduced her to Waxman."

"You never said no."

"Why should I have?" Vera sat down. "I trusted you."

"And I trusted Waxman." Caro frowned. "Something's gone very wrong."

Vera laughed harshly. "That's the fucking understatement of the month!"

"Calm the fuck down."

Vera jumped up. "You may be the world's best hacker, but as a human being you really do have a couple of screws loose."

Caro looked up at her calmly. "Well, aren't you the pot calling the kettle black."

Vera stared at her. "You are just so infuriating."

Caro shrugged. "And I should care what you think why?"

"Because we're family, damnit! And so is Alli."

"Is there a point you're trying to make?"

"Now you're mocking me!"

"No. Truly, Vera, I'm not."

Vera sat back down and took Caro's hands in her own. "We're *sisters*."

"Half-sisters, technically. And, by the way, when do you propose to get me the notebook that's in Father's possession?"

"I don't. That deal's off."

"What?"

"It didn't go very well for Alli, did it?"

"How could I have known?"

"Yes," Vera said acidly, "how could you have known?"

Caro's eye narrowed. "Are you saying that I was in on it?"

"What would you think if you were in my shoes?"

"Please." Caro shuddered. "To be in your shoes."

"You didn't answer my question."

"It's beneath contempt."

Vera struggled to keep her voice calm. She had been meaning to ask Caro to run the partial car tag number she had gotten off the Town Car, but now she changed her mind. She'd have to go a far more dangerous route. "Okay, let's move on.

"Alli hates Henry, too." All the childhood things—the selfishness, the enormous ego, the spiteful hatred that burned inside her—that she had forgotten about Caro came rushing back, slamming into her like a freight train. *Funny how we tend to remember the good things most clearly,* she thought. "It's time to come clean, Caro. Who the hell is this creep Werner Waxman? How do you know him, and what the fuck is going on?"

Caro rose. "I need a drink. You?"

"Brandy."

Caro nodded. "That seems appropriately bracing." Crossing to a side-bar, she poured two long shots from a crystal decanter into low snifters and brought them back to the sofa. She handed one to Vera, then sat and sipped hers.

A long silence followed. Vera was just about to prompt her when she said, "I'll come clean if you agree to tell Alli who you really are."

"She'll hate my guts."

"Maybe she will, but that's our quid pro quo."

"Goddamnit." Vera took a moment to agree to the inevitable. "Done."

"Okay, then." Vera nodded. "I was introduced to Waxman some time ago by a mutual friend."

"Name?" Vera gestured with her snifter. "Come on, Sis. Give it up."

"His name is Myles Oldham. I met him in London."

"So." Vera drained more brandy, her stomach already burning. "One of your lovers."

"Ex, actually."

"Everything's ex with you, Caro, do you realize that?"

Caro stared at her for some time. "I realize everything. I've spent most of my life learning to be an island. My survival dictated that. And yet, now I'm beginning to see that no one is an island. I relied on Myles, I relied on Waxman. They've both let me down."

Vera set down her glass. It was typical of her sister to be concerned solely with the repercussions to her own existence. But if that was the only way to get her to help Alli, so be it. "What I want to know is why Waxman wants Alli so badly that he used you and then betrayed you."

"That," Caro said, "is what I am determined to find out."

THERE WAS a time when Jack would have given just about anything to be away with a woman he cared deeply about, but he never could have imagined a nightmare like this.

"Where is she?" Gourdjiev said. "Where is Katya?"

Annika knelt beside him. She had recovered her equilibrium but had also acquired a rage that seemed to churn through her like a cloud of boiling vapor.

"Dyadya." She put a hand on his forearm. "Katya was pinned inside the Lada."

The old man stared straight ahead at the twisted, fiery wreck of the car.

"Jack and I tried, but we couldn't get her out."

A tear formed in the corner of one eye and spilled over, running down his seamed cheek. Others followed. No one said anything.

"What happened?" he said finally.

Jack, who had been talking quietly with the two men who had been waiting for them at the airstrip, crouched down beside him. "We were attacked with this." He handed over what the man named Lev had retrieved from the high ground on the other side of the road. "It's an M31 HEAT."

"An antitank rifle grenade," Gourdjiev said.

"The Lada was struck twice." Jack took back the M31 and gave it to Lev. "The second provided the lethal blow."

"The attackers?"

"Dead."

"Jack killed them before they could finish us off," Annika said.

"I want to see them."

"They were caught in the explosion," Jack said. "They're charred beyond recognition."

Tears rolled down the old man's cheeks again.

"Dyadya," Annika said softly. "It won't be long before the explosion and fire draw unwanted interest. We need to get going."

He nodded, his eyes fixed on the burning car. "A hand."

Lev and his partner lifted him. As soon as he was on his feet, he shook them off and walked unsteadily over to what was left of the Lada. Jack was about to go after him when Annika held him back, shaking her head.

Jack watched the old man standing at the edge of the scene of the crime, the toes of his shoes within the rough charcoal circle. Ash fluttered onto his head and shoulders, but he was too absorbed to brush them off. His head was bowed but his back was as straight as an arrow. He seemed both thinner and taller, though Jack could not think how that was possible.

Then Jack felt the brush of cool air on his cheek and knew Emma was close beside him.

"So much death," he said softly. "So much tragedy."

Everything changes here, Dad. There is no going back.

"There's never any going back," he said without a trace of sadness. "That's what your death has taught me."

Here I am in a place where past, present, and future run together, a place where time doesn't exist. I'm here; I was always here.

"That can't be true. You existed here. I held you in my arms, I fed you, changed you, rocked you to sleep. I peeked in at night and heard you breathing."

Yes, I was there; I was always there, too.

Jack shook his head. "I don't understand."

I'm trying to tell you in the only way I know how. Pastpresentfuture are all one, but that doesn't mean there aren't branches, where everything changes. This is one.

"Tell me."

Ask the old man. He knows. He understands.

Jack turned to her, but she was already gone, not even a wisp of mist to mark that she had ever appeared to him.

He felt his heart pounding, his pulse racing in the aftermath of his dead daughter's visitation.

"Jack?" Annika touched him at the small of his back. "You've gone white. Are you all right?"

He said nothing, feeling paralyzed and mute, as if he were in an alternate universe somewhere or inside his own dream; he felt detached from everyone and everything, as if some essential cord had been cut, sending him whirling free without gravity or any sense of how to return to where he had been before Emma appeared.

"Jack? Jack!"

Annika was standing in front of him, he was quite certain of that, but was it really Annika calling to him, or was it Emma? Emma never called him Jack, even when she was thoroughly pissed at him, so it must be Annika.

"What is it?" His voice sounded in his ears like a frog's croak.

"That's what I'd like to know."

"Something's happened." He cleared his throat. "Something . . . significant."

"I have no idea what—"

Walking past her, he picked his way through the rubble to where the old man stood silent and stiff. "Dyadya Gourdjiev."

He was surprised when the old man responded. "I'm listening."

"Something has happened."

"Yes."

"Something significant."

"Yes."

Jack sensed Annika standing at his shoulder, silent, observing. "What has happened?"

Dyadya Gourdjiev turned to him. By all rights he should have looked older, shrunken into himself. Instead, he seemed to have shed a decade or two.

"Look at what is left. Ash and bone, that's all we are, in the end. But she didn't deserve this."

"She must have known the risks when she agreed to come with you," Jack said.

Annika stirred and he scented her. "She knew the risks when she fell in love with my grandfather." She took a step out of Jack's shadow and kissed the old man on his papery cheek. "You promised to hold her in your heart and in exchange she emerged from the safety of anonymity."

"We spoke about this," Gourdjiev said, as if picking up an epic narrative. "At the beginning, I grew angry—my anger masked my fear for her safety. I wanted to push her away, and for some years I managed to keep my distance. But she persevered; she stayed close, refusing to ignore me. And she was wise. She knew my heart better than I did myself. I had imagined myself incapable of that kind of love again, I thought my time had passed. She showed me that I was wrong. *'Love comes in all shapes and sizes, and at all ages,'* she said. *'It's not just for the young.'* Well, she was right. In that, she was a constant."

He sighed. "All these years and I still haven't learned humility. My arrogance prevented me from learning to bow down and accept my fate." He took a deep breath; his eyes were pools of raw emotion. "I was a fool to think I could retire, that there would be a place for me in some beautiful spot in the world where I could live out the rest of my days with Katya in peace and happiness. I have lived my life in a certain way to make peace impossible. I fought against it, with the result that Katya is dead."

"Not because of you," Jack said. "Because of your enemies."

Gourdjiev grabbed Jack's elbow. "My enemies are part of the life I made for myself. They will not allow me to walk away. And now I do not want to. Retirement was a foolish pipe dream, a doorway to death." His eyes had become like coals into which someone had introduced a spark. Flames reared up, as they had to engulf the Lada and those inside. His hands curled into fists. "My enemies caused this—caused you and Annika to be hurt, caused Katya's death. Now everything changes, now the war begins in earnest. Payment will be rendered. Payment in fear, pain, and blood."

THIRTEEN

"THE PRESIDENT is worried that Three-thirteen has overstepped its bounds," Carson said.

Waxman shook his head. "We have done so since day one."

"Luckily, no one knows that. Still. According to Crawford there are individuals within the cabinet we're making nervous."

"The clockwork mechanism was set in motion weeks ago. You know that as well as I do. Now it's beyond even the president's power to stop."

The two men stood facing each other in a section of Rock Creek Park so remote even the daily joggers didn't venture into it. They were on a path that snaked its way alongside Rock Creek. Above their heads trees stretched their bare branches toward the buttermilk sky, tinged orange and dark red by the oblique light of the bloody semicircle of the setting sun.

"The president," Carson said as he turned his collar up against the increasingly cold breeze, "wants Three-thirteen shut down."

"The president," Waxman replied dryly, "is a nitwit."

"Ridiculing him isn't going to help." Carson's hands ached with the cold; he plunged them deep into his overcoat pockets, curling them into fists. "Of course we're not going to shut down. But the action needs to be accelerated, and fast."

"Tell that to the General."

"I don't have contact with the General," Carson said, a bit too stiffly. "You know that."

"Plausible deniability." Waxman curled his lips. "A broken record."

"You get it through his head. The president may be a nitwit, but he has the wherewithal to plow us all under, should he choose to."

"Which is why we have you, Henry, his best friend and confidant." Waxman softened his tone. "Listen, Henry, the best thing I ever did was to ask you to run interference for Three-thirteen with the president and, God forbid it should ever come to it, Congress. I've never lied to you about the purpose of Three-thirteen. You agree with us that the United States needs to insert its power into the Arab Spring before our enemies—Russia, China, Iran, and, more locally, the increasingly powerful Muslim Brotherhood. This president has proven that he doesn't have the guts to do what needs to be done. We need Three-thirteen to turn the tide in our favor, to return us to our rightful place as the world's premier superpower."

For a moment, Carson watched the failing light and wondered if it was a metaphor for the striving of human beings. In the end, no matter what you managed to accomplish, darkness fell. "Say this for you, Waxman, you're the only one of us who can handle the General."

"You're too kind." Waxman's voice was brittle. "The General is a vital part of us. Without him, this new incarnation of Acacia wouldn't get ten yards, let alone where it needs to go."

"If the president had any inkling that we had reconstituted Acacia—"

"Then it's a damn good thing he doesn't."

Waxman shifted his hips, shaking circulation back into his bad leg. "Your friendship with Crawford is a two-edged sword, Henry."

"Like most."

Waxman's lips twitched. "Which is why I don't court friendships."

"Nothing thaws you. You're a sad case, Werner."

"We're all sad, each in his own way."

Carson peered at him through the gathering twilight. "You'll get the message to the General."

"Good as done."

"I'll pass the good news along to His Nibs. With luck, it'll keep him quiet until Acacia is launched." Waxman looked out through the trees. "In the meantime, the General is putting the recruits through the last of their paces."

"Poor bastards."

Waxman barked a laugh that surely must have startled every fox in the park. "They'll be well compensated."

"The ones who come back."

Waxman pursed his lips. "You're in a particularly dark mood."

"My niece is missing. Again."

Waxman waved a hand. "Youthful indiscretion. I'm sure she'll turn up."

"She's a candidate at Fearington. This isn't youthful indiscretion."

"Have you spoken to your friend Crawford?"

Carson ignored the jibe. "I want this on the down low. The moment I tell Arlen he'll make calls and all hell will break loose."

"So you want my help?"

"In this area, you have contacts I do not." Carson hated having to ask Waxman for a favor. Being in his debt was not a desired position to be in. "Personally, I think she went off after Jack McClure. I don't think she can live without him, and, frankly, this troubles me deeply." Of course, he had contacted other members of Three-thirteen, first and foremost Lenny Bishop, but, strangely, Bishop could tell him nothing, other than that he had contacted Fearington's commander on background as to where Alli had been in the hours preceding her disappearance. Based on that intel, he had men canvassing Fearington and taking interviews with those who had seen and spoken to her.

"Even odder, however," he said, "is that she had been assigned a Secret Service agent to keep watch on her. He's nowhere to be found, either."

"Ah, yes, Dick Bridges."

Carson was surprised. "You know him?"

"He hung himself a couple of hours ago."

"What?"

"The General informed me. He wasn't surprised. Bridges had been despondent ever since your brother was killed on his watch. In fact, this wasn't his first attempt."

"First Edward and now Alli." Carson shook his head. "What a fuckup."

"I'm sorry. Bridges asked for the assignment." Waxman shrugged, leaning on his walking stick. "Lost out on what he saw as his last chance at redemption, is my guess."

Lights snapped on inside the park, strings of buttery light illuminating bits of trees, shrubs, and rocky outcroppings, while keeping the rest in blue-black shadow.

Carson lifted his head. "It's a long way home, in the dark."

"We'll find her, Henry." Waxman briefly squeezed Carson's shoulder. "You have my word."

FRAINE'S OFFICE felt both abandoned and stifling when he entered it. A stack of messages were waiting for him, along with a pile of reports that required his signature before they were filed. Frankly, he had no interest in any of it. His mind was filled to the brim with his work for Secretary Paull. As he looked out through the glass partition into the large room, all of Metro seemed gray as ash, and as he observed the detectives moving to and fro, alongside the familiar file clerks, support staff, and the occasional uniform from downstairs, he realized that he was living in another world altogether. He was no longer part of their universe, and good riddance. Thanks to Paull's faith in him, he had moved onto a larger playing field, one these people who worked for him scarcely knew existed.

He used his cell to call the kid.

"Still working," Leopard reported unhelpfully. "This thing's a fucking bitch."

"Take a break, clear your head," Fraine said. "And while you're at it, get me whatever you can on a Milton P. Stirwith."

"Who's he?" Leopard asked.

"No one."

Fraine spent a little over an hour making calls on legit Metro business and pushing reports from one pile to another without really knowing what he was doing. His mind was elsewhere. Day had lurched from gray dusk to charcoal evening, and he was wondering when he could get out of there when Detective Stoddart rapped softly on his door.

"Del, come on in." He beckoned with his hand. "What's up?"

Stoddart, a baby-faced man with pink cheeks and a fringe of ginger-colored hair, took a seat opposite Fraine. He had been Nona's first partner. He told Fraine about his interview with Vera earlier in the day, what she had claimed happened, how there were no bodies, no witnesses, nothing. Nevertheless, he'd written up the report.

"And Ms. Carson?"

"No one knows where she is."

"She's Henry Holt Carson's niece."

"That fact hasn't passed me by, boss. Which is why I checked out the area around the *Titanic* Memorial myself after I personally had delivered the report and the girl to Bishop."

"Find anything?"

"Nada."

"And Bishop?"

"He said the incident was now a matter of national security, that he was handing over the investigation to the Feds. He said to forget it ever happened."

"Yet here you are telling me about it."

Stoddart handed over a slim folder. "I made a copy of the report."

"Since when don't you follow orders?"

Stoddart's dogmatic MO was what had led Nona to request a new partner.

"The allegedly missing woman is President Carson's daughter. I liked Carson." He shrugged. "Besides, I take my orders from you, not Chief Bishop."

"You did good."

"Thanks, boss." He rose and crossed to the door.

Fraine looked up. "Del, by the way, how the hell did Bishop know the Bard woman had come to see you?"

"Info sarge in the lobby. She said he sent her up."

"Name?"

"McNulty."

Fraine nodded. "Thanks, Del."

"No biggie, boss."

Fraine started reading Stoddart's report. He was so troubled by it that he reached for his cell to call Paull. It rang.

"Dude," the Leopard said in his ear, "breakthrough."

"I'll be right over." *Yeah, baby!* Fraine thought.

NONA HAD just picked a gleaming, pearly morsel out of her lobster claw with a tiny fork when the maître d' passed a slip of paper into Leonard Bishop's hand. As she dipped the flesh into a small metal bowl of drawn butter, Leonard set down his knife and fork, opened the slip, and read it. It must have been brief, because he crumpled it immediately, pocketed it, and went back to his veal chop, which was thick as a brick.

Nona knew better than to make mention of it. In fact, she acted as if nothing had happened. They were seated in a prime booth in George's Pentagon, a white-tablecloth steakhouse on South Hayes Street in Arlington. It was one of Bishop's favorite dining spots, though as far as Metro HQ was concerned it was more than slightly out of the way. Maybe he planned it that way. Glancing around the warm, vaguely Colonial room with its crown molding and wainscoting, she recognized no one. It was as if Bishop did not want to be seen with her among his brethren. She could understand that. A man of his stature wining and dining a black woman could still cause some tongues wagging unpleasantly. He was taking no chances.

He took a sip of wine. When he set the glass down, he said, "I've been meaning to ask you whether you've had any contact with Jack McClure."

"What?" She was instantly on alert.

"Well, from what I've gathered, he and Secretary Paull were instrumental in getting you out of federal detention."

"Is that so? I've never met McClure. And I never should have been in detention in the first place."

"I understand that. I would have gotten you out, had I known." He took another sip of wine. "But you've met Paull." His voice was as light as if they were discussing the Nationals' prospects for climbing out of the National League East cellar.

"Once. He was there when I was released. He said, 'Congratulations,' I shook his hand and said, 'Thank you.'"

"And that's it?"

Nona made a face. "He's not my type."

"Neither am I, but here we are."

"Leonard, is there something—?"

"See if you can find out what McClure is up to."

"How would I do that?"

"Ask your pal Paull—he's McClure's boss."

"*If* I could even get to the secretary, he'll ask me why I want to know."

"Keep it simple," Bishop said. "Tell him you never got to thank Jack in person."

"What's your interest in McClure?"

"Just do it," he said sharply.

Five minutes practically to the second after he had received the note, Bishop wiped his lips, excused himself, and slid out of the booth. Nona followed him with her eyes until she saw him turn left past the bar to the bathrooms.

The moment he was out of sight, she rose and followed him. She paused at the curve of the bar, staring down the short corridor. There were only two doors, one for each gender. Otherwise, it was a dead end. Cautiously, she proceeded down the hall. A woman exited the ladies' room, gave her a cool look as she went past. Nona stopped, then glanced behind her. No one was looking. She pushed inside.

Silently surveying the long narrow space, she saw three sinks and mirrors on her left, beyond which were the urinals. To her right, a line of old-fashioned wooden stalls. In between, a narrow window in the wall facing her, its translucent pane cracked open. She saw no one, but an instant later she heard Bishop's voice, along with another, deeper, raspier one, emanating from the stall closest to the window.

Placing one foot carefully in front of the other, she crept close enough to make out what they were saying.

". . . are two things I can't abide," Raspy Voice said. "Incompetents and dissemblers. Which one are you, Bishop?"

"Neither, sir."

"Then how did you allow the Bard woman to slip through your hands?"

"I had her guarded by one of my best street sergeants. By the time I returned, she had caught him by surprise and was nowhere to be found."

"Surprised him? How?"

"She pretended to be nauseous, then broke his nose when he handed her a trash can to be sick in."

Raspy released a long-suffering sigh. "What was your response?"

"I have an all-points out for her."

"Results?"

Bishop cleared his throat.

"I see. Bishop, need I tell you—"

"You don't. Luckily, she didn't see our people."

"So she *says*. Do you believe her?"

"Impossible to tell. On a positive note, I'll have a dependable line on McClure by end of day tomorrow."

A significant pause.

"That's welcome news. But your primary assignment was to cover our tracks today."

"Apart from me, only one person in Metro is aware of the Bard woman. That's Detective Stoddart, who took her statement."

"No one else?" Raspy said with a good degree of disgust.

"Desk sergeant by the name of McNulty, and McKay, both belong to me."

"And this Stoddart? Who does he belong to?"

"He's part of Fraine's team, but he's such a straight fucking arrow he couldn't possibly belong to anyone."

"Fine and dandy," Raspy said. "Just make sure. Loose shoelaces trip you up."

"How d'you propose I do that?"

"Silence is golden."

"Are you—"

"Take the initiative, Bishop. With the Bard woman and with Stoddart. It's a rat-eat-rat world."

The voices had risen slightly in volume, which meant the conversation was ending. Nona unlocked the door, keeping the latch up at a midway point. Behind her, she heard the stall door rattle. Bishop and Raspy were coming out. Outside in the corridor, she closed the door softly, then slid in her credit card, bringing it down on top of the latch, relocking it.

She was back at the table when a man she didn't recognize emerged from the bar end of the corridor. She took a photo of him with her cell, sent it as a text message to Paull with the caption: *LB scrt rdv @ Georges Pent w/ ?,* then went back to her food until Bishop returned. His face looked pale.

"Are you all right?"

He shook his head. "Must've been something I ate for lunch." He put some bills on the table. "Let's get out of here."

"Where are we going?"

"Home."

"I still have some work to do." She needed to report what she had overheard.

"I say you don't." He tugged at her. "Not that kind, anyway."

As they left, Nona wondered how many more kinds of prison she would be in until she was free.

FRAINE SAW the empty grease-stained pizza box outside the door to their room and went inside.

"Thanks for saving me a slice," he said as he sat down beside the kid.

"Dude, I was starving!"

"Tell me what you've got."

Leopard's forefinger stabbed at the computer screen. "This dude Milton P. Stirwith doesn't exist."

"Tell me something I don't know."

Leopard hit a key and the screen showed some documents. "It's not the *name* that's so interesting. It's the docs that are being used to bring him to life."

"His legend."

"Hah, yeah, dude. His legend is *amazing*. I mean, look at the work." He zoomed in. "The detailing is absofuckingtastic!"

"How does that help us?"

Leopard hit more keys and other files popped up. "Here's a whole slew of docs—legends—with the same meticulous attention to detailing. You see the borders here on Milton P. Stirwith's driver's license— and here, the metallic holography on *this* one."

"Okay," Fraine said dully. Studying the minutiae of these docs that so excited the kid, all his initial enthusiasm had drained away. His lack of sleep and sustenance finally caught up with him. He'd been running on coffee and adrenaline for too long. He needed a break—a good hot meal—not fast food—and a solid night's sleep. Even a nap would help. "So what?"

"So *this*." Leopard's finger stabbed out again. "*These* legends were created by a group of ex-Nazis right after World War Two. They were brought over by the OSS and given the job of creating legends for agents who were then inserted inside the USSR. They called themselves the Norns, the weavers of fate from Wagner's Ring Cycle opera."

"How do you know all this?"

"The Internet, dude. How else?"

"There's all kinds of bogus shit on the Net," Fraine said. "I don't believe a tenth of what's flying around there."

"Yeah, but you've got to know the right sites, dude." Leopard's face was pink with excitement. "I had read about the Norns before, but I had my doubts about them being real—until you gave me Milton P. Stirwith."

"Even if what you say is true, how could a bunch of ex-Nazis still be alive and working at their highly specialized trade more than sixty years later?"

"Ah, that's the bone in the throat, dude. But, see, I think I've got the answer, or at least part of it." Midway through a new set of keystrokes, his fingers faltered, his face went from pink to red, and he began to choke.

"Kid—hey, kid." Fraine grabbed him before he could topple off his chair. Picking him up, he carried him to the bed and laid him down. Leopard's eyes were nearly popping out of his head and his hands were clawing at his throat. Clearly he couldn't breathe. Fraine pried open his jaws. The kid's tongue was swollen to three times its size.

Fraine was calling 911 when the kid spasmed off the bed, as if his body were trying to levitate. He made a terrible noise that sounded eerily like "Mercy," then his body went limp, his eyes out of focus. Bending over him, Fraine checked the pulse at the side of his neck, but there was none. He smelled garlic and tomato sauce.

The pizza! he thought, and ran for the door.

WHEN THE lights came on, they did so slowly and stopped long before they could blind her. The door clanged open and Herr entered.

"You stink," Herr said.

"I need a shower." So close to the food on the floor, her mouth continued to water.

Leaning forward, he sniffed her like an animal. "I like it."

Herr crouched down beside her, watching her with an evil stare.

Almost out of defensiveness, she said, "I'll tell you more about Morgan."

The evil stare blossomed into an evil smile. "You already played that card."

"Waxman is lying," she said, with more desperation than she intended. "That's all he knows how to do."

"Not interested."

"Then why did you come in here?"

Herr leaned in close and grabbed her. Alli cried out.

"You want to know what I've been doing in the hallway?" Herr's eyes darkened. "I've been daydreaming about the ways to cause you pain."

Herr leaned even closer, ran his hands roughly over her, exploring all her secret parts. Alli closed her eyes and gritted her teeth. Bound to the chair, there was nothing she could do to stop him.

"Open your eyes!" Herr commanded. "Open your eyes!"

When she refused to comply, he ripped off the straps, hauled her up, and batted her down onto the floor. He stood over her for a moment before he dropped onto her like a leopard from a tree branch. At the same time, his hand, worming its way between their bodies, pulled down her trousers and underpants. Alli squirmed beneath him, trying to find a way to free one of her arms or legs, but he'd pinned them with a combination of his free hand and his weight. When his mouth came down on hers, she bit his lower lip right through. He ignored the pain, the blood flowing, concentrating on freeing himself from his trousers. He was so hard he was near to bursting. When her teeth snapped at him again, he pulled his head away, rendering her helpless.

He was beginning to push himself into her when he suddenly arched his back and rolled off her, obviously in pain. Waxman's blood-darkened face loomed over them both.

"What did I tell you, Reggie? Not until I'm finished with her."

As Waxman aimed his walking stick at his navel, Herr batted it away, scrambling to his feet. The two men stood facing each other. Alli, panting like a steam engine, wriggled into her pants, then sat with her arms girdling her drawn-up knees. She kept her breathing slow in order to cut down on her shivering. She looked from one to the other, calculating the strategic advantages their enmity might provide.

Herr's eyes were as red as a demon's.

Waxman flicked the tip of his walking stick. "Do you know how absurd you looked lying on your back with a tent in your trousers?"

Herr glared at him. "There are times when you go too far. There's a line, and when you cross it—"

"What? What will happen, Reggie? You'll run away?" Waxman's laugh was ugly. "Where would you go? Who would take you?"

"Anyone in need of my skills. I could—"

"That's enough!"

The two men were locked again in a kind of kinetic stasis—their utter stillness inadequately masking the swirls of emotion coming off them.

What exactly is their relationship? Alli asked herself. Somehow, she could sense the importance of the answer.

"You're bleeding," Waxman said finally. "Go get your lip seen to."

Herr hesitated, standing his ground. Then he swiped at his lip, saw the amount of blood, and realized Waxman wasn't giving him an order, but rather attempting to calm the waters between them. He took a step backward, then another and another. When he was at the door, he hesitated. He found it difficult staring past Waxman, but when he did, he impaled Alli with his eyes.

Herr turned on his heel and left.

When Waxman returned to where Alli sat, she said, "He's far more difficult than his brother."

"Thank you so much for your expert psychological assessment." For the first time, he showed an upsurge of actual emotion.

Noting this, Alli rose; she'd had enough of him looming over her. "You'll never get what you want from me."

"Is that so?" Waxman limped to the door. As he was about to close it behind him, he turned and, grinning unpleasantly, said, "But, my dear, I already have it."

FOURTEEN

ANNIKA, HAVING piloted the Antonov An-2 across the border into Finland, guided them to a safe landing at Lappeenranta Airport. Jack's jet was waiting for them on the tarmac, having flown in from Tallinn.

They climbed down from the biplane, Jack helping Gourdjiev, while ground personnel jammed the wheels with chocks to keep the biplane from moving. The pilot from Jack's plane greeted him and then went off to inform the immigration people of the trio's diplomatic status.

As Jack turned back, he said, "We should board my plane as soon as possible. The fewer people who know we were here, the better."

The lowering sun was in Annika's eyes, turning their carnelian color luminous. "I can't go with you."

"Alli needs us," Jack said.

Annika smiled sadly. "She needs you. My grandfather needs me."

Jack looked around the airfield. The winter-shortened afternoon was clear, with a high blue sky that was almost purple at its apex. Even with little or no wind it was very cold.

"I don't like the idea of us splitting up. Not now, not after all that's happened."

"I wouldn't have it this way, either," she said. "But neither of us has a choice."

"Of course you have a choice." These were the first words Dyadya Gourdjiev had uttered since the Antonov had lifted away from the smoking pyre in which Katya had died. "You always have a choice."

Annika kissed him tenderly on both cheeks. "You of all people, Dyadya, so Russian, so stalwart, you know that duty obliterates choice. My heart may be with Jack, but my duty is clear."

The old man nodded. He knew better than to argue. He turned to Jack. "You've done me a great service, young man. A service I won't forget."

"You asked me to help you get out of Russia. But Katya—"

"Which you have done, most ably." Gourdjiev squeezed Jack's shoulder. "The rest is up to me."

They saw Jack's pilot returning across the tarmac. He gave a thumbs-up before climbing up into the jet.

"Almost time for you to go," the old man said. "Take these last moments together."

Jack watched him walk away, as precisely as any foot soldier, as confident as any commander. For a time, there was an uncomfortable silence.

At last, Jack said, "Why must it always be beginning and ending for us, nothing in between?"

"It is our fate," Annika said. "And our choice."

"Our choice? Really?"

She slid her hand along his chest. "We both carry pasts that make our present difficult."

"Is there to be no hope for us, then?"

Tears glittered in her eyes. "We are always together, Jack."

"Even when we're apart?"

"Especially then." Pressing herself against him, she whispered in his ear, "Think of Emma."

"Emma is dead." He tried to pull away, but she held him fiercely to her.

Her lips brushed his ear. "To some, perhaps. But not to you."

An inarticulate noise was all the sound he could make.

"We carry those we love inside us, always."

"And those we hate."

"I have let my father go."

"And everything he did to you?"

"A scar is a scar, Jack." She pushed him back now, so that their eyes locked. Her voice turned bitter. "You know that better than most."

"Emma's message is to let go—of hate, of guilt, of regret."

"And yet we can't, Jack, because we're human. We hate, we feel guilt, and we regret. We remember because sometimes memory is all we have."

"I don't believe that, Annika." He felt lost within her carnelian eyes. "It frightens me that you do."

She smiled. "I love that you're frightened for me, but there's no need."

"Truly?"

She nodded. "Truly."

Those were the last words she said to him. They kissed, and then she was walking away from him, sliding her arm through her grandfather's as they crossed the tarmac. He had neglected to ask where they were going. *Just as well,* he thought as he climbed aboard Paull's jet. She wouldn't have told him the truth, anyway.

The door swung shut, he walked down the aisle, and, taking a seat, strapped himself in. He peered out the Perspex window, but he could no longer see her. She and Gourdjiev had vanished as completely as if they had never existed.

The engines ramped up, their roaring filling the cabin, filling his mind, blotting out even their good-bye.

Then the jet sprang forward, hurtling down the runway, faster, faster, until, with a breathless rush, it lifted into the purple sky, on its long journey home to Washington.

VERA APPEARED at Carson's front door in a black Lurex dress that could have passed for a man's shirt. The hem ran straight across her thighs two inches below her pubis. She wore black Louboutins with four-inch heels and a splash of lipstick red on the part of the soles that rose up to the heel. Her lips were the same shade of red. Her coat was draped over her shoulders.

"What's happened to Alli? Where has she gone?" Her father drank in every luscious inch of her.

"Yes, I will come in, thank you." As she brushed by him, she pressed a thigh against his, and he leapt back as if poked with a cattle prod.

"Vera, answer me! There's very little time. I have company."

"Don't lie to me, Daddy. It's dead sad. You're all alone in this big house." Her shucked coat curled on the carpet like an animal. "And now that Alli has run off, I'm alone, too."

He stiffened. "So you know something about her disappearance."

She moved into the living room.

"Tell me!" He stalked after her, drowning in her silence. "You're supposed to keep track of her. If you haven't, of what use are you?"

As she settled herself on the deep leather sofa her dress rode up, revealing the apex of her triangle of hair.

Carson, cheeks flaming, tried to turn away, but the sight riveted him. "What a wanton. I ought to turn you over my knee and—"

"Oh, please, Daddy. Please."

Carson reddened all the more. "What about Alli?"

"I have no idea where she is or what's happened to her."

"Bitch!"

"I'm only what you made me, Daddy."

"Christ." Carson closed his eyes for a moment. A pulse beat in his temple. "What is it you want, Vera?"

"A favor."

"And why would I grant you a favor? You've let Alli slip through your grasp."

She slithered off the sofa, came up behind him, and wound her arms around his waist while she pressed her breasts against his back. "Because I'm your daughter, because you love me, and because I asked."

He turned and, with stiff arms, pushed her away. "It wouldn't be because it's important to you."

"You know what?" She yawned. "I just got bored." She stepped to where she had dropped her coat and, bending over with her buttocks toward him, picked it up. "So long, Daddy," she said without turning around. "Enjoy your exquisite aloneness."

"Hold it," he said when she had reached the front door. "Come back."

"Give me a reason."

He sighed. "What is it you want?"

She turned the knob, opened the door, and took a step across the threshold.

"Vera, please."

"Please what, Daddy?"

"Stay for dinner."

She shook her head. "No can do."

"A drink, at least."

"I don't want a drink."

"What—?"

"You know what I want."

"Come back in, damnit! I'll give it to you."

"Is that a promise, Daddy?"

"A promise, yes."

"But answer me this: How do you trust someone who lies for a living?"

"Are you talking about me," he said, "or you?"

She graced the gathering nighttime with a small secret smile, then wheeled around, closed the door behind her, and returned to the living room. This time she did not take off her coat, nor did she rub up against him. She was all business.

"Here." She handed him a slip of paper.

"What is this?"

"Part of a license tag. From a black late-model Lincoln Town Car. I want to know whose car it is."

His eyes narrowed. "Were you in some kind of accident?"

"A friend."

His eyes narrowed further. "You have no friends."

"That you know of."

"Who's this friend?"

"Doing it, yes or no?"

He sighed, picked up a cordless phone, and made a call. When he was done, he said, "Twenty minutes."

Vera nodded. "I'll take that drink now."

MIDNIGHT FOUND Grigori Batchuk, aka Myles Oldham, at High Vibes, one of the only late-night clubs in D.C. The nation's capital was not, strictly speaking, a late-night town—not publicly, anyway. But Grigori had a special talent for scenting out after-hours spots no matter what city he was in. And a special talent for attracting the tall, willowy, chicly attired denizens whose only ambition in life appeared to be to make themselves available to men like him. He had looks, wealth, and the necessary *je ne sais quoi* they could smell in their sleep.

Grigori danced and drank with a revolving quartet of these delicate jewels, and by the time he was ready to leave he had chosen the two he wanted for what was left of the night. Coatless, one arm around each, he emerged from High Vibes onto the sidewalk of Dupont Circle, sweeping them into the stretch limo that had been waiting for him. Its windows were blacked out and its wet-bar-equipped back cabin was separated from the driver by a thick sheet of opaque bulletproof glass.

The auto door locks engaged, the girls, giggling, anticipated the bottle of Dom Pérignon chilling in its silver bucket of ice, as well as other hinted-at delights. As Grigori settled back into the plush leather seat, the stretch nosed out into the street.

"Home, Serge," he said into the intercom, then cut all sound from up front. He and his two beauties were now sealed off from any and all distractions.

Speaking of which, Grigori was far too distracted by the unfolding layers of pleasure that piled up in direct proportion to the layers of clothes he peeled off the girls. He showered them with champagne while they squealed in mock alarm, then shrieked as he licked it off their bare flesh.

It was only when they came to a stop that he looked up and, peering through the blacked-out window, noticed they weren't at his apartment building. In fact, looking out at the block-square excavation pit, he discovered that they weren't even in his neighborhood.

Hitting the intercom key, he shouted, "Hey, Serge, where the fuck are we?"

When the black glass divider slid down he saw, not his chauffeur, Serge, but Caro behind the wheel. She was turned around to face him, a Bersa Thunder 380 pointed at his chest.

"We're not in Kansas anymore, Grigori." She hit a button and the door locks popped open. Without taking her eyes off Grigori, she said, "Girls, get the fuck out of here."

One of the girls looked around wildly. "What? Here?"

"Now!"

The girls scrambled for their clothes and fairly leapt off the seat and out of the stretch, slamming the doors behind them. When Grigori made a move to follow them, Caro waggled the Bersa. "Uh-uh. I have other plans for you."

"Caro, this is the wrong way to—"

Relocking the doors, she slid up the partition. A moment later, Grigori saw her picking the lock on the chain across the access ramp to the construction site. She returned behind the wheel and the stretch rolled down the ramp into a small city of concrete, rebar, and pyramids of sand and refuse-studded earth. When it reached the lowest point, it stopped. For a time, nothing happened. Then the partition rolled back down and Caro aimed the Bersa at him.

"Caro, what d'you think you're playing at?"

"I'm going to make sure that this is the last time you fuck me over."

"I don't know what you're—"

"Werner Waxman."

He shook his head.

"Okay, Grigori, since you're forcing me to spell it out, things will only get worse for you from here on out. That's a promise."

Grigori shook his head. "This isn't like you at all."

"See, that's the problem between us right there. It's *exactly* like me."

Grigori sighed. "Caro, can we at least move to a venue where we'll both be comfortable?"

"I'm extremely comfortable. You?" She tossed her head. "Oh, yeah, that's right, I don't give a fuck."

Grigori's eyes closed for a moment, as if he were trying to gather himself. "Okay, so what d'you want?"

She jabbed the Bersa at him. "Why did you introduce us?"

Grigori spread his hands. "Caro, that was so many years ago."

"Don't give me that, Grigori. You remember everything. What were you playing at when you put us together?"

"Waxman's a fascinating man with enormous political clout. I thought bringing you two together would be advantageous—"

"My bullshit meter has gone off the chart."

He glanced down for a moment. "All right. I thought if he was of some help, you'd be grateful, and that gratitude might one day turn to love."

Caro goggled at him. "Are you fucking kidding me?"

"Sadly, no."

She leaned forward. "Grigori, this fucker has kidnapped my cousin."

He lunged at the handgun, but she was prepared, chopping down on the back of his neck with the edge of her free hand. All the breath went out of him, and she shoved him back against the seat.

He ran a hand through his slicked-back hair. He was still having trouble breathing. "What are you talking about?" His voice was that of a hurt little boy. "Waxman isn't a kidnapper."

Grigori appeared genuinely shaken, which, in turn, flummoxed her. She had been so sure that he was in on whatever Waxman was planning.

"It's true," she said, trying her best to regroup. "For some reason, he has abducted Alli Carson, and, in the bargain, killed two Secret Service agents."

"That's absurd. How could he possibly get away with something like that?"

"I was hoping you could tell me."

Grigori was silent so long Caro said sharply, "You haven't developed narcolepsy, have you, Grigori?"

"Give me a minute, will you?"

"Assuming you're telling the truth—"

"I am."

"Well, that would be novel."

He glared at her, uncharacteristically silent. "I'm trying to remember how I met Waxman." He snapped his fingers. "It was before I left Russia, in Moscow—a gala thrown by an oligarch—Limov, Lementov, something like that, I don't quite recall. I never even met him. But I do remember the gala itself because that night I was alone."

"Poor you."

He made a face. "Anyway, Waxman was there. He and I hit it off right away."

"Knowing what I know now," she said dryly, "I'm not surprised."

"You're rushing to judgment. I don't know where you're getting your information these days—"

"And you won't know. You bumped into him?"

"No." Grigori shook his head. "We were introduced by an acquaintance of mine."

"Do I know him?"

"Probably not. He's a four-star general by the name of Tarasov."

"Russian?"

"No, American. Gerard Tarasov. But I assume his father, at least, was of Russian extraction."

"Meaning you don't know."

"I never looked into his background." He pursed his lips. "Anyway, I'd think his background is classified."

"Since when would that stop you?"

"It didn't seem important. I never bothered."

Caro wasn't certain she believed him, but now was not the time to push that particular button. She had more important questions to ask. "How do you know General Tarasov?"

"Well, that's a bit tricky, Caro."

"So's my finger on the Bersa's trigger. Tell me, Grigori. How are you and Tarasov in bed together?"

All at once, Grigori leaned forward, his head in his hands. *"Merde!"* he muttered. *"Merde, merde, merde!"* Then he shook himself like a dog coming in out of the rain and, sitting up straight, said, "Gerard Tarasov and I have a mutual interest."

"And that would be?"

"We have been after the same person for a very long time."

"A name, Grigori. Give me a fucking name."

"He's a Russian. Dyadya Gourdjiev."

"*Uncle* Gourdjiev? That's his name?"

"That's what everyone calls him," Grigori said. "But believe me, there isn't an avuncular bone in his body. He kills and destroys without remorse. The General and I both want him dead."

"GENERAL GERARD Tarasov." Dennis Paull was staring at the screen in his office where the slightly muzzy photo Nona had sent him from her cell was up. He pushed a button on a console and the photo moved slightly to the left to make room for a clearer color photo of the General.

"What the hell," he asked himself rhetorically, "is Leonard Bishop cooking up in a restaurant men's room with General Tarasov?"

He wished Nona were here to explain. He swiveled away from the screen, stared out at the nighttime view from his window. How he loved Washington, with all its warts and STDs, maybe even because of them. He could feel the power lines running under the city, fanning out like a spiderweb, not just from the White House, but from the lairs of all the power brokers, influence peddlers, and clandestine chieftains who, right this very moment, were scheming their schemes in an attempt to be king—or as close to it as America would allow.

A bitter taste had lodged in his mouth from the moment he had okayed the plan to send Nona undercover. Fraine had been right, he was whoring her out to Bishop in order to get inside this cabal. But at what price? Would Nona ever be the same? He contemplated these thorny questions even while he was perfectly aware that he should ignore them. Wasn't that what all good generals did—make decisions for the greater good that demanded sacrifice from the individual? Death was one thing, but dishonor . . . Had he asked too much of her? But she had accepted; that must stand for something.

He resisted an urge to pinch himself, as if unsure whether or not he was awake. All this meditation—even the identification of the General—was all to take his mind off the one fear that had been occupying it ever since he had received the news that Alli Carson was missing. At first he'd been angry with her. He had been the one to assign Dick Bridges to keep her safe, and Bridges had made it clear that Alli was fighting the protection tooth and nail. In fact, in his last phone call, he had said that Alli and Vera had discovered a lead to the identity of the person who had launched the rogue Web site. He'd seen the site before it was taken down; he alone knew what had freaked Alli out: the prediction of her death on the anniversary date of her abduction by Morgan Herr almost five years ago. Frankly, if he'd been in her shoes, he'd have been freaked out, too.

He acknowledged that he'd made a mistake in granting Bridges's wish to be assigned to her. The two of them were too close. She could talk him into most anything. But, if he were to be completely honest with himself, he knew that Jack was the only one who could talk her out of going off the grid when she felt the need arise. Jack was on his way home, but until then Paull had done everything in his power to discreetly find Alli. He had tried twice and failed to call Fraine, and was now concerned for the man's safety. The other problem was Bridges, who had been out of touch for hours now. That did not bode well for Alli's safety.

He swiveled back to stare into General Tarasov's face. First Alli went missing, now this. He felt as if events were running away from him.

His phone rang and he leapt at it, praying it was Fraine.

"Secretary Paull?"

Not Fraine. "Speaking."

"This is Detective O'Donnell over at the Twelfth."

"Yes, of course. I remember you, Detective. You helped my people pick up Ali Amoud last year."

"Yessir, that's right. I'm relieved to have gotten you. I didn't have your home number, of course, but I was hoping someone there would answer and let me know how—"

"What can I do for you?" Paull was staring at General Tarasov again. He was eager to commence his investigation of the General and,

as a result, had used a vaguely dismissive tone. He couldn't think of anyone he'd less like to chat with at this hour than a Metro detective.

"We've found a body, sir."

Suddenly focused, Paull could hear the thin line of anxiety that had
crept into the commander's voice. "Has Alli Carson been found?"

"It's not a female body."

Paull sat up straighter. "Then what?"

"Dick Bridges. Looks like a suicide."

"Where are you?"

"His apartment."

"What brought you there?"

"An anonymous 911 call."

"Traceable?"

"Nah. It came from a pay phone couple of blocks from the apartment. No fingerprints, and we swept the area with negative results."

Worse and worse. "I'll be right over."

Paull rose, grabbed his coat, and was on his way out of the office
when his cell phone buzzed again. He listened to Fraine telling him about
Leopard and his head began to throb painfully.

ARTURO'S PIZZA Parlor was getting ready to close when Fraine
pressed his badge against the glass door. A gangly kid as pimply as Leopard unlocked the door and stared at him blankly, his mouth half open.

"Manager," Fraine said, pushing past him.

"Mr. Sabatini!" the kid called from behind Fraine. "Cops!"

"Cops?" Sabatini, a rotund man with bandy legs and the dark skin
of the southern Italian, emerged from the rear, wiping his hands on his
smeared white apron. "What cops?"

Fraine gave him a look at his official ID. "You the manager?"

"Manager and owner." Sabatini looked at the empty pizza box Fraine
was holding. His eyes were like olive pits. "Wassamatta, you gotta com-
plaint?"

"Who makes the pies, Mr. Sabatini?"

"I do. I'm a third-generation *pizzaiolo*. I don't let no Hispanics near
my dough."

Sabatini said it with so much innate pride Fraine knew he couldn't be culpable. He held out the box and gave the address of the Dupont North. "Order must've been placed no more than an hour ago. Can you tell me who delivered it?"

Sabatini looked Fraine up and down. "Sure thing. Mickey."

"Where is he?"

"Right behind you." He meant the pimply kid.

Fraine whirled to see Mickey racing out the door and down the street. He tore after him, Sabatini's raised voice following him. "What'd that little prick do now?"

Up ahead, Mickey turned a corner to his left and, a moment later, Fraine followed. They were headed down a three-block decline, but a block later, Mickey darted left again, ducking left, through a chain-link fence. When Fraine reached the rubble-strewn area just inside the fence, he was confronted by a moldering brownstone too run-down even to be used as a crack house, though by the flux of human and chemical stink that assaulted him when he stepped through a front door hanging off its hinges, it must recently have been.

Just inside, he stood stock-still, listening. Hearing a floorboard creak above his head, he leapt up the stairs three treads at a time. At the top, a bullet whistling past his ear caused him to throw himself on his side. He drew his Glock and lay still, waiting.

A floorboard creaked again, and he rushed toward the sound, firing three shots in quick succession. No fire was returned, but he saw a blur of motion heading out the window of the room at the end of the hall. He sprinted into the room, fired again as Mickey grabbed the fire escape and disappeared upward.

As he cleared the window, he squeezed off a blind shot upward to prevent Mickey from firing his pistol while Fraine was vulnerable. Looking up as he climbed, he could see that the kid was as agile as a monkey. He'd never catch him in a footrace; time for Plan B.

Mickey hit the roof while Fraine was still a floor below. By the time Fraine came up over the low parapet onto the tar paper, the kid was on the other side of the roof. Fraine took the sharpshooter's stance, braced his Glock with his left hand, aimed, and fired. Mickey cried out and went down, grabbing his right thigh.

Fraine took off after him, feeling winded but gritting his teeth and pushing his body on its forward trajectory by keeping his center of gravity around his pelvis and his legs pumping. Mickey, hearing him coming, squirmed around and brought his pistol up.

Fraine aimed the Glock. "Don't be stupid, Mickey. Whatever you're into isn't worth dying for."

"What would you know about it?" Mickey shouted.

Fraine kept advancing, the Glock aimed squarely at Mickey's heart. "Don't make me pull the trigger, son."

"Fuck you!" Mickey screamed, but Fraine was now close enough, and he kicked the pistol out of the kid's hand. It was a cheap Saturday night special that broke apart when it hit the rooftop.

Fraine stood over the kid. "That pizza you delivered was poisoned, did you know that?"

Mickey looked up at him with red-rimmed eyes. "I don't know shit." He looked like he was about to burst into tears.

"Listen to me, Mickey. You're already in the shitter. Accessory to murder at the very least, first degree at the worst."

"What?" Now tears sprang out at the corners of his eyes. "What kinda trash you talking?"

"I don't have time to talk trash," Fraine said. "The young man you delivered that pizza to is dead, poisoned by whatever you put on the pizza."

"Jesus." Mickey ran the back of a shaking hand across his lips. "I didn't know. How could I know?"

"Tell me what happened. That's your only way out now. You talk to me and I'll see what I can do."

"They'll kill me."

"You'll be dead if you don't talk, trust me. I can protect you." He knelt beside the kid. "I can make you disappear."

Mickey hung his head. A dust devil whipped his hair into a brief frenzy. "I knew it, I knew it. I'm no fucking good at this."

"Meaning?"

"Being a hard-ass." His head came up, his expression bleak. "I don't have it in me."

"Then why go that route?"

His narrow shoulders lifted and fell. "Who the fuck wants to be in school, listening to gray-heads telling me what to think, when I can be pulling a grand a week?"

"And yet you do errands for a *pizzaiolo.*"

"Not for the money, that's for fuck sure. But, shit, you'd be surprised the things you pick up in a joint like that. The people that come in, talk in front of you to each other or on their burners like you're not there." He rubbed his fingers together. "Secrets."

"Makes you more valuable, huh?"

"Hey, I've gotta earn." He produced a weak smile. "I want all the things the big boys have, y'know? Flat-screen TV, iPad, bling—plenty of bling or you can't catch the bitches."

"Don't talk like that."

His attempt at ambition was so sad it almost broke Fraine's heart. Almost. "Okay, Mickey, you are what you are. Now you know. So give me what I want so I can help you."

The kid sighed and looked away, over the rooftops to the part of the city he scarcely knew and which would not accept him. "Rats're the only thing moving in this building now."

"Mickey."

"That's what he calls me, see. The Rat. I take it 'cause he's the one who pays me. He's the one who gives the orders."

"And he ordered you to—what?"

"Salt the pizza. Gave me a tiny packet."

"Still have it?"

Mickey tossed his head. "You kidding? He told me to get rid of it after the salting."

Fraine grew angry at the kid's stupidity. "And you didn't question this particular order? You didn't wonder what the fuck you were doing?"

"I thought it was coke. Anyways, I don't get paid to question or wonder. I did once, but he beat the crap outta me, so that was that."

"Beautiful. This sonuvabitch have a name?"

The kid ducked his head like he was in the ring, bobbing and weaving away from punishing blows. "Yeah, but I . . ."

"You stop now, I can't help you. You're a dead man walking."

Mickey held his head in his hands. "It all seemed so easy. All I wanted was for it to be easy."

That's what they all wanted, Fraine thought. These kids had no sense of work ethic, the value of money, or their own worth. How could they, when they were surrounded by gang lords and drug dealers raking in millions? It was a gangsta world; you lived and died by its code.

"So who is this guy, Mickey? This asshole who beats you, then gives you a grand a week for swallowing his shit?"

"His name's Moses, but, honestly, I think that's a moniker, not his real name."

"Moses got a last name, or is he like Paladin?"

"Who?"

"Sorry." Wrong cultural reference. "Madonna."

"Oh, yeah. Moses Malliot."

"You're kidding."

Mickey, so close to beating the rap, became panicky. "Fuck, no, I swear. Why?"

Moses Malliot was the name of the guy Andy Beemer, at Chesapeake BodyWerks, who serviced Leonard Bishop's car, had told Fraine knew who had given the chief of detectives his initial launch up Metro's ladder.

FIFTEEN

JACK ARRIVED in D.C. having slept all the way across the Atlantic. He had dreamed of Alli and of Emma, as they had been before Emma's death, two friends and roommates, inseparable and intertwined. He dreamed that he was the perfect dad, taking them to deafening rock concerts, then out for hot fudge sundaes, or on long weekends, walking the barrier islands, picking up seashells, and splashing in the surf. He dreamed he had gone with Emma to pick out a dog, a boxer she had longed for, that she named it Cleo, and he helped her train it, watching her laugh at the puppy's antics. He dreamed that, finally exhausted, she fell asleep in his arms, that he carried her to bed, and tucked her in. He dreamed of watching her sleeping face, pale in the puddle of moonlight slanting in through her bedroom window.

He awoke to the scream of brakes, the blur of motion out the window, and a catch in his throat that brought him to the edge of weeping. As he unbuckled, he recognized today as one of the days when he missed his daughter with an unbearable intensity, that this feeling would be with him all day, and that there was nothing he could do about it except put one foot in front of the other until, as in all the times before, it would fade into background chatter, impatiently anticipating its next flare-up.

JACK, HAVING been contacted by Dennis Paull while still at the airport, met him at the room in the Dupont North Paull had booked for Leopard and Fraine.

"What happened?" Jack said.

"Poisoned." Paull stood with hands on hips. "By a fucking slice of pizza, of all things."

Paull's forensics team had finished and were now loading Leopard's body onto a gurney. The room had been photographed and dusted for prints. There was little else to do but to pack up the two laptops, but Jack stopped the techs before they could do that.

"Take everything else back to the lab," Paull told them. "We'll join you later."

When the room was cleared, Jack said, "Any news?"

Paull shook his head. "She's off the radar, and so is her roommate, the Bard woman."

"No one knows what happened to Vera after she gave her statement at Metro HQ?"

"Unfortunately, no. Fraine told me Detective Stoddart was too busy typing up his report and bringing it up to Bishop."

"What the hell's Bishop got to do with this?"

"That's what I'm hoping Fraine or Nona will be able to tell me." Paull had briefed Jack on the taxi ride in from the airport, but the situation seemed to be changing minute to minute.

"I want to see where, according to Vera, Alli was abducted."

"Stoddart told me he already went over it himself—and I sent a team out there. They found nothing."

"I know Alli better."

"You think you'll find something my people missed?" Paull held up his hands. "Strike that. Stupid question. All right, as soon as we're finished here."

Jack turned to Leopard's laptop. "What was Leopard working on?"

"Trying to find out who provided the juice for Bishop's rapid rise to the top of Metro, among other hacked goodies."

"Well," Jack said, sitting down at Leopard's computer, "he must have hit a nerve."

"He also must have set off an alarm somewhere." Paull came and stood behind Jack. "Which worries me. Leopard was the best hacker I know."

Jack checked out what Leopard had been working on, but he was so upset by Alli's disappearance the letters swam away from him like frightened fish. His pulse rate went up and he felt the old, familiar anxiety grab hold of him again.

"Jack?"

"Give me a minute." Jack slowed his breathing, remembering the lessons taught him by Reverend Taske, concentrating on a spot just to the right of his head, a place of utter peace and calm. He looked at the computer screen from that spot and ever so slowly the fish returned, forming into letters, which became words, the words flowing into sentences, the sentences lining up as paragraphs, and he began to read.

"This doesn't have anything to do with Bishop," he said as his fingers worked the keys. "Who the hell is Milton P. Stirwith?"

Paull leaned over Jack's shoulder. "Damned if I know."

"This is interesting. According to what Leopard discovered, Stirwith doesn't exist. He's a legend—not just a legend, mind you, but a legend that bears all the hallmarks of those created by the Norns."

Jack turned to look at Paull. "Do you know anything about the Norns? Is it true?"

Paull took a breath and nodded. "The group did exist, yes."

"The point is, Dennis, according to what Leopard unearthed, the Norns still exist."

All the blood had drained out of Paull's face. "That's not possible. The group was officially disbanded after the end of the Cold War."

"Nevertheless, if we are to believe this, it still exists—unofficially."

"Do you?" Paull said. "Believe it, I mean. Because I don't see how this could be the case if the government shut it down."

"I think it's why Leopard was poisoned." Jack rose and began to gather up the laptop to take with them. "Dennis, it seems likely that the Norns, rather than ceasing to exist, migrated into a black ops organ."

Paull looked even more shaken. "The Norns require funding, which means they're working for someone very high up inside the government."

NONA WAS playing "Wichita Lineman" on an iPod speaker dock, a modern gizmo she had bought, resting side by side with Frankie's old-school cassette/CD player, when Fraine walked into the private room. Through the window, the meticulously manicured grounds of Bethesda Naval Hospital spread out in a showy display.

He stood just inside the door, watching her as she sat in the bed-side easy chair, holding Frankie's unresponsive hand. At least the music drowned out the metronomic hiss and sigh of the respirator that was keeping her brother alive.

"He loves Jimmy Webb," she said. "Go know." She always used the present tense when speaking about Frankie.

"And I like Kanye West."

Nona's laugh held a bitter knife edge. *She looks exhausted,* Fraine thought. He supposed nights with Bishop could do that to you.

"Any change?"

With infinite tenderness, she disengaged her hand from Frankie's, rose, and came over to where Fraine stood. Then she recounted in detail what she had overheard in the men's room of George's Pentagon—that Bishop was for some reason tracking Jack McClure's movements for the General, that they both knew about Alli's abduction, that Bishop had Sergeant McNulty on his private payroll. "As if all that isn't fucked up enough, this asshole General orders Bishop to take care of what he called loose ends," she concluded.

Fraine's eyes narrowed. "Meaning?"

"Vera Bard, if and when they find her."

"We've got to make sure we find her first. Any ideas?"

"Well, there's Stoddart," she said. "He took Vera Bard's statement, didn't he?"

Fraine looked up. "You're shitting me. This general ordered Bishop to kill a Metro detective?"

"That's what I'm saying."

Fraine's face broke out into a huge grin. "But this is fantastic news, Nona!"

"What? Stoddart is one of your own. How can you—"

"Don't you see?" He grabbed her and swung her around. "This is how we're going to bring Bishop down."

Nona began to laugh as he danced with her to the beat of "By the Time I Get to Phoenix."

"You hear that, Frankie?" she called. "Your sister's gonna be free!"

"IT LOOKS like Bridges hung himself," Paull said on the way over to the *Titanic* Memorial. "Broken neck, ligature marks are all consistent with suicide."

"Was Dick depressed?"

"He was in counseling after he returned home from Moscow with Edward and Lyn Carson. He took the president's death pretty hard. Then when Lyn passed away, and now Alli's missing . . ." He spread his hands.

"Who was Bridges's partner?"

"Lenny Betances. He's currently on leave."

"Where is he?"

"White-water rafting on the Snake River. Four days ago, according to the records. He's due back in a week."

"And where was Vera last seen?"

"Detective Stoddart took her and her statement up to see Bishop."

"Then he has her."

"No. Somehow she must've smelled a rat. She hightailed it out of there the moment he left his office."

"She's both smart and clever, but I still don't like it," Jack said. His mind was racing, fitting pieces of disparate information together. "Alli and Vera disappear, Dick is found hanged, and his partner is out of town." He turned to Paull. "Here's what I think happened: Alli's been abducted, Dick was killed—"

"Killed?"

"It would explain Vera's disappearance; she's in fear for her life."

"That would mean a cover-up at Secret Service."

"Yes, it would." Jack gestured. "Call your ME. Ten to one he'll find bruises and defensive wounds on Bridges's body."

Paull pressed keys on his cell, spoke briefly, listened for a longer time, said, "Thank you," and broke the connection. He looked at Jack. "On the money. It looks like murder."

Jack nodded. "And what about Carson? Why isn't he raising holy hell about his niece's disappearance?"

"Since he hasn't called or made a move, I have to assume that he doesn't know. You can be sure Bishop didn't tell him, and I sure as hell haven't."

"Good. Find a way to leak him the news about Alli and we'll see which way he jumps."

Paull regarded him with unconcealed skepticism. "You don't seriously believe that he could have had something to do with her abduction."

"I think Henry Holt Carson is capable of pretty much anything if it suits his purpose. Besides, there's no love lost between uncle and niece, of that you can be certain."

"You'd think—"

"But you'd be wrong. He resents Alli deeply because his own daughter is lost to him."

"Idiot." Paull thought of his own daughter, estranged for so long, who had come back to him with her young son, who he adored. "He should cherish her all the more."

"Human psychology," Jack said. "Its twists, turns, and distortions never make much sense in any rational way."

They arrived at the memorial, which, Jack was pleased to see, was still cordoned off with yellow and black crime-scene tape.

As they got out, Paull's cell buzzed and, standing by his car, he took the call, while Jack lifted up one section of the tape and entered the place where Vera claimed Alli had been abducted.

Jack stood in the center of the area and slowly turned in a complete circle. By that time he had created a three-dimensional map in his mind of where he was and where he needed to go. He began his search in the south quadrant, but there was nothing to see except dirt and the usual debris, which he sifted through on his haunches.

He thought he found something on the east side of the monument itself, but it turned out to be nothing. Having made the complete circuit, he closed his eyes and conjured up Vera's recounting of the report she had given to Detective Stoddart. When he reached the part where she described Alli looking out of the Town Car door, he opened his eyes and went under the west-side tape. Fifty paces on, he stopped at a spot and crouched down on his hams. There were two dark drops, not blood as he had first surmised, but motor oil. His fingertip smeared the oil. Though Vera hadn't made it clear, this was where the Town Car must have been idling when Alli was bundled into it. He continued his search in concentric circles, using the oil spots as a starting point.

As he went, he brushed leaves, sharp-edged gravel, and the odd crushed soda can away. That was when he saw something. He wasn't sure what it was at first, so he started taking pictures of it with his cell.

He felt the kiss of cold against his cheek at the same moment he heard her:

Waxman.

"Emma. You know what this means?"

I know Waxman.

"Is he the one who took Alli?"

Having finished his call, Paull came up. "Looking farther afield?"

Jack, no longer sensing Emma, changed angle and snapped another shot.

"Bishop knows something about Alli's abduction," Paull continued.

At that, Jack stopped what he was doing and stood. "If Bishop knows, then this group you're trying to follow is involved."

"My thought as well." Paull handed over his cell. "This fellow look familiar?"

Jack looked at the photo, shook his head. "Who is he?"

"Another member of the group. Bishop's superior. His name is Gerard Tarasov. He's a general."

"Your group's Secret Service connection?"

"Likely, isn't it? I was just starting to get a line on him when I got the call about Leopard. Are you finished here? I think we'd better go back to my office to find out all we can about Tarasov."

He gestured with his head. "What did you find?"

"Take a look." Jack pointed. "You tell me."

Paull stepped closer, then squatted down, peering at what Jack had uncovered. "Someone might have scratched something into the road-bed with a piece of this gravel." He looked up. "But wouldn't it be too hard?"

"Not here. The tarmac has been recently poured. It hasn't fully hardened yet."

" 'Waxman,' " he read. "It looks to me like graffiti. A gang moniker, maybe?" He rose. "You think it's significant?"

"I do," Jack said. "I think Alli left us a message."

THE AIR terminal in Tripoli was eerily quiet when Annika and Dyadya Gourdjiev arrived. Flying in, they had seen fighter jets banking, their trigger-happy pilots deep in electronic conversations with the pilot of the aircraft carrying them—a NATO cargo plane carrying relief supplies to the Libyan rebels. Once or twice the yellowish air was split by fluorescent lines of tracers, but the NATO fighter escort that had picked them up at the border kept them safe from harm.

Apart from their own hurried footfalls, the arrival hall was silent, eerily deserted. Outside, they were met by Bir Aziz, Gourdjiev's agent-in-place, who ushered them into an armored troop carrier, bristling with machine guns fore and aft.

"Apologies," Aziz said, "here this is the only way to get around."

"What news?" The old man was in no mood for idle pleasantries.

"The ongoing civil war has allowed us to make some progress of late." Aziz was a small, dark man, with a full beard, the nose and curious eyes of a hawk, and ringlets of black hair. A livid scar split his left cheek, which looked as if the underlying bone had been shattered and put back together in either a hasty or an incompetent manner.

"Ever since the chaos engulfed Tripoli, we have at last been able to infiltrate Gaddafi's palace and residence. Before she ingloriously defected, the Syrian's hacker expert had broken the Libyan encryption, so for weeks now we have monitored those communications. We know for an absolute certainty that what we've been looking for isn't in Tripoli. In fact, it's not in Libya at all."

The armored carrier reached one of the many checkpoints set up throughout the city, and they could hear the driver's tense, contentious exchange with the militiamen manning the checkpoint. Aziz lifted an assault rifle from its rack along one wall and checked that the magazine was fully loaded.

"The Syrian has provided us with the proper papers," he said as he set the rifle across his knees, "but you never know." He grinned. "Not to worry, worst case, we can blast any resistance to kingdom come."

A moment later, the altercation came to an abrupt end, and the carrier lurched forward.

"It appears," Aziz continued as he reracked the weapon, "that Gaddafi had advance warning of the uprising—enough time, at least, to move his entire fortune to a safer location outside the country."

"Do you know the origin of the warning?" Gourdjiev said.

"Not definitively, but I have a gut feeling."

"Please share it," Annika said.

"The Syrian."

The old man nodded. "It would be just like him to play both ends against the middle." He nodded to Aziz. "So tell me, have you learned his whereabouts?"

"Alas, no." Aziz clasped his hands together, as if petitioning Allah for continued life. "We intercepted only one message to him before the cipher was changed." His expression turned bleak. "However, if the text is code, we haven't been able to break it."

"What is the mysterious text?" The old man said.

"It's unpronounceable." Aziz drew out a pad and pencil and quickly scribbled on the top sheet. The he spun the pad around so they could see what he had written:

KWIFA

"At first we assumed it was a simple rearrangement of the letters, but we ran it through the computer program and nothing it came up with made sense." As he glanced from one to the other, he said, "Frankly, we're stumped. Does it mean anything to either of you?"

They shook their heads.

Aziz grunted. "Pity the Syrian's IT woman—what was her name?"

"Caroline," Gourdjiev said. "No one seemed to know her last name."

Aziz nodded. "It seems likely that she would have cracked this."

"Didn't the Syrian replace her?" Annika asked.

"Three times," Aziz said. "Not one could solve the encryptions she had created, so the Syrian shot them."

"Lovely."

Aziz said, "I must be going. Is there anything else?"

"No, good friend. Be at peace, and may Allah bless you."

"And you, as well," Aziz said as he clambered out of the vehicle.

"If the Syrian betrayed us once, he'll betray us again," Annika said when they were alone. She was smoldering. She'd had just about enough of being knocked around by forces she could neither see nor attack. She was itching to take action.

Gourdjiev shook his head. "I think not. You misunderstand him."

"I very much doubt that. He's a businessman, first, last, and always. He has no interest in ideology; money is his religion."

"Ah, darling, there you're wrong, though this is what he wants everyone to believe. My guess is he leaked just enough to Gaddafi to receive millions from the grateful dictator."

"But the money—"

"The Syrian has no interest in Gaddafi's fortune."

"Are you kidding me? Isn't that what we're in this for?"

The old man smiled indulgently.

Annika sat back in the uncomfortable metal seat, chewing over everything that had happened.

"What a partner we have!" she exclaimed at last.

"We have no partners," her grandfather said, "not in any real sense, anyway."

"But I thought—"

He patted her hand gently. "Pragmatism in all things, my darling, that is the first and most important lesson of the world we live in. Without pragmatism it is impossible to survive, let alone live to be my age. Without pragmatism it is also impossible to discern your enemy's motives."

"You know what the Syrian is really up to?"

"I do."

"Then tell me."

"Not yet." He leaned over and delivered a dry kiss on her cheek. "I would not have you die young."

VERA, HAVING switched over to flat-heeled boots, black jeans, and a man's white shirt under a surplus Navy peacoat, had no trouble finding the black Lincoln Town Car. Her father's contact at Metro had been thorough as well as punctual. He had not only gotten the name the Lincoln was registered to, but he also was able to place its current whereabouts.

Sometimes it was good to have friends in high places, as well as low, she reflected as she walked down H Street NW. Except for how many strings were attached, she'd have cultivated them herself, but she had no desire to be turned into a marionette, dancing to the tunes they dictated. That was for other people, not her. Not to say that she hadn't learned this much from her father: trading in secrets was much more lucrative that trading for mere money. Her father had ensured that her application was accepted at Fearington, all in the service of her becoming Alli Carson's roommate. But now that that assignment was over she could leave Fearington anytime she chose. The truth was, she had no desire to abandon the course of her career. She had done a ton of soul searching and had come to the conclusion that her father had done her an inadvertent service by linking her up with Fearington. Inside the FBI or whatever other federal clandestine agency she chose to apply for, she could amass secrets legally, and, when she was ready, she could begin to trade in them, all under the aegis of the government, the ultimate cover. It was the perfect situation.

She stopped across the street from Silicon Vault, Googled the phone number, and called.

"Yes?"

"Hi," she said. "I'm looking for Moses."

"Who's calling?"

"A friend of Werner's."

"Werner who?"

For a split instant, she wondered whether she was wrong. Then she said, with all the confidence at her disposal, "Waxman. But I've only called him Werner."

There was an infinitesimal hesitation, then: "This is Moses. What can I do for you?"

"LEOPARD WAS using an IronKey," Jack said, looking at the matte-black thumb drive sticking out of one of the laptop's USB ports. "Is it his own?"

"No," Paull said. "I bought it for him."

The two men had returned to Paull's office, where Jack had set Leopard's laptop onto a table and pulled up a chair. He plugged it in so the battery wouldn't run down. He had made certain to keep the laptop running on the way over from the hotel room in order to keep the open windows intact.

"Did you get it through the usual methods?" He meant through the DoD procurement office.

"I didn't want to chance it," Paull said, coming up behind him. "I had Galliardo buy it."

"Ask him to step in," Jack said.

Paull did so without a word; he knew Jack too well to query him. A moment later, a young man with sandy, brush-cut hair, a spray of freckles over his rather wide nose, and a ready smile entered.

"Sir?"

"Mr. McClure wishes to ask you some questions," Paull said.

"Sir!" Galliardo said, directing this crisp word at Jack.

Jack turned and studied Paull's aide for precisely thirty seconds before he said, "Secretary Paull tells me that he asked you to purchase this IronKey. Is that right?"

"Yessir, it is."

"You know the purpose of an IronKey?"

"Yessir. It's a microcomputer with its own Internet browser encrypted with military-grade software to allow total anonymity when surfing the Internet. The IronKey provides a dynamic ISP address that cannot be traced."

Satisfied, Jack continued. "Where did you purchase this particular IronKey?"

"At Silicon Vault, on H Street Northwest."

"How well do you know this store?"

"Exceedingly well, sir. I've been buying there for nearly five years."

"It's a secure venue?"

"Absolutely, sir. It's owned by an ex–Secret Service agent by the name of Moses Malliot."

Jack nodded to himself, and Paull, picking up the gesture, said, "That will be all, Galliardo."

"Yessir." The aide turned on his heel and marched himself out of Paull's office, closing the door behind him.

"Secret Service," Paull said, seeing Jack's expression. "Is that what you're thinking?"

"And more. Going on the assumption that Leopard was murdered because of what his cyber-snooping uncovered, it follows that he raised an alarm bell somewhere."

"Not through a firewall breach," Paull said. "Leopard was the best at that."

"Accepting what you say leaves us with only one other possibility."

He carefully disconnected the IronKey and, turning it over, used a tiny set of tools to dismantle it.

Paull bent over. "Where in the world did you get those?"

"Present from a distant friend." When Jack had the back off, he scrutinized the inside. "Through ATF, I took a course once in these things, just as they were coming out. Fascinating concept because they're completely self-contained. They repel any form of malware or virus picked up over the Internet."

"The IronKey is completely secure," Paull said. "Which is the idea."

"Correct. But see here?" Jack pointed to a spot in the interior. "What it can't defeat, however, is a hack from inside its circuitry." He looked up at Paull. "Someone at Silicon Vault sold your man an IronKey ready to be tracked."

SIXTEEN

FRAINE WAS in his car, coming into D.C. from Bethesda, when he caught the call from Dennis Paull.

"I need you to get over to Silicon Vault ASAP." Paull gave him the address on H Street NW. "Pick up the owner, Moses Malliot, and bring him directly to my office."

"What?" Fraine made a screeching U-turn. "The trail I've been following leads directly to that guy."

"Well, that's interesting. It's likely Malliot was following Leopard's cyber-tracks on the Net. If he didn't poison him, then he knows who did."

In turn, Fraine told his temporary boss everything that he and Nona had discovered. "So it's clear that Bishop and this general—"

"We got a name," Paull interrupted. "Gerard Tarasov."

"Doesn't ring a bell," Fraine said, taking a corner at speed. He was only three minutes away from H Street NW. "You know him?"

"Only by name," Paull said. "But as soon as you get Malliot here, I'm willing to bet that's going to change in a hurry."

Fraine pulled into a parking spot across the street from Silicon Vault.

"No problem," he said. "I'm at the target."

It was at that moment he saw a young woman turn a corner onto the street. She wore a peacoat and tight jeans. He turned off the engine and got out of his car. Though she had on dark glasses, he recognized her and his pulse rate went up dramatically.

"Fraine?" Paull's voice buzzed in his ear like an angry wasp.

"I've got eyes on Vera Bard."

"Say again?"

He watched openmouthed as Vera approached Silicon Vault. He thought, *No, it can't be.*

"Alan."

Then she vanished into the black maw of Moses Malliot's shop.

"Sorry," Fraine said into his cell. "Gotta go."

"VERA BARD wasn't taken with Alli," Paull said. "Fraine has eyes on her." He punched in another number on his cell. "Nona, get down to Silicon Vault ASAP to give Fraine backup." He gave her the address, then listened. He glanced at Jack. "Bishop has ordered her to get a line on your current whereabouts."

"They must know your plane has brought me back to D.C." Jack thought a moment. "Have her tell Bishop the truth, that I'm here in your office."

Paull relayed the message, then disconnected. "Was that wise? They'll watch for you, then tail you."

"I'm so hoping."

Paull shot him a curious look, Jack shook his head, and Paull shrugged his shoulders, resigned. "You were saying?"

"The Three-thirteen group designation was Acacia, according to what Leopard found."

The secretary grimaced from behind his desk. "But what they were doing in the Horn of Africa is anyone's guess."

"I very much doubt Acacia's deployment destination was anywhere within the Horn of Africa," Jack said. "That was just a jumping-off spot. They flew there with a battalion of Marines. That was simply cover, a way for Acacia to lose itself in the chaos of an ongoing war."

"So where did Acacia end up?"

"That was what Leopard was digging into just before he died. There are more files, but they're heavily encrypted. I can't read them." Jack pointed to the kid's laptop. "All I'm certain of is that a week later, no sign of Acacia remained in Mogadishu."

Paull swiveled his chair to look out the window of his office. The West Wing loomed large. "So we've lost Acacia."

"I'm afraid so," Jack said.

Paull glared at Jack, then rose and went around his desk to peer over Jack's shoulder. "Goddamnit! What in the name of holy hell is going on?"

"Whatever it is," Jack said, "we're getting closer."

Paull stood up. "Give me the laptop. I'm going straight to the president with this evidence."

"Consider whether that's wise, sir."

Paull rounded in him. "What d'you mean?"

"First, Acacia was a Three-thirteen mission. Second, what if the president is in on Three-thirteen?"

"I can't believe—"

"Third, there's no point going anywhere with the laptop until Leopard's files are decrypted."

Paull grunted like a pig who missed his truffles.

"Okay," Jack continued, "even if we assume Crawford doesn't know about Three-thirteen, do we really want our enemies to know how much we've found out about them? That will only drive them deeper underground and we may never find them, let alone discover what they're up to."

Paull turned on his heel, contemplating the view out his window. At length, he sighed. "To wield so much power and be so helpless."

"We're not helpless." Jack turned back to the laptop. "I'm convinced that a key to Three-thirteen is the Norns."

"Oh, come on. They're all dead."

"Leopard didn't think so, and neither do I." Jack worked the keyboard. He was zoned in. His dyslexia allowed him to make connections from the disparate documents Leonard had managed to hack. "This general . . ."

"Gerard Tarasov."

"Have you researched him?"

"I was just starting when, as I told you, Fraine notified me of Leopard's murder. Why?"

"There's something curious associated with the General. It's handwritten at the end of this doc."

Paull frowned. "What is it?"

"'KWIfA.'" Jack pronounced it carefully.

"Any idea what it means?"

"No. But what about Waxman?" Jack said, half to himself.

"The word scratched on the tarmac?"

"Waxman is someone's name," Jack said.

"If so, it's a poor clue." Paull began a global search of all the official databases. "It could be anyone."

"Even if he's associated in some way with the General?"

"The two of them would be careful to cover their tracks." Paull, staring at his computer screen, shook his head. "We need someone with Leopard's particular skills."

"There's no one else at your disposal?"

"Plenty," Paull said. "But none with his intuitive skills. Worse, I can't trust someone official. These people have their spies everywhere. I mean, look what happened to Leopard."

"Leopard must have had hacker friends—they're all part of some network or other."

"You actually believe any of them would speak to me, let alone take on his project?" He sighed and picked up the phone. "Still, I've got to try."

Moving on, Jack pulled up the last of the cached Internet documents on Leopard's laptop. "There is a line of warehouses," he said, "fronting the Washington Channel on First Avenue, between Fort McNair and the War College. They're long abandoned now, but during World War Two they were used to house warship building materials."

Paull turned from the phone to stare at him. "I thought they were torn down."

"Most of them were. But not all." Jack read down to the bottom of the documents. "In the decade after the war, two of them housed the Norns."

Paull's expression turned grim. "Alli was taken a block north of McNair."

Jack nodded. "And now I have a sneaking suspicion I know where she is being held."

MOSES MALLIOT had been in business all his life, or so it seemed to him. When he was six years old, he had sold lemonade on the street corners of his small southern Illinois hometown. By the time he was eight, he was selling candy he'd snatched from his supermarket prowls to his classmates. It wasn't much of a reach from there to stealing computers out of schools or buying weed in bulk and selling joints he rolled himself for a fivefold profit. Increasing money brought increased ambition. He had started early on the path of least resistance to making the most money. In his teens, money bought him girls and a degree of fame he instinctively knew was bad for business, so he dropped out of high school.

His parents hit the roof, obliging him to endure two years of twice-weekly psychiatric appointments meant to "cure" him of the "evil" that had "infected" him, according to his father. In no time at all, he had worked out what it was his doctor wanted to hear, and he began to have fun fabricating a curious inner life, punctuated with terrifying dreams, all of which fascinated her while entertaining himself.

She prescribed drugs, which his parents dutifully bought for him every month, and on which he made a tidy profit, pushing them onto rubes on the street. At the end of the two years, his doctor proclaimed him neurosis-free, and he promptly gathered up his ill-gotten gains and lit out for D.C.

He chose the nation's capital, inexorably drawn to power and to the people hollowed out by it. Politicians seemed to him the perfect marks: devious, compromised, corrupt, certainly, but not yet rotten to the core.

Then he joined the Marines and, by doing so, learned just how corrupt and stupid the government was. He'd found his way to the promised land.

People respected him, trusted him implicitly—*Semper fi,* baby!—and the contacts he'd made overseas provided the springboard into an entirely different and larger arena than he had ever mined before. He was bedazzled.

This was the man who greeted Vera as she entered his shop. He eyed her with the cunning professionalism he'd honed over decades in the villainous byways of the world.

"How can I help you, honey?" He was possessed of a baritone that would be at home at the Met or La Scala. In other words, it could charm people by putting them off their guard. This he expected because it always worked.

"I've got a nasty cyber-stalker I want nailed." Vera leaned over the wooden counter, but there was nothing to see in the windowless space, just blowups of photos Malliot had taken during his time overseas as a Marine. "What've you got for me?"

After peering at her for a moment, Malliot turned and selected two software packages. "I think I've got just the ticket for you, little lady." He turned back, his hands full. "Depends on how much you're willing to—"

Vera whipped out a stiletto and impaled his right hand to the countertop. As Malliot screamed, she said, in a gruff voice that eerily mimicked that of Pete Clemenza, "'It's a Sicilian message. It means Luca Brasi sleeps with the fishes.'"

Malliot's left hand swung out, but she deftly avoided the blow and punched him in the mouth. Blood spurted through his lips. "And so will you, unless you tell me where Alli Carson is."

"Who are you?" Malliot looked at her through narrowed eyes. "Do I know you?"

Vera sawed the stiletto back and forth. Blood erupted from the back of his hand and he gasped. "I ask the questions, Moses. You answer them. Where is Alli Carson?"

"Who's Alli Carson? I don't know what the fuck you're talking about."

Her eyes blazed. "Don't fuck with me, liar. I was there. I saw Waxman bundle Alli into your Town Car."

"Waxman?" He laughed. "I don't know any Waxman. There is no Waxman."

At the same time, he tried to extricate his hand, and she twisted the knife.

"Tell me what I want to know, motherfucker."

"All right, all right," Malliot said, clearly on edge.

She sensed that he was about to tell her when the front door opened and Fraine came in. Vera, startled, turned to see and Malliot clocked her with his fist. As she staggered back, he grasped the hilt of the stiletto and, pulling it up, freed himself. Fraine rushed at him, but Malliot pulled the .357 Magnum he kept at the ready under the counter for emergencies and leveled it at Fraine. But he never got to pull the trigger. Fraine shot him in the throat, then in the center of his forehead. Malliot slammed back against the wall, his surveillance and privacy gadgets showering down around him.

"Idiot!" Vera shouted at Fraine as she bent over Malliot. "He was going to tell me where they'd taken Alli, and now he's dead."

"Pity for you," the figure said, appearing from the shadows leading to the rear of the shop. "But not for me."

Vera looked from the figure to Fraine. "Fuck me. You two are identical."

"Hello, Alan," Chris Fraine said. "I've been waiting a long time for this moment."

He raised his left hand, which held a CZ 75 SP-01 Phantom with polymer grips. He squeezed the trigger, and shot his twin brother twice in the chest.

THE NOON fog had lifted in Rome, bringing in its wake the souls of the dead, wafting up like a dream from the buried layers, like dinosaur fossils beneath the bricks and cobbles of the modern city. Annika and Dyadya Gourdjiev arrived at the venerable Gran Caffè Doney on the Via Veneto, and were shown to a table. The wide, winding street was nearly deserted nowadays, a sad reminder of the faded fifties and sixties heyday of La Dolce Vita and Cinecittà, Federico Fellini, Marcello Mastroianni, Anita Ekberg, Sophia Loren, Sergio Leone, Clint Eastwood, a flood of paparazzi paying court, and a thousand and one starlets, sunglassed and wasp-waisted, draped over the tiny outdoor tables of its packed cafés. In those halcyon days, Cinecittà was the center of the film universe, outside Hollywood. Now its vast soundstages were kept afloat by Italian TV soaps and reality shows.

They ordered coffee and pastries, and glanced around the half-empty room strewn with tourists, heads huddled together, who didn't know the Venero's glory days were well behind it, laughing and partaking of the overpriced menu.

"He said he'd be waiting for us," Annika said.

"This is typical behavior." An unmistakable note of disdain soured Dyadya Gourdjiev's voice. The implied ending: *for this younger generation.* His expression grew grave. "You know what you must do."

"Of course, Dyadya."

"There is still time—"

"No." She shook her head. "There isn't." She tendered a tiny smile. "This is what—"

"Jack had not entered the picture then," he said sharply.

Her smile grew rueful. "Jack has changed nothing."

"And yet he's changed everything. For both of us."

"We go on, Dyadya. We are Russian, there is nothing else we can do."

"Perhaps Jack won't allow this."

"Even he cannot stop it."

He studied her for a moment, then nodded, albeit reluctantly. "It is interesting how humans can be pleased and sad, all at once."

"So." Annika, elbows on the table, took her grandfather's veiny hands in hers. "How are you doing?"

A movement on the darkened street caught his eye for a moment, then was gone. "There is no justice in the world."

"Don't say that." She squeezed his hands. "Justice is what we're seeking."

"Speak for yourself," Gourdjiev said. "As for me, I am seeking revenge."

"Then . . . now . . ." She looked into his pale blue eyes. "Dyadya, I'm afraid."

His smile contained the warmth of his confidence in her. "You are fearless, my lovely one. Of what could you possibly be afraid?"

For a long time, she did not reply. The coffee and pastries came. Their waiter ogled her surreptitiously. Out on the street, a drunk barked his displeasure at the phantom with whom he was conversing. A motor-cycle fled like time down the Veneto. She held on to her grandfather as if they were on the edge of a precipice, the crumbling rock on which they stood falling away.

"I am afraid of revenge," she said at last.

He seemed genuinely puzzled. "Why would that be?"

"I fear that revenge is the only thing with the power to kill you."

SEVENTEEN

JACK WAS running the name Waxman, which Fraine had relayed to Dennis Paull, through the available databases and getting nowhere fast, when the architectural blueprints for the First Avenue warehouses came up on the wall screen in Paull's office, including electrical, HVAC, waste disposal, and security systems. Jack looked up, but his dyslexia made deciphering them difficult. If he'd had time to build a three-dimensional model, he would have been all right. Instead, he memorized them.

Paull had summoned two commando types, young, brush-cut, square-jawed men, through whose eyes the world was reduced to danger zones, target points, and kill sites.

Before Paull could brief them, Jack intervened. "I don't need or want backup. Freeing Alli is a silent op."

"I agree it's a silent op," Paull said, "but these men aren't your backup—they're the insertion team leaders."

Jack was taken aback. "I think we need a private talk."

"That's just what we *don't* need." Paull came around from behind his desk. "Listen, Jack, this calls for a major operation. I'm not going to chance anyone escaping."

Jack shook his head. "You know how hostage situations can deterio-rate in a heartbeat. I don't want men swarming the warehouses, endan-gering Alli's life. No, the best way is my way. I'll find a way in without raising any alarms."

"I'm afraid that's not an option."

"I saved her before," Jack said. "I'll save her again."

Paull put a hand on his shoulder. The gesture was meant to be com-forting, but Jack wanted to shake it off.

"No one understands your love for Alli better than I do. But this is a different situation; this isn't a one-man abduction—it's part of a larger plan, it calls for a different approach. The plan of attack I've chosen has Alli's welfare as its top priority. Trust me on this, Jack."

RADOMIL, IN dark glasses and a white suit, slipped into Gran Caffè Doney like the shade of Marcello Mastroianni. Every woman in the café turned her head from her husband, boyfriend, or escort to take a long, greedy look at this apparition from the pinnacle of the Veneto's history. His dark hair was long, thick, and shining, obscuring the tops of his ears and the nape of his neck. His smile was wide, with that offhand flair only Europeans could muster without artifice. He might look identical to his twin, but that was where the similarity ended. Where Grigori's manner was sharp and probing, openly searching for the jugular, Radomil's was languid, placid, even, at times, diffident. On first glance, one could be forgiven mistaking him for an underachiever. However, that mistake would be lethal. Quiet as a panther, he made certain he was close enough to smell your breath before he pounced, claws sunk into your neck.

Annika did not look up while he wended his way between the ta-bles, though Dyadya Gourdjiev certainly did.

"Radomil," her grandfather said as the younger man slid into a chair opposite him, "it's always good to see you."

"I'm greatly relieved to see the reports of your death are exagger-ated." Radomil's voice was smoother and darker than his brother's—a bassoon instead of an oboe. "And I am most gratified that your escape from purgatory was successful."

Annika's head snapped up. "Cut the crap, Radomil. This veddy, veddy 'British gentleman' act of yours makes me want to puke. It might fool some people, but it won't make a dent in us."

"So you see even my attempt at civilized discourse is a threat to you."

"Threat?" Annika was truly enraged now. "You shit. You're a shadow of your brother."

"Humm." Unbidden, Radomil took a bite of her uneaten pastry. "And yet, my darling, it's me you're sitting here with, not him."

"Annika," Gourdjiev said, "will you force me to intercede between the two of you once again?"

Radomil chuckled. "Just like siblings the world over, eh?"

She bridled as he chucked her under the chin. "We're not siblings."

"Really?" Radomil cocked his head. "What do you call two children who share the same father?"

"Exceptionally unfortunate." She glared at him. "I killed our father, and was happy to do it."

"And I applaud you for that act of courage. We both hated him." Radomil sighed. "Annika, for the life of me I cannot fathom your continuing antagonism toward me."

"You cannot fathom . . . ?" Annika gave her grandfather an astonished look. "Do you hear, Dyadya?" she said, switching to Russian. "Can you believe this stupidity?" She rose abruptly. "I can't take any more of his lies and deceptions."

Gourdjiev reached out, took her hand in his. "Darling, sit down." His eyes searched hers. "I beg of you."

Wrenching her hand away, she stalked out of the café and stood on the Veneto, glaring at the young men on motorbikes grinning and whistling at her as they whizzed past. A moment later, she felt Radomil emerge and come up beside her. For a time, they both stared out at the dun-colored buildings of Rome—buildings constructed on the ruins of others, on and on, deeper and deeper, history become a physical thing you could both sense and touch.

"I don't want this, you must know that."

"When it comes to you, Radomil, I don't know a damn thing."

"Come, now." His voice softened. "Surely that isn't true."

"No?" She turned to him. "Where is your allegiance? Is it to my grandfather or is it to your brother?"

"You know I have nothing but contempt for Grigori."

"I know nothing of the kind. You can't believe a word your grandfather says."

Radomil spread his hands. "When have I ever lied to you?"

She stepped very close, her eyes entangled with his. "You never told us. *That's* a lie."

"I don't know what you're talking about." Nevertheless, Radomil's smile was forced.

She leaned toward him. "You think I don't know—but I *do* know."

"Know what?"

"I read the study notes on you and Grigori."

His face went pale. "You don't understand—"

"No, you want to believe I don't understand."

"Christ on a crutch." He licked his lips, his face now completely drained of color.

"Right you are, Radomil. I know what you are—or, rather, what you and Grigori were meant to be. But you can change that."

His eyes turned inward. "But that's the thing, Annika. I can't." All his surface polish seemed to have fled down the street, following the motorbike boys into the gunmetal Roman darkness.

"That's what you were *meant* to think."

"Because Grigori and I were made, not born."

She tossed her head, not shy to show her contempt. "Now you're being melodramatic. You were born the same way I and everyone else was."

He turned away, his face shadowed, but, unrelenting, she kept after him.

"Radomil, what happened to you? I mean you specifically."

"The experiments . . ." He bit his lip. "You weren't there. You didn't undergo . . . Even having read the notes, you cannot imagine what it was like."

"Radomil, look at me. Did he leave you without free will?"

"Wasn't that his purpose?"

"To be honest, even Dyadya doesn't know his purpose," she said.

Radomil nodded. "Only he knows, then."

"The one we're seeking." She stared at him, trying to worm her way in. "The one only you know how to find."

His head turned, the lamplight from the café firing his eyes. "Waxman. Werner Waxman."

"Now I can find out something about him."

"No, you can't." He sighed, all the air going out of him. "Because no one knows his real name."

"Someone must." She pulled him to her. "Radomil, will you help us find him?"

A significant change came over him, but it was too late to break away. Fear spread its batlike wings across his face, then pure aggression chased down the fear and killed it. He had a knife at her throat, a bead of blood running like a tear into the hollow of her neck.

"Annika, Grigori and I have been trained as killers, you know this."

"I also know, my brother, that you have fought your training. Now is the time for you to break away completely."

AFTER LEAVING Paull's office, Jack found a small park and sat on a bench, watching the pigeons come and go, like the shadows clouds make across hillsides. He closed his eyes and pictured the huge computer screen on Paull's office wall. Centering himself, he saw again the lines and markings, arrows and notations. Dismissing everything but the foundation outline, his mind began to build a three-dimensional model so that he could look at it from every angle. As soon as he did that, he began to make connections, then connections to those connections. Three minutes after he began, he had his point of entry.

He called a taxi, stopped first at REI, then made a number of purchases at shops selling electronics, car parts, Halloween costumes, and hardware, placing the items in the featherweight camping duffel he'd bought. The cab dropped him off at the Metro Green Line, which he took to Waterfront Station. From there, he headed due south toward the warehouses, skirting Fort McNair on the land side.

It wasn't that he didn't trust Paull—he knew his boss had Alli's welfare in mind—but he couldn't agree that the best way to approach the warehouses was with a show of force. Going solo into the house where Morgan Herr had imprisoned her had been the right approach. Unlike Paull, Jack saw no difference in this situation.

He didn't know why Alli had been taken, but it seemed to him that it must have been an act of desperation. No one in his right mind would abduct the daughter of a fallen president and expect to stay under the radar for long. Maybe, like Morgan Herr, her abductor had a secret death wish. But that, he well knew, could only cause more problems, because the perp wouldn't be afraid to die, or make a grand gesture that could only end in a wider form of destruction. The thought sent a chill down his spine.

Up ahead he could make out, glimmering in the dull sunshine, the northernmost wall of the warehouses—two long, low buildings, whose interiors had been completely gutted to configure and construct the of-fices for the Norns.

Seagulls banked and turned, cawing to one another, crying for food. Jack stood for a moment, surveying the scene. He stepped beneath the stippled shade of a thick-branched camphor tree. Reaching into his duffel, he affixed a theatrical mustache to his upper lip, then slipped a set of Halloween false teeth over his uppers. He checked his reflection in the mirror of the compact he had bought. These admittedly tacky pros-thetics changed the look of his face just enough to forestall anyone armed with a recent photo of him. They wouldn't fool someone for more than a few seconds, but that was all he calculated he'd need.

Stepping out of the shade, he made his way to the embankment that led down to the water's edge. The Washington Channel looked dark and sluggish, mucked at its edges. Paper wrappers and used condoms drifted along, bobbing like miniature boats.

He spotted the lookout. Studiously consulting the D.C. tourist guide he'd bought, he stumbled his way toward the man. When he was six yards away, he lifted his hand in greeting, and said in a passable upper-class British accent, "I say, pardon the intrusion, old chap, but I seem to have lost my way. Could you direct me to the nearest Metro Green Line station?"

As the lookout's eyes narrowed, focusing on his fake mustache, Jack made a short run at him, levering an elbow behind him. With a kick, he brought the man to his knees, whereupon he chopped down on his neck.

Jack grabbed him as he collapsed forward, and quickly dragged him over the embankment. Shielded by the low wall, he went through the lookout's pockets, finding his ID, an electronic access swipe card encased in plastic, and a CZ 75 SP-01 Phantom.

Pulling the lookout along behind him, he descended the steep slope of the embankment and laid him facedown in the water. Then he went along until he reached the water side of the warehouses. Because it was early, the canted shadow cast by the buildings lolled on the water side, and would cloak him temporarily.

He counted twenty-three paces from the northwest corner of the warehouse, then adjusted slightly for the conversion into feet. There, just as it appeared on the architectural blueprint, was the slipway to the water side. And there, just to the right and above it, was a video camera. Taking out a Fuji Instax camera, he circled around out of the lens's view and, standing just beneath it, took a shot of the gateway. When the photo hatched, he affixed it to one end of an extended car antenna, which he clamped to the video camera mount.

The first time he'd seen this trick was on an episode of the original *Mission Impossible* TV show. Since then, it had been repeated in films and TV shows so often it had become something of a minor espionage trope. He'd read that it had actually been the brainchild of William Joseph Donovan, the head of the wartime OSS. He had received a clandestine intelligence dossier, which he immediately marked EYES ONLY. The intel detailed the design and installation of a CCTV system in Peenemünde, for observing the launch of the Nazis' dreaded V-2 rockets. With his brilliant, forward-thinking mind, Donovan saw the future uses for CCTV systems guarding military installations, and, ironically, how to foil them.

Jack was counting to ten. He swung the photo into alignment, and heard the gratifying whir as the autofocus on the camera lens adjusted to the distance of the photo of the deserted slipway.

He had figured he'd have to pick the gateway's lock, but the look-out's swipe card made access that much simpler. Inserting the card, he waited for the telltale electronic double-click, then pushed the door in the slipway open and was immediately swallowed whole by the darkness of the interior. He switched on a pocket flashlight. Bringing out the newspaper and the clutch of fire starters he had bought, he separated the paper sections and crumpled them against the fire starters.

When he lit the pile, the flames shot up. He began to run.

"WHY DO you let him treat you like that?"

"Look at you." Reggie Herr stared at Alli. "I'm a fucking prince."

"I won't let Waxman intimidate me." She stared back.

"He was the bad twin." A sudden shaft of sunlight in the darkness. "I am the good one."

The misplaced pride in his voice caused her to shiver, and he, un-thinking, reached out for her. She could tell how much he still wanted to back her against the wall and fuck her. She pressed against him, her hands running down his sides.

"The good one," she whispered.

"Always."

"So that's why you obey Waxman." Her fingers wound and un-wound. "Who is he to you?"

The moment the words were out of her mouth, she knew she had made a mistake. Herr pushed her away and stumbled backward, as if her question had set off alarm bells inside his head.

"I'm really sorry, Herr. The good twin never needs to answer questions."

He nodded. "Damn straight."

"It's just that Waxman keeps asking me about you."

"He does?" Herr stepped closer; he didn't appear surprised. "Like what?"

"Like what you and I talk about."

Herr frowned. "You tell him?"

"Of course not. He doesn't have the right to know—"

"He's got a right," Herr said. "KWIfA gives him the right."

"KWIfA? What's that?"

A sly smile lit up Herr's face. "Only everything."

Just then the door swung open.

"Reggie, I've been looking for you," Waxman said as he stood at the threshold.

Herr was reluctant to take his eyes off Alli. "There was something that needed—"

"There's nothing here," Waxman said gently. "Nothing for you—or for me."

He gestured with his walking stick. "Come, now. It's time. McClure is in the building."

THE MOMENT the cell door clanged shut, Alli ripped off the tail of her shirt and threw it over the lens of the surveillance camera. Then she flicked open the gravity knife she had lifted from Reggie Herr's pocket. She had felt it the time he had almost succeeded in raping her. Now she applied the tip of its blade to the door's locking mechanism.

As she worked, she felt her heart lifting, her pulse drumming in her inner ear. Jack was here, he'd come to save her, just as he had before. But Waxman knew it, possibly also knew where he was. She had to get out of the cell to warn him.

The blade was too thick, she could only get the tip in. Retracting it, she slid the tip into the joint between floor and wall so the knife canted up at an angle. She stamped as hard as she could, bringing her heel down on the end of the hilt. The blade snapped, leaving a jagged edge, which she brought back to the door and inserted into the lock. Putting her ear against the door, she heard the tumblers falling into alignment the farther she worked the blade in.

A moment later, the door unlatched, and, swinging it open, she stepped into the corridor.

JACK HAD the plan of the warehouse interior in his head. It hovered like a theater scrim overlaying what he saw with his eyes. Quite soon after leaving the fire he had set, up a short set of metal stairs, he had come upon an illuminated hallway, carpeted in a dappled-gray, sound-absorbing material. He ran at top speed, knowing that his diversion would only give him a limited amount of time to find Alli and free her. Beyond that point, he was counting on the Escher-like configuration of rooms, staircases, and corridors, the staple of any black ops HQ, to keep him and Alli one step ahead of their pursuers until they got to the escape point he had chosen.

Hearing the clatter of boots descending a second flight of stairs, he shrank back into the shadows and, when two armed men came into view, he kicked one in the side of his knee and batted the other with the big, beautiful butt of the CZ. Jack smashed Knee Man in the mouth with the CZ's barrel, then disarmed both men.

As he leapt over their prone bodies, he heard orders being given on the upper landing, and paused, holding his breath.

". . . sure the girl is secure, then kill her," a voice came from above him.

Unfortunately, the sound-deadening carpet that had worked in his favor now kept him from knowing where the men had been dispatched. Rushing up the second flight, he found himself in a hallway identical to the one below—a key feature of the maze effect. He had just enough time to spot one of the men turning the far corner to his right before the man vanished. No sign of the order-giver. Jack took off after the men. He had to get to Alli before they did—and he didn't even know how many of *them* there were.

Owing to the high water table this close to the channel, the warehouses had no basements. That left the top floor. He was about to mount the stairs when he heard a voice and footsteps coming down. He could not afford the delay of another violent encounter.

Turning, he raced down the deserted corridor to the other end, where a back staircase, narrower and steeper, rose upward. This one must be the original, because it was old, abutting the original brick wall, which was covered with World War II graffiti. He paused midway up, shedding his empty duffel. It had one more use.

Reaching the top of the flight of stairs, he looked both ways. At the end of the corridor to his right, a metal ladder rose vertically through a cutout in the ceiling. Keeping the CZ at the ready, he reached it and climbed up. He paused with his head just below the lip of the cutout. He'd be going up blind, but what other choice did he have? He waited, listening intently, but heard not even the barest hint of a sound.

Poking his head up above the rim, he surveyed the empty corridor of bare, poured concrete. There was a distinct animal smell, as if emanating from a cattle pen. Four doors to his left led to what appeared to be a T, five to the right, with one at the end, thicker than the others, bolted: a cell door. That was where they were, with Alli! No time left. Levering himself into the corridor, he had taken two strides toward the cell when three men appeared from the closest rooms on either side, armed with handguns identical to his, holding him in what he could only surmise would, momentarily, be a lethal cross-fire.

ALLI, HIDING in a plumbing and electronic supply storeroom adjacent to her cell, saw it all, and her heart contracted. She had to do something. Now! She grabbed a large wrench and moved out into the hallway. Before she could fling it at one of the gunmen, Herr had her around her throat. He ripped the wrench from her hand and force-marched her with his knees toward where his men held Jack at gunpoint.

"Stop your infernal squirming," he said in her ear. But when she wouldn't obey he reached for his gravity knife.

Alli grasped the moment of his confusion at not finding it to slam her elbow into his side. He let up on his grip enough for her to deliver a backward kick into his groin. She ran toward Jack.

"No!" he shouted. "Alli, get the hell out of Dodge!"

"I'm not—" she began.

But he overrode her. "Just go, forget me, damn it. Cut your losses!"

One of the gunmen swiveled, leveled his CZ, and would have shot her in the stomach had not Jack's lunge knocked him off balance. Alli swerved as another gunman squeezed off a shot, which ricocheted past her shoulder, splintering a chunk of wall. Reaching the T at the far end of the corridor, she whipped to her left, Herr loping after her.

In all the chaos, Jack managed to draw his CZ, but the cold muzzle of a gun at the back of his head froze him.

"We can't have any of that, Mr. McClure."

It was the same voice that had given the orders. A dark thought swam into Jack's mind and he began to curse himself.

One of the gunmen reached over and disarmed him.

"I think we've had enough of your heroics for one day," the voice said from behind him.

"You're Waxman." It was a guess, but he felt a good one.

"Yes, and no," Werner Waxman said.

To his men, Waxman barked another order: "Take him to the cell."

The three men pushed and shoved Jack down the hall. When he stumbled, one of the men grasped his arm. Jack swung around, smashed him in the face, then spun, taking out a second guard. He saw the man with the walking stick out of the corner of his eye, tried to adjust his stance, then felt a needle enter his leg and something hot burning its way through his veins.

He tried mightily not to fall into the gunmen's arms, but it was useless. He was paralyzed. He could still see and hear, however.

"This is Alli's cell, one of three used during the war," Waxman said as the gunmen hurled Jack to the stinking concrete floor. "The cells stink of death even now, decades later. But you'll see for yourself as soon as Herr terminates her." He grinned. "He's been so patient, you know, waiting for this moment." The grin broadened like a waxing moon. "And so have I."

He limped to stand over Jack, who lay on his back, staring up at him. "It was never Alli I wanted, McClure, it was you. She was merely bait you couldn't resist." He shrugged. "I can't say I blame you, really. But you see how much of a liability she is to you. Better for all of us if Herr slits her throat."

He limped out, the door slamming shut behind him. From the hallway, Jack could hear Waxman's raised voice. "And here they are now."

"What do you want, Waxman?" Jack shouted. "Whatever it is, I'll give it to you." He struggled, but found it impossible to move. "Just promise you won't hurt her."

The door creaked slowly open and Waxman limped back into the room. "You mean that?"

"Of course I mean it."

"Then let us talk."

"Promise you won't harm Alli."

"A bargain struck." Waxman limped closer and leaned on his walking stick. "Your reputation precedes you, McClure. It is said there isn't a puzzle you can't solve." He began to circle Jack slowly, seemingly painfully. "Well, I have one for you. It's a puzzle disguised as a children's rhyme, and this is it: 'Ashur had a little horse, / Her mane as bright as gold. / And everywhere that Ashur went / The horse was sure to go.'" Waxman stopped directly in front of Jack. "What does it mean, McClure? What is the rhyme trying to tell me?"

"I don't know. How could you possibly expect me to know?"

"Who is Ashur?"

"I never heard of an Ashur."

"Who or what is the horse with the golden mane?"

"You're asking the wrong person."

"But, you see, I'm not, McClure. Because I believe the horse with the golden mane is Annika Dementieva, which is what Annika Batchuk calls herself."

"What would give you that idea?"

"Because in some way I cannot understand, her Dyadya Gourdjiev is involved."

"Whatever it is," Jack said, "I have no knowledge of it."

"Even though you were just with them in Moscow."

Jack said nothing.

"I see." Waxman limped to the door, opened it, and went through.

"Wait!" Jack called. "Remember our bargain!"

"You told me nothing. We have no bargain, McClure." Waxman's voice came through the door. "Besides, it's already too late. Blood has already been spilled."

PART THREE

December 13–December 19

Every generation rewrites the past. In easy times history is more or less of an ornamental art, but in times of danger we are driven to the written record by a pressing need to find answers to the riddles of today.
—JOHN DOS PASSOS, *The Ground We Stand On*

EIGHTEEN

"... HAS ALREADY been spilled," Waxman said into the empty hallway. He had waved his men back to their previous positions. He lifted his handgun and pulled the trigger, the report echoing through the corridor and, he was quite certain, through the cell door behind which McClure must be listening with every fiber of his body. The idea was to exterminate any hope McClure might have that Alli Carson could be saved.

"It's over, McClure," he said as he retreated down the corridor. "She died quickly, if not well."

"WHY AREN'T you afraid?"

With the knife at her throat and Radomil gripping her like iron bonds, Annika said, "Why do you want me to be afraid?"

"Fear makes everyone vulnerable. Even you."

"Radomil, let's stop this. You won't kill me."

He heaved a sigh from the depths. "You see how it is." He took the blade from her throat, wiped the blood off its razor edge with his forefinger. "You're a better person than I am. You have *his* genes." He gestured toward Dyadya Gourdjiev, inside the restaurant.

"What chance did you have, Radomil? Oriel Jovovich delivered you and Grigori into other hands."

"And I never stop asking myself *why*. Why did he do what he did?"

"Because you were boys. He had no interest in—"

"What he did to you."

"—abusing you."

He picked his head up and glanced down the Veneto. "Look where we are, in a section of Rome forgotten except by tourists who don't know that time has passed them by."

"Meeting here was your idea."

"It's secure."

"The overwhelming sadness makes it secure." She put an arm around his waist. "You did good."

One corner of his mouth lifted in a brief, ironic smile. "Life is like a train, each station bringing with it more sadness." He said this without a trace of self-pity, which had been burned out of him at an early age shortly after he and Grigori had been taken from their mother. He took a deep breath, let it out slowly. "That's another reason I chose this venue. Its sadness is all that keeps it from sliding into the Tiber and being swallowed whole."

Annika allowed a short silence to build, before she interrupted it. "Please let me help you, Radomil."

That ghost of a smile again. "What makes you think—"

"This has to be your decision, no one else can make it for you."

"But how can I be—"

"You can't be sure," she said. "Isn't that the point? About life, about everything?"

"You see this road? It twists and turns like a snake. It has shed its original skin, it has become something else. This is the truth, it is irrefutable." He watched her, tense and waiting.

"Nothing is the way we want it to be, nothing is the way it seems today. Even the snake, even Via Veneto. What lies around tomorrow's corner? You must have faith."

"Ah, now I understand you." He nodded. "But faith cannot exist without love. And you must understand what I mean because you have read the file that . . ." He faltered, his voice trailing off as he looked away again.

"That was the point of the experiments," she finished for him. "But I also know that we're all human beings, not machines." She touched his heart with her forefinger. "Somewhere in there is the child, no matter how damaged, who was born to Marion Oldham and Oriel Jovovich."

He made an animal sound in the back of his throat. "And what about Grigori?"

"Grigori is not like you."

"But that's the whole point of the experiment!" Radomil cried. "To make us identical in every way, to make us killing machines who would think alike, take orders—any orders—without question."

"And I repeat, Grigori is beyond redemption, but you are not. You are loved, Radomil. Your mother loves you, I love you."

He looked at her.

"Yes, it's true. You're my brother, my flesh and blood."

His eyes narrowed. "And Grigori?"

"We have spoken too much of your brother."

"He, too, is your flesh and blood."

"He has chosen his path, Radomil. You have chosen your own." She smiled gently. "So you see, love is alive. Only you can kill it." The bow of her lips parted. "Is that what you want? To destroy the thing you desire most?"

Radomil's hands curled into fists, the skin across the knuckles stretched and white. "This was the test to which Grigori and I were put. It was so easy for him, so difficult for me. We were meant to destroy the thing we loved most. That was our final exam."

"Good God!" she said, almost physically recoiling from his words. "Does my grandfather know this?"

Radomil shook his head.

"Then you must tell him," she said, linking her arm through his and leading him back to the restaurant.

Radomil peered in through the window. "I am afraid of him."

"Yes," she said. "We're all afraid of him."

———

VERA WATCHED, stunned, as Chris Fraine picked his way toward his twin. On the way, he paused, turning toward her.

"Don't move," he said.

She nodded mutely.

Alan Fraine lay where the bullets had propelled him, his back propped against the shop's side wall. He was still alive, breathing like a bellows full of holes, which just about summed up the state of his lungs.

Chris Fraine squatted down in front of him. "So it's come to this."

Alan Fraine opened his mouth, but only a low gurgle emerged, along with a thin drool of blood.

"This is your reward for taking the high road," Chris said. "You can't say I didn't warn you. I wanted you with me, despite what Vater Nacht planned for us. I went against the program and he never forgave me. But you—you were his bully-boy, weren't you? Bad genes reversed by whatever infernal methods he used. I'd kill him if I could, but I can't. His infernal methods are at least that strong inside me. Alan's breathing abruptly turned more labored. Chris sighed. "But I did the next best thing. I killed you."

He stood then and, turning on his heel, addressed Vera. "And what, might I ask, is your part in this passion play?"

By this time, Vera had regained a measure of both her equilibrium and her bravado. "I didn't know your brother and I don't know you. My concern is—*was*—Moses Malliot. It was his Town Car into which my . . . friend . . . Alli Carson was bundled."

Chris Fraine approached her, clearly intrigued. "Bundled?"

"She was abducted," Vera said, unsure how much to tell him. "Near the *Titanic* Memorial, by a man named Werner Waxman."

Chris shook his head. "Who?"

"The man with the limp," she said.

"I have no idea what you're talking about." He moved even closer. "But because you being here at the same time as Alan can't be a coincidence, I want to know." He reached out and grabbed her just as Nona burst through the front door, service pistol at the ready.

REGGIE HERR, racing down the hallway, realized that he had unaccountably lost the Carson girl. He brought himself up short. How had that happened? He was right behind her as she turned the corner, but now the hallway leered emptily at him.

Three doors, three possibilities. Methodically, he kicked open one door after another, checking the offices, the windows, any places the little rat could hide. Nothing. But in the last room, he found a window that had been cranked open. Leaning out, he saw that an intrepid person—especially one with minimum body weight like the little rat—could leap into the water without a problem.

Cursing under his breath, he turned on his heel and belted out of the room, along the corridor, clattering down staircase after staircase, and out the slipway door. He prowled the shoreline for a good ten minutes without seeing a sign of her. At last, forced to face facts, he stopped looking. She was gone.

THE MOMENT Chris Fraine saw Nona, he turned and fled into the rear of the shop. She might have gone after him, but she saw Alan propped against the wall, blood pooled around him, and she immediately dropped to her knees in front of him.

"Alan," she whispered. And then, as she placed two fingers against his carotid, "Alan!"

Vera started after Chris, but froze when Nona commanded her to stay right where she was.

"But that man—"

"Forget him," Nona said. She was already speaking to central dispatch, identifying herself. "Officer and civilian down." She wept as she gave their location. When she was done, she punched in Paull's number. He wasn't answering, so she left a message on his voice mail.

She put a palm against her boss's cheek. "What man, Vera?"

"You know who I am?"

"I don't know much of anything right now," Nona said, "but I know that."

Vera came toward her. "I need protection."

Nona gently closed Alan's staring eyes, and somehow thought about Frankie, lying dead to the world in his hospital room while a complicated mechanism breathed for him. "Christ almighty," she breathed, "don't we all."

ALLI, SUSPENDED above the open window, gripped the narrow overhang with the tips of her curled fingers. The toes of her shoes desperately scrabbled for purchase on the wooden siding. She sensed, rather than saw, Reggie Herr stick his head out the window and peer down into the Washington Channel. When she risked a circumspect glance down, she saw the window was clear, and, arms and shoulders aching, she clambered down and let herself back inside.

For a moment she sat on the sill, head between her legs, taking deep breaths. Then she rose and, crossing the room, opened the door and peeked out. The corridor was clear. She stole out, listening with every part of her body—voices, footfalls, vibrations, the small, sharp noises of metal on metal, like rats scurrying in the walls.

"*Get the hell out of Dodge!*" Jack had said to her, a coded message, one of several he had insisted she memorize. Knowing full well that at any moment she could be in danger, the two of them had set up a number of contingency codes. *Get the hell of Dodge* meant that he had left something for her—something that would help her escape. However, as she moved stealthily down the corridor toward the back stairs, she knew that she had no intention of escaping—not until she had found Jack and freed him. He had come for her twice, at extreme peril to himself. There was no way she was going to leave him here and run back to Fearington. As she picked her way along, she thought of Jack, of everything he had taught her, and she thought of Sensei and everything he had pounded into her.

Whatever she knew now wasn't going to be enough, she had no illusions about that, but for the moment, at least, it would have to suffice for the job at hand.

Reaching the narrow set of stairs, she cocked her head, listening intently. She heard no one moving up or down, so she began to descend from the top floor. Where would Jack have left whatever it was he had left for her? It had to be somewhere he felt would be safe; it would also have to be a place he had come across. She knew how Jack's mind worked, knew he would never have attempted to infiltrate this place without having a clear idea of the interior. If he'd seen architectural plans, Secretary Paull surely would have procured them for him, which meant Paull could very well be involved in the mission. But she also knew Paull never would have agreed to send Jack in alone. This meant that Paull's people must have already thrown a cordon around the area. All she and Jack needed to do was get themselves outside and Paull's men would do the rest.

She reached the landing of the next floor down. Jack had appeared near the other end of the corridor—he hadn't come this way. She began to creep slowly along, then paused, turning around. What made her think he hadn't come this way? She was thinking like Waxman's security people, not like Jack.

Retracing her steps, she peered down the back stairway to the next level. The brick wall was covered with graffiti. Midway down was a fuse-box door, set flush with the wall. The fuse box seemed to ripple and distort, and, the next moment, the image of Emma appeared, translucent, wavering, as if shivered by an invisible wind.

"Emma?"

Alli had only taken a couple of steps down when a security guard trotting up the stairs came into view. Seeing her, he opened his mouth to shout, but Alli threw the knife she had taken off Reggie. He put up a hand as it hit his cheek a glancing blow, but that was enough to give her the opening she needed. Flying down the stairs, she kicked him backward. He fell heavily, bouncing down the treads, and she followed him. It was well that she did, because his hand came up, pointing his gun at her. Her left leg flicked out, the side of her foot knocking the weapon out of his hand.

He leapt up and came at her, and she let him, just as Sensei had taught her in aikido class. As he reached out to grab her, she used his own momentum, grasping the extended arm, pulling him into her. Locking her leg behind his knee, she landed an elbow strike to the nape of his neck. His face crashed into the metal stair beside her, and he lay still.

Alli took possession of the knife and the fallen guard's CZ, searched for extra bullets, and pocketed them, then turned away to look for Emma. She was gone. Only the fuse box stared back at her, silent and enigmatic. Did it mean something? She stepped closer and saw a chalk mark, a small circle.

"Cut your losses and chalk it up to experience," Jack had shouted at the end.

Chalk. Reaching out, she rubbed off the chalk mark with her fingertip. Then she inserted the end of the broken blade into the door's lock and worked it gently back and forth.

The instant the door popped open, a nearly empty duffel bag, folded in on itself, fell into her arms. She moved beneath a light, unzipped the duffel, and peered inside.

"YOU'RE ON the wrong side of history," Grigori said. "Again."

Caro frowned. "Explain yourself."

He looked away, out the limo's smoked window, at the murky morning. "We've been in here for hours and I have to empty my bladder. Do you plan to hold me prisoner forever?"

"The quicker you give me answers, the faster I'll let you go."

"Not until you put away the gun. I've had enough of you waggling it in my face."

Caro set the gun down on the seat next to her, but she didn't put it away. Caro had driven Grigori's limo out of the construction site before the workers showed up. They were parked in a spot overlooking the World War II memorial. Caro wore a black baseball-style cap with a white FBI embroidered on it she had purchased from a vendor on Constitution. The bill was pulled low on her forehead, throwing her face into deep shadow.

When he leaned forward, peering through the partition at the weapon lying on the seat, she said, "Best I can do. Now spill."

" 'Spill.' What's become of you?" He shook his head. "You sound so damn American."

She shrugged. "It is what it is."

"I assumed—incorrectly, I see—that your time with the Syrian taught you things."

"Oh, it did, but not what you think. I learned I don't like being allied with the wrong people. I don't like getting their shit all over me."

"We're all tarred with the same brush, Caro. It's a matter of survival."

She made a face. "For you, maybe. Not for me."

"You're no better than the rest of us, Caro. You're fooling yourself if you think otherwise."

"If making my own decisions is fooling myself, then bring it on!"

"Sooner or later, the Syrian will catch up to you. And when he does—"

"Is that who you're taking orders from now, Grigori? The Syrian?"

"God, no! I steer as clear of him as I possibly can."

"And when that becomes impossible?"

"I go down on one knee and look away."

"Bravo! The perfect vassal!"

"I have a lot of my life left to live, Caro. What would you have me do?"

She snorted. "Please."

"So I should adopt your solution? Become a fugitive?"

She looked hard at him. "You still don't get it. For people like you and me, there *is* no solution. We're doomed by both genes and circumstance. The most we can hope for is a decent life until the violent end comes."

"You! Unlike me, you have an out. You can always go back to your father."

"With my tail between my legs!"

"But what a magnificent tail it is!"

She laughed then, puncturing the mounting tension that had risen between them like a medieval wall bristling with spears, catapults, and boiling oil.

"Always the charmer," she said, "even when holding a knife to my throat."

"It's you who has the weapon," he pointed out.

She waved away his words. "You were speaking about history and taking sides."

"I'd meant it as a threat, actually."

"Something's changed?"

He shrugged. "You have inexplicably aligned yourself with Alli Carson."

"She is my cousin."

"I can't see the relevance."

"Then look again."

"I've seen all I need to. She and Jack McClure are tight."

"And?"

"McClure is fucking Annika Dementieva. Her grandfather is Dyadya Gourdjiev."

"Who someone has convinced you is evil incarnate."

He ignored her. "McClure is the key—to everything."

"You'll have to explain that."

"Fuck you, missy!"

For an instant, her eyes flicked down to the gun. But as she reached for it, Grigori slammed the back of his hand across her cheek. She rocked backward while still scrabbling for the gun, and Grigori was upon her, launching himself through the open partition, his superior weight bearing her down onto her back. He knocked the gun away, but in such close quarters it was far too dangerous to fire.

He glimpsed his driver, dead in the footwell, as he hauled his legs through to the front seat. Then his hands fitted around her throat as if they were always meant to be there.

"You stupid, stupid bitch," he said as he throttled her. "I see you for the predator you are. You're heartless. You never loved me. And I loved you so very much."

His face was empurpled, his features distorted by the force of this rage erupting from the depths. "You stupid, stupid bitch. I gave you every opportunity to change your mind, to keep yourself safe, and what did you do? Did you accept? No. Did you ignore me? No, again. You mocked me."

He pressed down with a gathering strength that bordered on the berserk. The spark of reason had fled from his eyes, his mind was mired in a red haze that extinguished his connection to everything else, dislocated him from society, conventions, even history. He was exiled, alone with his rage—manufactured rage that, too late, Caro understood had been grafted onto him at an early age. He had become something else, something beyond or below human.

Her eyes were protruding, her lungs were burning, her windpipe nearly crushed. She stared up into the face of a creature completely unknown to her.

NINETEEN

APART FROM a Magic Marker and a piece of chalk, the duffel was empty. Alli plucked out the Magic Marker, curious. Then she turned the duffel inside out and discovered the map Jack had drawn of the interior of the warehouse abutting the Washington Channel. Not only had Jack shown her where Waxman had taken her, but he also had given her a way out. For the third time, she traced the route he had outlined on the map, committing it to memory. Then, returning the duffel to its original state, she zipped it up and stowed it back in the fuse box.

She wasn't going anywhere without him. Mounting the stairs, she reached the penultimate floor without encountering anyone. The corridor was eerily silent. She heard no voices as she approached the vertical ladder up to the floor where Waxman had kept her locked away and where she now assumed they were holding Jack. Moving hand over hand, she ascended, pausing on each rung to listen for voices or footfalls on the bare concrete. Nothing. But she knew only too well how Jack had been ambushed in the hallway, so she proceeded with extreme caution. She was so focused on what might be waiting above her that she was taken completely by surprise when someone grabbed her legs from below, ripping her from her perch.

REGGIE HERR strapped Jack to a gurney.

"I've learned over the years the human capacity to feel is as difficult to kill as a cockroach or a tick," Waxman said as he bent over Jack.

Reggie guided the gurney toward the open cell door. They crossed the threshold, into the corridor.

Waxman continued, "But imagine that ungainly mess of feelings burned out of you. Imagine what you would be like then. The purity of purpose to which you could dedicate yourself, like a monk or a guru, cleansed, ennobled, at last able to reach for perfection.

"This has been my life's work, McClure."

ALLI FELL against the bottom of the ladder, and almost immediately felt an arm around her throat as she was lifted off her feet. The man behind her braced for her to squirm, but instead she let herself go limp, forcing him to adjust his grip on her. Slamming the side of her handgun against the side of his head, she slipped from his grip, turned, and brought the butt of the weapon down on his forehead. He kept coming, ignoring the blood streaming down his face, so she drove her fist into his kidney. As he crumpled sideways, she struck him a vicious blow behind his ear. He went down and stayed down.

She was about to step over him to remount the ladder when she heard the whine of an elevator motor.

WAXMAN PURSED his lips. "It was your ill fortune that you landed in Annika Dementieva's web, eh? She got to you, turned you inside out. Pity for you—but not for me, eh?"

The gurney arrived in front of an elevator, Reggie pressed the Down button, and the car lurched into service.

"Annika and her grandfather have been a thorn in my side for some time. That ancient fucker is Nosferatu—he never dies. And now he has you as well as Annika as one of his guardian angels."

The elevator arrived and the door slid open. Reggie began to guide the gurney inside when Alli, hands gripping the top of the opening, swung out of the car, the impact of her boots slamming him backward off his feet. Reggie bounced off the opposite wall and, when he came back toward her, she scissored her legs around him, trapping his neck between her thighs.

Reggie tried to get his arms up, but Alli, gripping his ears, jerked his head around. Waxman, recovering from his shock, lifted his gun, but Jack, working his body, slammed the gurney into Waxman's side. He eeled his body so that the left strap rode up to his biceps. He swung his arm out in a shallow arc, catching Waxman's rib cage as he stumbled.

Alli, seeing there was no time, slammed the palms of her hands against Reggie's ears. His jaws opened in a nearly soundless scream, and she disengaged her legs. He took two staggering steps before collapsing, hands to the sides of his head.

Waxman still held on to his gun, but Alli, chopping down hard, took care of that. She held him at gunpoint and said, "Unbuckle the straps, Mr. Waxman." And when he hesitated: "It's now or never for you."

Waxman nodded and, turning to the gurney, freed Jack.

"Are you okay?" Alli asked him.

"Still a little groggy. Whatever the hell was in that cane packed a wallop."

"Tell me about it."

Jack swung his legs over and stood up, holding on to the gurney until he was able to try out his legs. They no longer felt like rubber bands.

Alli looked around nervously. "The sooner we get the hell out of here, the better."

"Not without him," Jack said, grabbing Waxman. He looked hard into Waxman's eyes. "You have a shitload to answer for."

He drove his fist into Waxman's solar plexus, doubling the older man over. Grabbing a fistful of hair, he pulled the older man erect as Alli bent to retrieve the walking stick Waxman had dropped.

"Forensics will have a holiday with this," she said.

Jack manhandled Waxman onto the gurney, strapped him down, and wheeled him into the waiting elevator.

When Alli was inside, he pressed the button for the first floor. "You got my message?"

Alli nodded. "Loud and clear."

It was then that he noticed the CZ stuck in the waistband of her jeans. "If you had a beard you'd pass for Che Guevara."

"Very funny."

As the lights counted down the floors, she stowed Waxman's walking stick under one arm, then drew out the CZ.

"Who the hell knows what we'll meet with when this thing comes to a stop."

"The warehouse is mostly deserted." Jack turned. "How many men do you have in here, Waxman?"

Waxman stared up at him, stony-faced. Reaching across him, Jack hit the Stop button with the heel of his hand.

"What are you doing?" Alli said.

He held out his hand. "Walking stick." When she handed it over, he took a quick inventory, found the button that released the dart. Hovering it over Waxman's chest, he said, "Tell me, Waxman, how many toxins does this thing hold? Still not talking?" He tapped his thumb lightly against the button. "I know what happens when this crap is injected into an extremity. Let's see what happens when it's shot directly into the heart."

"Wait!" Waxman licked his lips. "That would not be wise."

"The hell it wouldn't," Jack said, puncturing the cloth of Waxman's shirt. "You can tell me everything I want to know before your heart stops."

Alli plucked at his sleeve. "Jack, please, we can't stay here forever."

Jack stared down at Waxman. "How many?"

Waxman stared back. "How many what?"

Jack pushed the needle in farther.

"Six," Waxman said. "I have six men."

Alli snorted. "In addition to that shit, Herr."

Jack turned to her. "What?"

"Yeah, the fucker who abducted me, who you sent out the motel window, has a twin brother."

Waxman kicked out, the toe of his shoe connecting with the Stop button. The elevator lurched into motion and, before Jack could reach it, they had descended to the first floor. The doors slid open, revealing two of Waxman's men, handguns drawn.

GRIGORI BATCHUK was breathing like a bellows. The taste of bile was so bitter he turned his head and spat. Staring down at Caroline Carson's inert body brought waves of the past crashing against the ragged shore of his conscious mind. In the space of thirty seconds, he relived his entire affair with her, spanning both years and continents. His red-rimmed eyes saw her not as she was now, but as she had been the first moment he had seen her, walking down the rocky shingle, the pale froth of Nice's waterfront hotels behind her. Her hair had come undone, was fluttering in the sea breeze like a bird's wing. Her slim limbs were toasty-tanned. The sun was in her eyes. In that moment, his heart escaped the prison of his chest and took flight, arriving in her hand as she bent to lift a small oval stone, running the pad of her thumb back and forth over its water-smoothed surface.

Without another thought, he had gone up to her and introduced himself. She had gazed into his face for a moment, then, without a word, turned on her heel and picked her way back up to the pedestrian corniche. He stood, shoes and socks in one hand, his trousers rolled up to his calves, his toes squidging into the farthest edge of the water. He remembered putting his free hand up to shade his eyes, for he hadn't had the foresight to purchase either sunglasses or a hat. He watched her as she leaned against the iron railing while she stared at something—what, he couldn't tell—higher up in the city's streets. Then, again without warning, she turned, elbows on the rail, and stared down at him with what seemed to him the hint of a smile, an enigmatic expression.

After a moment of indecision, he went to her. The rocks hurt the soles of his bare feet, but he scarcely noticed. He watched her face come closer and closer, though, in fact, it was he who was drawing closer.

"You came," she said, when he had arrived beside her. "How nice."

That had been the beginning. He refocused his eyes on her body, draped across his lap like a Madonna. *Is this how it ends,* he wondered, *with my hands around your throat, squeezing the life out of you? What happened to my love for you? In what terrible fire did it burn? Where did the acid hatred, the wellspring of violence, come from? How did the murder happen? How have I landed here?*

When she stirred, coughing and gasping, he literally jumped. Then someone pounded on the window. Slowly and reluctantly, as in a dream, he tore his eyes away from Caro, thinking, *This can't be happening.* The pounding came again, Caro's arm fluttered like the wing of a bird. Her chest shuddered, her severely reddened neck pulsed. Her eyes opened, focusing on him. The hint of an enigmatic smile, that curious expression from the Nice waterfront, reappeared, annihilating time and space.

The smoked glass cracked inward, held together only by the thin sheet of anti-shatter film. Then even that was staved in by another titanic blow, and he was looking into the fierce, beefy faces of two uniformed cops. Their eyes darkened as they surveyed the scene. They drew their service pistols.

"You," one of them ordered. "Get your ass the fuck out of there!"

JACK SHOVED the gurney at the two men, and Alli shot one in the chest. The other ducked away and Jack went after him, but he slithered under the gurney and, grabbing Alli, threw her against the wall. She cried out, clutched her left shoulder with her gun hand. Jack leapt at the man, but he turned and fired.

Alli looked up to see Reggie Herr pounding full speed down the hall. She raised her good arm and squeezed off a shot, but she was in pain and shock—her aim was off. Reggie kept on coming.

"Jack!" she cried. "Behind you!"

Jack's gaze shifted, but the gunman slammed his fist into the side of Jack's head. They grappled at close quarters, Jack holding the gun at bay while the man pummeled him over and over. Glancing at Reggie, the man broke off his assault, rose off Jack, and began to run in the opposite direction. Jack shook himself, got to hands and knees, and then he was up, running after the man.

Alli had just enough time to spot Reggie pushing Waxman on the gurney into the elevator when the front door burst inward and a squad of heavily armed Marines in flak jackets thundered into the warehouse.

TWENTY

"DON'T TOUCH anything," Nona said as she guided Vera away from the bodies. She knew she should get the girl out of there, but she couldn't bear to leave Alan alone.

Vera nodded numbly.

"Who do you need protection from?" Nona asked.

"It's a long story."

"As of now," Nona said, looking into Alan's thousand-yard stare, "I've got nothing but time." She wondered what his last thought had been.

Vera felt out of time, drained of bravado, wanting now only shelter from the storm of violence that had been raging around her ever since she had spied on Alli's abduction. She heard the oncoming sirens, then stood silently by as the men and women piled into the shop. A pair of detectives spoke to Nona in lowered voices, nodding as they snapped on gloves and made their way to the bodies, along with the forensics people. Nona waited until the photos had been taken, everything bagged and tagged, and Alan was put on a gurney.

Then she took Vera outside onto the street. A pair of patrol cars, an unmarked car, two ambulances, and the crime scene forensics van were pulled up to the curb. The uniforms had secured the crime scene, keeping the gathering crowd at a safe distance. Now the police had begun to canvass the closest people to determine if anyone had seen someone running from the rear of the building.

Nona sent one of the uniforms to scare up a couple of Cokes and some chips. Then she led Vera to her car, where they sat with the doors open because both of them needed the fresh air.

They sat in silence, which wasn't what Nona wanted, but the specter of Alan's death clung to her like cordite. She could not believe he was gone, and tears sprang to her eyes, others following, and would not leave no matter how hard she squeezed her eyes shut.

As a distraction, she tried Paull again, and this time got him. She told him in broad strokes what had happened.

"How are you?" he asked.

"Fine," she lied. And to get him off the subject, "I'm with Vera Bard, taking down her statement."

"Bring her to the eighth floor of Bethesda when you're through. I've had the entire floor sealed off and secured." There was a pause. "Nona, I'm deeply sorry for your loss."

Nona could not speak, and broke the connection. She sat for a moment, rocking gently back and forth, as if to console herself.

An officer arrived, ducking his head and speaking softly. They all knew she had lost her boss. She thanked him, and handed a Coke to Vera.

Some time passed before she found her voice. "Okay." She cleared her throat. "Start at the beginning and don't stop until you've reached the end."

"Shit," Vera said, sipping her Coke, "don't I feel like Alice at the Mad Hatter's tea party."

Nona pulled open a chip bag and held it out to Vera. "How so?"

"Nothing makes any sense." Vera, guzzling down the soda, felt the caffeine kick in, and she crunched down on the chips, the salt cutting the sugar in her mouth.

"So we'll try to do something about that."

Nona, trying her best not to think about Alan, flipped open her pad and, as Vera began to talk, first slowly and haltingly, then in a gush of filthy memories, took down notes as fast as she could.

RADOMIL STARED into Annika's eyes. "There is only one way you can help me, and I know you will not do it."

"Try me."

His smile was both knife-edged and weary. "Your grandfather holds the key. Only he knows where it is."

Annika looked puzzled. "Where what is?"

Radomil's smile turned mocking. "You mean he hasn't told you?" He shook his head. "Sorry, Sister, I don't believe you."

"You mean his cache of secrets."

Radomil gave a soundless laugh. "That! My father told me what a lie that was." He grabbed her shoulders. "Listen, Annika, if that's what your *dyadya* has been telling you, it's a lie."

"I don't—"

He turned her so that she was looking through the café window to where Gourdjiev sat, drinking and talking on a mobile phone. "Oh, he's got a secret, all right. And a goddamned big one it is, too. He knows where the Gaddafi family fortune has been stored. That's billions, Annika. Billions. He knows where it is and how to get to it. My father wanted it and so does Three-thirteen. You've heard of Three-thirteen?"

"Yes," she said hoarsely. "I've heard of them."

"Then you know about Acacia."

"I know what happened to the original team. It was sent to find the Gaddafi fortune, ostensibly as a last attempt to bring him down. Without his fortune—"

"Three-thirteen couldn't care less about Gaddafi. In fact, it has investments with him all around Africa—hotels, casinos, seaside resorts. No, it's greed, pure and simple. When it comes to politics, Three-thirteen is totally agnostic."

He let her go, an expression of disgust on his face. "I know that look. You don't believe a word I'm saying, and why should you? Why should you believe that your beloved *dyadya*, who brought you up, would lie to you? After all, he came and saved you from Father, didn't he?"

"He was an angel, my savior."

He shook his head. "An angel with devil's wings. He didn't have the political strength to oppose Father openly, so he skulked around like a thief in the night." He puffed out his cheeks. "So. What did he actually do? He introduced a beautiful, highly desirable woman to Father, knowing full well the monster Father was. He sacrificed my mother in order to get you back, like a package of gold or diamonds stolen from him. He didn't want you, he wanted to win.

"And he did. Father couldn't have you around, couldn't afford to have Mother asking questions about you. Poor little orphan sister. No one wanted you."

"You can't manipulate human emotions like that. Love is chemical, not the result of intrigue."

"No? Isn't that what your kindly grandfather did with you and Jack McClure?"

"That's different."

"In what way?" He spread his hands. "Please tell me, I'd like to know."

"As I said, it's chemical. Sometimes you have no control whatsoever." Annika laughed uneasily. "In any event, I've heard your lies about your mother."

"From who? Your beloved Dyadya, doubtless."

"Marion loved Oriel, despite his cruelty and willfulness." She turned away from him. "I've had my fill. You disgust me."

"Annika, my dear sister, you haven't heard the whole story."

"More lies?" She whipped around to face him. "Go peddle them elsewhere. I'm not in the least bit interested."

"You're not interested in the fact that your grandfather recruited a foreigner named Marion Oldham, that he trained her, knowing as only he could all the intimate details that fired Father's erotic imagination?"

Annika was at once shaking and scarcely breathing.

"And when he was finished training her, he sent her out, just as he did you, to accomplish her mission and, in the process, be utterly destroyed."

———

WHEN HENRY Holt Carson entered his hunting lodge in Virginia, he knew he wasn't alone. Stepping to a side table in the foyer, he reached under it and drew out a 9mm Glock. Double-checking that it was loaded, he went carefully from room to room until he came upon the two men sitting in his library.

He dropped his gun hand to his side and walked in. "You look like you've been through the mill," he said to Waxman.

"Sit down, Hank," Waxman said darkly. "We need to talk."

"Really?" Carson seemed skeptical as he went over to a sideboard and poured himself a stiff single-batch bourbon and water. "Did you use your trainee to break in here?"

"It wasn't so difficult as all that." Waxman ignored the look Reggie shot him.

Carson returned to where the two were sitting without offering either of them a drink. "I don't like uninvited guests. Explain yourself."

A brief flush reddened Waxman's face, fading as slowly as a summer sunset. "I can no longer tolerate your intransigence."

Carson paused his hand in midair. "Meaning?"

"It is imperative that we deploy Acacia now."

Now Carson put the glass to his lips and took a sip, savoring the slightly sweet liquor. "A setback, Werner. You've suffered a setback."

"We're all in this together," Reggie growled.

Carson rounded on him. "Shut your mouth. Monkeys are seen, not heard."

Herr's black eyes smoldered and his fingers gripped the arms of his seat.

"If you score the leather, you'll pay for a new chair," Carson pointed out.

"This isn't about either Reggie or your precious chair," Waxman said.

Carson ignored him. He continued to stare at Herr.

Waxman sighed. "Reggie, please."

Herr rose. When he was on the other side of the room, Carson turned to Waxman. "Okay, Waxman, how did you fuck up this time?"

There was a small, deadly silence. Then Waxman stirred. "There's a problem with McClure."

Carson grunted. "There's always a problem with McClure." Finishing his drink, he turned and, at the sideboard, took his time pouring himself another. "And now you need me to haul your ass out of the crapper."

Waxman, uncharacteristically, said nothing. Crossing one leg over the other, he busied himself picking an imaginary bit of lint off his trousers. When sufficient time had passed to afford him some measure of face, he said, "McClure's involvement necessitates we move up the timetable. Time is now of the essence. I need the information."

"Because you fucked up."

Waxman remained mute. Not that that helped him.

"No other reason."

"It's been decided by Three-thirteen. Fetch the information."

Carson crossed to a humidor, opened it, and took out a cigar. He rolled it between his fingers, then held it under his nose. At length, he stuck it in his mouth, clicked open his lighter, and got the thing going. Waxman seemed rooted to the chair while this carnival sideshow was being enacted, but he did not look at Carson. His eyes were fastened on a section of empty space as if they could harness it and whip it until it bled.

When the cigar was going and great clouds of aromatic smoke drifted up to the beamed ceiling, Carson left the room without a word.

Reggie stirred. "Fuck. I think—"

"Damnit, you were supposed to take care of Alli Carson, and what happened? You let her get away. Now I have to take Carson's shit."

Herr's eyes glowed darkly. "I will get her back. Trust me."

Waxman levered himself out of the chair. "You'd better."

Carson, black notebook in hand, stood in the hallway, just out of sight of the two men. He found, after hearing his niece's name spoken by Waxman, that he was paralyzed. Though he wanted to take a step, he could not, neither forward nor back. His heart slowed to a glacial pace and his lungs refused to work. His breath was being squeezed out of him by an iron fist. His eyes began to water at the same moment the pain bloomed in his chest and slashed down his left arm. The world started to cant over.

God help me, I'm done, he thought.

"HER MISSION?" Annika said, slightly breathless. "What was your mother's mission?"

"What do you think? To get inside Father's head, to be the mole your grandfather so desperately needed to level the playing field between him and Father." He regarded her with a degree of cynicism. "So as to my mother's professed love for me, why should I trust it? She's been living a lie from the moment she met Father. And you—your entire existence is built of one lie on top of another. Why should I believe anything either of you say?"

"Because when it comes to love, no lies are possible. Love bares the bones of truth."

"And what can that mean to me?" he said with a good measure of contempt. "I, who have had love burned out of me. When it comes to love, I'm the perfect fool." The flat of his hand cut through the air between them. "Like the sirens who attempted to lure Odysseus, love seeks only to destroy me."

Radomil peered in again at the old man, who was still on his cell, either on the same call or a new one. "Ask him yourself."

Annika hesitated until her half-brother moved past her to the café door. "Wait," she said. "You tell me."

Radomil turned back. He crossed his arms over his chest. "Your grandfather was intent on using every means necessary."

"To get me back."

"For the fortune he was intent on accumulating."

Annika seemed shaken once again. "How would setting Marion down in the center of Oriel's life do that?"

He shrugged. "He thought Father knew where that fortune was."

"Did Oriel know?"

"Stop calling him Oriel. He was your father, too."

She ignored him. "He abused me in every way imaginable, then he abandoned me. You he simply abandoned."

"No. He sold us into slavery."

"Sold you?"

"Grigori and I were payment. In exchange, Father was to get the coordinates to the fortune."

"So Grandfather was right."

Radomil was about to answer when, peering through the window, he saw a figure emerge from the rear of the café, pick his way circumspectly between the tables, and slide into a chair opposite Gourdjiev. At once, the old man broke off his conversation and folded away his mobile.

As the two men put their heads together, Radomil said, "Who's that?"

"I don't know."

But he had seen that she hadn't bothered to look inside the café. "I think you know very well who it is."

"Sorry. You're mistaken."

"Like hell I am. Tell me—"

"Now that you've given me your reasons for hating Grandfather, it seems likely that you helped Grigori to keep us from leaving Russia."

"Don't be absurd." Radomil appeared taken aback. "My brother and I never collaborated on anything in our lives. We're polar opposites in everything we think and do."

"So it was Grigori."

"I'll tell you if you tell me who that man is talking with your grandfather."

She took a minute, as if thinking it over. "Who'll go first?"

"To demonstrate my good intentions, I will." He gave her a tiny mock bow. "I had fuck-all to do with hindering your flight out of the country."

"You hate my grandfather. You've admitted as much."

"I don't resort to violence, Annika—even by proxy. I'm not built that way."

"But your brother is."

"Indeed. Grigori is the worst kind of shit." He gestured with his head. "So who is that with your grandfather?"

"His name is Rylance. Perry Rylance."

"Who the hell is he?"

"Have you heard of International Perimeter?"

"The firm owned by Chris Fraine? Of course. IP handles security for half the multinationals in the world."

"Not to mention the U.S. government," Annika said. "Rylance is Chris Fraine's right-hand man."

Radomil took another long look at the man sitting across from Dyadya Gourdjiev. "What is that to me?"

"Chris Fraine founded International Perimeter with money he obtained from Three-thirteen."

Radomil looked thunderstruck. "Fraine is in bed with Three-thirteen?"

"Better than that," Annika said. "He's one of the members." Smiling, she pulled out a thick envelope.

Radomil frowned. "What's this?"

"Severance." Annika pressed the envelope into his hand. "You see, Radomil, darling, we no longer require your services."

WHEN HE heard the heavy thump, Waxman signaled to Herr, who crossed the library and stepped outside. A moment later, he called out softly. Waxman joined him in the hallway.

Henry Holt Carson was lying on the floor, curled up, one hand looking clawlike. His eyes stared up at Waxman, his mouth working soundlessly. Reggie had kicked the Glock away.

"Well, what have we here?" Bending over, Waxman pried the black notebook from Carson's rigid talons. "Could this be what you have been unconscionably withholding?"

As Waxman held the notebook up triumphantly, Carson managed a sound. Waxman looked up. "What's that, Henry? Speak up, I can't hear you."

"Help," Carson squeaked.

"Of course" Waxman stared down at the stricken man. "But first, I think I'll have a drink or two. Then a leisurely smoke of one of your fine Cuban Cohibas. It's only right that I return the hospitality you showed me and my—hmm, what did you call Reggie?" Placing one fine, gleaming shoe on Carson's neck, he applied judicious pressure. "Oh, yes, my 'monkey.'"

Observing Carson's eyes nearly bulging out of their sockets, he cocked his head. "What's that, Henry? Once again, you'll have to speak up, my hearing's not what it once was." He chuckled. "Dear Henry, you thought you had the upper hand. You thought you were smarter, more clever than me. In fact, it would hardly surprise me to learn that you held me in contempt. But, really, as we both know, contempt is your natural state, a sad testament to your upbringing. What a mighty pissant you must have been as a child." He gave a mock shudder.

"But now I—and my highly trained 'monkey'—must be off." He hefted the notebook. "After all, I have what we came for. I now know where to deploy Acacia, the coordinates of which you were so famously hoarding like a miser his stash of gold."

Waxman removed his shoe from Carson's neck. "I commend you, Henry. We all need something hidden to keep us safe when the shit hits the fan." He waggled the notebook. "And this is yours." He shook his head. "How you came by it is anyone's guess, but that's really irrelevant now. I have it. That's all that matters."

He smiled, showing the cutting edges of his teeth. "But even so, I have faith in you, Henry. I know you'll survive."

Waxman turned on his heel and, with Herr following in his wake, went down the hall, through the living room and the foyer, out the front door, and away.

Carson heard the echoes of their footfalls, but, like time slipping away, he couldn't do anything about it.

TWENTY-ONE

"DIPLOMATIC IMMUNITY?" Jack said. "What d'you mean? It's clear he throttled the woman to within an inch of her life."

"No one's disputing that," Paull said wearily. He pulled up an old green Naugahyde chair next to where Jack perched on Alli's hospital bed. "But the fact is Myles Oldham isn't his real name."

"He entered the country on a false passport. Another reason to detain him."

Paull settled the flaps of his overcoat over his thighs. "I couldn't agree more. Problem is, 'Myles Oldham' is a Russian political attaché. So is his driver, which is a joke. Oldham's got ties all the way up to President Yukin. And no wonder. His real name is Grigori Batchuk."

Jack, who had been watching Alli sleep, whipped his head around. "Grigori? Are you certain?"

"I am. The Russian ambassador presented his bona fides when he came to pick Batchuk and his driver up."

"The ambassador himself?"

"I told you, Jack. Batchuk is under Yukin's personal aegis."

At that moment, the surgeon who had taken care of Alli came in, paged through her chart, checked her pulse and blood pressure, as well as the monitors to which she was hooked up. When he was finished making notations, he looked up and smiled at Jack.

"Ms. Carson was lucky. Xrays show the hairline fracture in her left clavicle isn't all the way through. All she needs is some bed rest." He scribbled on a notepad, then tore off the top sheet. "Here's a prescription for a painkiller. She should only need it for a day or two, if at all." He handed it to Jack. "No operating heavy equipment while on this." He laughed. "You can take her home as soon as she wakes up."

Jack folded the prescription away as the doctor left.

"Forget Grigori Batchuk," Paull said. "We have Alli and Vera back, and Helene Simpson, the woman Batchuk almost killed, is recovering in a room just down the hall."

"Maybe she can provide some answers," Jack said.

"We'll certainly interrogate her the moment she comes to."

"I want to be the one to do that, Dennis."

Paull regarded him for some time. "What's up, Jack? What aren't you telling me?"

"It may be nothing."

"But on the other hand?"

Jack sighed. "We seem to be inundated with a tidal wave of twins."

Paull shook his head. "I don't understand."

"Alli says this man, Waxman—"

"As I've said, no such man exists in any official database."

Jack waved away his words. "Waxman's right-hand man is Reggie Herr."

"Herr?"

"Right. The late Morgan Herr's twin."

Paull sat up. "Go on."

"You already know that Gourdjiev and Oriel Batchuk were mortal enemies."

"I also know that Annika killed Batchuk."

"When I was in Russia this time, the old man warned me that his rivalry with Batchuk wasn't over because Batchuk had a son."

"Grigori." Then Paull caught himself. "Not Grigori."

"No," Jack said. "Gourdjiev was quite clear."

Paull tapped his fingers on the arm of the chair. "So now we have Grigori and his brother. You're saying another set of twins?"

"I'm positing the question, because we also have Alan and Chris Fraine."

"Chris shot Alan to death inside the store Silicon Vault." Paull shook his head. "Why would he do that?"

Jack wondered whether that was a key question. "Maybe we should ask Vera Bard. She was witness to the murder." He turned. "But first I need to debrief Alli. There's a pattern forming here, I can almost see it. But in order to make sense of it I need more information." He turned back to Paull. "Still no sign of Waxman."

"Or whatever his name is." Paull spoke on his mobile for several minutes, then killed the connection. "Nothing further. The Marine team scoured the wartime tunnel system you ID'd underneath the warehouse, but there's no indication that Waxman and the man Alli says is Reggie Herr took it."

"They must have," Jack said. "There's no other way out."

"Yeah, about that. You should have told me what you were planning."

"You shut me out, Dennis."

"I know, but—" He leaned forward. "Damnit, Jack, I don't know why I bother to give you orders."

"I don't, either."

The two men went eye to eye for a moment.

"Ah, fuck it," Paull said after a time, sitting back on his chair, but before he could get settled, his mobile buzzed. He looked at the caller ID, said, "I have to take this," got up, and went out into the hallway.

Jack returned his attention to Alli, to discover her eyes watching him. "How long have you been awake?"

"Thank you, Jack."

"Stop it."

"No, I mean it."

He shook his head. "If Dennis and I had been on the same page, I would have had a couple of his Marines guarding the other end of the warehouse tunnels. We would have gotten Waxman and Reggie Herr."

"Or they might have killed the Marines."

"Reggie is a highly skilled killer. I'm proud of how you handled yourself."

Alli gave him a sly smile. "Thanks. That means a lot." Her expression sobered. "While you were in the cell, Waxman pretended to shoot me dead. Did you believe him?"

"I might have," Jack said, "except that Emma appeared, and I sensed then you were all right."

She smiled.

"How do you feel?"

"Like I was hit by a truck."

"Close enough. But that's not what I meant."

"You mean Reggie Herr."

Jack nodded.

She closed her eyes for a moment. "Seeing him freaked me out."

"I can imagine."

"No, you can't," she said, not unkindly. "I didn't lose my head, I didn't fall back into the trap Morgan had set for me. I used everything I had learned to move past my fear, and when I got to the other side, it wasn't, you know, so bad." She stirred restlessly. "How's my shoulder?"

"Hairline fracture of the left clavicle. You'll be okay."

"Good." She moved, swinging her legs out. "Then I can get the hell out of here."

"The doctor ordered bed rest."

"Yeah, right."

Jack was scarcely surprised. He took her hand. "Lie back, honey. At least until I debrief you."

"I don't want—"

"And then you can see Vera."

Alli's eyes lit up. "You found her."

He nodded. "Now, come on, do as you're told, if only for the next fifteen or twenty minutes, and tell me everything you can about Waxman and Reggie Herr."

"DOCUMENTS," CHRIS Fraine said. "Your stock-in-trade."

Waxman, exhausted as he was, kept himself on an even keel. "What kind of documents?"

"The kind you and your gang conjure up for my people every day of the week."

"I hate when you use that term."

"But you and your people *are* a gang." Fraine looked behind him at Reggie Herr, who was pissing into an evergreen bush. "This one is for me, personally."

Waxman watched the road he had taken from Carson's lodge. He heard the sirens before he saw the ambulance, rising over the ridge, responding to the 911 call he had made just before Fraine had phoned to request an immediate emergency meeting. "Which means you're in trouble."

Fraine looked out across the Virginia countryside. "I killed Alan."

"What?" Waxman looked alarmed. "That wasn't supposed to happen."

Looking around, Fraine said, "You know something, Werner, it seems to me that none of this was supposed to happen." He regarded the older man. "How did we get here?"

"What on earth made you decide to kill Alan?"

"It wasn't a decision at all," Fraine nearly shouted. "It was an imperative, a blind—I don't know what—instinct."

"A *fratricidal* instinct?" Waxman shook his head. "I don't believe you. There must be another explanation. How badly did Alan provoke you?"

"You just don't get it." Fraine's hands clenched and unclenched, as if he were being kept from burning off excess adrenaline. "It's just one failure after another for you, isn't it?"

Fraine's words sent a bar of steel through Waxman's backbone. "Statements like that only reveal the depth of your ignorance," he said icily.

Fraine rounded on him. "I know enough. You put me and Alan

through enough, a fucking meat grinder." Realizing that Herr had come up behind him, he kept the animosity out of his voice. "Alan's death felt like some culmination, as if the act of pulling the trigger was a result of the cresting fever inside me. Now that fever is gone, there's nothing left, just a void."

It seemed like a child speaking, and Waxman said softly, "Keep it together, Chris. Something had gone wrong with the training. I don't know what yet, but you're not the first to turn on his twin. It doesn't matter now; I'll fix it. I'll fix you. Soon you'll be as good as new. Better than new. In the meantime, I'll manufacture the docs. The important thing to remember is that as soon as you're well again, as soon as you are relocated, you will resume control of International Perimeter." He engaged Fraine's eyes. "The important thing to remember is that nothing has changed."

"You're wrong, Werner. Everything's changed."

Waxman squeezed his shoulder. "Give me three hours. I'll have Reggie deliver the documents to you personally. In the meantime, make your travel arrangements."

"Who am I to be?"

"Who would you like to be?"

"Alan." Fraine licked his lips. "But since that's impossible, you prick . . ."

Waxman tapped a forefinger against his lips. "Let's see. You look like a Ted Callahan today."

Fraine nodded, almost distractedly.

Waxman, concerned, said, "Who are you?"

"Ted Callahan."

"Right." He patted Fraine reassuringly on the arm. "Drive to the safe house and book your flights. Whatever your destination, don't tell me. I don't want to know." He smiled. "Before nightfall, you'll be thirty thousand feet in the air, safe from all harm."

FOLLOWING CHRIS Fraine's departure, Waxman returned to his car, snapped open the latches on a beautifully made Italian cowhide briefcase. Inside, he found everything he would need. Setting up the portable makeup mirror, he selected a latex nose from the selection in the case, then set about expertly affixing it to his face. Then he regarded himself critically in the mirror. He scrunched up his face. The nose moved naturally. He peered at it more closely and saw the pores. Just like the real thing. Finally, he took out a small plastic case, unscrewed the top, and put dark-brown-colored contact lenses in his eyes.

Satisfied, he put everything away, wiped his hands on a moist towelette, and snapped the briefcase shut. Then he took out the black notebook that Carson had been hoarding. The man wasn't cut out to be in a group; he was an inveterate control freak.

Waxman paged through the notebook, with each succeeding blank page suspicion mounting that Carson had screwed him. Then, in the precise middle, he came upon four lines handwritten in Cyrillic. He could read Russian, of course. Quickly, he flipped through the remaining pages. All blank.

"Call the General," he ordered Reggie. "Tell him I'm in possession of the information we need."

Then he began to read the notebook's single entry, translating from the Russian as he went: *Ashur has a little horse, / Her mane as bright as gold. / And everywhere Ashur went / The horse was sure to go.*

That goddamned maddeningly indecipherable rhyme again! With a scream, he threw the notebook as hard as he could against the far window of his car.

"We're not done with Henry Holt Carson yet," he cried.

"What about the General?" Reggie said, hand over the speaker.

Waxman glared out the window. "Tell him to make the call."

"Are you sure?" Reggie appeared shaken. "If he makes the call, there's no going back."

Waxman leaned forward, his face flushed with emotion. "I don't want to go back. Tell General Tarasov to call the Syrian."

"Do I know you?" Caro said.

"Jack McClure, Ms. Simpson."

Caro, sitting up in her hospital bed, knew precisely who she was speaking with, and the knowledge sent chills down her spine. If anyone had the capacity to ferret out her real identity, it was this darkly handsome man sitting serenely on a chair by her bedside.

"Can I ask you why you were almost killed by a Russian cultural attaché?"

Caro swallowed. She still felt woozy and her throat was raw. "Russian? I know him as Myles Oldham."

"How long did you know him?"

"Oh, ages and ages. We met in—"

"Moscow?"

"London. At a political reception. We'd been lovers, off and on, since."

"Is that why he tried to kill you? Were you cheating on him?"

Caro's laugh turned quickly into a hacking cough, her face as red as the welt around her throat. Jack poured her a cup of cold water from a plastic jug on the wheeled table, and handed it to her. He waited patiently while she drank, and took the empty cup from her when she was finished.

Her eyelids fluttered. "I'm not used to being so thoroughly scrutinized."

"Sorry. Part of the job."

"Which is?"

"I work for the government."

"A description so very specific."

"*Specifically* for Dennis Paull, the secretary of homeland security."

Her eyes opened wide. "What shitstorm have I fallen into?"

He smiled, an expression so predatory it almost took her breath away.

"Let's return to the beginning. Why did the man you know as Myles Oldham try to kill you?"

"I don't think he was trying to kill me," Caro said in her most innocent voice. "We fought, it escalated, and I think he got carried away." She knew the false tone had betrayed her words the moment they were out of her mouth. No help for it now, she thought, but to spread butter on the trail. She sighed deeply. "Despite our long-distance relationship, the fact is Myles was always jealous. Finally, today, it had come to the point where he wanted me exclusively. I told him that was impossible."

"And why was that?"

"I'm not a one-man woman."

Jack sat back for a moment, continuing his study of her. Caro tried to relax, but the truth was he made her nervous—a first in her adult life. She fervently wished she were someplace else—anywhere but under his Xray vision.

"So, to sum up, you had no knowledge that Myles Oldham was a Russian cultural attaché."

"No."

"A Russian spy."

"Certainly not." Grigori wasn't a spy, at least, not in the sense McClure meant.

"Does the name Grigori Batchuk mean anything to you?"

"Should it?" *Damnit, I blinked. I never blink.*

"Here's what I think happened," Jack said. "You knew Grigori Batchuk before you knew Myles Oldham. You met him at a political function, all right, but it was in Moscow, not in London." He raised a hand. "Wait, let me finish. I believe you when you said that you and Batchuk have been off-and-on lovers, and I believe you two had a fight that escalated out of control. What I don't believe is that a man like Batchuk—trained for years— would fly out of control and expose himself just to settle a score with you." He smiled. "Now, Ms. Simpson, what did I get wrong?"

The way he said her name, the unnatural emphasis he put on it, caused Caro to suspect that he knew Helene Simpson was as false as Myles Oldham. What was she to do? How was she going to extricate herself from the snare McClure had set for her?

She was feverishly working on these crucial answers when he said, quite offhandedly, as if asking for street directions, "Don't worry. I won't tell your father that you're back in the country."

Caro felt her heart thud like a fallen stone within the cage of her ribs. "I don't—"

"Caroline," Alli said as she entered the room, "we don't have time to play this game anymore." She sat in a hospital wheelchair. The plain-clothes agent who had guided her in turned and left as silently as he had entered.

"You told him," Caro said.

"I trust him," Alli said. "And so should you."

Crossing her arms over her chest, Caro seemed to phase out, staring catlike at the shadows on the wall.

Alli turned to Jack. "Caro's a first-class computer hacker. Something else she neglected to tell you."

Jack leaned forward. "Caroline, we need your help."

Caro continued to stare at the wall.

Alli rose out of the wheelchair and moved into Caro's line of vision. "Is your life of so little value to you? Would you just throw it away?"

"I've been on my own for years. If I had been weak enough to think about anyone else, you wouldn't be talking to me now. I'd be dead." She shook her head. "Now the devil himself is after me. Because I made a rash decision. I ran. Sooner or later, he'll find me."

"Does your devil have a name?" Jack asked.

Caro bit her lip, silent.

"Please, Caro," Alli said. "Let us help you."

"I never asked anyone for help in my life."

"Things change, for all of us," Alli said. "We grow up, we learn we're not alone."

Caro shook her head.

"Vera and I were alone—alone for a very long time. But now we're not. Now we're best friends. We have each other, and I have Jack. Nothing will tear us apart."

"Wait." Caro shot her an odd look.

"What does that mean?"

"Just wait."

Alli shook her head. "Tell me his name, Caro."

"No." Caro took a breath, then a deeper one. She stared at her lap-top as if trying to find an answer there. At last, she let out a long-held breath. "His name is the Syrian."

"I know him," Jack said. "But not what he looks like."

"I wasn't kidding. He looks like the fucking devil—big, powerful, dark-skinned. He's got one blue eye and one green eye." Caro moist-ened her lips. "There's a Persian legend that Aesma Daeva, which means madness, the demon of lust and anger, wrath and revenge, had one blue eye and one green eye. He is the personification of violence, a lover of conflict and war. This is the man I used to work for. I managed all his accounts, hacking into bank subsystems, moving his money through a thousand unwitting financial institutions in a dozen different countries, until it could never be traced."

"And then?"

Caro sighed. "And then I saw the handwriting on the wall. I real-ized that I was nothing more than his slave. I realized I could no longer live like that. So I ran."

"No one leaves the Syrian's employ, so I've heard," Jack said.

"I wasn't just his employee," Caro said, "which, I expect, is the only reason I'm still alive. He wants to extract his pound of flesh from me before he kills me himself."

Jack watched Caro, and like a key turning in a lock, something clicked in his mind. "Is the Syrian known by any other names?"

"When we were together in bed, I called him Ashur."

The door in Jack's mind swung open, revealing a room burning with the children's rhyme recited to him by Waxman: *Ashur has a little horse, / Her mane as bright as gold. / And everywhere Ashur went / The horse was sure to go.*

Ashur, the Syrian. And Caroline Carson, his personal computer hacker, his lover, the horse with the golden mane. Caroline, not Annika, as Waxman believed!

His mind racing, working to fit pieces of the puzzle together, Jack edged closer. "Caroline, listen to me. I don't know what your friend Waxman told you, but that's not his name. We don't know what it is, which makes him all the more dangerous."

Caro remained silent as a sphinx.

"You met him at a political function."

"A party," Caro said. "Grigori told me who he was, and I went after him."

"Why?"

"Why?" Caro echoed, laughing. "Power. Limitless power."

Jack took out his mobile and called Paull.

"Dennis, anything from that police artist sketch you got from me?"

"Hundreds have it," Paull's voice said in his ear, "but without a name or any identifying—"

"I told you that he's got gray eyes," Jack said. "And that he's lame. He needs a walking stick to get around—"

"Even so."

"There's a good chance he's Russian."

"Ah," Paull said. "Now we're getting somewhere."

"I think you should come over here with Leopard's computer."

"Will do," Paull said, and broke the connection.

"You know Leopard?" Caro said. And then, responding to Jack's expression, "All the major hacker geeks know one another. It's like a secret club, a black ops."

"We had him working on a project for us."

"Had?"

"He got too close to something vital. He was poisoned."

Caro considered this for a moment. "Is Waxman involved in his murder?"

"I wish I knew."

"I'd like to take a look at what he was working on."

"Done," Jack said.

"About Waxman—"

"He abducted Alli to get to me, and he was willing to kill her to accomplish that."

"What did he want from you?"

Jack shook his head, judging she was not yet ready to hear about her own crucial part. Besides, he needed more information from her, untainted by more revelations. "However, I have a hunch it has something to do with twins."

"Twins?" Caro appeared dazed, as if she were caught trying to process too much information at the same time.

He nodded. "Do you know either Chris or Alan Fraine?"

Caro's brow furrowed. "I've heard of Chris Fraine. International Perimeter, right? Never met him. Alan's his twin?"

"Was," Jack said. "Chris shot him to death several hours ago."

"Christ. Why?"

"A compulsion, he said. We're still trying to determine what that means." Jack steepled his fingers. "To continue the subject of twins. Grigori Batchuk. He has a brother, Caroline, this much I know. His name is Radomil. I need to know whether he and Grigori are twins. The Russian records are unreliable, often doctored or stolen, even when we can get to them, which isn't often."

"Please, Caro," Alli said.

Caro looked from Alli to Jack. "Radomil and Grigori are twins."

PERRY RYLANCE, Fraine's right-hand man, sat down for dinner at a bustling Roman trattoria in the Prati. Radomil watched him as he ordered. From the calls Radomil had made, he discovered the following useful information: Rylance was booked on the 10:35 P.M. flight to Paris; he had engaged a car service to pick him up at 8:30 P.M. outside the trattoria and transport him to Fiumicino Airport. After making several more calls, Radomil had picked his way through swelling knots of tourists and a smattering of Romans, and sat down in the trattoria, where he ordered a glass of red Piedmontese wine and a pizza.

A swarm of tiny Japanese tourists, Nikon cameras clicking like cicadas in a field, passed by in lockstep, grimly marching from monument to ruin until it was time to return to their luxury, air-conditioned bus. Many of them wore white cotton gloves. Some had medical masks over their noses and mouths.

Rylance ate quickly, oblivious to everything around him. He might as well be in a McDonald's in D.C., Radomil observed with disgust.

The car arrived on time. Seeing it pull up, Rylance threw down some euros, rose, and got in. The driver put the car in gear, nosing out into traffic, heading for the airport via the Appian Way.

Radomil's car slid to the curb just as he was paying his bill. He climbed in, and the car took off, following closely behind Rylance's vehicle. Originally constructed in 312 B.C., the Appia Antica stretched all the way to the port of Brindisi, from which the ancient Roman Empire conducted lucrative trade with its far-flung colonies in the East. The initial stretch of bordering land five or ten miles outside Rome quickly became a popular burial site for wealthy Roman families after burial inside the walls of Rome itself was banned in the fifth century B.C. Later, Christians burrowed their way through the soft tufa stone, secretly burying their dead in miles of catacombs beneath the venerable highway.

When the car carrying Rylance stopped in front of the chained entrance to the catacombs, Radomil's car pulled in behind, and Radomil, armed with a 9mm Beretta, approached the leading car, wrenched open the rear door, and stuck his head and the Beretta inside. The driver, twisted around in the front seat, held his passenger at gunpoint.

"What is this?" Rylance said. "If it's a robbery, you should know I'm carrying approximately thirty euros, that's it."

"Get out," Radomil said, gesturing with the barrel of his handgun.

After a moment's hesitation, Rylance slid across the seat. As he placed one foot on the ground, his left arm lashed up. Radomil, anticipating him, avoided the blow even as he slammed the muzzle of the Beretta into the side of Rylance's head. As Rylance reeled back, Radomil stepped aside to allow his driver to reach in and haul Rylance out. A slash at his hairline was drooling blood.

"Whatever it is you want," he said, "I won't give it to you."

"You don't have a choice." Radomil signaled with his head, and the driver stuffed a wad of filthy cloth into Rylance's mouth, then he tied his hands behind his back. "You simply made the wrong deal with the wrong person."

He shoved Rylance, stumbling, up to the old iron gates and stood with him while Radomil's driver, a large flat package under one arm, opened the padlock. Once Radomil had discovered which car service

Rylance had hired, it had been child's play to substitute one of his men for the company's driver. No questions had been asked. The original driver was at this moment enjoying an expensive dinner alongside a stunning twentysomething, whom he soon would bed, all at Radomil's expense. Money well spent.

The gates swung open and Radomil pushed Rylance up the rough, dusty driveway and into a small entry building on their left. The two drivers activated powerful flashlights and they all descended into the catacombs, past horizontal burial niches once filled with the bodies of two or three family members. Here and there could be seen the ghostly outline of Christian art that had once adorned the open crypts where centuries before family members came weekly to picnic and feel closer to their departed loved ones. The atmosphere was thick with history and the dead left like detritus in the wake of the ages' inexorable march onward.

Radomil stopped them when they came to a rough-hewn stairway down to the lower levels. From a chain across the entrance hung a red no-admittance warning sign. Years ago, tours were allowed into the lower levels. But that was before one of the guides got lost down in the depths and never returned.

Turning Rylance around so he faced the stairs down, Radomil took the 9mm Glock his driver handed him and shot Rylance point-blank in the back of his head. Radomil's driver unfolded the package he had been carrying to reveal a body bag. He and the second driver manhandled the corpse into the bag, sealed it completely, then pitched it down the stairs into the lower catacombs.

The entire operation had taken less than ten minutes.

AN HOUR later, Radomil rode up in the Hotel Borghese elevator and knocked on Annika's door. He heard a rustling from behind the door as she peered through the peephole at him. He grinned at her, and, a moment later, she opened the door.

She was wearing a plush terry-cloth robe with the hotel's logo like a medieval coat of arms on the left breast. Her wet hair was turbaned in a towel, her feet were bare.

She stood squarely in the doorway, one hand on the partly open door. "This is something of a surprise."

"I'd like to speak with you. May I come in?"

For a long moment her eyes studied him, and he had the uncomfortable feeling that she was evaluating his motives. Abruptly, she nodded and stepped aside. The room was spacious, ornate, high-ceilinged. The heavy drapes were drawn, revealing the black foliage of the Borghese gardens through the thick panes of glass.

He crossed the thick carpet to the windows. "It must be beautiful in daylight."

"I wouldn't know."

"In the morning you will." He turned back into the room, smiling, only to discover her holding a small, pearl-handled .22 aimed at him. "What is this, Annika?"

"You tell me."

He spread his hands. "I just wanted to give back the severance money you gave me."

"Don't bother. It's yours."

He slowly and deliberately moved the thumb and forefinger of his left hand into his breast pocket, lifted out the envelope she had given him, and dropped it on the floor between them. "I didn't even open it."

Using the toe of his shoe, he slid the envelope across the carpet toward her. "I want my old job back."

"Sorry, it's been taken."

"Yeah, but no, it hasn't. I have a hunch Mr. Rylance isn't going to show up for work tomorrow."

She lifted the .22 to aim at his head. "What did you do?"

Radomil shook his head.

"What the fuck did you do, Radomil?"

"I have it on good authority that Mr. Rylance had . . . well, what should we call it? . . . a date with destiny."

"You killed him."

"He's no longer available to you . . . or to anyone else, for that matter."

Annika pulled out the desk chair and sat down. "Well, this changes everything."

"Yes." He stood silent for a moment, hands clasped in front of him, like a respectful mourner at the funeral of a distant relative. "I think now would be an opportune time to renegotiate the terms of our deal."

TWENTY-TWO

"I SCREWED the pooch with Alan Fraine," Paull said. "He called in, said he was being followed, and asked for help. The person he spoke to got the address wrong. My men showed up at the wrong spot and Alan had to deal with things himself."

"Which he did," Jack said.

"Yes, but I think it put him in a more perilous position."

The two men were in a situation room Paull had had set up on the eighth floor of Bethesda, rigged with a large-screen monitor linked to Leopard's laptop. Caro had been moved into the room and Alli was standing beside her, while Caro plundered the hard drive.

Jack understood his friend's remorse. "None of us could have anticipated that Alan would be shot dead, let alone by his twin brother."

Paull nodded morosely.

"Were you able to find any trace of Werner Waxman?"

"I called in more favors than I would have liked to, all to no avail."

"Can you trust the results?"

"From these people, yes."

"Who the hell is he?"

"One thing I can tell you right now," Caro piped up from behind Leopard's laptop, "Waxman isn't Waxman. His name is Werner Ax. At least, according to the intel Leopard gleaned, that's his last pseudonym."

"Jesus Christ!" Paull ran his hand through his hair. "This man's like a fucking ghost. Looking for him is like trying to stop sand from running through an hourglass."

He blew air out through his lips, then pulled Jack aside. "There's something else," he whispered. "Henry Holt Carson is currently in surgery. He had a heart attack. I had him brought here."

"What's the prognosis?"

"It's too soon to tell," Paull said.

At that moment, Caro called them over. "Leopard was looking into the background of someone named Leonard Bishop."

"Bishop is currently Metro's chief of detectives."

"I got that," Caro said without looking up. "Previously, Bishop was in an elite unit, designated Acacia, which was the operational field arm of an SBO group known only as Three-thirteen."

"SBO?" Alli repeated.

"Shielded black ops," Paull said in a wooden voice, "the designation given only rarely, to a black ops group so secret its existence is shielded from everyone except those directly involved."

"Even the president?" Alli asked.

"It's my understanding that Three-thirteen was unknown to the presidents up through Edward Carson."

"But you've heard of it," Jack pointed out.

"Only in passing, as a rumor."

"But you're the secretary of homeland security!"

Paull, ignoring her, nodded at Caro. "Please continue."

"On July third, 2002, Acacia was deployed to the Horn of Africa, according to the DoD file Leopard hacked into, but it didn't stay there long. Forty-eight hours later, it was flown by a local, nonmilitary transport to Baghdad."

"What was Acacia doing in Iraq?" Paull said.

"Looking for WMDs," Alli said with a smirk.

"Plenty of unaccounted-for money over there," Jack said.

Caro's eyes scanned the screen. "But Acacia was a kill squad."

"It was sent to take out Saddam," Alli offered.

"Maybe." Paull seemed thoughtful. "Caroline, what do the Three-thirteen files say about Acacia's mission?"

"They don't. The files are compartmentalized. Leopard hadn't gotten that far."

"That must have been when he was poisoned."

"No." Caro shook her head. "He was poisoned later." Her fingers flew over the keys. "He broke off his search to look for someone named Milton P. Stirwith, who, as it turns out, doesn't exist." She looked up. "Leopard dug up Stirwith's false ID documents; his identity wasn't just any legend. The quality of workmanship bears all the hallmarks of the legends created by the Norns."

"But that's impossible," Alli said. "All those guys have got to be either in old age homes or dead and buried by now."

"Yeah, that was Leopard's thought also." Caro worried her lower lip. "But he discovered something that really excited him. He was a World War Two fanatic, so he knew a lot about the Norns working under the aegis of the OSS."

"Not the intelligence service's finest hour," Alli said acidly.

"There were a number of questionable decisions made at that time," Paull said. "Security was the overriding issue for the people at the top of OSS."

"I'm sorry." Alli shook her head. "I don't buy it. No Nazi should have been given a free pass."

"In a perfect world, I'd agree with you," Paull said. "Caro, what else did Leopard discover?"

"First, that this Werner Ax guy is somehow involved with Three-thirteen. Second, Leopard was in the process of accessing a particular file when he was stricken."

"What's in it?"

"I'll have to get back in through the DoD firewalls."

"This is scaring the hell out me," Paull admitted. "We need better security than this."

"Whatever you come up with, believe me, I'll be able to get through it." Caro's fingers danced over the keyboard again. "Okay, here we go. Bingo! Here we have the rest of Acacia's itinerary. Baghdad wasn't their destination. Another plane—also nonmilitary—flew them out of Iraq to a small airfield outside of Yerevan."

"Where the hell is Yerevan?" Alli said.

"Armenia," Jack said immediately. "Surely that wasn't Acacia's final destination?"

"No," Caro said. "So far as I can make out, it was Lankaran."

"In Azerbaijan."

"That's awfully close to Iran." Paull rubbed the stubble on his cheek. "From there it's only, what, a couple of hundred miles to Tehran."

"Three-hundred-eighty-five-point-one-four, to be exact," Caro said. "Assuming their route would keep them over the Caspian Sea for as long as possible."

Paull nodded. "Excellent assumption."

"Was Acacia's mission to assassinate Iran's supreme leader?" Alli asked.

"If it was," Caro said, "they failed."

"Still, even the hint that Three-thirteen would sanction such a dangerous and reckless mission is cause for alarm."

"Why?" Alli shrugged. "This all took place in 2002."

"But Three-thirteen is still active." Now Caro did look up. "There's a notation here that Acacia has just been redeployed."

"Where?"

"It doesn't say."

"See if you can find out." Jack turned to Paull. "It looks like we're on someone else's timetable. We've got to find out where Acacia is headed." He gestured to Caro. "Do you think Acacia's legends were dreamed up by the Norns?"

"In 2002 and now?" Alli said. "How?"

"What if some—or all—of these master forgers had offspring?" Jack said. "That would account for the Norn's continuation without, strictly speaking, ever having to go outside the group."

"But how could these people guarantee that their children would have their talents, let alone follow in their footsteps?" Alli said. "Nowadays, kids almost never do."

"That's true." Paull nodded. "It seems implausible that these people could control the future to that extent."

"And yet," Caro said, "judging by the work done on Stirwith's legend, I can't think of another explanation."

Alli twisted her torso to get a better look at the laptop screen. "But it's impossible."

"Nothing's impossible." Jack shook his head. "Caro, is there anything else in this file?"

"Yes, but I can't read it—hang on a sec, there's something. There's an appended file, it's small and, curiously, also encrypted."

"A double layer of protection."

She nodded. "I have the first line, but it still doesn't make sense. "K-W-I-F-A," she spelled out the word. "Anyone have a clue?"

A shiver of recognition ran down Jack's spine.

"Those same letters were appended to an eyes-only file on General Gerard Tarasov."

Caro pursed her lips. "A Russian military officer?"

"No. Tarasov is American."

"So both Ax and Tarasov are connected to Three-thirteen," Alli said.

"Nona Heroe observed a clandestine meeting between the General and Bishop," Paull said. "It was clear by the nature of their conversation that Bishop was taking orders from Tarasov. Caro, see if the name Moses Malliot appears anywhere in those files."

She nodded, then after several tense moments she nodded again. "He's a member of Acacia."

"Alan Fraine was running him down for information on Bishop's mentor."

"I think it was General Tarasov," Jack said.

Paull nodded. "And now we have Tarasov directly linked to a Three-thirteen file. He may very well be running the group."

"Without any oversight whatsoever," Alli added.

"But where does the mysterious Werner Ax fit into the picture?" Jack said.

Paull stirred uneasily. "Unless or until we unearth his real name, that's a question without an answer."

CHRIS FRAINE had just finished booking his flights when he heard someone outside the safe house door. He pulled out his Beretta and stood stock-still, listening. Then a rhythmic knock on the door: a staccato three-one-two.

Gun pointed down at his side, he crossed to the door, unlocked it, and stepped back. Reggie Herr pushed the door open and strode inside. Outside, the blue winter twilight was sweeping the foreshortened afternoon into the gutters.

"Thought you might be hungry, holed up here," Reggie said, setting down a white paper bag on a scarred wooden table.

Fraine peered in, shuddering at what he found. "A Big Mac? Really?"

"And double fries." Reggie shrugged. "If you don't eat 'em, I will."

Fraine's arm swept out. "Be my guest."

Reggie unbuttoned his thick coat and handed over a slim packet.

It was all Fraine could do not to recoil. "God, you stink."

Reggie shrugged, sat down heavily on the frayed flower-patterned sofa, and, pulling the bag toward him, lifted out the Big Mac and fries as Fraine opened the packet and examined the legend documents. "Looks good," he said.

"Damn good." Folding back the foil, Reggie attacked the Big Mac with his large, sharp teeth. "Nothing better," he said around the food.

Fraine didn't know whether he was talking about the documents or the Big Mac. Maybe he meant both. Checking his watch, he said, "My flight's at seven-fifteen. I'd better get going."

"You've got time. Sit." Reggie pushed over the greasy packet of fries. "Have a couple. Relax. I'll get you there in plenty of time."

"I'm not hungry," Fraine said, looking at Reggie's ketchup-stained lips with distaste. "Come on. I want to get to the airport."

"Wanna stretch out in the first-class lounge, eh?" Reggie shrugged. "Okay. No problem. Just let me wipe my hands." He reached into the bag, drew out a .45 HK MK 23, and shot Fraine three times in the chest.

Fraine's body slammed backward against a chair, then crumpled, his legs folding under him like a dropped marionette.

Reggie set the .45 down, picked up his Big Mac, and resumed eating while contemplating Fraine's astonished expression. "Kinda weird you and me being here like this, huh, Chris? But, you know, in a way it makes perfect sense. I never did like you, you arrogant sonuvabitch." He finished the burger, stuffed his mouth with a handful of fries, chewed and swallowed convulsively. "Now you've got what you deserved, it's time for me to saddle up." He stuffed the HK into his waistband and rose, sucking morsels of food from between his teeth. "Be seeing you. Or maybe not."

His laugh seemed to echo in the safe house even after he had slipped, unnoticed, out the back door.

"I DON'T renegotiate deals," Annika said.

Radomil shrugged. "Then I'll speak to your grandfather."

"You won't," she said with such finality that he rose and went to the hotel window.

At length, he turned around to face her again. "You'll renegotiate this one, Sister." He came toward her at a slow and deliberate pace. "Grigori wasn't the one trying to stop you and your *dyadya* from leaving Russia."

"It wasn't you, either."

"No." He smiled. "It wasn't."

"Cut the crap," she said abruptly. "I'm not in the mood."

"Then get in the mood, Annika, because I know who's behind all of this, who your enemy really is."

"How could you know this?"

A slow smile spread across his face. "What d'you imagine I've been doing all these years since I fled the program? I've been keeping track of its creator. I hate him as I hate no other human being."

"Wait a minute, you told me that Grigori was responsible."

"I wasn't lying," Radomil said. "But Grigori is the beginning, not the end."

She watched him, silent, brooding darkly.

"If I tell you what I know, will you renegotiate my deal?"

"Impress me."

He grabbed a chair and sat astride it, opposite her. "Grigori is a front man, a foil, a—what's the American slang?—flunky."

"He would be very unhappy to hear that."

"Yes, he would. But my brother has an uncanny facility for self-deception, not to mention delusions of grandeur, so he wouldn't believe you. He thinks of himself as a playboy of the world, a man of mystery, in the most old-fashioned sense of the word."

"So." Annika crossed her arms over her breasts. "Who's pulling the strings?"

"I want the renegotiation."

"I'm listening."

"That's not enough of a commitment."

She shrugged. The ensuing silence became a test of wills between the half-siblings.

At length, Radomil nodded. "I'm continuing as an act of faith. Faith in you, Annika. The man who created the twin program is Werner Ax. Inside the program, however, we called him something else: Father Night."

"I SUPPOSE you've used face recognition programs," Caro said.

Paull nodded. "We have. Trouble is, we're going off a drawing of Ax. Without a photo, the programs are notoriously unreliable, so basically we haven't been able to get off square one in identifying him."

Jack moved closer to Caro. "Caro, I'm going to recite a children's rhyme to you. 'Ashur has a little horse, / Her mane as bright as gold. / And everywhere that Ashur went / The horse was sure to go.' Does that sound familiar?"

"In what way? I've never heard it before."

"If the Syrian is Ashur, then I think you're the horse with the mane as bright as gold."

Caro shook her head. "I don't understand."

"Werner Ax was so desperate to decipher the meaning to the rhyme that he devised a plan to capture me. He knew quite a bit about me, especially my ability to solve seemingly unsolvable puzzles. I want to know why he was so desperate."

She shrugged. "I don't know how can I help you."

"I think you know something—something you came across when you were working for the Syrian."

"But I don't—"

"You said you were in charge of laundering the Syrian's money through a maze of international banks."

"That's right."

"How much would you estimate the Syrian is worth?"

"I don't have to estimate, I know," Caro said. "It's over fifteen billion dollars."

Alli gasped.

Jack nodded. "I think Werner Ax is after the Syrian's money."

"That's crazy. How could he—?"

"You tell me. You're the horse with the mane of gold. I'm betting you know how to access the account."

"But that's just it," Caro said. "I don't."

"You set the mechanisms in place. You must know—"

"'And everywhere that Ashur went / The horse was sure to go,'" Caro sang to herself to the tune of "Mary Had a Little Lamb." She snapped her fingers. "That's it! The electronic key to withdrawing the money is always with Ashur, but in case he was killed or incapacitated I created a backup."

"What is it?"

"A medallion. I had it made with a secret compartment, and then gave it to Taroq as a present. He's the Syrian's chief bodyguard. He wears it night and day on a chain around his neck. He never takes it off, but he has no idea what's inside it."

"If you created the electronic key, you must know it yourself," Alli said.

Caro smiled. "If only. The electronic key is a tiny instrument with a readout. Every three minutes the array of fifteen numbers changes randomly."

The door opened and Nona came in, one hand on Vera Bard's shoulder. Alli rose and ran to Vera, the two young women embracing, murmuring to each other. Then they both came across the room.

"We're all happy to see you," Jack said. He gave a quick glance in Nona's direction. Her face was drawn and pinched. He could see that she had been crying.

"Vera has something important to tell you." Nona's voice was all business.

Vera looked from Jack to Dennis Paull and back again. "After Chris Fraine shot his brother, he went over to him and knelt down. It seemed to me that he wanted, or maybe needed, to talk to Alan before he died."

"Could you hear the conversation?" Jack asked.

Vera nodded. "It wasn't much of one. Alan couldn't really talk. But Chris said, 'You can't say I didn't warn you. I wanted you with me, to carry out what Vater Nacht planned for us. I went against the program and he never forgave me. Bad genes reversed by whatever inferned methods he used. I'd kill him if I could, but I can't. His training is at least that strong inside me. I killed you. I don't know why. I saw you and felt a compulsion. I couldn't help myself.'"

Apart from the soft hum of the computers, the room was enveloped in complete silence.

At last, Jack turned to Vera. "Chris said 'Vater Nacht'? You're sure?"

"Absolutely certain."

"'Father Night.' Could he have been referring to Ax?" Paull said. "If he is German it would be odd to choose Waxman as his legend's name."

"Depends on his ego," Alli said.

Jack nodded. "She's right. Even the cleverest of criminals often can't give up every single part of them." He gestured to Caro. "Let's start with the sketch, then add Werner, and the notion that he might be a German national."

"It'll take a moment to access all the relevant databases and cross-reference them."

As her fingers danced over the keys, they all waited breathlessly. Alli, noticing that Vera and Caro were avoiding each other, turned to her friend and roommate. "What's going on between you two?"

"Nothing." But a flicker of fear crossed Vera's face before winking out.

Caro, seeing the expressions on both their faces, found the hint of a smile creeping into her lips. Then she turned back to the computer.

"I've found something," she said. "It may be nothing, but . . ." She pressed a key on the laptop and a photo appeared on the large monitor. "A man similar in build and face shape passed through immigration at Dulles forty minutes ago. You can see that his nose is different than in the photo, and his eyes are dark, not gray."

"Then it's not him." Alli moved closer to the monitor. "And yet—"

"Yes," Caro said. "There's something familiar about him."

Jack used the laptop keyboard to merge the sketch with the photo.

"I can't tell for sure," Alli said to Jack. "Can you?"

Jack dispensed with the sketch, concentrated on the photo, bringing it in for a close-up. "There we go." He pointed. "See this hairline shadow here? He's used a false nose." He moved closer still on the eyes. "And there's a tiny corona of light along the left side of his irises."

"Yep. Colored contacts."

"What's the name he's traveling under?" Jack asked.

Caro squinted at the screen. "Werner von Verschuer."

Jack heard a bell tolling in the back of his mind. Why? Did that name mean something to him? He couldn't bring it into the light of his conscious mind.

"And you're right," Caro continued. "This legend has him as a German national."

Paull opened his cell. "I'm calling airport security. We got him."

"Don't bother." Caro swiveled the laptop back to face her. "His flight's already left."

"Destination?" Jack said.

"Rome."

"What's he going to do there?"

Caro shook her head. "I've no idea."

"Damnit!" Paull opened his phone. "Let's pick General Tarasov up, at least." He began to bark orders into his mobile.

The idea of flights caused something to click in Jack's mind. "Caro, you said the Acacia team was flown out of the Horn of Africa by local transport. Do you have a company name?"

"Just a moment." Caro screened through page after page. Yeah. Mirage AirTransport."

"See if you can find out who owns Mirage."

Caro nodded.

Paull had just completed his call when his mobile buzzed. He listened for a moment, then looked at Jack. "We're needed elsewhere."

Out in the hushed corridor, Paull said, "Carson's about to go into surgery. He's down the hall. We should take a look-see."

As they went, Paull opened his mobile. "I'll alert the authorities at Fiumicino. As soon as the plane lands, Ax or whoever the hell he is now will be picked up and extradited back here."

"Hold on," Jack said as they reached the doorway to Carson's prep room. "I think we should do nothing but follow him."

"Are you kidding?"

Jack tapped the side of his head. "I think Ax is going to meet his partners. We find him, we find them. I'll use your plane, and we'll track him through your contacts at Fiumicino and the FAA. Whatever planes he takes, the pilots will have to file flight plans. As long as we don't lose Ax, we'll be fine."

Paull nodded. "All right." He was getting used to following Jack's intuition, though he was never quite comfortable with it. "My plane is fueled and ready to go. You can leave now."

They were about to enter the room when they saw Alli striding down the hall toward them.

Her face was flushed. "I know you're going after Ax, Jack."

"And, of course, you want to go," Paull said.

"Is that right?" Jack said.

"No, I'm needed here to protect Caroline. The Syrian isn't going to let her go quietly."

Paull gestured. "This place is crawling with Secret Service agents."

At that moment, she moved so that, inadvertently, she had a line of sight into the room. "Is that my uncle?"

"He's had a heart attack," Paull said. "He's about to have emergency bypass surgery."

The two men followed Alli into the room where Henry Holt Carson lay. A pair of surgical nurses were monitoring his vitals while the anesthesiologist administered a Valium drip. Carson's skin was ashen and slack.

Paull bent over, peering down at him. "Too late to wish him good luck."

Alli approached the bed with some hesitation. "He looks old."

"He is old," Paull said.

"No, I mean *really* old, as if his body has collapsed in on itself." Alli stepped closer. "It's weird to see him like this, drained of all his energy and power. It's like a dream I've had about him."

Jack, standing behind her, put his hands on her shoulders. "Wish fulfillment."

Alli nodded. "You could say that."

He turned her around to face him. "I'm glad you've made the decision to stay. You're the one I trust."

Carson was wheeled out by his retinue of hospital personnel.

"Alli," Paull said, "these agents don't know Caro or Henry. You do. That's crucial now."

Alli looked at him critically.

Paull laughed. "My days of underestimating you are gone, trust me."

"Alli," Jack said, "before I go, I just wanted to know . . . is everything okay between you and Vera?"

"Yeah, sure, why d'you ask?"

But Jack saw the sorrow in her eyes, and she knew he did. Their deep understanding of each other was revealed in that one glance. Jack knew something was wrong, but he also knew her too well to push her. She would tell him if and when she was comfortable enough.

Still, he said, "Walk with me."

"We'll be in constant touch." Paull followed them out the door. "I'll be going back to the office, the better to monitor the intel coming in." He tilted his head toward Alli. "Another reason you need to be here as my eyes and ears."

Neither Jack nor Alli said a word in the elevator, on the way down. As they crossed the lobby, he said, "Caroline may be jealous of your relationship with Vera."

"Why should she care?" But Alli started to mull this idea over in her head.

"I don't know, but she does."

As usual, Jack was on to something important, she thought, even without having full knowledge of the situation.

"Maybe if you talk to her, you'll find out."

They had reached the front doors. The twilight had gathered like the shadowed strands of a spider web.

"I don't know which I hate most," Alli said, eyeing the street, "your leaving or my staying."

Jack smiled, signaling Paull's car. The driver started the engine.

"Jack . . ."

He turned back to her, his smile fading.

She shook her head. "Nothing. Just get Ax, or whoever he is."

"Don't worry."

She stood on her tiptoes, gave him a kiss on the cheek. "I won't let you down."

"I know you won't. Careful of that shoulder."

He ducked into the car, the door slammed shut, and it nosed down the driveway. Alli, her heart aching for so many different reasons, watched until the car vanished into traffic. Then she turned and, taking a deep breath, went back inside to begin the task Jack had set for her.

"I WANT double what we originally agreed upon."

"I can do that," Annika said, "but you'll have to work for it."

Radomil grinned. "I've never run from work. Unlike my brother, I prefer to earn my keep."

They were sitting at a black lacquer table in a nook of the bar to one side of the ornate hotel lobby. Lamps spread golden dollars of light across the deep-red carpet. The long polished teak bar gleamed, and glasses and bottles twinkled like stars in the night sky. Radiohead was playing softly from well-concealed speakers in the low-ceilinged room's four corners. The windowless space felt warm and sheltered. Voices murmured like the wind in the willows.

Annika turned her vodka rocks around and around, making interlocking rings of moisture on the table. "You won't like what I'm about to ask you to do."

"I don't have to like it," he said, taking a sip of his whiskey. "I just have to do it."

"Just so." Annika nodded. "I want you to take me to where the Syrian is."

Radomil reared back in his barrel chair. "You're not serious."

"On the contrary. I've never been more serious in my life."

"But why the hell would you want that?"

"He and my grandfather are partners."

"Then you should know where he is."

"I trust the Syrian," Annika said, by way of an answer. "It's Ax I'm concerned with."

"I don't want any part of Werner Ax."

"Neither do I, but we all need to play the hand we're dealt."

Radomil's eyes narrowed as he cocked his head. "You're planning something, aren't you?"

She sipped her drink. "I want you to understand that you work for me now," she said. "No one else."

Radomil nodded.

"I also want you to know that if you cross me—"

"What? You'll kill me?"

"No," Annika said. "I'll do much worse than that."

The look in her eye caused Radomil's laugh to die stillborn. He swallowed. "All right. I get it. You're the boss now."

"Yeah, well, I have to wonder whether that means anything to you."

A wry smile cracked open his dour expression. "Not much, to be honest."

"Then you have some serious learning to do."

"They say change is extremely difficult to handle, especially for a man."

"Are you up for the challenge?"

"I'm up for the money," Radomil said.

"That isn't enough." Annika pushed a thick packet across the table, but did not take her hand off it. "Not for me, at least."

He spread his hands. "What would you have me say?"

"That's entirely up to you." She tapped the packet of money. "Everything is different now. Either you understand that, or you don't. The money is irrelevant."

Radomil seemed to roll her words over in his mind. At length, he nodded. "You're talking again about an act of faith."

Annika nodded. "Start small, Radomil." She took her hand off the packet. "Don't look inside. Trust that I won't cheat you."

Radomil took possession of the packet. For a moment, his fingers twitched, as if of their own accord they wanted to open it. Then he looked up at her. "The Syrian is here in Rome."

"What the hell is he up to?"

"Something. I don't know."

"I have to find out. I don't know where he is, and it's obvious you do. I want you to take me to him."

"Are you serious?"

She stared at him, silent, enigmatic as a sphinx.

Radomil grunted in surrender. "I get you there, I light the way for you to see him." He blew air out through his lips, shook his head, then glanced at his watch. "Okay. If you're serious, we'd better get started. There isn't much time."

Annika's arm froze with her vodka halfway to her lips. "Until what?"

"I told you I don't know. But he's been planning something—something very complex, very big, very dangerous."

"Can you make an educated guess?"

"With the Syrian, who the fuck knows?" Radomil stood and pushed his chair aside. "Maybe light the sky on fire, maybe burn cities down, maybe World War Three."

TWENTY-THREE

FOR HENRY Holt Carson, the world kept flickering like a firefly at the periphery of his vision. All else was darkness—and the pressure of colossal pain pressing down on him, as if trying to flatten him entirely.

There was a moment when he thought he saw Dennis Paull's face, heard Paull's voice echoing, "Get him to the eighth floor," as if from the other end of a house with many rooms through which it was impossible for Carson to negotiate.

Darkness.

Finally, only the pain remained, making him want to scream, never stop screaming.

Then the abyss.

HE AWOKE, or rather his eyes opened, gluey, his vision blurred. He stared up at a white ceiling. He heard the suck and sigh of machines, and knew he was in a hospital. What had happened to him? The last he remembered . . .

"Mr. Carson. Mr. Carson, can you hear me?"

His eyes, adjusting, fell upon a face.

"My name is Dr. Delany. I'm the surgeon who operated on you. You had a myocardial infarction, Mr. Carson. In layman's terms, a heart attack. You've had a double bypass, but you're going to be fine. Do you understand?"

Carson nodded. His tongue felt swollen, glued to the roof of his mouth, and his throat was raw, as if he had been screaming for hours.

Dr. Delany smiled. "You're in Bethesda Naval Hospital."

His head turned and Carson sensed he was speaking to someone else in the room.

When Delany turned back, he said, "There's someone here to see you. Think you're up to it?"

Carson nodded. He was acutely aware of his heart beating. He felt very alone.

The doctor moved aside and Carson saw the familiar face of Dennis Paull.

"Hello, Henry."

"I must look like hell."

Paull smiled. "I want you to know that Alli is safe."

Carson felt like laughing. He had lost Caroline; his relationship with Vera was based on estrangement, hatred, and the endless tiny revenges they took on each other. Death by ten thousand cuts. But Alli, worst of all, was a constant reminder of his brother, Edward. Edward, who had become president, who was so admired, so beloved, so much the favored son. But Carson was the successful one, the wealthy one, the brother with real influence. Where would Edward have been without his help? The truth was, he despised Edward, and now that Edward was gone, every time he saw Alli, he saw Edward as well.

"In fact," Paull continued, "Alli's here at Bethesda."

Paull smiled. "You can see her in a while, if you like."

"Don't bother," was all Carson could manage. He felt exhausted. His eyelids fluttered, despite his efforts to keep them open.

"That's enough now," he heard Dr. Delany say. "He needs his rest."

Instantly he was overcome by a deep sleep, where he dreamed of

314   Eric Van Lustbader

climbing an enormous, mazelike tree, and falling before he could reach the top.

GENERAL TARASOV took off from a private airfield in a private Gulf-stream G450, a long-range jet owned by Mirage AirTransport. That was an hour ago, just about the time Dennis Paull was ordering him taken into custody.

Tarasov knew that he narrowly missed capture, but the funny thing was that he didn't seem to care. Staring out the Perspex window at the city of gray clouds below him, he wondered where his life had gone. It wasn't as if the years had passed through his fingers like grains of sand. It was more that he'd taken handfuls of those years and thrown them into the sea, where they had immediately sunk, drowned beneath the waves, as if erased off the face of the earth. In a strange way, he existed only in this moment. Whatever had occurred during those years belonged to the past of some other Gerard Tarasov, one to whom he was not even remotely related. It was as if he had been born from the head of Zeus, or, more appropriately, Wotan, the sad, defeated one-eyed god of German mythology beloved by Wagner. In any case, he had erased all memory of his parents from his mind. He'd had a sister once, but she was dead, blown up on the West Bank by an Islamic extremist. It was his attempts to keep her alive in his mind that had led him to this moment in time, all the sinister threads of his life pointing the way to failure. Cause and effect, that's all life was. He had loved his sister. He had never recovered from her death. From that moment on, his life had become a single strand he followed blindly through the darkness, looking neither to the left nor to the right.

Below him, the cloud city rolled by. But above, there was only the blue-black sky, clear and unblemished, at the apex of the world.

WERNER AX, traveling under the name Werner von Verschuer, German national, arrived at Fiumicino Airport in Rome, where, the moment he passed through immigration, a car was waiting to drive him to a walled-in villa on the city's outskirts, complete with a private airfield from which he could take off when Acacia's mission was accomplished sometime tomorrow night. On the way, he called Reggie Herr.

"Where are you?" he said curtly.

"With the kill team."

"Good. And Fraine?"

"Full fathom floorplant."

Ax nodded to himself. "What's your ETD?"

"We're going over the architectural plans for Bethesda now. I've got Fillin figuring the work-arounds on the hospital's security systems."

"There's bound to be extra security personnel, undoubtedly Secret Service, but you can't discount a contingent of Marines."

"I'm so hoping Marines," Herr said with obvious relish.

"No fuckups this time, Reggie. That comes direct from the Syrian. You know the consequences of failure."

"I don't plan on dying today, or anytime in the foreseeable future."

"Good. You need to be out of there within the hour; your expertise is required elsewhere."

"No problem. Reeder can take it from here."

"A Bell X-1 helicopter will pick you up at the rendezvous point. A Mirage Gulfstream is standing by to take you the rest of the way. An envelope with your instructions, encoded in the usual manner, will be waiting."

He cut the connection, sitting in brooding silence as the car headed to the villa. It was a pity his plan to capture McClure had fallen apart. He would not now be able to find the meaning of that damnable children's rhyme.

The guard watching the CCTV image, having identified the car and driver, opened the electronic gates, and the car rolled up the long driveway. Far to his left, on the edge of the private airfield, Werner could make out the silhouette of the Mirage Gulfstream G450 crouched like a cougar, waiting.

The car drew up to the villa's entrance, the driver hopped out, and opened his door, and he emerged. Lights blazed from the perfectly manicured pencil pines. He trotted up the steps, the gigantic wooden door opened soundlessly, and he was welcomed into the villa by a tall, svelte blonde from somewhere in Russia, who looked like Anna Kournikova. She had a face meant for sex. *Leave it to the Syrian,* he thought, as he took the glass of champagne she offered.

"This way," she said. "You are expected."

He followed her, his gaze drawn to her buttocks swiveling provocatively beneath her tight skirt. Werner was quite certain she wasn't wearing underwear. She led him into an enormous study, outfitted with desk chairs, upholstered sofas. An antique sideboard was topped with a large arrangement of fresh flowers in a cut-crystal vase.

"Please make yourself comfortable," the blonde said with a smile.

Werner lifted his glass as he returned her smile. "Pour one for yourself, while you're at it, and come join me."

"Certainly."

Moments later, full flute in hand, gazing into the blonde's cornflower-blue eyes, he heard the front door slam and footfalls on the oak floorboards.

Werner clinked his glass against hers. "To us, my dear," he said.

The blonde giggled and leaned forward. Her lips parted.

ALLI RETURNED to Bethesda's eighth floor without incident. Every Secret Service agent knew her on sight and, furthermore, they had watched her accompany Jack out the front door. As an added security precaution, Paull had arranged for only one elevator to access the eighth floor, and manned barriers had been set up between the seventh-, ninth-, and eighth-floor stairwells.

The makeshift situation room held an odd, soulless feeling without Jack and Dennis Paull. Caro was working Leopard's laptop with continuous, compulsive stabs of her fingertips. Across the room, Vera was sitting with her arms crossed over her breasts, staring at the wall. Nona Heroe had left with Paull.

The moment Alli walked in, Caro looked at Vera. She also closed the laptop as Alli came across the room. "It looks like you and I are the only ones talking to each other. Grumpy over there hasn't said a word since you bugged out. Where did you go, by the way?"

"I wanted to make sure this place was totally secure."

Caro nodded. "Satisfied?"

"For the moment, anyway."

Caro snorted. "Yeah, you've got so much experience."

"I stayed here to protect you," Alli said, with such gravity the ironic smile died on Caro's face.

Ducking her head, she opened the laptop and continued her work.

"I have something to tell the two of you." Alli tried looking at Vera, but at that moment it was too difficult. "Your father has had a heart attack."

"What?" Vera, rising, looked as if Alli had just delivered an electric shock.

"He's had a double bypass."

"Who gives a shit?" Caro said without raising her head.

Vera rounded on her. "Yeah, that would be your response."

"Happy to hear I'm an open book to you."

Two discs of color bloomed on Vera's cheeks. "You really are a little shit."

"You're the one who flaunts herself in front of him," Caro said, "and *I'm* the shit? What the hell did he ever do for us?"

"We're here because of him."

"My point exactly." She glanced up then. "At least I don't lie about my feelings . . . or other things."

Vera's cheeks were flaming. "Shut up!"

Alli looked from one to the other. "Caro, please—"

"I'm sick of all this adolescent sniping. I was better off when I had no family." She rounded on Alli. "You and Vera are such buddies? Well, guess what, she's been lying to you from the moment she met you."

Vera blanched. "Caro, no!"

Caro's eyebrows raised. A cruel smile spread across her face. "Tell her, Vera. Go ahead."

Vera was trembling visibly. "Shut up!"

"If you don't tell her," Caro said, "I will."

"What the hell is this?" Alli said, looking from one to the other.

"Listen, Alli, I . . ."

Caro snorted. "Your *best friend* has something to tell you, Alli."

Alli did not like the way she emphasized those two words. The silence stretched on for so long she felt compelled to say, "Vera, what is it?"

Vera took a deep breath, let it out in a hiss. "I've been lying to you."

"About what?"

"About who I am." Vera's face was bleak, her eyes pleading. "I'm your cousin. Caro's half-sister."

Alli stood in stunned silence before finding her voice. "You mean . . . ?"

"Henry Holt Carson's my father, yeah."

"Good God!" Alli jolted away, pulling her hands free. "Now I understand why my uncle chose you to be my roommate at Fearington, why you became my friend."

"Now you're getting it," Caro said.

Vera gave her sister a sharp look before turning back to Alli. "No," she said, "you don't."

"It was all part of my uncle's scheme. He wanted you to get inside my head, he wanted to control me, to—"

"Alli, stop it! Please!"

"Why? Why should I stop? Am I wrong?"

Vera's face was contorted. "Not in the beginning. I hated you in the beginning, but, Alli, that was before I got to know you. You have to believe me."

Alli backed away. "Who are you? I don't know you at all."

"But you do." Vera came after her. "You know me better than anyone in the world. Nothing we ever shared is false."

"Except the most important thing!"

"I wanted to tell you. You can't imagine. Every time we were together, just the two of us, that's all I could think about."

"And?"

"Somehow the words would never come out."

"Coward!"

"Yes, absolutely. I admit it. In this I am a coward. But you have to understand you're my only friend, the only person I ever felt safe with. I couldn't—there was no way I could jeopardize that, and then the longer the lie existed, the more afraid I became."

"Everything we spoke about, every moment of our friendship, was based on a lie. When is a liar not a liar, Vera?" Alli turned and walked away.

"No, please, Alli." Vera lurched after her. "Tell me what to do. I don't know how to make this all right."

"I don't think there is a way."

"Please don't say that. Please, please, please."

"And you talk to me of trust?" Caro said to Alli. "I learned never to trust anyone, and neither should you."

Alli was silent.

Vera, stricken all over again, turned away.

Caro snorted. "Nice surprise, isn't it? But what the hell, we're all fucking liars. Might as well get used to it. Every member of this family has been living a lie, yeah?"

"That's enough," Alli said. "I'm sick to death of both of you."

She stalked out into the hall and stood, hugging herself, feeling tremors race through her uncontrollably. Her mind was roiling at Vera's betrayal. She wished she could think straight, but emotions kept clogging the lines of communication.

She felt a presence, did not have to turn her head to know that it was Vera.

"Alli—" Clearly, Vera was about to go on, but maybe she felt the frost coming off Alli, so she abruptly changed her mind. A silence fell between them. Alli was about to return to the situation room when Vera said, "Do you know anything more about my father?"

"No." Alli's voice was cold, as removed as her emotions.

"You'd tell me, though, wouldn't you?"

"Why d'you even care?"

"He's my father."

"When has he given any of us a reason to care about him?"

Vera made an animal noise in the back of her throat. "Caro's a fuck-ing psycho."

"Maybe it's in the Carson genes."

"Yeah, we're all psychos on this bus."

At any other time Alli would have laughed, but not now.

"Alli—" Vera tried to begin again.

"Don't. Just leave it alone, okay?"

Vera nodded silently. She stood rigid, tears welling in her eyes, splashing down onto her shirt. Alli, contriving to ignore her, turned and was heading back into the situation room when Vera said very softly, "You know, just then you sounded exactly like your uncle."

DYADYA GOURDJIEV, risen, showered, shaved, and dressed, used the hotel's interior phone to ring Annika's room. Not receiving an answer, he went out of his room and down the hall to hers. Using a spare key card, he entered her room and performed a thorough search. Satisfied that she was gone, he took the elevator down to the lobby and went out into the late Roman night. It had been a full day since he and Annika had arrived in the Italian capital. Events were moving at an accelerated pace elsewhere in the world, but they were moving forward here as well. He strolled down to the Roman Forum, stood across the wide street with its swirling traffic, contemplating the adjacent Colosseum. Astonishing, to see these relics of a bygone age risen in the middle of the modern city, retaining all their Caesarean grandeur and power, as if both the emperors and the gods of the ancient empire were still gazing down on their descendants.

He crossed the street, following a Roman, so he wouldn't get run over. As in most of Rome, there were no traffic lights to be seen. The physical eruption of the past filled his mind with memories of Oriel Jovovich Batchuk. Once again, he wondered how, by their decisions, the divergent roads taken, two close friends had morphed into impla-cable enemies. Time had a way of warping one's spirit, if not one's soul, he thought. He wondered if the past could have happened any other way, if, by making other decisions, the two of them could have avoided the deaths from ten thousand cuts they had inflicted on one another, boiling away every emotion except hatred, distilled like a venom of immense potency.

At that precise moment he sensed that he was being followed.

He kept to the periphery of the Colosseum, which was lit up like the onion domes of the Kremlin and St. Basil's. Iconic structures always were. Drawing a stiletto, he proceeded past the first two ancient entrances, heading around toward the flank of the structure. His bones hurt and the soles of his feet ached from walking on the Roman cobblestones, but he ignored these disturbances. Ducking behind a column, he waited for his tail to come abreast of his hiding place. Having lost sight of his quarry, the man's gun was out, a discreet .22, whose discharge would easily be mistaken for a vehicle backfire.

Gourdjiev stepped out and, as the tail's head swiveled toward him, he slipped the stiletto blade, angled slightly upward, between two ribs. The tip pierced the heart, and Gourdjiev withdrew the blade before the tail could topple over, taking Gourdjiev with him. He was wiping the blade down on the tail's coat when he spotted the backup. Then the second and third men came into view, quickly converging on him.

"WE LOST General Tarasov," Paull said in Jack's ear. "He vanished into the wild blue yonder."

"What about Reggie Herr?"

"Gone to ground."

Jack stared out the plane's Perspex window at the jet-black nothingness of night. There was no sense of forward motion, let alone speed. Something was swimming around in his head, some connection between twins and the name of Ax's new legend, von Verschuer.

"Dennis, do me a favor. Look in Wikipedia for a Werner von Verschuer."

"Hold on. . . . Okay, the site's up. Typing now. . . . Hmmm."

"What is it?"

"Well, there's no Werner, but there's an entry for . . . Good God. A Dr. Otmar Freiherr von Verschuer was a leading scientist best known for his research in genetics with a particular interest in twins."

Jack felt his head about to explode with possible scenarios. "There's more, isn't there?"

"Christ, yes, and I hope you're sitting down."

"Go on."

"In 1937, at the Institute for Hereditary Biology and Racial Hygiene in Frankfurt, one Josef Mengele became von Verschuer's assistant."

That was it! Jack thought. Now he knew, but before he said anything he needed one more bit of confirming evidence. "Dennis, what does it say about von Verschuer?"

"Quite a bit. He was married, he had a daughter named Margarethe, who became Mengele's mistress."

And there it was in all its dreadful detail. "Mengele worked at the Kaiser Wilhelm Institute of Anthropology, Human Heredity, and Eugenics, or, in German, Kaiser-Wilhelm-Institut für Anthropologie, menschliche Erblehre, und Eugenik. In other words, KWIfA, the notation you found in General Tarasov's Three-thirteen file."

He heard Paull's swiftly indrawn breath. "What are you saying?"

"I think it's possible that Josef Mengele may have secretly gotten his mistress pregnant. I think it's possible that Margarethe von Verschuer had a son. I think it's possible that Werner von Verschuer isn't another legend, I think it's Ax's real name."

"Ax is Joseph Mengele's son?"

"Do you get the sick joke, Dennis? Where better to hide out than among the Norns, a cadre of ex-Nazis cleared by the OSS? They created the Werner Ax legend for him. Beautiful, right? In a sense, he didn't even exist—officially, surely not. His father would have seen to that."

"So the sets of twins are his—what?—experiments?"

"I'm very much afraid so, Dennis. I'm willing to bet that Acacia is made up of these twins."

"Goddamn."

"It looks as if we've had a continuation of the Nazis' most infamous and horrifying experiment on human beings bubbling under our noses for decades."

Twenty-four

NONA KNEW she ought to be paying attention to the phone conversation Dennis Paull was having with Jack McClure, especially when he said, "So the sets of twins are his—what?—experiments?" And then, a moment later, "Goddamn," but she could not get the image of Alan laid out on the coroner's slab out of her mind.

Perhaps she didn't want to. It was still difficult to get her head around the fact that her friend and mentor was dead. It seemed so ironic—she was the one on the streets. If anyone was to die, surely it should have been her. And yet here she was, sitting in the office of the secretary of homeland security while Alan was a million miles away, lost to her forever. Why was it, she thought, that you never truly appreciated how much someone meant to you until they were gone? Was that a common human trait? If so, it was one she'd rather not be burdened with. Unbidden, her mind reached back to past incidents, moments she and Alan had shared, intimate pieces of the past that now, abruptly, had lost their luster, going slightly out of focus, as if her memories of him were already slipping beyond her grasp. It was this thought that finally brought tears to her eyes, and she bent over, face in her hands, as if she needed to hide away from the world.

"Nona," Paull said, through with his call, "are you okay?"

"Don't talk to me."

She could hear him come around from behind his desk, watched him approach through eyes clouded with tears. "Why did you rope Alan into this mess? You got him killed."

"I suppose that's one way to look at it."

Wiping her eyes, she stood up. "Is there any other?"

"Nona, I am truly sorry for your loss. Alan was a great asset—"

"That's not all he was!" she cried.

"Sorry." Paull raised his hands. "That came out wrong. Of course he was more than an asset, much more. But the fact remains that he wanted this assignment, I didn't twist his arm."

"With your power you didn't have to twist his arm."

Paull shook his head. "Why don't you take the rest of the day off? We can talk about—"

"I have nothing more to talk about with you," she said, turning on her heel and stalking out of the office.

"FRANKIE, WHAT d'you think of your sister now? I just crashed my career." Nona came and sat beside her brother. "I just screamed at the secretary of homeland security, can you beat that? I'll probably be black-balled off Metro and any other law enforcement organization in the country." She shrugged as she took his limp hand in hers. He looked just the same as he had for years, the machines sucking air in and out of his body, keeping him alive—just barely. "Oh, fuck it, Frankie. Just fuck it." She stared at his placid face, trying to remember the funny, happy, brave person he once was, but there seemed no relation to the hunk of meat lying in the bed beside her. "Damnit, Frankie, why don't you come back to me? What are you waiting for?"

As she did from time to time, when his near-death state became too much for her to bear, she went through his zip bag she kept under his bed. There was nothing of real value in it, so she wasn't worried about it being stolen. But each and every item inside was invaluable to her because they were all mementos of her brother's life. As she took out each piece and handled it, his life returned to the real world, anchored by these bits of flotsam and jetsam that he had collected over the years.

There was an admission ticket from Disney World, a rabbit's-foot key chain, so old the fur had been worn away, a couple of faded color photos of Frankie and Nona as kids, in summer shorts, their arms around each other, squinting into the sun, some dyed feathers and a yellow and blue polka-dot bikini bottom from a particularly raucous Mardi Gras. A song mix Nona had made for him before he shipped out to the Horn of Africa in 2002. She held the label up, reflecting on the string of songs she had selected, concluding with Fleetwood Mac's "Go Your Own Way."

She slipped the CD out of its plastic case and into the portable player she had brought, clicked on the Play button. While Mick Jagger sang "Start Me Up," she looked over the small carved wood elephant charm Frankie had picked up in a bazaar in some unnamed African country, a couple of machine gun bullet casings strung onto a beaded-metal chain, his ring of keys to a car and apartment she had finally sold, and several coins from different African nations. There was also the SSD card she had sent him, filled with e-mails, photos of her, friends he'd asked to see, and a couple of MP3s of songs he'd requested, Prince's "Do It All Night" and Marvin Gaye's "What's Going On."

She had never looked at the material on the SSD card, feeling that it might be too painful, but now, with Alan's death, her desperation to feel closer to Frankie had reached an intolerable level. Her hand trembled, feeling the SSD card on the tops of her finger. It was so small, so light, and yet brimming with the last moments of the life that had flowed back and forth between her and her brother.

Her vision blurred, she inserted the tiny card into her mobile, wiped away her tears as she waited for the information to appear on the screen.

Dear NaNa . . . the first e-mail began. NaNa was what Frankie had called her when he was little; for whatever reason, he could not pronounce Nona, and between them the nickname had stuck. She read the e-mails, back and forth, first him, then her response, on and on. Slowly, inexorably, his life in the Horn of Africa resurrected itself. And yet, as she reread the correspondence, she was struck by the spaces that should have been filled up but weren't. She knew that there were things he couldn't tell her while over there, but for the first time she wondered what it was he had really been up to.

She looked up, her gaze falling on his placid face. Frankie, who was no longer Frankie. Her heart broke all over again, but this time she didn't think she would ever be able to piece it back together.

After a time, she returned to the files on the SSD card. She played "Do It All Night" and "What's Going On." Both of the songs reduced her to tears, head down, forearms on knees, like the lost little girl she once had been.

But her head came up when the last note of "What's Going On" faded out and the first bars of Prince's "Darling Nikki" came on. *That's interesting,* she thought. *I never sent him this track.* Then she remembered Frankie's lifelong girlfriend, Nikki. What was her last name? Harris, that's right. Hadn't Nikki Harris broken up with him while he was still in the Horn? Hadn't he told her it had happened right after he'd sent her a proposal e-mail because he couldn't get a call through? Or was it before he had a chance to send it?

This idea sent her poring through the rest of the files on the SSD card. She found nothing pertaining to Nikki, but she did find an odd file, or at least part of one. It was an e-mail addressed to her, but never finished, and, therefore never sent. In many of its expressions it seemed rushed.

> NaNa, the weirdness here continues unabated 2 b honest I don't know how much more I can stomach. I want to come home but I don't want to be branded a coward or think of myself that way. I will if I come home now, and yet there's something in the pit of my stomach that tells me this is all wrong, no matter what Lt. Bishop says. . . .

Abruptly unable to draw breath, Nona stopped right there. Her hands were shaking so hard she had to rest them on her knees, but then her knees began to shake. Her mouth was dry and she poured herself a glass of ice water from the plastic pitcher on the movable bedside table. She had insisted one be there every day in case Frankie woke up, even though there was no chance he would ever wake up. Its presence made her feel a sense of hope where none existed.

She drank convulsively, almost choking on the first gulp. Her head was pounding in time to the hammering of her heart. She forced herself to continue reading.

We're about to ship out, don't know where but its not where the Marines we came with r going, that's for damn sure. I caught a peek at the plane taking us. Its not military, not even American. MimicAir. Sounds like a joke, right? Except nothing heres a joke. Took a look on the net & found MimicAir is a subsid of Mirage AirTransport, who the fuckre they? Did some digging in Bishops work orders—ill be fucked for sure if anyone finds out—& found a company Cakra Holdings being billed should ck it. Bishop coming finish later

And that was it, the end of the e-mail that Frankie hadn't finished, hadn't sent, and had been lying at the bottom of his bag for years, waiting to be found.

Bishop, she thought murderously. *Fucking Bishop.*

A sound caused her to look up.

"Secretary Paull."

Paull stood on the threshold to the room.

"What are you doing here?"

"May I come in?"

"Of course."

He came across the room to stand by the bed. Frankie lay still, inert between them.

"I regret what I said before."

He waved her words away. "I can only imagine how upset you are."

She nodded. "Thank you."

"Any change?"

She was surprised. "I wasn't aware you knew about him."

Paull studied Frankie's face. "He was a good soldier."

"He was."

"A brave man." He cleared his throat. "I was worried about you."

She caught the note in his voice. "You mean you were worried about Bishop."

He smiled. "What you might do to him, more to the point."

Nona let out a deep breath she had been holding. "Now I have more reason than ever to want to wring Bishop's neck."

Paull's eyes lit up. "Tell me."

REEDER WAS not a man to suffer fools. He was both a thinker and a doer—that odd duck, so valuable to those who understood the full scope of his talents. He had been many things in his thirty years: a carpenter, an architect, a teacher, a killer. He was entirely self-taught, haunting both libraries and the Internet, studying when he might have been sleeping. In fact, sleep was as foreign to him as Mandarin was to the average American. He had come to Reggie's attention through a series of multiple killings Reggie was following, along with the police and the FBI. Eleven women in West Texas, then another eleven three years later on Long Island. All dark-haired, Hispanic, or dusky-hued. All prostitutes. Neither the police nor the FBI had as much as a single clue. This dual outbreak was what sparked Reggie's attention; he was both admiring and envious. He found Reeder where law enforcement could not. He went to Werner, wanting to bring Reeder into the fold. At first Werner was reluctant, and Reggie knew why.

"He won't be like the first one," Reggie said, forestalling Werner's objection. "We won't have another Incident."

"That first one almost did Acacia in," Werner said darkly. "It was a miscalculation to insert a control twin into the mix. I sincerely regret that. It might have gotten all the way up the line to Three-thirteen and me. It could have been the end of everything."

"Could have, yes," Herr agreed. "It's a good thing I ordered Bishop to put a stop to it, and he did. There was minimum danger, and this time, none at all." He grinned. "You should see this guy. Fucking killing machine."

"Really?"

Werner was intrigued, as Herr knew he would be. Killing machines were his business, his only business.

"All right. Let's see this prodigy in action."

Herr arranged a demonstration—the victim was not a prostitute, not a woman at all. He knew Werner was expecting a real test, so he chose a Marine.

"Too easy," Werner had said. "I want him to really show me something. Have him take out a SEAL."

"A SEAL?" Herr had been momentarily taken aback. "Won't that cause a shitstorm of an inquiry?"

"Leave that to me," Werner had said. "You concentrate on this killing machine's target."

The result impressed even Werner. Three days later, Herr met Reeder for breakfast and offered him a job. Reeder had a newspaper open to an account of the brutal murder of a Navy SEAL outside a downtown bar at the hands of a pair of wacked-out meth-heads, both shot to death by responding members of Chief of Detectives Leonard Bishop's High Crimes Unit. The story perfectly delineated, accepted by the press without hesitation. Twenty-three victims had for the moment sated him; he was ready to move on to fresher abattoirs.

In Herr's mind, if there was a negative about Reeder it was that he took his own sweet time. Reggie would have preferred that Reeder and his team begin their assault on the eighth floor of Bethesda immediately upon studying the plans, but this was Reeder's MO, the one that had allowed him to feast off of twenty-three people without leaving behind the slightest clue for law enforcement to discover.

"Just get it done," he had told Reeder just before he left to rendezvous with the Bell X-1. It was a needless command—Reeder had never failed an assignment Reggie had given him—but it gave Reggie a sense of being in control.

Now Reeder, meticulous and dogged, addressed his team of four people he had handpicked from the pool Herr had provided, and gave them their final instructions. All four were, of course, one half of twins from Werner Ax's project, though Reeder had no knowledge of this, nor, if he had, would he know what to make of it. Only Werner and Reggie, himself a member of that special fraternity Werner had created, knew and understood.

Still, Reeder could sense a certain homogeneity of both concentration and purpose in the four individuals, as if they had trained at the same facility, which was what they had, in fact, done, all their lives. Reeder looked from one to the other, and briefly wondered what it would be like to possess their indefinable, almost godlike fervor.

Then, shrugging off such useless introspection, he once again took them through the stages of the assault from first moment to last. Reeder was bald, a man with wide shoulders, a barrel chest, and the demonic eyes of a goat, perhaps a direct consequence of having witnessed too much death, most of it inflicted by himself. Apart from those eyes, it would be difficult to pick him out of a crowd, which was why he often wore sunglasses, and often a hairpiece, in public.

As the team finished its last run-through, Fillin, the electrician, said, "I've said it before and I'll say it again, I don't like it."

Reeder fixed him with his goat's eyes. "What don't you like?"

"This here." Fillin's forefinger stabbed out. "You've given me thirty seconds to get to the main junction box and bypass both the main and the backup alarm circuits."

Reeder cocked his head. "That's not enough?"

"No, it certainly is not."

Reeder's left hand was a blur, connecting with Fillin's jaw. As Fillin stumbled back, grabbing his face, Reeder said, "How about now, cocksucker?"

Silence, apart from Fillin's harsh, uneven breathing, like puffs of smoke from a brush fire.

"As for the rest of you, get some sleep," Reeder said, fixing them one at a time in his animal stare. "When I wake you, we go."

"I'M OUTTA here," Vera said when she encountered Alli just outside the situation room.

"You need to stay right where you are." Alli tilted her head.

"Please, Alli. I can't stand another minute with that cold-hearted bitch."

"You two need to find a way to get along."

Vera tossed her head. "Fuck, has the whole world gone crazy?"

"Come on," Alli said.

When they reentered the situation room, Caro was busy on Leopard's laptop.

"Find out anything new?" Alli asked.

Caro glanced up, then back down again. "Nothing of interest."

"Then what are you doing?"

"Waiting for my father to die."

Alli watched Caro working away for a moment, then, without a word of warning, snatched the computer from out of her lap.

"Hey!"

She glanced down at the screen, which was filled with text concerning Mirage AirTransport and one of its subsidiaries, MimicAir. "What the hell is this?" she said.

Then she saw that both companies were owned by LightFast Optical Networks, which was part of Owl Offshore Trust, which, in turn, was owned by Hyde Rubber & Tyre, Ltd., which was owned by Picketline Metalworks GmbH, which was owned by Linolean Properties Pty HK, on and on, through a maze of more manufacturers, corporations, trusts, and holding companies, until reaching the center.

Alli looked up. "Damnit, Caro, what is this?"

Caro passed a hand across her face. "I don't —"

"Come on, Caro. Spill."

"I guess there's no point in . . ." Caro hesitated, then nodded in acquiescence. "It's a map of the Syrian's holdings."

"EVERYONE YOU asked for is on this call," Paull said. "We reestablished contact. Werner von Verschuer is in a villa on the outskirts of Rome that has its own airfield."

"Rome," Jack said from his seat on the plane. Putting Paull on hold, Jack called a flight officer over, told him to inform the pilot of their new destination.

"We'll have to refuel, sir."

"Quick as you can," Jack told him.

The officer nodded and went back up the aisle as Jack returned to his call. "I think I know Acacia's target."

"The Iranian supreme leader."

"It would seem that Acacia's been re-formed to succeed where the previous iteration failed."

"I don't have to tell you what an insane plan this is. With no clear successor or plans for the aftermath, the attack has the very high risk of setting off a nuclear war, even if it succeeds. China and Israel are certain to become involved, then Russia. We'll be sucked in, and devil take the hindmost. I'm scrambling a SEAL team to the area, but there's no telling if they'll arrive in time. Thirty hours from now we'll have a night of low loom." That was military-speak for low moon luminosity, the ideal moment for a night raid. "Acacia is von Verschuer's baby. He controls the group. It's up to you to stop him at all costs."

"I understand."

"Still, I'm at a loss to understand why all this is being undertaken."

"One step at a time," Jack said. "Cakra Holdings is owned by the Syrian. Alli and I found that name in his villa we raided last year."

Paull made a noise in the back of his throat akin to that emitted by a lion prior to an attack. "From the information Caro and Alli wrested from Leopard's laptop, the local African airlines used to transport Acacia are owned jointly by Three-thirteen and the Syrian."

"That can't be a coincidence." Jack switched his mobile from one ear to the other. The plane had started its steep descent. "Three-thirteen, Acacia, Werner von Verschuer are all connected with the Syrian."

"An unholy alliance if ever there was one. But why would Three-thirteen ally itself with the Syrian?"

"He's got unfathomably deep pockets."

"True enough," Paull admitted, "but that doesn't explain what the Syrian gets out of the alliance."

Jack thought a moment. "Alli?"

"Here, Jack."

"What's your read on Caroline? Is she still secretly working for the Syrian?"

"Hard to say for sure. She's devious enough, so it's certainly possible.

What I do know is that she didn't want me to see the information on Mirage and MimicAir."

Jack considered for a moment. "I had asked her to find out who owned Mirage."

"Right," Alli said. "I don't think she was going to tell you."

"Why?"

There was a small silence, Alli thinking. "She must still be connected with the Syrian in some way."

"Or," Jack said, "she's been using Leopard's laptop to rechannel the Syrian's fortune into her own accounts." He considered. "I think she's in real and imminent danger."

"Alli," Paull said, "lock down the eighth floor now. Absolutely no one in or out."

"I'm on it. Anything else?"

"Yes. Try to find out whose side Caroline is on."

"Caro is on Caro's side."

"Get confirmation, then. I want to know what she's up to."

"Right."

"Nona," Jack said, "are you on?"

"Yes, Jack. Secretary Paull and I are both in my brother's hospital room."

Jack felt the plane begin its descent toward the airfield the pilot had chosen for refueling. "I'm so sorry about Alan. I know what the two of you meant to each other."

"I appreciate that."

Her voice was soft, subdued, and Jack imagined her tamping down hard on her emotions.

"I'd like you to go over with me everything in Frankie's kit bag."

"Okay."

Nona went through the list. When she came to the coins, Jack said, "Stop right there. Tell me what countries they're from."

"Eritrea, Somalia, Djibouti, Iran, Sudan—"

"Wait." Jack was pressed back as the plane hit the runway, then the pressure came off as they began to taxi. "Did you say Iran?"

"That's right."

"Frankie was part of Acacia?"

"I . . . I don't know."

A sudden revelation bloomed in Jack's mind. "Are you and Frankie twins?"

"Yes, but—"

"I think he was part of Acacia."

"How could that be? He never made it out of the Horn of Africa."

Good question, Jack thought. "Do you know what happened to him?"

"He was hit in a mortar attack on the compound. He was very near the epicenter."

"That jibes with the official record," Paull interjected. "I've checked."

"I'm not interested in the official record. Nona, how did you hear about Frankie?"

"A general came by to see me. He was there. He sat with me and answered all my questions."

"General Tarasov?"

"Yes. How did you know?"

"This is all one gigantic spider's web," Paull said. "But I'll be damned if I know what's at the center."

The plane rolled to a stop, overalled mechanics jumped off the truck as it pulled up beside them, and they began the refueling process. The pilot must have put the fear of God into them, because they were working as fast as a pit crew at the Talladega Superspeed way.

"I have a feeling that only Werner von Verschuer can tell us," Jack said.

"Maybe," Paull said. "But I still don't see the connection with Iran. I maybe see the insane logic of neocons wanting to assassinate the Iranian supreme leader, but the Syrian is a businessman and a terrorist. What could he possibly gain from a regime change? He has many interests throughout the Middle East. It seems to me that an areawide destabilization and a possible nuclear war would be the last things he'd want."

Paull was right on all counts. So what weren't they seeing? Jack wondered whether Frankie held the answer in his impenetrable mind.

"One thing that bothers me," Jack said now. "If Acacia was made up of members of von Verschuer's twins program, why was Frankie recruited?"

"Frankie and I are twins," Nona said.

"Yes, but neither of you were in von Verschuer's program," Paull said.

Refueling complete, the jet began to race down the runway, lifting off in a precipitous climb into the clouds.

"Dennis, take care of her."

"Then there's the matter of Bishop. We have no solid evidence to charge him with. All we have is Nona's word against his regarding the meeting with General Tarasov. It's not enough to—"

"I'll take care of Bishop," Nona said.

"I don't think you're in any state of mind to—"

"No offense, Mr. Secretary, but you don't know me well enough to accurately assess my condition."

"She's right, Dennis. Neither of us knows that part of the equation like she does. Nona, do you need backup?"

"That will only complicate matters, Jack."

"Dennis?"

Paull gave his grudging consent.

"Okay, then. As soon as either of you has anything more, call me."

Jack sat back, staring out the window. Rain slanted down from a darkened sky, the drops striking the Perspex window and juddering down. Then the darkness lifted. They pierced the cloud bank, flying into absolute stillness.

He had yet to understand what role Dyadya Gourdjiev and, by extension, Annika had in all this. For some reason he was not looking forward to finding out.

TWENTY-FIVE

"DAMNIT, ANNIKA."

Radomil looked from the Syrian to Annika. They were confronting each other, appropriately enough, in the pool house in the Syrian's Roman villa. Outside, the wind gusted fitfully, moaning through the pencil pines, sending tiny ripples across the water of the heated Olympic-sized pool. Steam rose from its surface, swirling like dust devils in the desert.

Annika smiled. "It has been a long time, Iraj."

The Syrian was an anomaly in the postmodern world: willing to work with anyone of any race, religion, or creed in order to achieve his goals. His was a method of inclusion, rather than the exclusion that these days had become the norm. But after all was said and done, what was the Syrian? Incredibly wealthy businessman, international criminal, terrorist? None of those, or all of them? He was an enigma, reclusive to the point of obsession, patient to the point of sainthood. More than anything else, he resembled an immensely careful spider, spinning his web for years, encompassing people in far-flung corners of the globe, who would, at the moment he chose, work unwittingly to fulfill his design. In all these traits, he resembled Dyadya Gourdjiev. They both had grand designs, thought as strategically as chess masters, and planned for the future.

"How is your grandfather?" Iraj said.

"Old."

"But not ill."

The Syrian missed the slightest tremor in the corner of her eye. "Thankfully, no."

"Praises, then." The Syrian was a big man as well as tall, his shoulders and arms knotted with muscle, as if he had been a hod carrier or a bricklayer all his life. His hands were big and square, callused, their backs ropy, dark as coffee. But his eyes held the talent of a sculptor. It was, of course, his eyes that were most remarked upon. One green, the other blue, each seemed to be buried in a different head or, more accurately, connected to a different brain. The Syrian instilled fear, even within his own cadre.

Radomil felt his head swimming. "What is this, Annika? You *know* the Syrian?"

"Iraj and I have been friends for many years." She laughed. "Well, perhaps 'friends' is not the correct term."

The Syrian grinned, his strong white teeth gleaming in his handsome, dusky face. "Radomil, will you please excuse us now?"

When they were alone, the Syrian turned to Annika, his features hardening like cement, and said, "Why have you disobeyed your instructions never to come?"

"I WANT a piece."

Caro looked at Alli with a puzzled expression. "A piece of what?"

"Whatever you've planned to steal from the Syrian."

"What?" Caro barked a brittle laugh. "Steal from the Syrian? You're nuts."

Alli, who had returned to the situation room from the unused lounge where she had joined Paull's conference call with Jack, placed Leopard's computer on Caro's lap. "Go on. Keep on with what you're doing. Only this time, I want a cut."

"You," Caro said with derision. "You're not someone to take a cut of anything."

"In the Syrian's case, I'll make an exception."

"I don't believe you."

Vera, curious about the direction their conversation was taking, had hauled herself out of her self-imposed mental exile and, glancing from one to the other, approached the narrow desk where Caro sat.

"Listen, Caro, last year, Jack and I were in Albania, we penetrated the Syrian's compound, but he had already fled. We found your desk, though at the time we didn't know it was yours. You had ripped out all the pertinent drives and backups. We almost got you, we almost got the Syrian. You both beat us there, so, you bet I want a piece of the action you're planning to take from him."

Caro looked fixedly at Vera. "And what d'*you* want?"

Vera lunged at Caro, but Alli, moving quickly, intervened, stepped between them.

Vera's mouth, teeth bared, snapped at her. "Let me go, you controlling bitch!"

Still, Alli held her back from reaching across the desk, watching them both with a maddeningly diffident expression.

"Look at her!" Vera cried. "She doesn't give a shit about us, she doesn't give a shit about anything but herself."

It occurred to Alli that if she didn't put aside her pain at Vera's betrayal, there was no hope of the three of them ever speaking to one another civilly, let alone aid in this mission. Much to her surprise, she found that she wanted them to get along. These two young women, difficult as they were, were still family, her flesh and blood. She had known too many siblings and family members who were estranged, and she had found it disturbing. Besides, there was knowledge, strength, and potential power if they could find a way to work together. She just didn't know how that was going to happen.

"NOTHING'S CHANGED," Annika said. "You can still bullshit with the best of them."

The Syrian cocked his head. "I consider that a compliment."

Annika inclined her head. "As it was meant."

The Syrian watched her carefully. "I took great pains to keep myself hidden from you and your grandfather. This is necessary to our plans. It was agreed upon by the three of us. So again I ask, why have you sought me out?"

"My grandfather and I were almost killed several times while escaping Russia."

"So I heard. It pained me to hear it."

"It pained me, too, especially when I discovered that Grigori was working for Ax."

"Grigori was part of Ax's experiments, what would you expect?" Then he frowned. "Why would Ax want you and Gourdjiev killed?"

She shrugged. "Does he know that we are allies?"

Iraj considered the idea for a moment. "Perhaps we should ask him."

"Ax is here?"

Iraj spoke softly into his mobile. A moment later, the door opened and Radomil ushered Werner Ax in.

"Why have you brought him here, Iraj?"

"Iraj?" Werner frowned deeply "I don't understand. Iraj is an Iranian name."

"So it is, Werner." The man the world knew as the Syrian rose. "You see, I was born in Sedeh. Now it is known as Khomeyni Shahr and has been engulfed by the city sprawl of Isfahan."

Werner's voice was hushed by shock. "You are Iranian."

"An Iranian who repudiates the 1979 revolution. An Iranian who means to restore order in the current chaos of my long-lost homeland." Iraj's right hand clenched into a fist.

Annika stood up as she looked from one man to the other. You only had to glance at Werner's face to know how completely Iraj had snowed him.

"Wait a minute, Iraj. You made a deal with this man?"

"Don't be angry, Annika. He had no idea what my real aim was. Until this moment, I kept him at a remove. Radomil was the go-between; your brother has a certain talent I find useful." His hand rose, gestured obscurely. "It seems that Werner and his coterie of spies and military folk were so desperate for America to fill the power vacuum in the Middle East, they would have made a deal with the devil in order for his country to gain power in the region." He turned to Ax. "That's the dream of all Americans, Werner. But, hold on, you're not American."

"I most certainly am."

"No, no, no," Iraj said, circling. "Your real name is Werner von Verschuer. You're a fucking Nazi."

Annika laughed, and continued laughing until tears came to her eyes. "Really, Iraj? Really? Bravo!" Then she turned to the white-faced von Verschuer. "I'm immune to Iraj's bullshit. There isn't a snowball's chance in hell that he has a single altruistic bone in his body. He wants a regime change in Iran, just like you. That's true enough. But he wants it so he can have his handpicked followers take over. He has all the clandestine infrastructure already in place, not only inside Iran, but in the Arab world as well. The Saudis love him; they'd be overjoyed to see him as the power behind the ancient peacock throne."

Werner looked stunned. "Is this true?"

The Syrian threw his arms wide. "Let my people go!"

Werner, recovering, laughed sourly. "Right. The Iranian people will be free—to do what? Obey you."

"Why not? I will have freed them from all the ritual insanity that has made their lives a living hell. And from the Americans." Here he touched Werner on the shoulder, in mock comraderie. "I haven't forgotten you. An uncle with such deep pockets is as rare these days as a hen's tooth."

"Yes, your opportunism is another valuable trait," Annika said. "The Americans never learn." She regarded Werner with pity. "Did you think he would do your bidding, like the shah? Such naïveté!"

Iraj called out and one of his men stepped in, took hold of von Verschuer.

"You used me!" Werner shouted.

"We all use each other," Iraj said. "It's part of the game."

Werner was furious. "I want my pound of flesh. I want McClure. He fucked up everything for me."

"You'll get your time with him, Werner. Ten minutes, no more. Make the most of them."

"He'll fuck everything up for you, too, unless—"

"But he won't get the chance," Iraj said with equanimity, as Radomil hustled Werner out of the building.

When they were alone, Iraj held out his hand, and Annika allowed it to slide against hers. "Here is the proof of it," he said. "When it comes to foreign policy the Americans keep making the same mistake over and over. They keep arming rebels in an attempt to overthrow regimes they don't like, then, when the rebels are in power, they're shocked when the newly installed regime turns on them. It's happened so many times—in Vietnam, Iraq, Afghanistan. There would be no Taliban had the Americans not armed them to fight off the Russians."

"Which they did," Annika said. "Once they pushed out the Russians, they turned on the Americans. In that part of the world, who likes capitalism?"

"Who even understands it? All anyone sees are Crusaders and Jews invading their sacred land."

"And yet, Shia and Sunni, Islam cannot stop tearing itself apart."

"In religion, I cannot take sides," the Syrian said. "No matter that I was born Shia. To choose is to make enemies beyond numbers. Radicals of either sect are dangerous. What I need now, more than anything, are allies."

"What you need," Annika said, "is to turn down another path, embrace a semblance of pragmatism."

"I am nothing if not pragmatic."

"On the contrary, you are one of the radicals you pretend to shun because you loudly and persistently claim they're too dangerous."

"Nonsense."

"You don't consider an outright attack on the supreme leader of Iran radical?"

"I consider it a necessity."

"No, what is necessary is for you to take a step back. When you do, you'll see that the prime consequence of what you are about to initiate is nuclear war."

The Syrian shook his head. "This will certainly not lead to nuclear war. It is a precisely guided surgical strike, just like what was initiated with bin Laden, after which my network inside Iran will take care of the army leaders while the radical imams are killed or jailed."

"Listen to yourself, Iraj. You're already talking like a god."

"Perhaps it takes this kind of god to make these decisions."

"'The battleline between good and evil runs through the heart of every man.'"

"Now you quote Solzhenitsyn at me, one of your Russian pacifists?"

"This line exists in everyone, Iraj, even you."

"No, no, I cannot countenance such drivel. I have more important matters to attend to, and so do you." He took her hand in his. "What I wish for, more than anything, is for you to be with me. I've wished for this for years." Registering the expression on her face, he added, "You didn't know?"

"I admit the thought occurred to me, but I dismissed it."

"Why would you?"

"You're the human equivalent of quicksand."

He threw his head back, laughed. "Then we are ideally suited."

She smiled.

"But—" His expression was abruptly serious. "You have been see-ing someone else." He rubbed the back of her hand. "Haven't you?"

"On my grandfather's orders."

"What does Jack McClure have that I don't have?"

"He has access to the United States secretary of homeland security."

"Access to the upper echelons of American government was always an obsession with Gourdjiev. Why?"

"He doesn't trust Americans."

"Neither do I." Iraj laughed. "And you?"

"I follow Dyadya's wishes in all things."

"Admirable. I admire the familial devotion the two of you exem-plify, possibly because it's something I never had."

"There are other forms of devotion." She squeezed his hand. "I could show you."

"Yes, I imagine you could."

For the first time she realized that the gaze of his green eye was warm when he willed it, but the blue eye's gaze was always cold. This revelation sent a tiny chill through her.

Iraj was just about to add a thought when his mobile buzzed. "Excuse me." He let go of her hand and walked to the other end of the pool house to take the call. He listened, spoke three words, then, glancing at Annika, listened some more.

When he put the phone away, he returned to her, took both her hands in his, and said, "As it happens it's fortuitous you're here now. Come with me."

She reacted to his expression. "What is it? What's happened?"

NONA, NO more than a shadow, stood in a midblock doorway on Twelfth Street NE. She had chosen this particular doorway because it had a view of the entire street. She knew Del Stoddart well, they hung out together from time to time. She knew his habits. Every night after leaving the office, he'd drive down here to Gilly's for a couple of beers, a round or two of pool, and, if he got lucky, a roll in some woman's bed.

True to form, Stoddart's blue, beaten-up Ford Focus rolled down the street and pulled into a space at the curb. Stoddart got out from behind the wheel, checked the parking meter for stray quarters, and began his round-shouldered shamble up the block toward Gilly's.

Tonight, however, he was not alone. A figure in black jeans, a hoodie, and premium black kicks emerged from a doorway on the other side of the street. As the man crossed diagonally to get closer to Stoddart, Nona saw a shiny black face, the eyes intent on Stoddart's back. One arm was held close to his side. Nona saw the glint of a Saturday night special gripped in his hand. No doubt the grips were taped so as not to pick up prints and all serial numbers had been filed off.

Hoodie was behind Stoddart now. He risked a quick glance around to ensure no one was paying attention. The street was nearly deserted. Nona unholstered her Glock and waited until he swung the Saturday night special up, then she stepped out into the streetlight and shouted, "Police! Stop! Put down your weapon!"

Both Stoddart and his would-be murderer turned. Hoodie swung his gun around, aimed it at Nona as she came toward him across the street.

"Put it down!" she said. "Drop it and no one will get hurt."

"Fuck you, bitch!" Hoodie said as he fired wildly. Then he dropped the gun and took off.

Stoddart sprinted after him.

"No, wait!" Nona ran after them and was close enough when the two shots rang out to see Stoddart pitch backward. The first bullet penetrated his chest, the second took the side of his head off.

Nona recognized the sounds and, from the direction in which Stoddart fell, immediately extrapolated the direction of the marksman. She looked to the roof of the building across the street, saw a blurred shape, then raced back across the street to the side of the building. Reaching up, she pulled down the fire escape ladder and climbed up, taking the rungs three at a time.

Glancing up, she saw the figure, dressed in a plaid wool winter coat, sneakers, and a Nationals baseball cap. As he leaned over, she fired her handgun. His head snapped back out of sight.

She resumed her climb, keeping to the shadows as best she could. She caught a glimpse of him. He carried the sniper rifle he had used to kill Del Stoddart, a Savage 10FCP. His face was blackened, camouflaged Marine-style. Professional through and through. She fired again as she took the rungs three at a time, but her angle was bad, and she missed. Still, she must have wounded him because she was gaining on him.

He appeared again, closer this time. As she raised her gun to shoot, she caught a glimpse of his face. It was Bishop! He had hired Hoodie, but, clever as he was, he had had a backup plan, which, due to her intervention, he had had to implement. Now, despite her best efforts, Del Stoddart was dead. Having lost her chance to fire, she launched herself upward after him. She called after him, called him by name. He ignored her, heading across the roof. She aimed and squeezed off two more shots.

Seeing him vanish over the parapet, she redoubled her efforts and, soon thereafter, began to lever herself over it. Bishop sprang up from where he crouched and slammed his fist into her chest. She rocked backward, then fired again at point-blank range. Bishop went down and stayed down.

She knelt in front of him. His mouth was opening and closing like a landed fish. His eyes stared at her in disbelief. Blood drooled out of his mouth.

"Look at you," Nona said. "Look what you've become."

Bishop tried to answer her, but only a thick gurgle emerge from his mouth, along with clots of fresh blood. As he stared at her, his eyes glazed over.

Nona, watching him die, wanted to feel some satisfaction, but at the moment there seemed to be nothing left inside her. Turning away, she sat beside him with her back against the parapet. Hauling out her mobile seemed like a Herculean task. With palsied fingers, she called in. While she waited, she took off her jacket and ripped off a sleeve of her shirt.

As she began to apply this makeshift tourniquet she thought about the last time she had been up on a roof. She and Frankie were seventeen. It was a stifling summer night in New Orleans, when sad jazz, which could have been funeral music but wasn't, wafted up from below, along with drunken shouts and crazy laughter. Now and again the crack of beer bottles against the sidewalk punctuated the night like fireworks.

She had come up to the rooftop, its thick tar warm as taffy, in order to be by herself. But she saw the tops of some shapes, lumpy and moving in the shadows of the water cistern. Picking her way silently forward, she saw Frankie with a young girl she would come to know as Nikki. Their bodies were coiled together like snakes, but the moment they noticed her, they sprang apart like repelled magnets.

"Nona!" Frankie exclaimed.

"Who the hell is that?" Nikki asked plaintively.

"My twin sister."

"You never told me you had a sister." Nikki scrambled up, buttoning her blouse. "What she doing spying on us?"

Nona's mouth was dry. "I'm not spying."

"Yeah, I'll just bet." Nikki strode past her. "You look like a fucking natural." She slammed the metal fire door behind her and clattered down the stairs.

Brother and sister stared at each other. The frayed music welled up from the street, lurching as drunkenly as the laughter. A shouting match commenced, a bottle shattered, the music rose to a crescendo of volume. Finally, Frankie put his back against the parapet. "I've got a couple of cold Cokes here. One of 'em's gonna go to waste."

Grinning, Nona sat down next to him. He handed her a bottle, and she rolled it across her forehead before popping it open and taking a deep, satisfying swig.

"The thing of it is, Nona, you *are* a natural."

"Shut up." She took a longer swig, stared at her distorted reflection in the faceted glass bottle. "What, you like that girl?"

"I do," Frankie admitted.

"She's a slut."

"Fuck, yeah," Frankie said, and they both laughed in such perfect synchronicity it could have come from one throat.

Nona, brought back to the present by the hastening sirens, lifted her head and smiled into the night.

"THE EIGHTH floor is in lockdown," Reeder said to his team members as he pocketed his mobile phone. "One more hurdle to overcome." He studied the architectural plans, then checked his wristwatch. "Mallory, it's time for you to leave us."

Mallory, who was dressed for her part, nodded and exited the room at the flyblown motor lodge near Bethesda that served as the group's staging area.

Reeder heard the car start up and drive out of the motor lodge grounds. Pulling the curtain aside just enough to peer out, he saw the medical supplies truck parked outside. "Now climb into your uniforms," he said. "In thirty minutes we begin the final assault."

DENNIS PAULL had a car with diplomatic plates standing by, and Jack transferred to it without incident. There was a man named Weaver in the car riding shotgun with Lorenzo, the driver.

"Good evening, Mr. McClure. Welcome to Rome," Weaver said after he had made the introductions. "We have made all the necessary arrangements with immigration, so no worries there. Also, we know precisely where this villa is and will take you there now."

"Who owns it?" Jack said as he settled himself in the backseat.

Weaver shrugged. "Cakra Holdings, whatever that is. We're running checks through multiple channels, but I wouldn't hold my breath."

"Cakra Holdings is owned by the Syrian."

"Good to know." Producing a briefcase, Weaver swiveled around and handed it to Jack. Inside was a selection of handguns. Jack chose a 9mm Beretta. He checked that it was fully loaded. Lorenzo gave him two more magazines.

"Expecting a firefight?"

Weaver shrugged, accepting the briefcase back.

By this time, they had left the vicinity of Fiumicino and were on the ring road that encircled the city, on their way south.

"Anything you need to brief me on?" Weaver said.

"Yeah." Jack stared out the window. As on the flight over, he was thinking of Annika and why she hadn't returned his calls. "Don't get in my way."

JUST AFTER three A.M., the shift at Bethesda changed. A pair of surgeons emerged from the operating theater on the eighth floor where they had been working on Henry Holt Carson. The pair was met by the duty nurse, who had just checked in.

Alli, who, along with Caro and Vera, had been asleep, was loitering in the hallway outside the situation room where the other young women were still dozing. She peeled her back off the wall and went down the hallway.

"Did he die?"

The head surgeon turned, puzzled. "How did you know?"

"What happened?"

"We had gone in prepared to do a double-bypass, but a third artery was completely blocked. While we were attempting to bypass it, Mr. Carson suffered from another myocardial infarction. This one was massive; he was gone before we had a chance." Behind him, two nurses pushed Caron's body out of the OR.

"He's usually so fortunate," Alli muttered.

The head surgeon gave her a quizzical look. "We did everything we could to keep him alive."

Alli was visited by an image of Henry Holt Carson in a wheelchair, a drooling semi-vegetable. "He wouldn't have wanted that."

The surgeon nodded in the particular way of a funeral director. "You have my deepest condolences. He'll be well taken care of by Ms. Mallory, the head duty nurse, until the funeral parlor comes for him. Will you make arrangements?"

Alli looked at him. "Why bother?" But for all her bravado, she knew she would.

REEDER BACKED the medical supply truck into the loading bay at the rear of Bethesda Hospital. As expected, he was met by Whelan, the head of procurements, and a pair of beady-eyed Secret Service agents, who asked for and received IDs from everyone aboard the truck. There was no doubt that Whelan's welcome of the crew gave them an excuse to perform only a cursory examination of the truck's interior before moving on to other matters.

Reeder and his team, carrying a number of legitimate cartons of supplies, were led into the bowels of the hospital. Whelan was one of Reggie's people on the inside, a man who did his job in sterling fashion while collecting his monthly stack of Benjamins against just such an occasion.

The drugs delivered to the pharmacy, Reeder's people ripped open the remaining three cartons, each of which contained a backpack. Whelan turned his back as if they did not exist, and the team, slinging on their backpacks, got down to their real work. Down in the basement, while Fillin went to the electrical room, the other two followed Reeder to the bottom of the elevator shaft. He unlocked the access door, and they all slipped soundlessly inside. He was about to give the deployment signal when his mobile vibrated. Clawing it out of his pocket, he saw a text message from Mallory: *C on 8 fl, 2 rms dn from target.*

Reeder smiled to himself. Well, how about that? They had been scouring the world for that traitorous bitch and she washes up at Bethesda. Two targets in the same place. It was his lucky day.

"WHAT HAPPENED?"

"A hit-and-run," the Syrian said. "It sometimes happens in Rome, but only, I'm told, to tourists."

Annika stared down at the body of her grandfather. She was very still. Iraj's men stood back at the corners of the coroner's cold room, which was windowless, metallic, bleak. One of his lieutenants had made inquiries, handed over packets of money to ensure that no one would be around when the boss arrived. Outside, unseen, the nighttime glow of the city turned the sky a livid purple-gray, as if Rome were in the midst of a thunderstorm.

"He must have stumbled crossing the street," Iraj said. "It's terribly dangerous here for an old man."

"This isn't possible." Annika's face was as white as chalk. "He can't be dead. After all we have been through together, it's just not possible."

The Syrian put his arm around her. "I'm truly sorry, Annika. He was an invaluable ally. Frankly, I don't know what I'll do without him."

"Neither do I." Tears welled up.

TWENTY-SIX

BETHESDA HAD a bank of three elevators. Reeder and his two men each went to a cable and, drawing on thick work gloves, began the dangerous process of climbing hand over hand up the parallel cables. Once or twice they were able to ride on the top of the cars as they rose from one floor to another, but for the most part they were fully engaged in the arduous task of ascending by hand to the eighth floor.

Twenty minutes after they had begun, they reached their goal. Before exiting through the service door, they donned gas masks and checked their sidearms. Then they drew small canisters out of their knapsacks. Reeder checked his wristwatch, counting down the seconds. Then he nodded to his team and, in perfect unison, they moved out.

THE VILLA was lit up like an airport.

Weaver leaned forward, checking his .357 Magnum. "Looks like they're expecting us."

"If they're being that vigilant," Jack said, "we'll give them something that meets their expectations."

Weaver turned to face him. "Like what?"

Jack smiled and gave Lorenzo instructions. The driver nodded. It was very quiet—too late for birds, too cold for crickets or tree frogs. Fog lay pale and low, like a sleeping girl, wrapped in a ghostly cloak. Inside the villa walls, rows of pencil pines nodded their heads in unison. Outside, the deciduous trees spread bare-knuckled branches, grasping fingers, disfigured by pain and time.

Lorenzo motored slowly, with the headlights extinguished. At that moment, Jack felt his mobile pulse. He had a text from Paull: *Herr located.* He immediately deleted the text and pocketed the phone.

Several hundred yards on, Lorenzo pulled off the road and rolled the car to a stop.

"A little farther," Jack said.

"Right here will be fine," Lorenzo said, as he shot Weaver. Jack had just enough time to raise the Beretta before Lorenzo turned and squeezed the trigger of his handgun a second time.

Jack was slammed against the backseat, then his torso canted over as he was assailed by waves of vertigo, and he plummeted headlong into impenetrable blackness.

ALLI WAS in the toilet attached to the situation room when she heard Vera and Caro start to cough. Then her eyes began to water. She heard a flurry of shots being fired, then a kind of vibrating silence. She turned on the cold-water tap and, grabbing three towels, soaked them in water. When they were saturated, she tied one over her nose and mouth, then ran out. The tear gas was worse. Vera was already on the floor. Kneeling, Alli tied the second towel over Vera's nose and mouth, then she did the same with Caro, who had been trying to crawl off the bed with the sheet over the bottom half of her face.

Alli, gun out, sprinted into the hallway. All the Secret Service agents were shot or coughing up a lung. Smoky gas was coming from the fire stairs; she'd get no help from the agents stationed there. She pulled the alarm lever on the wall, but nothing happened. Her cell was useless, as well—no signal. Grabbing a sidearm from the closest agent, she returned to the situation room, and wrapped Vera's hand around the grips.

"Keep Caro safe till I get back," she said in Vera's ear.

When she returned to the hallway, she had just enough time to register figures moving when one of them took a shot at her. She ducked back, then, lying flat on the floor, eeled out and squeezed off two shots. The first threw the shooter back against the far wall, blood spurting from his chest. The second gunman aimed and fired at her, forcing her back inside the situation room.

"What's happening?" Vera's voice was thick, muffled by the wet towel.

"We're under attack," Alli told her. "Secret Service is down; there's only us now."

Vera crawled over. Her eyes were red and tearing, her breathing labored. "I'll give you cover."

Alli nodded and they both crawled to the doorway. Unprotected, Alli's eyes were tearing and some of the tear gas had seeped into her lungs, making them burn, but the women had no other protection.

"I saw three of them," she said. "I shot one. If I can get to him—"

"You can put on his gas mask," Vera finished for her. "Gotcha."

Vera crawled past Alli and began shooting. Alli rose to a crouch, tapped Vera on the back, and sprinted out. She immediately saw a second man heading for her uncle's room, brought her gun to bear, and shot him twice. As he pitched sideways, she heard a shot emanate from her uncle's room and her heart lurched heavily in her chest. The snout of a gas mask emerged from her uncle's room and, with unerring aim, she put a bullet through it.

The figure recoiled. Then the now-useless gas mask was chucked into the hallway. A moment later, a figure lunged out of her uncle's room. She fired on the run, but missed him. He turned on his belly and fired at her, twice. She felt shards of plaster and wallboard whiz by her ear, one of them drawing blood as it nicked her.

REEDER, BLOOD gushing from his ruined nose, lunged for the gas mask on one of his downed men at the same moment the girl did. She looked no more than sixteen, but she had killed two of his highly trained men. Who the hell was she? He elbowed her aside and ripped the gas mask off Johnson. Johnson groaned, still alive. Reeder finished him off with one blow; no loose ends, those were Herr's orders. Eyes tearing, lungs wanting desperately to clear themselves, he began to fit the gas mask over his head.

He saw the girl. Roaring, he launched himself up. She fired her gun, and he was struck in the chest as if by a pile driver. Flung backward across the hall, he lay there, half stunned. He looked down in disbelief at the blood pouring out of him.

With consciousness flickering and dying, he stared up at the damned girl who had killed him.

JACK AWOKE with a massive headache and a pain in the side of his neck. He reached a hand up, felt a sore spot where he thought he had been shot. He swam slowly into full consciousness. There had been no noise when Lorenzo had shot Weaver, no recoil, no smell of cordite. He'd just had time to register those facts when the driver had shot him.

At the moment, he was lying on a sofa in a richly appointed library. The far wall was lined with shelves of books. To his right was a huge fireplace in which flames cracked and sparked merrily. Above, a carved marble mantel held an ornate ormolu clock in the style of Louis XVI.

The sofa on which he lay was covered in midnight-blue satin. A painted porcelain coffee service on a low Carrera marble table gleamed in the buttery lamplight. Swinging his legs down, he sat up, but his head pounded so painfully he was obliged to sit perfectly still as he deepened his breathing, pushing through the pain. The aromatic scent of freshly brewed coffee invaded his nostrils.

"*Krankheitsgefühl, sind wir?*" *Feeling poorly, are we?*

Jack raised his head, his eyes focusing on the figure sitting in a high-backed chair upholstered in the same fabric as the sofa he was sitting on. Werner von Verschuer.

"*Ich fühle mich wie Scheiße,*" he said. *I feel like shit.* "What did your flunky hit me with?"

"I needed to make certain you wouldn't come out of it prematurely," von Verschuer said by way of answer.

Baring his square teeth, von Verschuer lifted back one of the lapels, revealing an enamel pin: a swastika, along with the double-lightning-bolts insignia of the SS.

"*Mein Vater ist.*" *My father's.* Von Verschuer let go of the lapel. "To keep his memory alive."

"That's not all you've kept alive of his."

Von Verschuer shot a quick glance over his shoulder at the closed door. He frowned. "You seem to have figured out quite a bit about Acacia."

"Everything except its true purpose. Attempting to assassinate the supreme leader of Iran once is insane enough, but twice?" He shook his head. "That wasn't why you created Acacia."

"Of course not. The assassination was to be a training, that's all." Von Verschuer smiled again. "Tell me, McClure, have you ever heard of Louis Simpson?"

Jack stared at him, unblinking.

"Simpson was an American Pulitzer Prize–winning poet, but before that he served in the 101st Airborne Division and fought in France, the Netherlands, Belgium, and Germany. You'd do best to mark his words. I did. He wrote that 'the aim of military training is not just to prepare men for battle, but to make them long for it.'" Von Verschuer's smile broadened. "That, in a nutshell, is the aim of Acacia, to create a class of modern-day warrior who longs for battle, who is so proficient in mind, body, and, most importantly, spirit, that he is virtually undefeatable."

"But twins?"

"You know nothing of my late father's work, do you? Well, neither do most people, even historians who pawed through the wreckage of the Kaiser Wilhelm Institute of Anthropology, Human Heredity, and Eugenics."

"That's how you got your nickname: Your father was given that code name within the SS high command: *Vater Nacht.*"

Von Verschuer shuddered like an old lady. "I detest nicknames, especially that one."

"Twins," Jack prompted.

"Yes, twins." Von Verschuer leaned forward. "Coffee? It was just brewed. No?" He shrugged, poured himself a steaming cup, and continued. "One of my father's aims was to create the perfect soldier, not simply the perfect Aryan. Twins have special qualities, whether it's chemical, physical, or ephemeral, my father did not know. But that was the journey he was on, the one I picked up, refined, and extended. I had his notes, you see—all of them. He was far too clever to keep them at the institute."

Von Verschuer sat back. "And he was right, *mein Vater war brilant*. Sadly for us all, he wasn't privy to the advances in science I was. The genes of twins are subtly different and this, in turn, gives rise to shared enzymes in their brains. This has been my work for decades."

"Gene manipulation."

"Precisely."

It was at that moment that Jack realized just how demented von Verschuer was. How he had seduced other people to his way of thinking was beyond Jack's comprehension.

"So the Fraine twins."

"Washouts."

"And the others—Batchuk's sons."

"Loony as Coney birds. Too much manipulation, a dead end, so to speak. The Batchuks ended up being at war with each other, as did the Fraine twins, instead of hating a programmed enemy they could be sent out into the field to destroy."

"Yet you allowed these time bombs to roam free."

"First of all, they are my children, so to speak. Dear God, one doesn't harm one's children, McClure! Second of all, they were still in the experiment. Their ongoing behavioral patterns were closely monitored, the better to refine my system."

"And what about Frankie Heroe?"

"Who?"

"Frankie Heroe, the twin who Acacia took to the Horn of Africa in 2002."

"Oh, him." Von Verschuer shrugged.

"In what way was Frankie a part of your experiment?"

Von Verschuer winked obscenely. "You're the clever one, McClure. You'll figure it out."

Jack considered for a moment, and then the entire dreadful scenario blazed clearly in his mind. "Frankie was recruited to be the exception that would prove the validity of your rule."

Von Verschuer had adopted an equally obscene professorial air. "Continue."

"He was the *control* in the Acacia experiment on human beings."

"No. Frankie Heroe is a twin, but he's also black. He proved himself incapable of channeling his thoughts the way my own children could. My experiment was validated."

"Aryans." Jack felt disgust clog his throat. Von Verschuer was so arrogant he hadn't bothered to try training Frankie. "And then he had to be eliminated."

"Naturally. Only, well, the incident became a bit problematic when he didn't die in the directed mortar attack. Still, when he was sent home he was more dead than alive."

Jack barely restrained himself from attempting to throttle the demonic creature so effortlessly confronting him. "Which leaves us— where?"

Von Verschuer spread his hands. "Here. Your last stop, McClure. As for me, I have shut down Three-thirteen, rather than have its constituents interrogated. I will leave here, to continue my experiments elsewhere."

As if on cue, the heavy wood-paneled door to the library swung open, revealing a large, powerful-looking man with one blue eye and one green eye. According to Caro's description, this was the Syrian. Then Jack's blood turned cold.

Striding in, at the Syrian's side, was Annika.

ALLI RIPPED the gas mask off the man she had shot and slipped it on. For the next fifteen seconds she experienced the immense relief of breathing normally. Then she rose up, staggered a bit, and had to hold on to the wall while she regained her equilibrium.

"GET THE hell away from him," Iraj ordered.

Like a soldier, Werner kept his position. "But you promised."

The Syrian grabbed him and threw him bodily onto the sofa.

"Jack," Annika said, for the moment ignoring the two other men, "my grandfather is dead."

"Dead?" For the first time in his life Jack felt as if his mind were moving in slow motion. "How?"

"Hit-and-run."

"What? I can't believe it. He seemed indestructible."

"Mortal," Iraj said, "like all of us."

Jack focused his attention on Annika. "What are you doing here?"

"Was machst du mit diesen Leuten zu tun, meint er." What are you doing with these people, he means. Von Verschuer's smile had turned sardonic.

"I am upholding my grandfather's alliance with the Syrian."

"What alliance?" Jack said. "I don't believe you."

"That is your prerogative," the Syrian said as he stood in front of Jack, "but the truth is staring you in the face." He shrugged. "What you think is no concern of mine." His fingers snapped. "Now come, stand up and meet your fate like a man, not sitting down like a child."

As Jack rose, he hefted the porcelain coffeepot and smashed it into the Syrian's face. The Syrian cried out, staggering back, hands over his burning skin. Von Verschuer leapt to his feet to help the Syrian.

Annika drew a small-caliber handgun, but before she could aim it, von Verschuer knocked it away and shoved her. Jack dived after the gun, grabbed it, and fired once, twice. Von Verschuer reeled into him with such force the gun flew out of his hand, skittering to the other side of the room. Blood burst from von Verschuer as if from a dam. He clutched himself, his eyes wide and staring.

The Syrian, having regained his balance, wiped his face, trying to clear his vision. He had hauled out a CZ Phantom, and was trying to find a target. Von Verschuer, lying sideways where he had fallen onto the sofa cushions, tried to speak, but only bloody bubbles emerged from his open mouth. He was drowning in his own blood.

Jack took hold of Annika's arm and, before the Syrian could regain his sight completely, hauled her out of the library.

"CARO, WHAT'S wrong?"

Vera had heard shots being fired and had been undecided about sticking her head out or staying put as Alli had asked her to do. Now she put her arm around her half-sister as Caro bent over, head between her legs.

"I can't . . . catch . . . my . . . breath."

"It's the tear gas." Vera, trying to keep her breath shallow and losing the battle, wiped her eyes. "I'll get us both new towels."

She slid off the bed and was crossing to the bathroom when Ms. Mallory, the nurse she had been introduced to, stepped into the room and said, "Back away from there." Vera recognized her under the gas mask she had clamped over her face.

It was only then that Vera saw the 9mm Glock pointed at her. Out of the corner of her eye she saw Caro move, a blur of motion as she grabbed the water pitcher. Mallory swiveled, aiming the Glock at Caro.

"No!" Vera shouted, tackling the head nurse, slamming her to the floor. By some horrific miracle, Mallory retained her grip on the Glock, and now brought the barrel down on Vera's forehead. Blood spurted and a bolt of pain shot through Vera's head. She gritted her teeth and, drawing up her right leg, jammed her knee into the nurse's jaw. Ripping off her gas mask, Vera broke her nose. The Glock waved in front of her face, and she crushed down on Mallory's throat with both her thumbs. The nurse's mouth opened, filled with blood. She arched up, almost dislodging Vera, but Vera bore down with all her strength. With a muffled *crack!* Mallory's throat cartilage shattered.

Vera rose and, leaving the head nurse to gasp out what was left of her life, slipped the gas mask on Caro, then staggered to the bathroom, put her face under the cold water, and rewet her towel, once again masking the lower half of her face. She was wringing it out when she heard a thud, and raced out to find Caro leaning against the wall nearest the door.

"Caro, what are you doing?"

"The Syrian's people are here. They've finally found me."

Vera tried to pull Caro back to a chair, but Caro was so agitated and Vera was so debilitated from the tear gas that she merely sat down in the doorway with Caro leaning against her.

"Where are the alarms?" Caro said. "Where's the Secret Service?"

The second question was answered as they crawled out into the hallway and saw the bodies strewn all around.

"Good God," Vera said. Gaining her feet, Caro helped Vera up. Caro reached one of the downed intruders first, ripped off his gas mask, and adjusted it on Vera's face.

"Thanks, Sis."

"Anytime."

As she stepped over one of the bodies, Vera reached down and took the gun. They moved on.

"What the hell happened here?" Caro said.

Vera peered into every room. "Where's Alli?"

They found her in a room farther down, where Henry Holt Carson lay. Alli turned, Glock at the ready, but she relaxed visibly when she saw them.

"You two okay?"

Vera nodded. They all looked so odd with their snouty masks on.

"We're isolated up here for the moment," Alli said. "All the lines have been cut or bypassed and they must have set up a cell blocker like what's done at some hotels, because my mobile won't work."

Vera stood stock-still. "There he is."

Alli nodded. "Henry Holt, yes."

Caro turned away, shaking her head. "I don't want to even look at him."

"He's dead," Alli told them. "He died on the operating table."

Vera stared down at him. "I don't feel anything—not a fucking thing."

Caro shuddered. "Why should you? He was a monster."

Caro, staring into the corridor, cried out as a figure emerged from the elevator service door. Vera lurched past her as he aimed a handgun at Caro. Alli pushed Caro aside, saw the figure, heard the shot. Even as Vera was spun backward into Caro, she squeezed off two shots, both into the left side of the man's chest. He dropped as if poleaxed, and did not move again.

Agents in gas masks and riot gear, brandishing assault rifles, now began pouring out of the fire stairs and elevator service doors.

Caro sat, her legs beneath her. Vera's head and shoulders were cradled in her lap. Alli came and knelt beside them. She reached out, pushing Vera's damp hair away from her face.

"It's nothing." Vera smiled, raising her left arm and wincing. Despite her bravado, her face was very pale. "Just a flesh wound."

There was a stricken look in Caro's eyes. "Damn me, Vera, I don't know what I would have done if—"

Vera raised her good arm, her hand caressing her sister's cheek. "Look at her," she said softly.

Alli ripped off a sleeve from her own shirt and, using it as a tourniquet, wrapped it tightly above the spot where Vera had been shot.

"Alli," Vera said, "does it still hurt?"

Alli called to one of the agents for an emergency medical team, then looked at Vera steadily. "I imagine it still hurts both of us."

Tears, glittering at the corner of Vera's eyes, spilled over, running down her pale cheeks.

"I can't."

In the hallway of the villa, Annika pulled away from him.

Jack stared at her. "You can't what?"

"I can't go with you, Jack."

"What?" He heard heavy footfalls. "What are you talking about? Come on, Annika, the Syrian is coming."

"I know he is, Jack. That's why I have to stay."

"I don't—"

"Get out of here." She shoved him toward the front door. "Now!"

Jack came back for her. Reality was shrinking down to the space between the two of them. "Forget it."

She glanced nervously over her shoulder. "He'll kill you."

"He wants too much from me to kill me." Time seemed to slow, grinding to a dreadful halt. "Anyway, I don't care about him. It's you—"

"Jack, you don't understand."

"I'm not going to leave you here."

She looked at him with something akin to pity. "You never did."

At that moment, he got it, reality collapsed like a house of cards, and his heart shattered. She wasn't coming. She didn't love him. Like her mysterious grandfather, she had aligned herself with the enemy. It seemed incredible, and yet, as the Syrian had said, he was confronted by the truth.

And still a part of him clung to hope, though hope seemed to have abandoned him. "Annika—"

"Good-bye, Jack."

"You fooled me completely," he said, before racing out the door, onto the villa's brightly lit grounds. The gates were locked up tight. Dogs began howling and a pair of German shepherds came racing around the corner of the villa, eyes set on Jack. Radomil Batchuk emerged from beneath a pencil pine and, as if he had been waiting for Jack, stepped into his path. "This way!" he said.

Jack stood rooted to the spot, undecided until Radomil put a strange-looking whistle to his lips. Jack couldn't hear the sound it made, but the dogs were brought up short.

"Come on!" he urged, as the dogs began to snuffle and back away.

Jack had no choice but to follow Radomil as he threaded a devious path through the pines. Shouts rang out behind them, and among them Jack recognized the Syrian's voice. Radomil headed out of the pines and straight toward the villa's perimeter wall. He unlocked the gardener's door.

"There's a black Fiat parked off the road five hundred yards to your left, the keys are in the ignition," he said, standing back. "Good luck."

"Why are you doing this?" Jack asked, but Radomil had already disappeared into the shadows, and Jack sprinted through the door, vanishing into the enfolding night.

EPILOGUE

December 20

GENERAL TARASOV had arrived in Sharm el-Sheikh right on time. He breathed in the curdled Egyptian air, dense with palm and cardamom and diesel fumes. The hub of the city was an insane cacophony of noise and movement, but at the coast, where the waves lapped against the piers of glimmering luxury hotels and the hulls of sleek pleasure craft, a luxuriant sense of ancient calm prevailed.

General Tarasov had checked into a glitzy resort and went immediately to Room 202, which had been preassigned. Twice a day, he used his mobile to call Werner Ax, as planned. Ax's line went directly to voice mail, which was odd, since Ax was expecting his call. Tarasov could not move ahead with Acacia's final deployment without Ax's go-ahead.

He left a coded message, then picked up the hotel phone and ordered room service. Levering himself off the bed, he went into the bathroom to relieve himself and wash up. Refreshed, he pulled a beer out of the minibar, snapped open the can, and took a long slug. There were no messages on his mobile. While he pulled open the sliding glass door, he redialed Ax's number. Voice mail again. Stepping out onto the expansive terrace, he felt the warm, wet air wash over him. Moonlight gilded the crests of the small waves. He could smell salt and phosphorus. By long-ingrained habit, he once again checked the terraces to left and right; they were empty. He wondered why Ax wasn't answering his mobile. For security reasons, Tarasov had no other way of contacting him. How long could he continue to wait? Ax must have his reasons for staying out of touch this long—he always did.

Off in the distance, a muezzin began his call to prayer, the tinny loudspeakers distorting the voice. Others took up the call. A pair of guards, one tall, the other quite small, strolled down the beachfront toward his side of the resort. They seemed to be chatting with each other, their faces in shadow. Tarasov took another long swallow and belched deeply. He was beginning to relax. He knew Koenig and the Lintel twins were here at the resort, but, again for security reasons, he was enjoined from contacting them. Not that he wanted to. What he wouldn't give to bed another female tonight. He had just decided to go down to the bar to see what was available and at what price when there was a knock on the door. His stomach rumbled emptily, reminding him that he had ordered a meal. Hopefully, these Egyptians wouldn't fuck it up. Setting the half-empty can on the top railing, he turned and went inside, crossing the room to open the door.

A waiter pushed a laden cart into the room and Tarasov closed the door behind him.

"Where would you like it?" the waiter said with his back to the general.

"Just leave everything where it is," Tarasov said, coming toward him.

"As you wish, General." The waiter turned, a CZ, suppressor attached, in his hand. "Everything where it is now."

Just before the bullet tore through his chest, Tarasov's eyes opened wide in shock. The waiter was no waiter at all, but Reggie Herr, grinning at him like a death's-head as he pumped another round into his victim. The General fell to his knees.

"What . . . what?" was all he managed to get out.

"Shutting down the pipeline." Reggie happily stood over the soon-to-be corpse. "Orders from Father Night. Three-thirteen is out of business."

Those were the last words General Tarasov heard, in this world, at least. His eyes grew fixed and he toppled over onto the carpet. Reggie bent over and checked his pulse. Happily, there was none.

Reggie turned and, a moment later, had vanished through the open slider onto the terrace. Once there, he climbed atop the railing. He crouched, about to leap to the terrace to his left when an unopened beer can came flying at him, striking him on the temple. At once, he lost his balance, tumbling down to the sandy beach below.

Even as he was gaining his feet, he saw the tall guard rushing toward him. As the man passed through a pool of light, Herr recognized him as Jack McClure. He raised his CZ 75 Phantom, but McClure swerved just as Herr squeezed off a shot. The bullet, intended for the chest, struck the shoulder instead, spinning McClure around. Up on one knee, Herr took careful aim and was just about to fire a second time when a figure crashed down onto him from above. He writhed on his back, but all he got for it was a mouthful of sand. He saw Alli straddling him, and swatted at her, as if she were a fly or a gnat. She rocked back, but kneed him in the throat. Using the suppressor as a cudgel, he swung at her again and again. With satisfaction, he heard her grunt in pain. He had never wanted anyone dead more than he wanted her dead. She wrestled the suppressor away from her face, just as he supposed she would, and he grabbed her throat with his free hand, clutching her so hard she started to retch.

Now I have you, he thought.

ALLI'S EYES were watering and there was bile in her throat. She felt her consciousness wavering, a blackness coming and going. The area around her fractured clavicle throbbed dreadfully, weakening her further, but at the moment that seemed the least of her worries. The pain from Herr's grip was so excruciating she wanted only to cry out, to have it end.

Then the pressure came off her and she saw Jack hauling Herr up, Herr turning to deliver a blow.

To have it end.

She saw Herr attacking Jack again, Jack striking back so ferociously that Herr stumbled backward against her. She jammed her thumb into his eye. Herr leapt like a fish on a line and almost threw her off him.

Jack slammed his solar plexus. As Herr doubled over, she fought to keep her grip, twisting her thumb harder, deeper, her breath hot in her lungs, sobs coming out of her. There was a timeless moment when she met Jack's eyes, and in them she understood what she needed to do to purge herself of the nightmare the Herr twins had thrust her into.

Jack hit Herr again, staggering him. This was her chance! She snatched the CZ out of Herr's grip, pressed the muzzle to his chest, and pulled the trigger again and again. Then Jack was prying her gently away from her nemesis, who lay unmoving, unseeing, on the sand in a widening pool of his own fluids.

"It's done," Jack said in her ear as he held her with his good arm. "It's done."

FINALLY ALONE, in the cold room of the coroner's building, Annika stood over the white corpse of her grandfather and wept without restraint or self-pity. Cradling his cool head in her hands, she placed a kiss on his forehead and thought of all the days and weeks and years of their life together. He had served as her father, mentor, savior, protector, and now he was gone forever. There would never be another Dyadya Gourdjiev, nor did she want there to be.

"I did what you asked," she whispered, tears streaming down her face. "I've always done what you asked. But this is so very hard, harder than I thought possible. I've trusted you my whole life. I still trust you, but goddamn you for what you've done to me, what you made me do to Jack. You knew I loved him and yet you persisted. I understand, but I don't understand you. I don't know how you can use people the way you have—people you love, people who love and trust you."

She stood up, wiping her eyes. But the tears came again, harder this time, and she sobbed out her pain and misery, safe within these four windowless walls, where no one could hear or know her anguish. By the time she left here, she would be dry-eyed and iron-willed again, but now she was lost, alone, vulnerable, and so very, very sad.

Reaching out, she touched her grandfather's temples, where, inside, his brain had been eaten alive by cancer. She was the only one he had confided in; everyone else believed him to be invulnerable. He had known the end was near; he chose the way he would die, the way that would serve him best by bringing her closer to the Syrian. That had been his plan—the long con, something he was so adept at. Her acting had convinced Iraj that she had bought his fiction of the hit-and-run. She knew the truth; that was all that mattered.

At least she had instructed Radomil to ensure Jack got out of the villa alive. But it wasn't nearly enough; she could never tell him, and he must despise her for betraying him. How thin the line between love and hate, like tissue, shredding.

She bent, as if genuflecting, and kissed her *dyadya*'s stone-cold lips. She had done everything he wanted. Now she was at the end. But also at the beginning, the last phase of Dyadya's grand design. If, in the coming months, all went well, she would gain the world. But in the process she had lost everything.